A PIRATE'S PREY

Unable to bear what she'd just seen, Celeste fled the slave auction, rushing blindly into the night, sobs catching in her throat. As if from a long distance, she heard her father call her name, but she couldn't stop her stumbling run into the sheltering darkness. She was just seventeen, a child in many ways.

She fell on the path up from the bayou, ripping her skirt, but got up and scrambled on.

Suddenly, there was a collision with a hard man's body, a growling exclamation. Pinning her arms, the man clutched Celeste, trembling, to him.

"Where bound, little bitch?" His breath was rank and scorching-hot on her upturned face.

"Let me go!"

Laughter rumbled deep in his chest. "McCoy's brat."

Celeste's knees turned to water. It was Gambini, the pirate, her father's blood-enemy, cruelest of all the captains who sailed with Laffite.

He scooped her up in his arms and slung her over his shoulder, chuckling as if unable to believe his luck.

So begins this saga of the McCoy women, born to desire and danger, swept by their own passionate natures from the depths of degradation to the heights of passion—and beyond.

CANNONS & *Roses*

Rosetta Stowe

A. DELL/BRYANS BOOK

Published by
Dell Publishing Co., Inc.
1 Dag Hammarskjold Plaza
New York, New York 10017

Copyright © 1979 by Rosetta Stowe

All rights reserved. No part of this book may be reproduced in any form or by any means without the prior written permission of the Publisher, excepting brief quotes used in connection with reviews written specifically for inclusion in a magazine or newspaper.

Dell ® TM 681510, Dell Publishing Co., Inc.

ISBN: 0-440-01027-6

Printed in the United States of America
First printing—January, 1979

CANNONS
&
Roses

BOOK I

Celeste & Paul

PART ONE

1

*T*he Temple in the swampland below New Orleans had been a sacred place for the Choctaw, those Indian descendants as cruel and fierce as their Aztec ancestors, but in 1825 this oyster-shell ridge was a mart of trade for the Laffites and their Baratarians. There slaves pirated from Cuba-bound slave ships were sold to the highest bidders. Here Creole and American plantation owners mingled with the mongrel Baratarians; some of them descendants of runaway slaves, others the spawn of pirates and their captured women.

On the bank of a turgid bayou, the Temple rose like a half-mile-long island. The long and narrow slave barracoon on the crest of the ridge heightened the illusion. As he poled his borrowed *pirogue* toward The Temple, Jamie McCoy wondered if it hadn't been a mistake to bring Celeste to the auction. He stole a glance at his dark-haired daughter. She sat erect in the bow of the burned-out cypress log, her shoulders back, the long hair streaming down her back.

"So this is The Temple, Daddy." Celeste turned from the waist as she spoke, careful not to disturb the shaky balance of the *pirogue*. "It doesn't look like much, does it?"

"God, but she's a beauty!" Jamie murmured to himself.

Hair as black as ebony, the delicate features of her French-English mother, a generous mouth over a stubborn little chin. In turning, Celeste's small breasts moved restlessly under the sheer fabric of her dress.

"I've told you why it's called that," Jamie said. "What is it you were expecting?"

"I don't know." Celeste shrugged her slender shoulders. "More than this."

"You'll not get out of my sight tonight," Jamie cautioned. "I'm thinking it was a mistake to bring you here, Celeste. Jeanette will kill me if she finds out."

"Oh, Mother!" Celeste swung her hair, and made a face. "She's seen plenty of naked black men and women on the block. I'm seventeen, Daddy." There was a glint of mischief in her eyes. "I've learned how men are made in the quarters at Great Oaks, and what they do with women and girls."

"You're a forward enough wench," Jamie accused. "I should have blistered your backside more often."

Celeste laughed. "Like you do to Mother every so often?"

Jamie flushed, and Celeste recognized the signs of a rising Black Irish temper. "You'll not be spying on your mother and me when we're behind closed doors, young woman."

"How am I to learn?" Celeste asked, all innocence.

Jamie glowered but didn't answer.

Cannons & Roses

* * *

Celeste helped her mother with the accounts at Great Oaks, but with 150 slaves now, and more than 1,000 acres in cotton, Jamie McCoy had decided to buy an educated slave to help the women. In New Orleans to arrange a loan, and to meet with a British factory owner, Sir Douglas Dunn, he'd learned that such a slave would be put on the block at The Temple this Saturday night. Celeste had come down the river with her father to shop. They were taking coffee in The Royale, guests of Jean Laffite, when Jamie mentioned his purpose.

Jean snapped his fingers. "Exactly what you want will go on sale at The Temple, McCoy. Gambini brought him in. He's a handsome young mulatto who claims he was a bookkeeper in Philadelphia."

"Gambini!" Jamie spit the word. "He's probably kidnapped a free nigra. The only sort of business I'll do with the Italian would require cutlasses or pistols. The man's scum, Jean. That cruel bastard is going to stab you in the back one of these dark nights."

Celeste noticed a dangerous glint in the handsome Jean's dark eyes. "I watch my back, McCoy. You know that. Gambini's nigra belongs to me in payment of a long-overdue debt. My brother Alexander has him tamed by now, so Paul will be a safe investment."

"No doubt," Jamie said. "I've watched your brother use the whip."

"Paul's not damaged merchandise," Jean said. "Gambini didn't have him long enough."

"Who is this Gambini?" Celeste asked the men.

"I first heard of him while I was privateering in the Caribbean," her father told her. "Vincent Gambini comes from Naples. The man's a degenerate! In a camp his men had just left on a Florida key I found a Spanish woman—a duenna—naked and nailed by her hands and feet to a plank. Gambini had crucified her so she could witness the rape and mistreatment of her young charge."

Celeste shuddered. "Did she die?"

"Yes, but not soon enough. Other things had been done to her."

Jean seemed unmoved. "Gambini and I have in common our hatred of Spain and the Spanish."

"He's going to bring you down," Jamie warned.

Jean touched the points of his waxed moustache. "Perhaps. Gambini would like to see me driven from Grande Terre and Grand Isle." These islands at the mouth of Barataria Bay, Celeste knew, were Laffite fiefs. His considerable fleet of prizes was anchored in the bay, off their shores. "But that won't be."

"You should get rid of the bastard," Jamie advised. "It isn't like the old days. Governor Claiborne will have you yet."

The danger glints were back in Jean's eyes. "The incorruptible American!" Jean leaned forward and said confidentially, "As a former captain of mine, you know how often he tried to get me on trumped-up charges." Jean slapped his palm on the tabletop. "I've tried more than once to call him out, but the man is too cowardly. Have you influence with him?"

Jamie shook his head. "We've met only once."

At their boardinghouse on Royal Street, Celeste announced, "I'm going with you to the auction."

"You'll not," Jamie said. "The Temple is no place for a child."

"Child!" Celeste flared. "For heaven's sake, I'm seventeen—old enough to marry. Mother and I will be working with this Paul. It's only fair I should have some say before you buy him."

"Your mother will skin me if I take you to The Temple," Jamie said.

"She doesn't have to know, Daddy."

"Jeanette will find out sooner or later," her father told Celeste.

"She won't from me. Please?" When Jamie hesitated, Celeste smiled. "So it's settled. What do you suppose I should wear?"

"You're as headstrong as your mother," Jamie said gloomily. "It's only fair to warn you. You'll probably be the only respectable young woman down there. Planters don't take their wives and daughters to a slave auction."

"Which is exactly why I'm going," Celeste said.

Cabin barges used to bring prospective buyers and their companions to The Temple were drawn up on the bank of the bayou. It was just dusk. As they wound their way up the narrow footpath to The Temple, Celeste's excitement mounted.

I must be depraved, she thought. She'd never seen Negroes bought and sold before; all fresh slaves were smuggled now. Because of the demand of the planters, striving to grow more and more cotton for British textile mills, authorities winked at the smuggling of slaves, but couldn't countenance public sales.

Jamie was climbing the path behind Celeste. He touched her elbow. "Stay in my sight," he warned her. "Something about a slave auction heats the blood, as you'll soon enough find out."

"I'm anxious to see this fellow Paul," Celeste said.

"He won't be offered at first," Jamie told her.

Cannons & Roses

"Women and children are sold off before they put up the prime stock."

Celeste found more than a hundred men, and as many women, at The Temple anticipating the auction of slaves. Baratarian women and girls, with their colorful head scarves, or *chignons,* were serving crawfish, shrimp and clams from boiling caldrons, to be washed down with liquor and wine.

Shacks lined a broad stretch of ground that reached the auction block at one end of The Temple. Tobacco, jewelry, and other luxuries were for sale in these shacks —privateering loot supposedly, taken under a Cartagena flag from Spanish ships.

"It's a Laffite policy to never touch American ships these days," Jamie confided to Celeste, "but much of this stuff comes off Dutch and British ships, I suspect. Some Laffite captains aren't too choosy whom they board."

"Vincent Gambini, for instance?" she asked.

"That one!" Jamie looked around. "I see some of his men are here tonight." He touched the butt of the pistol thrust in his wide belt. "I hope the Italian is somewhere else."

"I'd like to see the man who would crucify an old woman," Celeste said.

"The duenna wasn't much beyond thirty," Jamie said grimly.

"What other things had been done to her?"

Jamie grimaced. "I'll not be telling you."

"Was she raped?"

Jamie nodded. "There's Alexander Laffite," he said, pointing to a swarthy man with a gold ring in one ear. "We were shipmates once. Dominique You is his *nom de guerre.*"

Cannons & Roses

Alexander had seen them. With a wide grin that showed white teeth, he shook Jamie's hand and slapped his shoulder. "It has been too long since you and I served on Chalmette with Jackson, my friend," he said. His dark eyes appreciated Celeste. "And who is the little one?"

"My oldest daughter," Jamie said. "I probably should have left her in New Orleans."

"Ah, no." Alexander favored Celeste with a clumsy but sweeping bow. "We need such fresh beauty to grace The Temple—a rose among thorns." He turned back to Jamie. "Jean has told me you are interested in the one named Paul."

"If he can cipher and keep accounts," Jamie said.

"I assure you this one can, my good friend."

"How much do you think he'll bring?" Jamie asked.

Alexander considered. "Before the unfortunate Flora Gaines affair, I would say two thousand American dollars, but you know how it is now. Few planters are willing to trust an educated nigra around their womenfolk. I'd say a thousand dollars."

"Who was Flora Gaines?" Celeste asked.

"A planter's wife who claimed she was raped by a house servant," Jamie explained. "In my opinion, she lied in her teeth."

"Who can say?" Alexander's was a noncommital shrug. "The wretch confessed."

"After being stretched on the rack for an hour, and having his joints crushed," Jamie said. "I think the woman should hang."

"There will be entertainment before the auction begins," Alexander said. He glanced at Celeste. "It may not be suitable for her to watch."

"She stays with me," Jamie said.

Cannons & Roses

Alexander shrugged again. "As you see fit, my friend. It is better that she doesn't wander tonight. Let's meet for a friendly glass after the auction."

"What sort of entertainment?" Celeste asked, when Alexander was gone.

Jamie scowled at his daughter. "You've seen Carroll slaves punished, courtesy of Richard, I hear."

Celeste flushed. Bliss! Richard had invited her and the twins to see a recalcitrant field hand lashed. No whipping was allowed on Great Oaks, and the first thing her father had done, when he bought the plantation, was to tear down the whipping shed near the quarters.

Bliss was named after a black body servant who had helped Jeanette McCoy escape the bloody slave revolt on Santo Domingo in 1803. Jeanette had seen the result of extreme cruelty practiced on slaves. No slaves she owned would ever feel the whip, Celeste's mother had resolved, and good-natured Jamie respected his wife's wishes.

It had been a lazy summer afternoon. With Richard, they'd sneaked down to the Carroll quarters and hidden near the whipping shed. Stripped to his drawers, Celeste had seen the husky Negro strung up by his wrists, to receive thirty lashes on his bare back.

Jamie Two was disgusted with the spectacle. Celeste was strangely unmoved. Bliss watched with glittering eyes.

My sister is a strange little bitch, Celeste admitted to herself. She remembered that the next day she found Bliss and Jamie Two naked in the summer house on Great Oaks. She was stunned.

"Jealous, sister?" Bliss asked, as Jamie fumbled for his pants. She caught her hands behind her neck and made no move to cover her nakedness.

Cannons & Roses

"No, you little fool! Cover yourself!"

"And why should I?" Jamie Two had fled. "You'll not tell Mother or Father, will you?"

"I just might."

Bliss smiled. "No, you won't, virgin sister."

"Why are you so sure I'm virgin?" Celeste asked.

Bliss reached for her clothing, her back to Celeste now. "Because Richard hasn't seduced you yet."

"How would you know that?"

"I know things," Bliss said.

Celeste hadn't told either her mother or father, and Bliss claimed riding astride one of their stallions had ruptured her maidenhead. Jamie believed her, but Celeste was certain her mother didn't.

It had to be Bliss who had told on them.

"A bit more of the same shouldn't bother you too much," Jamie said.

Celeste smiled at her father. "I have a strong stomach."

The auction block was a square slab of granite dragged to The Temple by the Choctaws. Jamie let Celeste examine it. Channels had been chiseled into the stone. "What are these for?" Celeste asked, scuffing one with her foot.

"Blood."

Celeste looked up, startled.

"Human sacrifices were made here in the Aztec fashion," Jamie explained. "The hearts were cut out of men and women prisoners, to be eaten raw by the priests."

Celeste shuddered. Square wooden timbers had been sunk in the ground on either side of the granite slab. A crosspiece was bolted to the top of each pillar that spanned the stone. Iron rings were sunken into this timber, and other rings were sunk into the granite beneath them.

"Why the rings?" Celeste asked.

"You'll discover soon enough," Jamie said grimly.

Crude wooden benches ringed the block, and men and women were filing into the amphitheater. The men were unsteady, and their companions giggly-drunk.

Jamie led his daughter to a front-row bench, knowing full well what sort of entertainment Alexander promised.

Let her get a bellyful of torture, he thought. *Let her hear the screams, smell their sweat.*

Of his three children, Celeste was more like her father, with blond and brown-eyed Bliss taking after her mother in appearance, as did Jamie Two. There was a hard core in Celeste.

Like her mother there, Jamie decided.

But he was only partly right. He, too, was a born survivor, and Celeste had that quality in abundance. Melded with it was Jamie's reckless streak.

The excitement she'd first felt upon arriving at The Temple was at a fever heat now. Celeste's calm appearance, as she inspected the gathering crowd, belied the turmoil inside her. She recognized mulattoes, quadroons, and octoroons among the women.

Mistresses every one, she thought. *They probably think I'm Daddy's mistress.*

This thought amused her.

"When does this so-called entertainment start?" she asked her father.

Jamie licked dry lips. "Soon enough."

A husky slave, naked but for a breechclout, had mounted the block with a drum made from a hollow cypress log. He squatted with the slender drum clasped between his knees. Torchlight reflected off his ebony skin, rubbed to a fine sheen with palm oil.

"Oh!" Celeste said, disappointed. "Dancing."

2

Great Oaks, one of the oldest plantations in Louisiana, antedated only by The Columns whose acreage adjoined it, slumbered in the afternoon sun. Even the rasping cicadas were enjoying a siesta.

And it's no wonder, Jeanette McCoy thought. *All that love-song scraping of their legs for the poor males, and their females tone-deaf.*

With Jamie and Celeste gone to New Orleans, Jeanette was restless as she prowled the empty house. DeWitt Scott, the Great Oaks overseer, was in the fields with the slaves. DeWitt would come to the house this evening to go over accounts with her in the small office adjoining the living room with its huge stone fireplace. That would be a welcome diversion.

I'd be stupid if I didn't realize the poor man is hopelessly in love with me.

Jeanette promised herself that tonight she wouldn't flirt with DeWitt. It wasn't fair. She wished the poor man would divert himself with one of their more-than-willing nigras, but he was hopeless. Sundays he preached to them. Nigra morale on Great Oaks was so good that other planters resented DeWitt's gentle methods of working their slaves.

The man's some sort of blond saint, Jeanette thought.

Which was more than anyone could say about Delray Bone, the young overseer Jamie had hired to clear the ground and plant the acreage along the Red River in cotton. Jeanette shivered. It would take a man like young Bone, Jamie had convinced Jeanette, to net a profit on the Red River acreage.

Delray Bone. Razor-sharp features, with a long, pointed nose. Thin lips that exposed tobacco-stained teeth when he flashed that shark smile. Pointed ears matched the tip of his nose.

"I'm a real nigger-driver," she'd heard young Bone tell her husband. "You'll get your quota and me my bonus."

Jamie had stripped their cash reserves and gone into debt to obtain the Red River plantation, traveling all the way to Charleston to buy slaves from Wade Hampton. Prime, fresh stock, just off the boat from Africa, Jamie had told her.

Wild nigras.

Jeanette had reached the uneasy conclusion that Jamie knew what he was doing when he bought the Red River acreage and hired young Bone. It would take a man of Bone's caliber to tame Africans just sold into slavery.

What was it Alicia Carroll had whispered about the young slave-driver's father, Ulric Bone? Jeanette wrinkled her forehead, trying to remember. Poor Alicia, married to Colonel Carroll of The Columns. The man stayed too drunk on his precious peach brandy to ever

Cannons & Roses

satisfy her in bed, Jeanette suspected. Lacivious gossip was Alicia's stock in trade.

Jeanette remembered. "They say Ulric Bone owns the most notorious brothel in New Orleans," Alicia had whispered. They'd been alone in the house, except for the servants, but Alicia always whispered her choicest gossip tidbits. "He *sells* white women as if they were nigger wenches! Can you imagine?" Alicia giggled. "They say he hates women and rules his brothel with an iron fist. That's a joke of sorts, Jeanette. One of his hands *is* made of iron."

The next time she stayed in their New Orleans town house that Jamie had bought after their last crop, and was having remodeled, Jeanette determined to find out more about Ulric Bone.

Bliss and Jamie Two would be staying at The Columns tonight because Richard Carroll was back from a trip to Virginia. A marriage between Celeste and Richard would link Great Oaks and The Columns.

Jeanette frowned. She supposed every mother had her favorite child. Celeste's quick intelligence and resemblance to her father should have earned her that role, Jeanette realized.

Then why was wanton little Bliss her favorite? The child had no shame. If Jamie ever found out that she'd lain with Jamie Two! Jeanette was pretty certain that Celeste had surprised the pair of them in the summerhouse. Why hadn't the sly little minx come to her? Jamie Two had.

The twins were identical in appearance only. She'd talked long and earnestly with her son about incest. She'd made her point, Jeanette was sure, because Jamie Two had a sense of right and wrong his twin sister never would have.

Cannons & Roses

Bliss. A grasping little bitch!

But I truly love the brat, Jeanette admitted to herself. *Somehow between the way I loved her black namesake, now probably an African queen, and Edith Radcliff, with whom I shared Thomas.*

Jeanette sank into a window seat and looked through the shimmering heat haze at the alley between ancient oaks that reached the river landing, then closed her eyes.

Singapore. A moonlight nude swim with Edith. Thomas, naked, joining them. Before that, poor, battered Bliss. Straying hands and lips.

"You, my dear, are a depraved and wanton little bitch," she told herself. She shivered. "Jamie should be enough man for any woman."

He is! she thought. *He is!*

Stella picked that moment to enter the room. "You be wanting your tea soon?" the lissome black girl asked.

She was barefoot, and only a thin shift covered her nakedness. House servants knew they had Jeanette's tacit permission to wear few clothes when Jamie and the children were gone from Great Oaks.

"Soon, Stella," Jeanette said.

"I bring him now?"

"Please do." Jeanette studied the proud thrust of the girl's breasts, with the nipples so obviously erect. "In here."

Not upstairs in the bedroom!

"It's your damned fault, Jamie McCoy!" she muttered, when Stella had gone to do her bidding, with an insolent twitch of her hips. "Come home! Our female house servants are beginning to look good to me."

Jeanette wondered if Bliss had seduced Richard Carroll yet.

Cannons & Roses

* * *

The cue for their captors to lead the tall Mandingo man and his woman to the block was a tattoo on the drum. They'd come from the barracoon stripped naked, wrists bound behind them, a grinning Baratarian with his nose missing driving the woman, a hulking brute of a man marshaling the male Mandingo.

She's magnificent, Celeste thought.

Full but firm breasts, flat belly, tapering long legs, the haughty carriage of a queen.

The man, too, was a fine specimen, rippling muscles in his arms and legs, a broad chest, but Celeste stared at the shaft of his manhood. She sensed that was the focus of all the other women, too. Their men would be gloating over the woman, of course. Even her father, a quick side-glance told Celeste.

She pressed her thighs together.

On the block, the man was quickly triced up by his wrists, legs jerked apart and fastened to the rings in the granite, so that he hung spread-eagled. His attendant was fitting a leather pouch, drawing it tight to be secured by a leather cord around his waist. Palm oil had been rubbed into his skin; his nakedness glistened in the torchlight.

The woman struggled with her disfigured captor. A ripple of laughter swept the spectators. The swart little Baratarian had his hands full!

The hulking brute solved the problem by looping an arm around the woman's neck, pushing a knee into the small of her back, and strangling her into submission. The two of them triced her up like the man, and she hung, gasping, trying to get her breath back.

Both victims faced Celeste.

I'm enjoying this!

Celeste's vagrant thought startled the girl, and she

locked her thighs more closely. A sweet, warm sickness coursed in her veins.

There was a pile of whips on the block. Now the Baratarians were making their selection. This whole spectacle, Celeste realized, was carefully staged and designed to arouse the spectators.

The noseless man had selected a wicked affair with three braided thongs, each tipped with lead. The brute was satisfied with a wide, thick strap.

"Why don't they protect her down there?" Celeste whispered to Jamie. "Like they have him," she explained. "It isn't fair!"

She'd never forget her father's harsh burst of laughter.

The audience was hushed.

Before taking up his station behind the victim, the brute dipped the strap into a bucket of saltwater to make it more pliant.

The whippers faced each other behind their victims. Some woman in the audience giggled, half-hysterical.

The crouched drummer tapped his drum, raised his fist, hesitated, then struck the taut drumhead. On cue, the brute swung his strap, with its two-handed handle, and there was a wet, meaty smack. He'd caught the Mandingo man squarely across his buttocks.

Celeste would never forget the red, gaping mouth of the Mandingo, or his strangled scream of pain. It seemed to echo.

"The idea here," Jamie said calmly, "is to let the poor bastard strung up there get the full benefit of each lash before he's hit again."

It was the woman's turn. At the next heavy drumbeat, she was lashed across her bare shoulders, but the thongs curved around to bite her right breast, leaving

Cannons & Roses

globules of blood. Celeste had heard the sound that burst from her throat before!

One of their husky field hands, covering a girl, and thrusting into her hard. Pain was mingled with wild ecstasy in the sound the girl made. So it was, Celeste realized, with this Mandingo woman!

Celeste herself felt the bite of the whip!

"Mon Dieu, she liked it!" cried a Creole dandy.

Celeste clenched her hands. Nails dug into her soft palms, but she didn't notice.

The strap, swung up between the man's parted thighs, caught the leather pouch squarely before the end of the strap licked his belly.

No scream of agony this time—the man was hurt too badly. It was the sound of a tortured animal, and Celeste felt sick to her stomach.

"Let *her* have it there!" A woman's screech.

The noseless man was grinning as he waited for the next drumbeat. The thongs whispered in the air before the upward cut of the whip struck between the Mandingo woman's open thighs.

It was a vicious stroke. The lead tips drew blood from the rounded base of her belly. She stiffened, her eyes rolling up. But only a long-drawn moan escaped her lips.

Celeste's knees knocked together involuntarily. Somehow she'd caught the Mandingo's stare. Their eyes locked. Celeste couldn't look away. Nor could the woman.

We must buy her! Celeste thought.

The woman smiled, as if she'd read the girl's thought. Her head was up. The man's chin was on his chest as he heaved for breath. His swelling belly snapped the cord around his waist, and the leather pouch fell to the granite block.

Cannons & Roses

On the next drumbeat, the brute struck again, a vicious cut up between the man's thighs, and the heavy, saltwater-soaked strap, emasculated the Mandingo.

Retching, Celeste fled. As if from a long distance, she heard Jamie call her name, but she couldn't stop her stumbling run for darkness, with sobs catching in her throat.

The drum throbbed again. She heard whistling, catcalls, women's screamed exclamations, and somehow knew the noseless man had circled his victim, to lash her breasts.

Blind instinct led her to the narrow path up from the bayou. She fell, ripping her skirt, but scrambled to her feet, and blundered on down the path.

Celeste jolted a sharp exclamation from the hard man's body with which she collided in her headlong flight. Pinning her arms, he clutched Celeste's panting body to him.

"Where bound, little bitch?" His breath was hot and odorous on her upturned face.

"Let me go!"

Laughter rumbled in his chest. He'd jammed a thigh between her legs. "McCoy's brat!" She saw cruel recognition dawn in the man's eyes, sunken in a thin, pockmarked face.

Other men were close in the warm darkness. How many? Celeste went limp in the arms of the man who was holding her.

"Hey, Vincent!" The speaker's hands were fumbling at her skirt. "I have her second."

"To hell with you, Roberto!" A second man there in the dark. "We share her after Vince."

So she'd run into the arms of Vincent Gambini! He scooped her up in his arms. Over his shoulder, he told the other two men: "You, Alain, and you, Roberto, get along to our barge. Tell the Goddamned slut we got a fresh pigeon." Gambini's chuckle was wicked. "McCoy's brat!" he gloated, as if unable to believe his luck.

In the cramped, stuffy cabin of a barge, Celeste had been dropped on the single wide bunk. A heavy-set woman with an unwashed body had her elbows pinned above her head. Celeste arched her hips. It was no use. Her skirt was ripped off, then her blouse, all three men grasping at her.

In moments she was stark naked.

"Turn up the lamp," Gambini ordered.

Yellow light flooded the dark cabin. Gambini gloated down at her. The back of Celeste's head was in the woman's lap, between her heavy thighs.

"Please!" she begged the woman. "Don't let them!"

"Helena." Gambini was in charge. Alain and Roberto were standing back, waiting. And watching. "See if she's a virgin."

"I am!" Celeste was frantic with fear. In her panic, she grasped the woman's name as if she was drowning, and it was a straw. "Don't let them hurt me, Helena! Please!"

Gambini had motioned to Alain and Roberto, and now each man seized an ankle. From opposite sides of the bunk, they folded her legs until Celeste's heels dug into her buttocks, then splayed her legs while Gambini, stripped to his shirt, mounted the bunk.

Helena bent her head to slobber a kiss on the girl's gaping mouth. "You and me, *chérie,* when these pigs have finished," she whispered.

Celeste fastened her teeth in the woman's lower lip and tasted salty blood.

Cannons & Roses
* * *

Until the Mandingo woman had been lashed across her breasts, Jamie didn't realize Celeste had fled out into the darkness. He knew she'd left the bench and had called after her, but he thought she'd return immediately. When he finally realized what had happened, Jamie knocked men and women out of his way with a curse to go after her.

He bumped into Alexander Laffite just beyond the circle of torches.

"You are in the great hurry, my friend." Alexander's hands brushed Jamie's clothes. "And what has happened to the little one?"

"She ran off. We've got to find her."

"She will no have gone far," Alexander said in a consoling voice. "Our little entertainment, I think, was too strong, no?"

But Alexander's slip—speaking English, because he made so much a point of speaking his adopted language carefully—alarmed Jamie. He grasped the man's shoulders. "We've got to find her, do you hear? What have you seen?"

Alexander pointed. "A woman says she ran that way, toward the bayou path, and I come to find you."

Both men loped off into the darkness, Jamie in the lead.

"Celeste's all right," Jamie muttered to himself. "She can take care of herself."

He wished he believed what he was saying.

When the men reached the head of the narrow path from The Temple to the bayou, Alexander halted and said, "Are you armed, my friend?"

"Yes." Jamie felt for the reassuring butt of his pistol—only to discover it was lost. "No."

Cannons & Roses

Alexander pressed a slender-bladed knife in Jamie's hand, a wicked poniard. "I'll follow you," he said in a grim voice. "There is this feeling in my *estomac* I do not like."

3

Helena's hand closed convulsively on Celeste's breasts as she jerked back her head and howled with pain. Celeste threw herself off the bunk and started to rise, but Gambini had her long hair knotted around his fist.

"You slut! You bitch!" Helena screamed. Blood dripped from her chin.

Laughing uproariously, Gambini dragged Celeste back up on the bunk by her hair and stunned her with a vicious slap.

"I'm going to kill you!" Helena promised. She'd snatched up a handkerchief to stanch her bleeding lip. "Let me at her, Vince."

"Gag the bitch," Roberto suggested.

Helena leaped on the bunk astride Celeste. This time it was Alain or Roberto who pinned her wrists above her head. Helena's pendulous breasts had burst from her loose bodice. They swung from side to side as she slapped Celeste's face back and forth.

"There!" She'd stuffed the bloody handkerchief in Celeste's mouth.

Gambini watched with an evil grin.

Reaching behind her, Helena sank fingers into Celeste's most sensitive flesh, and twisted—hard. "Like that, *chérie?*" she mocked.

With the back of his hand, Gambini knocked the woman off Celeste. "Get her ankles again!" he ordered Roberto and Alain.

Only half-conscious, Celeste would have trouble remembering what happened next.

Jamie and Alexander Laffite were galvanized by Helena's scream. Jamie pounded down the path, the poniard in his hand, but Alexander, more cautious, followed at a trot.

Springing to the deck of the barge, Jamie framed himself in the cabin doorway.

"Look out!" Roberto and Alain, not as intent on the business at hand as Gambini, saw Jamie first, and shouted the warning.

Poniard held low, poised for a gutting upward stab, Jamie lunged for Gambini as the man gained his feet and whirled around with the quickness of a cat. It was Helena's bad luck to scramble from her hands and knees between the two men in time to receive Jamie's vicious stab in her stomach.

Clutching air, she staggered back into Gambini, and he had her as a shield.

The poniard fell from Jamie's hand when he tried to snatch it back. When he stooped to regain it, Gambini shoved the heavy woman into Jamie, and he fell back, her weight on him.

Cannons & Roses

Roberto and Alain bolted for the cabin door, jostling each other in the small cabin, but Gambini, with a snakelike gesture had Roberto's broad-bladed knife from his belt.

Jamie heaved the bleeding, gasping Helena off him, and on his knees, the poniard lost, grabbed for Gambini's wrist. When it slipped from his grasp, Gambini drove the knife into the hollow of Jamie's throat and scrambled over him.

Roberto and Alain, bursting from the cabin to the barge deck, had knocked Alexander reeling. They were gone up the path when Gambini came through the cabin door, still wearing only his shirt, the knife in his hand. When he saw Alexander, who was braced against the rail, Gambini faced him, on the balls of his feet, knife ready.

"We quarrel?" Gambini spit in Italian.

Alexander raised his empty hands. The gesture was enough. Gambini vaulted the barge rail and was gone after his followers, naked white legs flashing in the moonlight.

Alexander swore in French.

In the cabin, he found Jamie already dead, with torrents of blood still gushing from his throat. Helena hunkered in a corner, arms clasping her belly as she made mewling sounds.

Celeste sat on the edge of the bunk, dazed, the bloody gag in her hand.

The poniard was on the cabin floor at his feet. Moving with deliberation, Alexander stooped to pick it up, eyes on Helena.

Murder here at The Temple, and the victim a wealthy planter, his daughter raped, would finish the Laffites in Louisiana. It was all the excuse Governor Claiborne needed to send another naval expedition to

Cannons & Roses

Grande Terre and Grand Isle, but this time there wouldn't be another Andrew Jackson who needed the Baratarians to rout the British.

The Battle of New Orleans had gotten him out of The Cabildo, and made his brother Jean a folk hero, but Alexander knew better than vain Jean Laffite that they were in Louisiana on sufferance.

"Help me!" Helena was gasping.

Alexander hadn't served in the Napoleonic Wars, when he wasn't a pirate and privateer, and survived until now, because his wits were slow. McCoy was gone. By the yellow lamplight he saw that now Helena's intestines were spilling out over her hands and arms. The girl, clasping herself, rocked and moaned on the edge of the bunk.

Alexander stepped over to Helena, grasped her hair to raise her face. *"May God have mercy,"* he said in French, before he sliced her throat and crossed himself.

He turned to Celeste. She'd seen what he'd done.

It is too bad she had to see this, he thought.

The lamp. Extra fuel for it in a corner. The barge timbers were old and dry. It would make an excellent funeral pyre for McCoy and the woman.

And the girl, too?

She met his steady gaze as he wiped blood from the knife on his clothing.

Celeste wasn't afraid. She wasn't in shock, either. Alexander admired the beauty of her nakedness as if she were a statue.

"This becomes a most unfortunate situation," Alexander told her.

Celeste nodded dumbly, and crossed her arms to shield her breasts. Alexander sensed she wouldn't beg for her life.

"Have you been raped?" he asked.

Celeste shook her head. "No." Her voice was normal. "There wasn't time."

"*Bien*."

Celeste's eyes strayed to the bloody body of Jamie, and widened, but there was acceptance in them. "If you must kill me," she told Alexander, "please get on with it."

Alexander considered.

"Shall we say this?" he said finally. "Helena was a woman-loving whore and a procuress for Ulric Bone. This is common knowledge."

Celeste waited.

Alexander tucked the knife into his belt. "Your father found you here with Helena. This is truth."

Celeste nodded, and waited again.

"The lamp uspet, this barge was burned, only you escaped. Helena and McCoy . . ." He let the sentence drift, and Celeste was amazed to see tears in his limpid dark eyes. "*So unfortunate*," he said in French. "I loved your father. He has saved my life, and me, his. We were shipmates and comrades on Chalmette."

Alexander blinked away the tears. "Is it agreed?"

"Yes."

"Your word?"

"You have it."

Alexander wrapped her in a tattered blanket and lifted her in his arms. Celeste could smell his tobacco scent and welcomed the comforting warmth of his body. She was so cold!

"You will not leave The Temple unrewarded," he said. "Laffites always pay their debts."

Alexander carried her back up to The Temple and stopped at a shack removed from the others.

"Mother?" he called, *sotto-voce*.

Cannons & Roses

An elderly woman, with cloth bound around her gray head, turban-fashion, shuffled out of the shack. She glanced briefly at Celeste. "This one is about to drop a child?" she asked in patois French.

Celeste had learned French from her mother, before she knew English. She had to swallow hysterical laughter.

"Gambini tried to take her," Alexander said in careful English, "but that is our secret, no?"

The woman nodded.

"You will care for her and find clothing." This was an order. Alexander set Celeste on her feet, to press coins into the woman's outstretched hand. "I myself will take her back to New Orleans tomorrow. Is this understood?"

The woman touched a finger to her lips.

Alexander turned on his heel and disappeared into the darkness.

The interior of the hut was clean, the dirt floor swept. Celeste wondered if this woman was a gypsy. Stretched out on the only cot, Celeste let the woman bathe her and cover her with a clean blanket, but not before the woman had examined her intimately with gentle hands. No words had been spoken between them yet.

"*What is your name besides 'Mother'?*" Celeste asked in French, when a mug of some hot liquid was cupped in her hands.

She'd startled the elderly woman. "*You are French?*"

Celeste shook her head. "My mother was."

"Ah!" The smile that split her leathery, wrinkled face showed missing front teeth. "Drink. You sleep, no?"

Cannons & Roses

Celeste finished the bitter liquid in the mug.

The woman reached under the blanket. Her warm hand cupped Celeste's womanhood. "It is still safe, little one, for the man you will love to have for himself." The withdrawn expression in the woman's eyes was something Celeste had never seen before.

She's in a trance, Celeste thought.

"I'm called Amalie. Your man is near tonight."

If it was a trance state, it was quickly gone. "Sleep." It was a command. "Forget." The woman lapsed into French again. "You will have revenge."

Celeste closed her eyes.

All of this is only a nightmare, she thought. *Daddy isn't dead.*

She fell into a drugged sleep.

Paul Wright, his slender body naked, lay on a mat apart from the Africans, sore in every muscle, and with his back and flanks just beginning to heal. The auction was over, and he hadn't been put up for sale.

The Mandingo man was dead. They'd hauled his lifeless body from the dim barracoon an hour ago, two men dragging him away by his heels. The woman they'd whipped lay only a few feet away from Paul, stretched out face down. Paul wished he could speak her language. He studied the proud curve of her buttocks, the arch of her back, the tapered black legs.

Only a few slaves were left; the old, the lame, the halt and the blind. Paul wondered what their Baratarian captors would do with them; then with a sigh decided he really didn't care.

Three weeks ago he'd been a free man, walking the streets of Philadelphia. The memory was getting vague. Was there really a dry-goods house up there named

Cannons & Roses

Barnes, Gaines & Son? After weeks of job-seeking, had a pontifical gentleman named Adolph Barnes hired him as an assistant bookkeeper?

That night Paul had left his dingy rented room to celebrate. He'd turned into a corner saloon, as much for the free lunch as a drink, because only a few coins jingled in his pocket.

The rest of it? Paul couldn't remember. But he'd never forget the swarthy man who'd flogged him the first time he'd insisted he was a free man after being brought to this God-forsaken place in the swamps. He'd been tied embracing a post.

"You're a slave, my friend." A cut of the whip across his shoulders. "You are a slave." The lash struck his buttocks. "Tell me, my friend. Are you a slave?"

"No!"

Another slash with the whip, across the small of his back.

The man was patient. "I don't wish to mark you up too much, my friend." The whip snapped across the back of his legs. "Admit you are now a slave."

"No!"

"You will be fed, you will be clothed, black wenches where you're sold will be very willing, since you are nearly white. Is this the bad life?"

"I'm a free man!" Paul winced when he remembered this hysterical scream.

He'd tensed, waiting for the searing pain of the lash, but it didn't come. Instead, a callused hand found him between the thighs. "You still are a man," his tormentor said, and squeezed, but not too hard. "Do you want to be deprived of these? This can be easily arranged."

"No!" Paul was sobbing. "*I am a slave!*"

Cannons & Roses

The man's hand was gone.

"*Bien*. Do well and remember it, my friend." The man patted his bare shoulder. "We'll find you a good master."

The Mandingo woman moaned in her sleep, turned her face toward Paul, came awake to stare at him. Her face, with its high cheekbones, was impassive. The woman's back, flanks and even her breasts were striped, with dried blood where the leaden tips of the lash had bitten her, but she didn't seem to care.

Her unblinking stare studied Paul.

Paul sat up, clasping his knees. "How do you feel now?" He knew she couldn't understand the words, but hoped his tone of voice would comfort her.

The woman blinked. With a sigh, she laid her head on her arms again, and was back to sleep.

A booted toe nudged Paul's back. He looked around and up to find the swarthy man who'd whipped him standing there.

"I've made you a gift, my friend," the man told him. "Come." He reached down to help Paul to his feet, then handed him a pair of loose cotton drawers. "Put them on," he said, as if speaking to a child.

The Mandingo woman was awake, watching.

The man spoke to her in her own language, a harsh command. Slowly, wincing, she came to her feet. He motioned for her to follow.

A hand touching her cheek brought Celeste awake. Her start was involuntary, but she relaxed and managed a smile, when she saw it was only Alexander Laffite who stood beside the bed.

"What do you want?" she asked.

"The slave, Paul, your father wanted," Alexander said. "He is outside, a gift from me and Jean, and

Cannons & Roses

the woman you saw whipped last night—we give her to you and your mother, too. It is little enough reward for your silence." He paused, then said, "There was a most unfortunate fire during the night. You are now fatherless. We Laffites send condolences to your good mother." Alexander crossed himself. "May his soul rest in peace."

Celeste was groggy and couldn't focus her eyes, but she saw a blur of clothing laid on a stool near the bed.

"Dress," Alexander commanded. "My men will take you and your new slaves through the bayous in my barge. You will sleep in New Orleans tonight. The slaves will be cared for in the house of Pierre Laffite until you claim them."

"Pierre?" Celeste hadn't realized there was a third Laffite brother.

Alexander's white teeth flashed when he grinned. "Our older, most respectable brother," he said. "Pierre lives with his mistress in New Orleans. She's an octoroon, but you will like her, I think."

Celeste sat up, holding the blanket to cover her breasts, because Amalie had tucked her in naked. Drug fumes were clearing. *This is unreal. Only last night Daddy brought me here!*

Last night? A century ago!

"What's been done about Gambini?" she asked.

Alexander's was a typical Gallic shrug of the shoulders. "Vincent and his men are gone back to Grand Isle, and I have sent a message to Jean. Vincent is no longer welcome here at The Temple."

This is the way my father is avenged!

Celeste's expression must have betrayed her bitter thought.

"Jamie McCoy, I understand, has a son," Alexander said.

"Yes. Jamie Two."

"When he challenges the Italian, I am at his service to serve as a second."

4

The men Alexander Laffite had assigned the task of getting Celeste and her gift slaves to New Orleans were the whippers of the night before. The brute was named Antoine, his noseless partner (he explained to Celeste that a saber cut had cost him his nose), was Jules. The shallow-draft barge had a small cabin aft, and another forward, with stern and bow decks for the other two Baratarians who would pole the barge.

Paul and the woman, shackled together, back to back, were locked in the forward cabin. The aft cabin with its comfortable bunk was at Celeste's disposal.

Celeste was still too stunned by the course of events to feel grief. Reporting her father's death to Jeanette, she would keep her word to Alexander. Anticipating the impact of her mother's shock and grief, Celeste winced mentally.

Jeanette will blame me.

Cannons & Roses

It was no use trying to shunt out of her conscious mind the trauma of near rape. Or the bloody death of her father, and the sight of Helena with her throat cut. She considered what had happened with a cool and calculating mind.

Confronted with the same helpless situation again, Celeste decided she would handle herself differently. Her struggling and pleas had only inflamed the men further. Who was the Biblical woman, faced with rape, who entranced her captor with her body, then cut his throat when he slept?

Celeste couldn't remember. But she determined, faced with last night's situation again, she knew what she would do. She should have groveled to Gambini and begged him to take her any way he so desired.

I'm tired of being virgin!

Richard Carroll was most anxious to relieve her of virginity. For what she'd done to him when they were twelve, Celeste decided she owed Richard, so let him be first.

Celeste smiled. It would serve Bliss right. But Jamie Two would be the really jealous one. Celeste suspected that Bliss was the reason for Jamie Two's sexual preferences. At sixteen he was a handsome enough young man, and every nubile virgin in the parish was setting her cap for Jamie Two, but his young body servant, Moses, slept in his bed.

Jeanette didn't suspect. Her father had never known. Jamie Two had no idea that Celeste knew about his sleeping arrangements.

She wondered what Jamie and Moses did together in bed? She'd walked in on them one morning, and found the pair sound asleep, clutched in each other's arms. She made a tiptoe exit.

Cannons & Roses

Celeste couldn't despise Jamie Two. In a very different way, she loved her brother. And she'd seen him, often, following Richard with his eyes.

Richard Carroll. Blond hair, sky-blue eyes, a silky moustache that tickled when he kissed, and he moved with the grace of a panther. Celeste could do worse than marry Richard, as her mother wanted, and Alicia Carroll, too.

Maybe she would.

She did owe him.

It was in a shed down near the quarters at The Columns that Richard had suggested they both take off their clothes. She had been invited to his twelfth birthday party.

"It's a dare," he'd said.

Celeste didn't have to pretend interest, as many naked black boys as she'd seen. She doubted Richard had ever seen a naked black girl. Alicia Carroll was too strict about the quarters where Richard was concerned. But a naked white boy, well, she felt she owed it to herself to study the difference.

"You first, Richard," she told him.

"Then will you?"

"I promise," she'd lied.

With trembling hands, Richard dropped his pants, and ducked out of his shirt, removing his undergarments, and standing before her naked, hands stiffly at his sides. He couldn't meet her eyes.

"Oh, Richard!"

"Now you."

Celeste had picked up his pants. She knotted the legs as she saw Alicia Carroll coming down the path from the house. Richard's back was to the half-open door of the shed.

"No thanks, Richard," she'd said sweetly.

Cannons & Roses

And, leaving him there in the shed, Celeste had met Alicia Carroll on the path.

"Good evening, Miss Alicia."

"Where's Richard, dear?"

"Getting dressed, I think," Celeste had said.

There was no birthday party.

Richard didn't ride his favorite horse for more than a week, and Miss Alicia apologized to Celeste profusely, swearing her to secrecy about the depravity of her young son.

"He takes too much after his father," she'd said, in a burst of confidence.

Remembering, Celeste laughed.

The McCoy town house in New Orleans, two blocks from Congo Square where slaves were allowed to congregate and dance on Sundays and holidays, was at the corner of St. Claire and St. Paul streets. Creoles called it The Spanish House. It was commonly supposed that the spirit of Maria Castellano haunted Spanish House.

Don Francisco Castellano had murdered his bride there when the Spanish owned New Orleans. It was said that his housekeeper, Madame Oliveaux, betrayed the young woman to her jealous husband and assisted in the murder of Maria, afterwards disposing of the body.

Don Francisco fled back to his estates in Spain, near Madrid. Madame Oliveaux was mulatto, and, some said, a former mistress of Don Francisco. Left alone in Spanish House, she was arrested by the authorities, and tortured in The Cabildo, on a rack and with the instruments imported from Spain for an American Inquisition, but never used. New Orleans Spaniards didn't care to have their own Torquemada.

Cannons & Roses

The New World had mellowed its attitudes toward sin and the Mother Church. But what the authorities did to Madame Oliveaux to obtain a confession was gossip for years afterwards.

When what life she had left was extinguished by breaking on the wheel, it was a gala occasion. There was a *baile,* or dance afterward, and nine months later, a surprising rise in the birthrate.

When Jamie McCoy bought Spanish House, it was a deserted ruin. Built in the Spanish style, blank walls facing St. Claire and St. Paul streets, except for narrow, barred windows, the house itself surrounded a paved courtyard with a central fountain.

Spacious rooms with many windows fronted this courtyard, above across a balcony.

Jamie McCoy had bought Spanish House at a bargain price, after a good cotton season when his fortunes were flush. It had been a surprise present to Jeanette.

Celeste knew her mother missed the house on a Port-au-Prince side street where she'd been raised, before going to England for an education. It was in that house on Santo Domingo that her mother's parents had been murdered by poison at the instigation of Hippolyte Verlaine, the sadistic monster who married Jeanette before her parents were cold in their grave.

Spanish House, her father had told her, was ready for occupancy. When they'd returned to Great Oaks, Celeste knew her father planned to bring her mother to the town house and New Orleans. He couldn't now.

Celeste wished she could cry, but it was too soon.

She decided to take possession of her new slaves when the barge reached New Orleans, and groom them at Spanish House for the upriver trip to Great

Oaks. She didn't want to become involved with another Laffite.

Vashti was the biblical queen in the book of *Esther* who refused to answer King Ahasueras's summons to share his bed. Remembering how the Mandingo woman, stripped naked and strung up before an avid audience, had savored the sting of the lash, Celeste chose the stubborn Vashti to be the Mandingo woman's namesake.

It was mid-afternoon and she'd rested, so Celeste went to the small forward cabin of the barge to inspect Vashti and Paul.

Paul, chin on his chest, was dozing when she stepped down into the cabin. He was naked and sweating except for the drawers Alexander had furnished him. But Vashti was awake and looked up boldly.

Antoine had followed Celeste and stood on the deck just outside the cabin.

There was a bucket filled with brackish water, and a tin dipper. "Drink?" Celeste asked the woman, pointing to the bucket.

The woman nodded. Celeste held the dipper to her lips while Vashti gulped the water. It took a second dipperful to satisfy Vashti's thirst. Standing over the shackled pair, sitting back to back on the cabin floor, Celeste studied the fresh whip marks on the woman's thrusting breasts and flat belly. She resisted the temptation to kneel and touch them.

"Your name is Vashti," Celeste announced to the woman. She pointed a finger at her. "You're Vashti. Vashti is your new name. I'm Miss Celeste," she said, poiinting to herself. "Celeste. Do you understand?"

The woman nodded, her somber eyes still studying Celeste. "Vashti." She licked her thin lips to moisten them before trying the harder word. "Miss Celeste."

Celeste smiled. "That's right." She reached down to pat the woman's head.

Paul was still dozing, but Vashti jerked him awake when she lunged in an attempt to bite Celeste's hand.

"No you don't!" Celeste snapped.

Antoine threw back his head and laughed. "That wench—she's the one," he said. "You want her whipped? Jules and me, we flip a coin."

Celeste shook her head. "No."

"Why not?" Paul asked quietly. There was nothing thick-tongued about his speech. "She's your property, and so am I."

Antoine brushed Celeste aside to aim a kick at Paul's groin, but Celeste shoved the man back, so his boot struck Paul's chest. "Get out of here!" Celeste ordered.

Antoine smirked, but he left Celeste alone with the pair.

"Thank you," Paul said gravely, when he'd regained his breath. "I don't believe he broke any ribs."

He could almost pass for white! was Celeste's startled thought.

Paul's eyes were gray. They'd cropped his hair short, but it wasn't kinky, like the woman's. Nor was there the hint of blackness in Paul's even features. There was a shadow of beard on his face.

"What's your full name?" Celeste asked him.

"Paul Wright. Your name besides Miss Celeste, or is that my business?"

"It's your business," Celeste said. "You will be helping Mother and me keep the books at Great Oaks. I'm Celeste McCoy."

Paul, to Celeste's amazement, jabbered a few words to the woman in her own clicking language, and when she answered, told Celeste, "She'll be good if you untie us. I have her word."

"Where did you learn to speak her tongue?" the girl asked him.

"In Liberia and along Africa's west coast," Paul told her. "The American Colonization Society sent me down there in 1822. I taught school for two and a half years."

"Why didn't you stay?" Celeste asked.

On her knees, Celeste was busy unknotting the stout cord that shackled Paul and Vashti, wrist to wrist.

"It wasn't home," Paul said.

She'd freed them. Vashti stared at her hands, as if she was surprised to find she still had them, then winced as the blood began flowing again, cradling the hands against her stomach.

Paul sighed and dry-washed his tingling hands.

"If I'd stayed on in Liberia," Paul mused, "I wouldn't be in this mess."

Celeste caught her breath when she saw the healing whip scars on his light brown back.

Vashti, her hands normal again, stretched full length on the cabin floor, threw an arm over her eyes, and promptly went to sleep.

"She claims she was a queen with many slaves of her own," Paul told Celeste, regarding the naked woman with downcast eyes. "She whipped them all on a daily basis, or so she'd told me. Africans have the exaggeration habit. But I do believe she can handle a whip."

"The man who was whipped with her at The Temple," Celeste said. "What happened to him?"

"He's dead, of course. Your Vashti shed no tears. She said he was useless to her now."

Paul eased his stiff body off the cabin floor, groaning, and stepped over Vashti to sit on a bench along the cabin wall.

Celeste watched his awkward movements, then asked, when he was settled on the bench, "Isn't Vashti a bit cold-blooded?"

"About her man dying?" Paul shook his head. "No. She's African. Tribal wars are the rule along Africa's west coast. The slavers provoke them so they can buy fresh stock from the various tribes."

"That's terrible!" Celeste said.

"It's a profitable business, Miss Celeste. Many tribes would otherwise eat their captives. An enterprising slaver bought Vashti and her man just before they were to be tortured, then served up for supper."

Celeste regarded the sleeping naked woman. "Slavery is better than dying that way, certainly."

"I don't know," Paul said. "Vashti was a bit disappointed."

Celeste nodded. "I guess she likes to be hurt, but being cut up for the cooking fire . . ." She shrugged. "Not a really pleasant ordeal."

"No," Paul admitted.

Even white teeth flashed when he smiled.

Celeste stepped out of the ruffled petticoat Amalie had given her. She handed it to Paul.

"Use that to wash where the whip has cut her," she ordered. "I'll try to find salve somewhere on this barge."

"Rum or whisky will do," Paul said.

"All right. I'll get you two fresh drinking water."

Celeste left them. But before she left, she told Paul, "Try to get her to wear my petticoat."

"I'll try," he promised.

Paul's seeming acceptance of his plight bemused Celeste. In his situation, she knew that she would have railed bitterly. Paul was cool and rational. She wondered if he was planning to break for the North and freedom again; in his place, she knew she would be making careful plans. She must warn him of the folly of trying to escape the South and the cruel penalties should he be caught.

Bliss decided that Richard Carroll was a gentleman. "Too damned gentlemanly!" she swore to herself.

The hot and humid afternoon was her excuse for unbuttoning her blouse to reveal a daring amount of deep cleavage. Fanning herself, Bliss blew blond hair from her eyes as she and Richard sat on the grassy levee, gazing across the river.

Today the dark river water looked as if it was barely moving. The late afternoon sun sent a wide silver path across the water to where they sat. Vagrant wisps of wind ruffled the water here, then there. The cicadas in the trees behind Bliss and Richard were nearly deafening.

"Why do they make *so much* noise?" Bliss asked.

"What?" Richard asked in a lazy voice.

"The blessed locusts!" Bliss clapped hands over her ears.

"Actually, they're cicadas, and not locusts," Richard told Bliss. "I'd guess this is their mating season." He leaned back on one elbow, facing Bliss. A stem of grass bobbed from the corner of his mouth when he spoke. "When are Celeste and your father coming back up the river?" he asked.

"I don't know and couldn't care less," Bliss pouted. Her brown eyes were angry. "Dear sister always gets to go to New Orleans with my father, while Jamie Two and I rusticate here. It isn't fair."

Bliss shifted her weight, turning more toward the

lounging Richard, and in so doing, didn't appear to notice that one breast had nearly escaped her loose-fitting blouse.

"How long must we rest the horses?" she asked him. The two mares were cropping grass at the landside foot of the levee.

"Hey!" Richard said softly. "You're losing something." With his cupped hand, Richard lifted the breast free of her blouse. "Does this one match the other?"

Bliss made no effort to move away from his touch. "Why don't you see for yourself?" she whispered.

"With your gracious permission, I do believe that I will," Richard said, but bent his face to the breast lifted in his hand.

"You're tickling me with your moustache," Bliss protested. "Oh!"

5

At the French Market on the riverbank, Celeste had clothed Paul and Vashti, buying a black broadcloth suit for him, boots and a white shirt, and a calico shirt for Vashti. When they reached the bustling city, Vashti was amazed and cowed. Celeste was glad of that. She'd anticipated trouble in handling the woman.

She'd ignored the invitation that Pierre Laffite had sent by one of his house servants to hire a carriage and pick up the luggage she and her father had left at the boarding house. From there the carriage took the three of them to Spanish House.

Before dismissing the Negro driver, Celeste sent word by him to Ludwig Wagner, the German who was in charge of the remodeling. Until he came with the key, the three of them were stranded in the street.

Celeste was exhausted and hungry. So were her slaves. Vashti had turned sullen. Paul leaned against

Cannons & Roses

the front wall of the house, arms crossed on his chest, and studied the toes of his boots.

The man who rode up to them on a chesty black stallion and dismounted, was dressed in a fashionable frock coat. He was, Celeste thought, one of the ugliest men she'd ever seen.

Over a protruding lower jaw, a lantern jaw, there was a wide slit of a mouth. Bony eye sockets framed yellowish eyes, and smallpox had scarred his hollow cheeks. He was clean-shaven. Black hair fell to his shoulders.

A massive torso, and muscular shoulders were mounted on short, thin legs, so that he looked somehow deformed. He kept his left hand tucked out of sight inside the frock coat, a peculiar Napoleonic gesture, Celeste thought.

"At your service, Miss McCoy, is Ulric Bone." His smile was mechanical—more of a grimace than anything else. He produced a heavy iron key from the pocket of his coat. "Ludwig is otherwise engaged, so I've come instead."

"Doesn't your son work for us?" Celeste asked.

"Delray? He certainly does. By the by, I've just had the shocking word about your father. Please accept my condolences."

"Thank you."

Key in the palm of his hand, Bone stripped Celeste with his eyes, running the tip of his tongue around his thin, liverish lips. "You're as fine a figure of a woman as your mother," he told her.

"The key, Mr. Bone," Celeste reminded him.

Instead of giving it to her, he thrust it in the lock of the door to the courtyard. His left hand came from inside the frock coat to push the door wide. Celeste saw it was a clenched fist made of iron!

Bone followed Celeste into the courtyard, and stood aside with her to let Paul and Vashti enter. "Two prime niggers," he said. "I intend to buy the woman from you."

"Vashti isn't for sale," Celeste said in a cold voice.

"You'll sell her," Bone said.

"I'll not," Celeste countered. "Now I have to buy food, and settle Paul and Vashti here for a day or two. We thank you for coming, but I'll have the key now."

Laughter rumbled in Bone's chest. "I've arranged for your provisions on my way here. They will be coming shortly." Stepping up to Vashti, Bone peeled her single garment over her head. When she tried to resist, he knocked her down with a blow of his iron hand.

"Stop that!" Celeste snapped.

Bone jerked the naked Vashti to her feet by her kinky hair. She cowered away from him. He calmly inspected her, as if the two of them were alone in the courtyard.

"You enjoy a good whipping, I hear," Bone told the woman.

Vashti must have understood. She drew herself up, no longer afraid. She turned for Bone's inspection. Poking out her lower lip, like a pouting child, Vashti met Bone's gaze with smoldering eyes.

"Get out of here!" Celeste ordered.

Celeste never would have guessed that the slender Paul was a match for Bone.

Stepping between Celeste and Bone, he caught the man's good hand as it reached to tweak one of Vashti's breasts. Grasping the man's first and second finger, he jerked them apart, ducking the swing of Bone's iron hand. With a grunt, Paul used all his wiry strength,

Cannons & Roses

disjointing the fingers as he tossed Bone over his hip. When the man started to rise, Paul calmly kicked him unconscious.

Grabbing Bone by the heels of his boots, Paul dragged him to the street, slammed and bolted the courtyard door, then turned to Celeste, dusting his hands.

Vashti stared, wide-eyed. Paul stooped and tossed her the red calico shift. "Put it on."

Vashti did as she was told.

Bone was pounding on the courtyard door with his iron fist and screaming curses.

Celeste finally caught her breath. "Where did you learn to fight like that?" she asked.

"They call Philadelphia 'The City of Brotherly Love,'" Paul said. "It isn't if you're a nigger."

Celeste was thinking fast. They'd heard Bone give up and gallop off, still cursing. "You've just injured a white man," she told Paul. "We can't stay here. Bone will be back."

Paul nodded. "How do we get out of the city?"

"Horseback. There's no boat upriver until the day after tomorrow."

There was a soft knock on the courtyard door. Celeste hurried to peer through the judas, then opened it for a slave woman with a full market basket.

"Thank you." She took the basket, and pushed the woman back to the street, bolting the door again, and standing with her back to it.

"Horses?" Paul asked. "Where do we get them?"

"I'm thinking."

Would Pierre Laffite help them? Celeste didn't know where he lived, but she could ask.

"Back there are the slave quarters," Celeste said, pointing. "Paul, you and Vashti can hide there while

Cannons & Roses

I go to fetch horses. I'll have to find Pierre Laffite. He can help us if he will."

Paul was undecided.

"Have you a better idea?" Celeste asked, now impatient.

Paul nodded. "You have clothes here. Let me dress as a woman. Have you money to hire horses? We passed a livery stable on the way here."

"That's best," the girl agreed. "I'll wear your clothes. No one will recognize us."

"Your hair?" Paul asked.

Celeste was caught up in the escape plotting. "Damn my hair. I have a knife in my belongings. We'll cut it off."

Paul inspected her figure. "We're just about the same size," he said.

"We'll bind my breasts."

"Right." Paul was in the spirit, too. "We should hurry."

In the partially furnished bedroom, with Vashti an interested spectator, Paul and Celeste stripped down, backs to each other. When they'd swapped clothes, Celeste found the knife with a jeweled handle Jeanette had brought from Santo Domingo. She handed it to Paul, turning her back.

"Do it," she ordered.

His body pressed to hers. "A shame!" she heard him mutter.

Black hair cascaded to the floor around her ankles.

Paul's clothes fitted Celeste, the coat loose enough to disguise her breasts.

Celeste stuffed handkerchiefs in Paul's bodice, and gave him a wide-brimmed hat with a veil.

Paul had explained to Vashti what they were doing, and why. Her sullenness was gone. Celeste realized

Cannons & Roses

the woman now recognized Paul as her new master.

"You're a white woman," Celeste told Paul. "We walk arm in arm, with Vashti following. Remember not to lift your veil."

"You'll have to see for both of us," Paul said. "I'm not used to a veil yet."

Celeste laughed. "Get used to it. It's going to be a long ride up the trace." She felt free and light-headed without her long hair. "Vashti, you carry the basket."

Vashti stooped, picked it up, balanced it on her head.

"No. Carry it on your arm," Celeste ordered. "Your *arm*. Do you hear? We don't want people staring. Tell her, Paul."

Paul explained to Vashti. It was no use. As soon as they were on the street, the woman raised the basket to her head. Paul spoke to her sharply, but Celeste said, "Leave her alone."

Bone and two other men pounded past them on horseback before they reached the livery stable.

In a low voice, Celeste had hired a horse and wagon, without telling the livery stable owner their destination. They'd discovered that Vashti was deathly afraid of horses. Getting her on one would have been an impossible feat.

It was late afternoon when they started up the trace, Celeste handling the reins. Paul was beside her, while Vashti huddled in the back of the wagon.

It was close to seventy miles to Baton Rouge, and beyond that, Great Oaks. Celeste had never slept in the open a night in her life. The three of them munched on dry bread and cold meat as the horse jogged along. Celeste decided she'd never seen such a miserable animal. He was spavined, swaybacked, and thin as a rail.

Cannons & Roses

The river was on their left.

"We're never going to make it this way!" she wailed to Paul.

If they did, Celeste knew word of Jamie's death would reach Jeanette long before she did.

Long stretches of the trace were forested and sometimes infested with outlaws who preyed on travelers.

Mr. Albert Grymes, the lawyer from Boston! Why hadn't she thought of him? Jamie had retained him for years. He'd know what to do.

"What are you doing?" Paul asked. He'd discarded the hat and veil and now squirmed uncomfortably in Celeste's clothes.

"We're going back. I know who can help us," Celeste said. "Remember that inn just after we left the city?"

Paul nodded.

"We'll stay there tonight. In the morning I'll send for Mr. Grymes."

Paul didn't question her decision.

A gentle rain dripped from the eaves of the summer house at The Columns. Alicia Carroll was confined to her room with one of her sick headaches. Colonel Carroll and Jamie Two had ridden out that morning to stay the day with the Johnsons, who owned a small plantation six miles from The Columns. Sted Johnson made the best peach brandy in the parish. Bliss had encouraged Jamie Two about Nettie Johnson.

"She's crazy in love with you," she'd confided to her brother.

It's probably true, Bliss thought.

Jamie Two was handsome enough, and his soft-spoken, gentle ways intrigued girls. One McCoy hel-

Cannons & Roses

lion was enough! She qualified for that role. Bliss had Richard Carroll's word for that.

They'd dragged a mat from one of the benches, after the door was bolted, and now Richard slept beside her. Raised on an elbow, through half-shut eyes, Bliss studied the naked Richard. Now it drooped between his muscular thighs. Bliss touched it with a finger, and Richard moaned.

Bliss laughed silently. She moved so she could stretch out, resting the nape of her neck and head on his stomach. She crossed her legs, and clasped her elbows, humming.

She wondered if Richard knew he slept with his mouth slightly open, and each breath fluttered his silky moustache.

Amused, Bliss remembered how it had been on the crest of the levee, in full sight of anyone who might have come along! She was thankful no one had. He'd rucked her blouse up under her chin, and peeled down her riding skirt and undergarments, but they'd tangled with her boots.

"Don't hurry," she'd urged Richard. "I'm not going anywhere."

She might as well have been talking to a runaway horse, or a stallion in heat! His spurs ripped her skirt, and the undergarments, too. She couldn't spread her thighs properly. But somehow Richard managed.

Bliss had been the one who managed this time. She'd made him try to lie still while she fluttered kisses all over his body, with very special attention to his swollen manhood.

She'd pinned *his* shoulders this time. "No hurry, Richard," she'd breathed. "We'll teach you to take your time."

And she had. How long had she tantalized him

Cannons & Roses

from the saddle of his flesh? Bliss was sorry she couldn't see the watch on top of her neatly folded clothes. Richard's were strewn all over the floor around them. She'd have to teach him neatness.

Bliss decided Richard had slept long enough. Flopping over, raised on her elbows, she studied his limp and wrinkled manhood.

"We fixed you, didn't we, little friend?" she whispered. "Do you want to be kissed again? All right."

Richard stirred this time, and so did his manhood.

Bliss raised her head to study his face. His breathing was even again.

"All right, buster!" she hissed.

She lowered her face, and nipped with her sharp front teeth.

Richard awakened with a galvanic start, and his drawn-up knees knocked Bliss back. "Why, you bitch!" Scrambling to his hands and knees, he grabbed her shoulders and pushed her down. "Who taught you to *bite?*"

Bliss was laughing.

Richard, straddling her waist, jerked up her arms and pinned them above her head. "Two can play that game!"

"No!"

"Yes." His teeth worried a nipple.

Bliss groaned.

He nipped her other nipple.

"Ouch!"

Richard was grinning. Bliss raised her head enough to stare down their bodies. "Hello, there!" she exclaimed. "Come in out of the cold, little friend."

"No hurry, Bliss," Richard mocked.

"You're a beast!"

"You're wanton," he said, grinning wolfishly.

Cannons & Roses

"Kiss me."

Richard did her bidding, and it was a long, lingering, exploring kiss. Bliss no longer minded his tickling moustache.

"You're poking my stomach!" Bliss exclaimed.

Richard slid down her body, Bliss locked her ankles behind the small of his back, and met his hard thrust with one of her own.

"Oh!" The cry shuddered out of her. "My God, Richard!"

His mouth swooped and crushed hers, bruising her lips, and her nails tore at his back.

"Richard?"

"What?"

Exhausted, and damp with sweat, they lay side by side on the mat.

"I think someone is coming," Bliss said.

He raised his head to listen. "You're wrong. Mother won't be wandering around today. When she gets one of her headaches . . ."

"Richard?" There was a sharp rap on the door. "Are you in there?"

Stricken, Richard touched a finger to his lips, but Bliss got up, holding her dress in front of her, and unbolted the summerhouse door.

"It's all right, Miss Alicia," she said, and she smiled. "Richard and I are going to be married."

She hoped he'd never discover that she'd bribed the house girl, Eulalia, to awaken Mrs. Carroll after a suitable interval, and tell her "something" was going on in the summerhouse.

6

Albert Grymes had come to New Orleans in 1806, but the Creoles still considered the Bostonian a newcomer. The stocky little middle-aged bachelor, with a ready smile, was well liked nevertheless. He understood their easy way of life better than most of the American newcomers, and spoke fluent French and Spanish. He was also a good friend of the American governor, Claiborne.

With New England shrewdness, Albert served the Laffites as a lawyer, and many times acted as a buffer between them and their mortal enemy, the irascible governor.

Lately he'd taken young Raoul Arcenaux as his law partner. Raoul was the oldest son of a rich and influential Creole family. Grymes & Arcenaux was the most prominent law firm in the Crescent City.

From Pierre Laffite, Albert learned of Jamie's death at The Temple.

Cannons & Roses

"It was a most unfortunate circumstance," Pierre said. "Both Alexander and Jean are desolate that he died accidentally while rescuing his daughter from a notorious madam."

In Albert's opinion, Pierre's account of the barge fire didn't ring true. But he didn't probe. He knew the truth was like quicksilver when dealing with a Laffite.

Jamie had retained Albert four years ago, and the men had become good friends, as well as lawyer and client. Jamie McCoy's death at this time was extremely unfortunate. Great Oaks and Spanish House were mortgaged to the hilt. Jamie had needed cash to buy the new Red River acreage and stock it with slaves.

Recently a most disturbing circumstance had come to Albert's attention. It was Raoul who'd come to him with the rumor about Ulric Bone.

"The whoremaster has bought up all of your good friend's obligations," Raoul reported. "His son is an overseer for McCoy, driving slaves on the Red River acreage. This does not look good, yes?"

Albert knew Bone personally; he had refused his retainer to foreclose on a prominent Creole family. Bone wanted their secluded home just outside the city. Albert knew why Bone wanted that particular home.

Bone posed as a cotton broker since coming to New Orleans from the notorious Five Points section of New York City, but his main source of income was tribute from prostitutes and madams. It was whispered that he was a man with depraved tastes. The Fortier home, located as it was on a bayou more than a mile from the nearest neighbor, was ideal as a place where Bone and his henchmen and friends could indulge in every conceivable depravity.

Cannons & Roses

It was rumored that more than one girl or woman was at the bottom of that bayou.

"I've heard," Raoul had told him, "that now Bone wants Spanish House, as well as land and slaves."

With Jamie McCoy dead, and Delray Bone already established as overseer on the Red River property, Albert knew Bone would very likely get what he wanted.

God help the McCoy women, he thought, *if they get in the man's way!*

It was late, but Albert was still in his law office on Bourbon Street. That afternoon he'd gone to Spanish House when Pierre advised him that Celeste and her new slaves would be there. But Spanish House was locked up and empty.

Albert was too disturbed to keep his mind on the brief that Raoul had prepared for Jean Laffite—another effort to get back from the United States property of his that Claiborne had seized just before the British came to New Orleans.

"It's a hopeless cause anyway," Albert muttered, and pushed aside the lengthy brief to light his pipe.

At the last quadroon ball, Albert had arranged with her mother for a nubile young daughter to live with him. Clarice was the joy of his life these days. She'd be waiting for him, with a late supper on the table, and the bed already turned down.

Clarice had come to him a virgin, but not untutored in the many ways her lithe, brown-skinned body could be used to please a man.

At forty-one, now Albert felt more virile than he'd felt at twenty-one.

The doorbell jangled. Albert found a ragged Negro boy waiting in the street with a message from Celeste,

65

urging him to come to her at the inn right away. Albert knew the inn. If the girl was there, with her slaves, she was in deep trouble.

Albert's new carriage was down the street, with his free Negro driver dozing.

Remembering that Clarice could neither read nor write, Albert swore.

"See here, lad." He seized the boy by his thin shoulders. "You're to run to my house." He gave the boy careful directions. "Tell Missy Clarice I'm gone on urgent business."

"Yassuh. Business. You gone." The boy seemed smart enough.

"She's to feed you. Understand?"

"Yassuh!" The boy grinned.

Albert fished his heavy gold watch from the pocket of his floral-patterned vest. "Twelve now," he told the boy. "Tell Missy Clarice I'll be home by two."

"Yassuh." Still grinning, the boy held up two fingers.

"You stay with her until I come home."

"Yassuh."

"We'll get you back to the inn then."

With a pat on his back, Albert dismissed the boy, and walked to his carriage. He patted a side pocket to make sure that the small pistol was still there.

Celeste hadn't waited until morning to send for Albert because she'd just had time to steer the wagon off into underbrush before Ulric Bone pounded by on his lathered black horse. He was alone.

The grubby innkeeper, surprised to have two young people of quality stopping at his establishment, with their body servant, took Celeste and Paul up a dark, narrow flight of stairs. Vashti followed him.

Cannons & Roses

"We don't get much quality here," he apologized. "I'll fetch a pallet for your slave. It ain't safe to put her in the stable," he growled. "The boys drinking here tonight would wear her out before morning, if they had to hog-tie her."

"We won't be here long," Celeste told him. "Have you a bright boy who'll carry a message into the city?"

"Sure have. Sam. Bright as a dollar, and you can depend on him. You can pay me for his services. I guarantee Sam."

"Never mind the pallet," Celeste said.

Paul was hunkered down on his heels in a corner of the room, arms crossed on his chest. With Celeste's permission, Vashti was stretched out on the filthy bed and had gone to sleep.

Celeste paced the narrow room, thinking.

"Mr. Grymes should be here by now," she'd just said.

Wood crackled. The latch exploded. The room door swung open, banging against the wall. Ulric Bone was framed in it, a pistol in his hand.

Celeste sprang back. Paul jumped to his feet. Vashti snorted awake and sat up, staring with sleep-blurred eyes.

Bone's thin lips twisted in a grin. The pistol swung to cover Paul. *"You're a dead nigger!"*

"Don't!" Celeste sprang toward Bone, but he easily knocked her aside with his iron fist.

On the floor, stunned, she saw his finger tightening on the trigger.

"You, dear sir, are going to be a very dead white man if you pull that trigger," Albert announced, stepping into the room and pressing the muzzle of his pistol to the back of Bone's neck. "Uncock it."

Bone froze.

"Uncock it, I say!" There was a click as Albert cocked his pistol. "Oblige me, Mr. Bone."

Bone uncocked his pistol. His arm dropped to his side.

"Young woman, take the weapon," Albert ordered Paul.

Celeste was back on her feet. "Young man, are you all right?" Albert asked.

"Yes." Celeste rubbed the shoulder Bone had hit. "Only I'm not a young man, and Paul isn't a young lady."

Albert's jaw dropped. "Great good God! What is all this?"

Paul had Bone's pistol, had cocked it, and was now covering the man. "You came in the nick, sir, and I do thank you," Paul said. "Miss Celeste will explain."

"Stop pointing that weapon at me, mister," Bone snarled.

Albert had uncocked and pocketed his pistol.

"Lay the pistol aside," Albert advised Paul. "Mr. Bone, please sit in that chair over there. Let's discuss this matter like reasonable human beings. I'm sure we can find an equitable solution."

Vashti lay back down and turned on her side to watch the four people in the small room. Her sleepy stare was lackluster, as if she'd lost all interest now that they had quieted down.

"That McCoy nigger tried to kill me," Bone said, pointing to Paul.

"Did you report the matter to the authorities?" Albert asked.

"No." Bone was surly. "I planned to kill him myself."

"Is this true, Miss McCoy?" Albert asked.

Cannons & Roses

"No. Paul used only enough force to protect me," she said.

"He knocked me down and kicked me in the face," Bone said, rubbing the lump on his jaw.

"That's a very serious charge. Do you have witnesses?" Albert asked Bone.

"Her and the wench on the bed." Bone had jerked a thumb toward Celeste.

"I have a very poor memory," Celeste said in a sarcastic voice, "and Vashti can't testify."

"Against another nigger she can," Bone said.

Albert nodded. "That's quite correct."

Bone was thoughtful, staring at Celeste, then glancing at Vashti. "I offer Miss McCoy one thousand dollars —cash—for the African wench on the bed," he said, in a conciliatory voice. "If she'll sell the woman, here and now, I won't bring charges against her male nigger."

"And if I won't sell?" Celeste asked.

"Grymes and I take the nigger to The Cabildo, and the wench, too. They'll wring the truth out of her, and hang your nigger as an example."

Celeste turned to Mr. Grymes. "Would you do this?" she asked.

Not meeting her eyes, Albert said, "I'm an officer of the court, but if I refused, Mr. Bone would get someone else, and your servant might not reach The Cabildo alive."

Bone showed his teeth in a derisive grin. "Do you accept my offer?"

Celeste realized Vashti was watching her. She didn't try to meet the woman's stare. "Do you have the money?" she asked Bone.

"I'll write you a bank draft."

* * *

Cannons & Roses

In the carriage, with Paul outside on the seat with the driver, Albert Grymes told Celeste the financial situation her father had left behind. Ulric Bone was after all the McCoy property.

He also explained to her the inheritance laws of Louisiana.

"As his widow, your mother inherits only half of the estate. You, your sister, and your brother, by law, which is based on the Napoleonic Code of France, divide the other half," Albert said. "That is, unless the four of you can arrive at an agreement."

"That includes slaves?" Celeste asked.

"Oh, yes. They are real property."

"We'll work something out so that my father's estate remains intact," Celeste said wearily. "What we can do about Bone, however, is another matter. All these obligations you mention come due in ninety days?"

"That's right."

Celeste thought. "We'll need $80,000. The Red River plantation is still being cleared. Our crop at Great Oaks should bring that much, I think. But that's going to leave us nothing to live on until we make another crop."

"Your father knew that," Albert said, "but the cotton broker who took the mortgages and notes promised him extensions. It was a gentleman's agreement. There is nothing in writing. I'm afraid Bone has you where the hair is short."

"Why does he want to ruin us?" Celeste asked.

"Because Bone wants the social standing of a planter, probably," Albert told her. "He's been south long enough to envy you slave owners. Money isn't enough for him any longer."

"Where are we going?" Celeste asked.

"To my home for the rest of tonight. A packet is going up the river tomorrow morning, and I suppose

Cannons & Roses

you want to reach your mother before the news of your father's death does," Albert said, then asked, "What really happened at The Temple, Miss Celeste?"

"What did you hear?" she countered.

Albert told her. He mentioned that he had the news from Pierre Laffite.

Celeste didn't know if she could trust Albert Grymes's discretion. "My father did have to come to my rescue," she said, "and consequently died in a fire. My mother is going to blame me for his death!"

"I see." Albert's eyes were hooded. "This is a terrible thing, especially coming at this time. I want to help you and your mother anyway I can."

"I'll remember," Celeste said, "and thank you."

"You'll have to bring your mother downriver to sign papers so I can arrange the succession," he said. "Shall I see to it that Spanish House is made ready for occupancy?"

"If you would, please," Celeste told him.

DeWitt Scott took the sobbing woman by her plump shoulders and shook her. "Stop this blubbering and mumbling, Sarah! Speak up. What are you trying to tell me?"

The black woman gulped back her sobs. "Lord have mercy, Master Jamie, he be dead! Now we all be sold away."

They were in the separate kitchen, a square brick structure at the end of a walkway from the main house, and DeWitt was alone with the cook, Sarah. The woman sat down on a chair that creaked with her weight, and covered her head with her apron.

"Lord have mercy!"

DeWitt considered the shaking shoulders of the woman, stroking his jaw with a hand. This wasn't his first experience with the slave grapevine. If anything had happened to Jamie McCoy, the house servants would know about it first.

And their information was usually accurate. He knew, for instance, that Bliss had seduced Richard Carroll yesterday afternoon and trapped him into some sort of marriage proposal. As yet Jeanette didn't know about this development, and DeWitt didn't plan to tell her. Slaves at Great Oaks confided their gossip to him because he kept their secrets.

"Sarah?"

The woman uncovered her tear-wet face. "Yes, Mr. DeWitt?"

"Who else on the plantation knows what you've just told me?"

The woman wrinkled her forehead. "That twitchy Stella, she know." Sarah counted on her fingers. "Robert, he know." Robert was what in a British home would be called the majordomo. "Stella sneak off last night to meet Jackson, that half-white nigger who belong to Mr. Fuller." The Fuller plantation was below Great Oaks. "That's all, I guess. Robert, he tell me."

"All right, Sarah. Now I don't want this rumor to reach the quarters, do you understand? It may not be true. Master Jamie and Miss Celeste should be coming home this evening."

"Master Jamie never come home!" Sarah wailed.

"Stop that."

"Yes, sir."

The gentle walking horse Jamie had brought down from Tennessee was tied to the rail outside the kitchen, browsing grass. DeWitt stood beside his horse, undecided, still stroking his jaw.

Jamie McCoy dead?

Jeanette would come to the kitchen later this morning

Cannons & Roses

to go over the food supplies with Sarah. DeWitt patted the horse's flank, then strode up the walkway to the back door of the Great House.

Better to warn Jeanette, in case the rumor was true. In his bones, DeWitt felt that it was.

7

Jeanette said, "DeWitt, I don't believe it! You, of all people, should know better than to listen to servants' gossip."

But Jeanette had paled and clenched her hands. She and DeWitt faced each other in the small office off the Great House living room.

"I thought you should know what's being said, Mrs. McCoy." DeWitt shifted his feet uncomfortably. "It was Sarah who told me. Robert and Stella are the only others who've heard the rumor."

"Stella!" Jeanette spit the name. "I'd like to blister her brown backside! That girl is like a bitch in heat! Sometimes I'm sorry we spare them the whip here at Great Oaks. If I had my way, there would be a little harsher discipline around here."

DeWitt knew, of course, it was Jeanette who'd insisted no whip should touch a slave on Great Oaks.

Jeanette brushed hair away from her forehead. It

was a typical gesture when she was disturbed, DeWitt knew. He loved her the more for it.

Jeanette's smile was shaky. "I'm sorry, DeWitt. You did right coming to me with this rumor. I have a bit of news for you. Richard Carroll rode over early this morning to say he and Bliss are engaged. And all this time I thought the boy was after Celeste." She laughed. "Jamie will be pleased, I think. He's never had anything against young Richard, except that ridiculous moustache, and that Jamie thought the boy was after his favorite daughter."

"When Great Oaks and The Columns are merged," DeWitt mused, "we'll have the largest plantation in the state."

"Yes." It was an absentminded answer. "Pray that the bottom doesn't drop out of the cotton and rice markets."

"I'll be about my chores," DeWitt said.

"If Jamie and Celeste come up the river today, come to the house this evening," Jeanette said. She smiled. "I listen to servants' gossip. I've heard some ugly things about Delray Bone."

"I have, too," DeWitt admitted, "and I've been anxious to discuss them with Mr. McCoy."

"We'll reach our landing right after supper," Celeste told Paul. She was dressed as a woman again, with a *chignon* to hide her cropped hair, which drew askance glances from the other women passengers.

"I thought only slave women wore those," Celeste had heard one woman remark to her male companion, "but isn't that Celeste McCoy?"

"I do believe it is," the man answered. "But who but another woman would notice what she wears on her head?"

Cannons & Roses

The remark earned him a sharp tap with his companion's fan. "Naughty, Herbert!"

Celeste and Paul, clothed again in his black broadcloth suit, were on the hurricane deck of the small steamboat. Because he was a house servant, this was permitted. But he had to take his meals, such as they were, on the lowest deck with the slave hands.

"I've always wanted to see the Mississippi and New Orleans," Paul said in a bitter voice. "Seeing it as just another slave, however . . ." He shrugged. "Does Albert Grymes know my story?"

"Yes. I spoke to him. He's going north next month, to Washington on business for the Laffites, I believe. Mr. Grymes has promised to spend a day in Philadelphia. I gave him the names you suggested. I keep my word, Paul."

"I didn't doubt it," Paul said.

Celeste confided to Paul what Albert Grymes had told her about Ulric Bone. As she did so, the girl realized she wasn't only treating him as an equal, she was thinking of him that way.

This, Celeste knew, was dangerous, not so much to herself as to Paul. "Until we get matters squared away, Paul, you've got to act the part of a born slave," she told him. "Never stare directly at my mother or me when others are around. Remember to call her Miss Jeanette, and me, Miss Celeste. It's important, Paul. You don't know much about the South yet."

"Yassuh, this nigger do what you say, Miss Celeste," he drawled with the thick-tongued Negro speech. He ducked his head and touched his forelock.

"Let's not overdo it," Celeste said, laughing. "Just show proper respect."

"I'll try to remember, Miss Celeste."

* * *

Cannons & Roses

When the steamboat rounded a bend in the river, and the Great Oaks landing was in sight, Celeste felt as if a hand were squeezing her heart. How to tell her mother?

The landing was empty in the dusk, which was strange, because she knew the hands were out of the fields, and the steamboat's whistle, when it was rounding the bend, should have brought some of the men, most of the women, and all of the children in the quarters racing down to the landing.

Then she saw in the shadow of one of the oak trees DeWitt Scott sitting his horse. His flat-crowned, wide-brimmed hat was shoved to the back of his head.

What was wrong? Celeste was sure word of her father's death couldn't have reached Great Oaks this soon.

The steamboat wouldn't tie up. The pilot would simply nudge the piling that supported the timber platform long enough for Celeste and Paul to step ashore. She saw DeWitt swing out of the saddle and stride toward the landing, slapping his boot with the riding crop he always carried.

Paul took her elbow to assist Celeste stepping from the boat deck to the landing, then jumped the distance as the pilot swerved away toward midstream again.

DeWitt raised his crop in greeting, but his face was somber. "Where's Mr. McCoy?" he asked.

Celeste bit her lower lip. She avoided DeWitt's probing blue eyes. It wasn't within her to answer the man's simple question, because once she did, Jamie's death would become a fact.

It was Paul who answered DeWitt. "Mr. McCoy is dead. He was killed at The Temple."

"Who are you?" DeWitt asked, not unkindly. "I don't believe we've met."

"Paul is the servant who will help Mother and me with the accounts," Celeste explained. She told Paul, "Mr. DeWitt is the overseer here at Great Oaks."

DeWitt adjusted his longer stride to Celeste's as they started up the grassy alley between the oaks for the Great House. "Bring my horse along," he told Paul over his shoulder.

"How much does Mother know?" Celeste asked.

"I heard that he'd been killed this morning from Sarah, who got it from Robert, whom Stella had told. She met Jackson last night."

"Jackson?"

"One of the Fuller nigras."

"Oh, yes. The man Stella sneaks off to meet. How much were you told?" Celeste asked.

"Nothing beyond the fact that Mr. McCoy was dead. I reported the rumor to your mother before she wormed it out of Sarah. She's waiting for me now to go over some accounts in the office. I'll go on ahead."

"You'd better," Celeste said.

"Take my horse to the barn," DeWitt told Paul. "Miss Celeste will tell you where it is. Sam is the groom. He'll take over. Then come to the house."

DeWitt strode up the tree-shadowed alley.

Celeste told Paul where the barn was. Paul swung up in the saddle, leaned to shorten the stirrups, then loped off. He rode as if he'd spent most of his life in the saddle. Celeste guessed he must have learned in Liberia.

It was Robert who opened the front door for Celeste, when she'd crossed the wide front porch, with its portico and five Doric pillars.

"Welcome home, Miss Celeste." Robert's lined face was solemn. He was an old man—seventy at least, Celeste guessed—and had been at Great Oaks all his life. Only slightly stooped shoulders and a cracking voice told his age. His step was as lively as a youngster's. "Master Jamie is dead, Miss Celeste?"

"Yes, Robert, he is," she said.

It touched Celeste to see Robert's eyes fill with tears.

Celeste crossed from the broad hallway that ran from the front to the back of the house, through the living and ballroom, so seldom used, to the cozy office she shared with her mother.

Celeste expected DeWitt would have broken the news to her mother, but she found him, his back to her and Jeanette, staring out the window.

"Where's your father?" was Jeanette's sharp question.

"Daddy is dead." Celeste completely forgot the soft words she'd rehearsed coming up the river. "He was killed by Gambini . . . in a duel. Oh, God damn it!" she burst out, when she saw her mother's stricken face. "I'm going to kill the Italian!"

Celeste lost control. Tears gushed. Words spilled out, stumbling words, and between sobs, she told the whole story, the flogging of Vashti and the Mandingo man, how she fled when the strap emasculated him, how close she had come to being raped.

"And Alexander Laffite burned the barge with Daddy's body and the woman's in it," she finished. "We can't even have a funeral!"

The last was a wail.

Celeste heard Paul's step behind her.

Jeanette had listened to Celeste's recital, clenching and unclenching her hands. Her face was dead white. Her lips drew back in a rictus, when Celeste finished, and DeWitt, watching now, took a step toward her.

"You little bitch!" Jeanette screamed. *"You've killed your father and my husband!"*

Jeanette shrugged away from DeWitt's reaching

Cannons & Roses

hands, and flung herself at Celeste, who stood shocked and frozen.

Paul stepped around Celeste, to put himself between the girl and her mother, so it was Paul she hit in the face.

Paul protected his face with his arms but didn't draw away from Jeanette's pummeling, moving to stay between the mother and daughter. DeWitt finally captured Jeanette's wrists. Grasping her, DeWitt pinned her arms.

"Leave us," he ordered Paul and Celeste. "It's going to be all right, dear lady," he murmured to Jeanette.

Robert was hovering in the hallway, wringing his hands, his brown face glistening with tears. "It's so bad!" he was muttering as Celeste and Paul passed him. "Poor master!"

Robert sank to his knees, closed his eyes, and began to pray. Celeste paused in the doorway to the porch to listen.

"God, you just ain't been kind," Robert scolded. "Why do you take Master Jamie? It ain't fair!"

"Robert?" Celeste said.

Robert rose from his knees. "Yes, Miss Celeste?"

"Pray later, please. Where are the twins tonight?"

"At The Columns."

"Send someone for them. Then tell Sarah to fix me a meal and to feed Paul in the kitchen. We'll put him in the downstairs bedroom, near the office."

"Yes, Miss Celeste."

With a shrug, Paul followed Robert. When they were gone, DeWitt came, carrying Jeanette in his arms. Sweat beaded on his forehead and upper lip.

"Where are you taking her?" Celeste asked.

"Upstairs. To her room."

Cannons & Roses

Celeste started toward them, but Jeanette buried her face in DeWitt's shirt. "Keep her away from me!" she said in a muffled voice.

"All right, Mother." Celeste was resigned.

"Send up brandy," DeWitt ordered, and mounted the wide circular staircase, holding Jeanette tight.

"There's brandy and whisky in their room," Celeste called after him. "I've sent for the twins."

Ulric Bone had taken Vashti from the stable at the inn to his secluded house on the bayou and turned her over to the husky women slaves dubbed Bone's Amazons by the select group who patronized his establishment.

This pair of women, just recently imported from Africa, were both over six feet, and as muscular as any man. They'd learned their trade from a harsh Arab slave trader.

While he waited for the groomed Vashti to be brought to him by the Amazons, Bone relaxed on the curious table bolted to the floor in the center of the room.

This was a low table, the wood surface covered with black leather, and there was a thick iron ring screwed into each of the four corners. Bone had seen one like it when he visited Spain. This one he'd managed to obtain from the Ursuline nuns!

Toward the end of the Spanish reign in New Orleans, a fine array of torture instruments had been imported by overzealous Spanish friars. They planned to bring the Inquisition to the New World, but the easygoing Creoles quickly vetoed this idea. The table and assortment of torture instruments had been gathering dust in the convent storeroom since.

Bone had convinced the Mother Superior he was a

collector of such artifacts, and she'd sold him the table in good faith.

This rather small room had once been for the storage of vegetables and other perishables. It was windowless, with a low ceiling. Bone had installed mirrors on three walls, and the ceiling.

Against the bare wall, on either side of the heavy oak door that could be securely bolted from the inside, hung an array of whips, ranging from a cat-o'-nine-tails to wicked little whips, and there were also straps and thongs to secure wrists and ankles. Vents in this wall permitted some air to circulate.

Beside his Amazons, only Ulric Bone's victims had ever seen the inside of this room. Sometimes it amused him to let them help him with a particularly recalcitrant woman or girl. But the horrors of being conducted to this room for what Bone called *"discipline"* were whispered by prostitutes up and down the levee.

Bone stripped himself to the waist and hung his iron fist by the straps securing it on a hook put in the wall for that purpose. No man—and only a few women—had ever seen Bone unclothed below the waist. Tonight he was barefoot and wore tight-fitting black broadcloth pants.

Hands behind his thick neck, Bone lay on his back, staring up at his mirrored image. He grinned, thinking of Vashti in the hands of his Amazons. It was a woman who'd cost him his hand. In a basement near Five Points, where he'd been dragged by a rival gang, she'd driven a railroad spike through his hand, pinning it to the dirty floor.

Unable to find that particular woman again, Bone had been revenging himself on her sex ever since. Here in New Orleans, Bone quickly discovered he could turn a neat profit by catering to a select group of other men who shared his taste in depravity.

He knew Vashti wasn't the ordinary black wench. Word quickly reached Bone from several patrons of his establishment that there was a slave at The Temple who enjoyed the lash. He'd arrived there too late to buy her from Alexander Laffite. From experience, Bone knew such a woman would also derive enjoyment from punishing other women—or men.

Bone had to have her in his stable! Bone had seen Jeanette McCoy twice when she visited New Orleans. Now he was also acquainted with her daughter. A spirited pair of females!

Bone hadn't had a hand in the murder of Jamie McCoy, but he'd rewarded Vincent Gambini with enough money to leave the country and set himself up as a slave trader on Africa's west coast. He'd be Gambini's silent partner. It wasn't right that the Laffites and Wade Hampton in Charleston should have the illicit traffic in black flesh cornered.

A plan to get both Jeanette and her daughter in his power had begun to mature in Bone's mind. Vashti would be an important part of such a plan, Bone knew, but he hadn't decided yet exactly how he would use her. But he was satisfied that inspiration would come.

There was a knock on the door. Bone unbolted and opened it. The grinning Amazons shoved a naked Vashti into the room. They'd shaved her head and oiled her body.

"That's all," Bone told the women, and laughed at the disappointed expressions on their faces. He slapped each rump. "She's been drugged?" he asked.

The Amazons nodded.

"Good." Bone closed and bolted the door.

Vashti, hands fastened behind her, was studying herself in the mirrors. There wasn't the slightest flicker of fear in her eyes.

Bone, admiring her, rubbed his dry hands. Then he untied her wrists. "Crawl up on the table," he ordered. "Let's find out how much pain you can stand, wench."

8

After the first wild storm of grief, Jeanette pulled herself together and began the preparations for the wedding. It would take place within the month, she and Bliss decided. The drawing room at Great Oaks was turned into a sewing room, and every girl and woman who knew how to sew was drafted into service. But so soon after Jamie's death, it would be a quiet wedding, with only family and close friends invited.

After she had made a halfhearted apology to Celeste for that first furious outburst, Jeanette avoided the girl as much as she could. But it was agreed they'd both go down to New Orleans to stay while Albert Grymes worked out the legal details of the succession.

Celeste had explained to her mother the financial mess Jamie had left behind him and the danger of Ulric Bone's foreclosing.

"He's a monster," she told Jeanette. "I don't believe he'll stop at anything to get what he wants. We shouldn't have Delray Bone working for us."

"Talk with DeWitt about this," Jeanette said.

Immersed in the wedding preparations, Jeanette left the management of the plantations to Celeste and DeWitt. Celeste wondered if her mother was too stunned to realize how dangerous the situation was.

DeWitt realized. Until late at night, he and Celeste worked over the accounts, until they were both satisfied that with economy, and a good crop, they would be able to meet Jamie's obligations, but barely.

During the following year they would have to borrow again to buy seed and provide food for their slaves.

Paul worked with them to familiarize himself with the problems involved in running the two plantations. Some suggestions he made were readily adopted by DeWitt and Celeste.

They advertised in the New Orleans, Alabama, Mississippi, Georgia, and Virginia newspapers for an overseer to replace Delray Bone. But it would take time to find one. They would have to depend on him until the first Red River cotton had been picked and ginned.

DeWitt traveled by horseback to the Red River plantation twice within two weeks. He reported to Celeste what he'd found.

"Young Bone is a driver, all right," he said. "He's flanked himself with two big bucks just off the slaver from Africa. He's working the slave crew seven days a week, from dawn until dusk, cultivating and clearing new ground. We should get our quota, and Bone should earn a good bonus, according to the agreement your father made with him."

"Those slaves should be dropping in their tracks!"

Cannons & Roses

Celeste said. "Have you told him they must have one day a week free?"

"No."

"I thought we agreed on that, DeWitt," Celeste said.

DeWitt flushed. "We did," he admitted. "But we need every ounce of sweat Bone can wring out of the wretched blacks if we're going to save Great Oaks for your mother."

"What about provisions up there?" Celeste asked.

"Bone had them on a quarter of a pound of bacon a day and a quart of meal."

"That's a starvation diet!" Celeste exclaimed. "The man must be mad."

DeWitt nodded. "I suspect in some ways he is. I've had their bacon ration increased to a pound for the men, and three-quarters of a pound for the women, and three pints of meal for everyone. I bought the additional supplies in Shreveport. We'd be too short here if I sent them up the Red River from Great Oaks."

Paul had been listening to this discussion. "I notice here that every cabin in the quarters has a garden plot," he said. "And then there's the big garden to supply our kitchen."

"That's true," Celeste said. "What are you getting at?"

"We have two men now working full time in the kitchen garden. One man with a helper or two could do the work. Right?"

DeWitt nodded thoughtfully.

"Why not send one of those slaves up to where Bone is, with a couple of helpers, and let them make a big garden there? That would supplement the diet of those slaves."

"I think we should do it, DeWitt," Celeste said. "And send along a few barrels of rum for Bone to ration out."

On Great Oaks, the slaves were allowed rum only on Sunday, their day off. But DeWitt decided that Paul and the girl were right.

"I'll take care of it," he promised, "and go back up there to see Bone carries out his orders."

"Does he know we plan to replace him?" Celeste asked.

"Not from me," DeWitt told her.

Richard Carroll could understand neither Celeste nor Jamie Two in the way each reacted to his engagement to Bliss. After all, it was Celeste he originally planned to seduce and marry, and he had reason to feel he was on the brink of her conquest. He wanted her dark beauty in his bed and in his life.

Not that Richard wasn't willing now to settle for her blond sister, who had so many tricks and ways of stimulating a man. And whether it was Celeste or Bliss, marriage would link the fortunes of the Carrolls and McCoys. Richard had talked with his father about that. He had political ambitions.

Colonel Carroll had served two terms in the legislature and one in the senate. Richard had read some law, planned to read more, and on being admitted to the bar, to follow in his father's political footsteps. But he resolved to stay reasonably sober if he ever reached Washington, uninvolved with other women, and to become a conscientious legislator.

Bliss was eager to go to Baton Rouge, and then Washington, and had promised Richard she would do anything to further his political career. When Richard

Cannons & Roses

tried to discuss politics with Celeste, she had only shown faint interest.

So Richard was comfortably reconciled to marrying Bliss. But Celeste's lack of jealousy puzzled Richard. She would be delighted, Celeste promised Bliss, to be her maid of honor. And she already treated Richard with easy informality. It was almost, he decided, as if Celeste was relieved that he'd be marrying her younger sister.

"Damn the girl!" he muttered, and then laughed at himself.

Richard had been a bosom friend of Jamie Two. They rode together, hunted together, swam together, and drank together. But the moment Jamie Two learned of the engagement, he turned cold and aloof.

"Sorry, fellow," Jamie Two said, when Richard asked him to be best man, "but I'm working on some other plans."

Jamie Two had decided on a military career. Within a week he planned to be on his way to Washington College in Lexington, Virginia, to join the cadet corps.

Only Celeste suspected the real reason for Jamie Two's sudden decision. She helped him with his packing. "Bliss certainly trumped both of us where Richard Carroll is concerned," Celeste told Jamie.

They were alone together in his room.

"Do you plan to take Moses with you?" she asked.

Jamie looked up from strapping the last piece of luggage. Earnest was the word for Jamie, Celeste decided.

"No, I do not," Jamie said.

Celeste smiled. "I think that's a wise decision, Jamie."

Squatting on his heels, Jamie studied her for a long

moment, then said, "Remember when you caught Bliss and me?"

Celeste noticed the flush in his cheeks.

"I remember," she said casually.

"I don't suppose I should talk like this to my own sister," Jamie said, "but ever since, I haven't been able to . . . satisfy another girl or woman."

"You don't love Bliss that way, do you?" Celeste asked.

Jamie shook his head. "No. Sometimes I think I hate her." He stood up, and stretched. "I need to be away a long time," he said. "Away from Richard as well as Bliss. Do you think I'm sick?"

"No." It was a prompt answer. "You need a strong woman who is older than you are, Jamie. You'll find one."

Jamie was thoughtful. "I've thought along those exact lines," he admitted. He grinned sheepishly. "I want such a woman to seduce me."

Celeste laughed, but not unkindly. "I suspect you'll get your wish before too long," she said. "If I weren't your older sister, I might take on that job myself."

"God forbid!" Jamie groaned, and they both laughed.

Delray Bone lived in a crude log cabin, near the sheds that sheltered the slaves when they weren't in the fields.

Near Bone's cabin, a tent had been pitched for the sweating women who cooked for the crew. Bone had his own cook, Charles—the only slave he allowed to touch anything he ate.

The sheds, the cabin and the cooking tent were on a high bluff overlooking the Red River, with fields stretched out behind nearly as far as the eye could see.

Cannons & Roses

The Red River had shrunk to a pool; so shallow, and with so many red-clay bars above the surface, that a long-legged man could wade across to the opposite shore. When work was finished, Bone allowed the slaves to rush down the bank, strip, and bathe in the river.

Today the slaves clearing new ground and burning the brush had finished the task Jamie McCoy had laid out for them. Now the whole crew could concentrate on chopping cotton, hoeing the weeds away from the thriving plants.

Delray Bone was satisfied with the progress made. That fool, DeWitt Scott, should have been, too, Delray thought. Slouched on a crude bench in his cabin, he spat a stream of chewing tobacco on the hard dirt floor. Scott had come yesterday and was gone this morning.

Rum would help.

The slaves had become increasingly surly as more men and women collapsed from exhaustion during the heat of the day. Bone's husky bodyguards had tired themselves swinging their bullwhips, and there were a lot of raw backs in camp tonight.

Yes, the rum would certainly help, and the increased rations.

"Your people are a sorry-looking bunch of nigras," Scott had told Bone yesterday. "I don't like it, and I'm sure Miss Jeanette won't. Ease up a little, man. These are humans, not animals."

"Well, now, I don't know that, Mr. DeWitt," he'd said. "I got sent up here to do a job and to get it done. I've had to work them like animals. It means money for Miss Jeanette, and you, too, I suppose."

Bone considered Miss Jeanette and her daughters. "God almighty, I'm getting randy!" he muttered. "Right

Cannons & Roses

now I'd like to get my hands on all three of them, and teach them what a real man can do."

Bone thanked his stars he wasn't handicapped as his father was. Once in a while, when the mood was on him, and he had a gut full of raw liquor, Delray liked to flog a saucy girl or insolent woman, just for the hell of it.

I'm that much my father's son, he thought.

But the things he knew his father did in that small room with the table made Delray Bone feel queasy. He wondered how many prostitutes and slave women were at the bottom of the bayou, feeding the alligators? Someone, somewhere, Delray knew, was going to catch up with the Old Man and put a final stop to his nasty sex habits.

Not that he gave a good damn.

Charles was opopsite Delray cooking supper on the wood range. Alligator tail tonight. Delray, like the blacks, and the Indians, considered the firm white meat a delicacy.

After supper, what?

There were too few girls and women with this crew, and most of them were stinking workhorses. Bone stretched and spat again. One of the girls he'd noticed in the fields today wasn't bad. What was her name?

"Charles, who was that girl I sent in early today?" he asked his cook.

"That one be called Martha, I think, Mr. Bone. She about twelve, maybe thirteen."

"That's old enough. Send her up when I've finished eating, and remember what I told you about doling out rum tonight."

"I remember, Mr. Bone. One dipper for the womenfolk, two for each man."

Charles glanced over his shoulder at Delray. "That Martha, she told me she ain't ever laid with no man, Mr. Bone," he said. "Sure you want her up here tonight?"

Delray grinned. "Why do you reckon I sent her in early, you black rascal? Sure, I want her. How's she going to learn if I don't teach her?" He paused to spit. "Dip her in the river before you bring her, Charles."

"Yassuh, Mr. Bone."

"You'd better dip too, Charles, because you're getting a little gamy in this heat."

"Yassuh."

Delray knew his father depended on him to burn the crop they were making in the field, as soon as he sent word. For doing it, the Old Man had promised to double any bonus he might have earned.

Delray was no longer sure he was going to burn the ripe cotton. He wanted DeWitt Scott's job at Great Oaks more than he needed the extra money. How else would he be able to sniff around the mother and the girls?

With McCoy killed—and Delray wondered if his father had taken a hand in that—he considered his chances of getting rid of DeWitt to court the mother and daughters better than ever.

There was no shadow of doubt in Delray Bone's mind that he couldn't seduce at least one of them, it didn't matter which one, although he'd prefer that black-haired witch called Celeste.

"Hurry up supper, Charles."

"Yassuh."

Arms crossed on his bare chest, leaning against a mirrored wall, Ulric Bone watched Vashti at work on

Cannons & Roses

the chubby woman who called herself Mercy. Mercy and her girls had cheated his collectors once too often.

She was strapped by wrists and ankles to all four corners of the low, leather-covered table, and a bolster thrust under her hips raised the fleshy globes at a provocative angle. Mercy was face down.

Vashti was using a stiff riding crop as he'd trained her to do. Vashti knew well enough by this time how it felt to her victim!

Mercy's buttocks were already crisscrossed with welts, vivid red against the woman's pale skin. Bone had stuffed a rag in Mercy's mouth. The only signs of her pain were her pleading eyes and what muffled sounds she could make each time the crop whistled down to streak her flesh with another welt.

Power over a helpless woman! This was Ulric Bone's aphrodisiac. He'd watched his Amazons use Mercy, submitting the woman to one indignity after another. Mercy was too cowed to fight their advances, and tried to satisfy them and Bone in any way she could. He might not take her to The Room!

But he had.

Vashti paused to wipe her brow. There was a pouting, sullen look on her face, but it was obvious she delighted in doing to other women what Bone had done to her.

Vashti is going to be worth a fortune to me, Bone thought.

Vashti studied her handiwork, traced a welt with the tip of her finger, frowning slightly.

"Legs, Vashti," Bone ordered. "She's had enough there, I think."

Vashti raised the stiff crop, and brought it down with a snap of her wrist across the top of the woman's thighs.

Mercy managed to spit out the gag.

"Please, Mr. Bone!" Mercy pled between gasps for breath. "I can't stand any more of this!"

She'd chewed her lips bloody.

Bone wiped her lips with a handkerchief he'd had tucked into the waist of his black tights and slapped her inflamed buttocks. He laughed at Mercy's squeal of new pain.

"Please!" she begged.

Bone took the crop. He touched Mercy with the tip of it, in the cleavage between her thighs.

"Oh, no!" Her voice rose to a scream. "Not there, Mr. Bone!"

"Just a lick for luck, Mercy," he taunted, and the crop whistled, struck, the woman stiffened, snapping back her head, but there was no cry, this time.

Her forehead struck the table with a thump. Mercy had finally fainted.

Bone tossed the whip to Vashti. "She's had enough for this time," he said.

9

Celeste and her mother took Stella and Paul with them to Spanish House. Within just a few days Albert Grymes was leaving for Washington on a ship that would also unload cargo in Philadelphia. With the help of his young mistress, Clarice, Albert had tastefully furnished the remodeled house, and they found it ready for occupancy.

Bliss had seemed a blond angel in her white wedding dress. Reverend Holloway had ridden up from Baton Rouge to perform that service, and, at Jeanette's request, a memorial service for Jamie.

Richard and Bliss would visit Washington, New York, and Boston on their honeymoon, spending the better part of two months.

Jamie Two had matriculated at Washington College, and from his letters to Celeste and Jeanette, was very enthusiastic about a military career.

We are going to need every military officer with a

Cannons & Roses

southern background we can get in this next two decades, Jamie Two had written Celeste. *I predict there will be a war with Mexico, before we can claim Texas as another slave state. The few Yankees I've met here can't see beyond the end of their nose! Our southern race will have to fight this country's wars.*

To his mother, Jamie Two wrote: *John Quincy Adams, our sixth president, is a crusty old cuss, those who know him say, but people here in Virginia begin to like him. Nobody talks about anything but the Erie Canal! What a waste of money, I think. Thank God we have Old Muddy to move our cotton and rice.*

There was a cryptic postscript to the last letter Celeste had received from her brother.

Remember that woman we spoke about, sister? I do believe that I've met her.

Celeste and DeWitt had given up hope of replacing Delray Bone as overseer. The few answers their advertisements brought were completely unsatisfactory. And on his last visit DeWitt had found conditions better. DeWitt didn't approve of Bone's young black mistress, and had said as much to the man, but so far as he could see, she wasn't being mistreated.

They decided to leave that situation alone until the first crop was in, and then make any changes that were necessary.

DeWitt Scott burned with desire for Jeanette, and he couldn't hide this fact from Celeste. They worked together too closely. One evening, she said, out of a clear sky, "DeWitt, were you to take a mistress, I believe my mother might sit up and take notice."

Paul was in the office and gave the pair an amused glance when he overheard that remark.

Celeste continued. "My father used to say, to get

Cannons & Roses

a stubborn mule's attention, so you can sweet-talk him, you first hit him between the eyes with a two-by-four timber. Mother is so damned stubborn!"

DeWitt had flushed beet-red. "My feelings for your mother, and our relationship, are private, Miss Celeste."

"Pardon me," Celeste said, "but think in terms of a mistress, will you? Mother needs a man, whether she knows it yet or not."

And so do I, Celeste thought. *But not you.*

Near-rape—the kind she'd experienced,—should have made the thought of sex a private horror, but it hadn't. Celeste was plagued with a recurring dream.

Sometimes the setting was her bedroom at Great Oaks; other times she was on that filthy bunk again, on the barge. But it wasn't Gambini who was going to rape her.

It was Paul. At The Temple she'd seen him nearly naked. When changing clothes at the inn, Celeste had sneaked a glance at his back and slender brown flanks. In her dream, Paul was always naked.

"This won't hurt," he would promise in her dream, and smile in a lazy way he had. "Just lie still."

Was Paul made the way she saw him in her dream? Celeste wondered every time she looked at him.

That damn dream! Celeste always woke up just before Paul thrust into her. *Then* try to fall back to sleep!

Damned if she'd relieve herself!

"Paul is a nigger," she would say, pacing her room, the nightgown in a heap on the floor beside the bed. "Nigger, nigger, nigger!"

Just one drop of black blood made him that, and Paul had quite a few drops, Celeste knew.

She'd returned to Great Oaks determined to seduce

Cannons & Roses

Richard Carroll and let him initiate her into the rites of sex. Strangely, Celeste had been relieved to discover Bliss had seduced Richard first.

There was a shameless hussy! The night before the wedding, Bliss had confided her stratagem to her sister, gloating over the details. Celeste listened quietly, then said, "So what that's new and different are you and Richard going to do on your wedding night tomorrow?"

Bliss pretended deep thought, poking at her cheek with a forefinger. "Tease him until he's half-crazy," she decided. "You just don't know how we women can make a man crawl and beg, sister! It's such good fun."

"I'm sure," Celeste said.

"You're just jealous."

Men could have their pick down in the quarters, and Celeste knew some plantation wives encouraged this sort of activity—Alicia Carroll for instance. Why shouldn't a southern woman have the same pleasure? It wasn't fair!

But it just wasn't possible.

Or was it?

Couldn't she have Paul, taking all the precautions Jeanette had learned on Santo Domingo, and passed on to her girl children?

Celeste was certain Paul wanted her.

The trouble was, Celeste finally admitted to herself, that she didn't feel toward Paul as her slave. How did she feel, where Paul was concerned?

"No white woman can love a nigger!" Celeste insisted to herself.

So she couldn't be falling in love with Paul. *That was impossible!*

Or was it?

Cannons & Roses

Celeste had insisted that Paul accompany them to New Orleans and Spanish House. Jeanette wanted De-Witt to sit in on their conferences with Albert Grymes, and had protested about taking Paul downriver, but Celeste had had her way.

Colonel Carroll consented to accompany the women and their slaves because he knew of the problems they faced and had a solution. Jeanette decided that De-Witt should stay at Great Oaks after all, with cotton-picking time almost on them.

So it was Colonel Carroll who sat in on their first conference with Albert Grymes. And both Jeanette and Celeste were glad to discover that Colonel Carroll had come to the offices of Grymes & Arcenaux reasonably sober.

"I can raise the necessary sum of money, sir, to save the McCoy holdings, with the exception of mortgaged Spanish House," Colonel Carroll told Albert. "It is the least a man can do for his son and daughter-in-law."

"What security for such a loan would you want?" Albert asked.

Jeanette spoke up. "In time Richard and Bliss will come to live at Great Oaks, Albert," she said. "There is no reason why we can't merge the two plantations now, is there?"

Albert thoughtfully pinched his lower lip, his eyes on Celeste. "Do you find this solution agreeable?" he asked her.

"Mother has discussed it with me," Celeste said.

Albert studied Celeste more closely. "You haven't quite answered my question," he said.

Celeste spread her hands. "I can't think of a better way to meet our obligations."

Colonel Carroll broke in. "Mrs. McCoy and I have

discussed the young lady's best interests," he said. "When she marries, the Red River plantation with sufficient dowry to erect a new great house there, and the slaves, of course, will become her property."

"I see," Albert said, and called in Raoul Arcenaux, telling him how to prepare the necessary legal papers. Then he asked Celeste, "Do you still want me to make inquiries in Philadelphia?"

"What inquiries?" Jeanette asked in a sharp voice.

Celeste flushed. "A personal matter, Mother. No," she told Albert. "Leave it alone."

Albert shrugged.

Ulric Bone was in a white-hot rage! Albert Grymes had just left his office in the Bayou House, after paying Jamie McCoy's obligations in full.

Ulric was just returned from a trip up the Red River to consult with his son. Delray had coolly told him that the cotton would be picked, ginned, and sold through another cotton broker in New Orleans.

Grymes intimated that he would get Spanish House. "Unless," he'd qualified, "the women realize enough from this next crop to pay you off on time."

Bone planned to make Vashti his mistress of ceremonies when he moved into Spanish House. He would leave the Amazons here.

Too many of the riffraff infesting New Orleans— men with special tastes—knew their way to Bayou House. Ulric was a snob. Spanish House would be reserved for Creole gentlemen and well-to-do Americans in the city. He planned cruel entertainments for these men whom he considered guests or patrons, but not the sordid sort of spectacles now staged at Bayou House.

Bone suspected that the McCoy women would be

Cannons & Roses

able to save Spanish House from him unless he took drastic steps. Even if Delray had gone along with the plan to burn the Red River crop, Bone was sure the McCoy women would have found a way to save Spanish House.

Bone never let senseless rage get in the way of his mind. He'd promised his Creole gentlemen and well-to-do American patrons another auction soon. At these events white women were put up for sale, as if they were slaves. They were virtually slaves, kidnapped from the northern parishes, or lured to New Orleans by his agents.

Almost all of them were poor girls from large families, or orphans. When the highest bidder tired of his purchase, Bone took back the female merchandise, and put them to work along the levee, under the tutelage of women like Mercy.

But the last woman who'd mounted the auction block had been an aristocratic Cuban, purchased undefiled from Vincent Gambini. Gambini had raided a *finca* on the coast of Cuba, to kidnap slaves for resale in Charleston or at The Temple. In this sweep he'd caught the eighteen-year-old daughter of the family.

Bone had paid him $2,000 for the girl. When her virginity and lineage were proven, bidding became frantic. Old Don Miguel had finally bought her, for the sum of $15,000! Bone decided the old man must be getting his money's worth. It was three months, and he'd made no attempt to return the girl.

Bone wondered what sort of price would be paid for a young woman like Celeste McCoy? He knew she'd survived her ordeal at The Temple still a virgin. Bone licked his thin lips and grinned. She'd made a fool of him once and had seen him humiliated by that white nigger, Paul.

Cannons & Roses

Bone wanted both Paul and Celeste and was just insane enough to begin planning ways and means of getting them in his power. He could already envision Celeste nude, and on the auction block, before a select audience of bidders.

Paul?

With an involuntary wince, Bone remembered the other thing the woman who nailed his hand had done in that basement. His lacerated organ had healed, and he'd lost only his hand to gangrene.

Bone wondered what Celeste McCoy would do to save her white nigger from the torture he'd undergone and survived.

Bone determined to find out.

When she'd been sold off, and freely used, Bone knew what he could do with Celeste McCoy and her white nigger. Ship them both on a returning slaver to Vincent Gambini. The Italian would be delighted.

Bone rubbed his palms. He was no longer angry. Planning revenge was nearly as enjoyable to Ulric Bone as finally accomplishing it.

He sent for Vashti.

Regardless of what Celeste said, Albert Grymes was determined to make inquiries about Paul Wright when his ship reached Philadelphia. It was obvious to Albert that she was falling in love with Paul. There was no way that could bring anything but grief to his clients.

Albert suspected that Paul's story was absolutely true.

Albert had written a minute description of Paul when Celeste brought his problem to Grymes & Arcenaux, and, lawyer-wise, embellished it from direct observation when he visited Celeste and her mother at Spanish House.

The night before he sailed, Albert had talked at length with Governor Claiborne about Ulric Bone. But the good governor, he discovered, was only interested in his personal vendetta with Jean Laffite.

Albert had no direct evidence of Bone's criminal activity to present to the governor and decided to drop the matter until he'd returned from Washington. Albert already knew of Jean Laffite's ambitious plan to move from Grande Terre and establish a port of entry for Texas on Galveston Island.

Pierre Laffite planned to migrate north and would probably marry his pregnant mistress. Alexander would stay on in New Orleans, but he'd become almost a folk hero, and probably would enter low-level state or city politics. By the time he returned, Albert suspected Claiborne would know he was finally rid of the Laffite brothers.

That would be time enough to interest Claiborne in ridding New Orleans of Ulric Bone and his henchmen. Albert planned to stay north for at least a month or two, visiting Boston and his New England relatives. Clarice would pose as his young *French* wife.

Any marriage was strictly against the law in Louisiana—Clarice was a woman of color—but Albert toyed with the idea of a secret marriage, in New England, or perhaps more liberal Canada.

At his age, Albert couldn't abandon his New Orleans practice of law, even if he'd wanted to do so, so he could never acknowledge Clarice as Mrs. Grymes down here.

But Clarice would know she was his wedded wife. That was all that mattered. He hadn't yet dared mention any sort of marriage plans to the girl, or—God forbid!—her mother. They both expected Albert to support Clarice and any children she might have if he married a white woman.

But marriage? The mere idea would shock Clarice and her mother out of their shoes!

Philippa Randolph had lost two husbands by the time she was thirty. Randolph was her maiden name, which she'd assumed again after each bereavement. She had no children, for which she thanked God, from either marriage.

"Young children bore me out of my mind," she'd admitted to a woman friend. "What I don't want out of this life is a flock of the little buggers."

Philippa's salty language and sharp tongue were the talk of Richmond society. She'd been raised by a rakehell father whom she dearly loved. David Randolph could outdrink and outwench every other man in Virginia. He broke his neck trying to take one fence too many on his hunter, a horse imported from England.

"I'm gone, but is the damned horse all right?" were David's last words.

Assured that Charger was still fit, David Randolph died with a relieved grin.

"What every man really wants for a wife," he'd advised his daughter, "is a saint by daylight, but a whore at heart when the sun goes down. Your mother was so damned good in bed, I could never get it up for another woman while she was alive, and I tried, by God!"

Philippa's first husband, a Washingtonian, confessed that he was impotent before they were married. Philippa sought out the most notorious madam in Richmond. On their wedding night, her husband discovered he wasn't as impotent as he thought.

Cannons & Roses

At the champagne breakfast the next morning, the dazed man said, "For a virgin bride, Philippa, where did you learn all the tricks of whoredom?"

"Do you really want me to tell you?" she asked.

Her husband laughed. "Don't you dare!"

Her second husband was a Hampton who got himself killed in a duel. To his amazement, she'd gone to him a virgin. He never knew that the tricks she'd learned from the Richmond madam made actual intercourse with her first husband unnecessary for his satisfaction.

10

Philippa Randolph was the most handsome woman in Richmond—no one ever called her pretty. Her Randolph nose was sprayed with freckles Philippa disdained to hide. Dark red hair crowned her high and broad forehead. Philippa had a stubborn mouth and chin.

She carried her high-breasted body proudly, and was seldom seen out of her man-style riding clothes, for Philippa careened through the streets of Richmond on a hunter sired by Charger. She was tall for a woman of her time—taller than the average man.

Philippa lived alone, except for an indentured Irish girl, in the town house she inherited after her first marriage. Both of her husbands had left her substantial sums of money.

Mrs. Brady, the Richmond madam who'd instructed Philippa in the arts of oral sex, remained her good friend. She often took tea with Mrs. Brady, with her

Cannons & Roses

horse tied to the hitching rail outside the woman's establishment. Philippa knew and befriended all of Mrs. Brady's girls.

It was a tribute to Philippa Randolph that the *good* women of Richmond considered her only eccentric, and not depraved. But after they'd had tea together, Philippa usually enjoyed a langorous hour or two with a selected pair of Mrs. Brady's "young ladies," as the woman called them.

"Sex is a damned inconvenience for a widow," Philippa confided to Mrs. Brady, "if she thinks she has to have a man. Every time," she added. "I've nothing at all against a lusty young man laboring to satisfy me, you understand."

Philippa's younger brother attended Washington College. Chester introduced her to Jamie Two. Chester and Jamie McCoy were roommates.

The second time they met, Philippa and Jamie Two became lovers.

Philippa stopped taking tea with Mrs. Brady.

"I want to have a baby by you," Philippa told Jamie Two the third time they met. Raised on an elbow, she admired the boy's body, and her own, too. "Not a boy, but a girl." She cupped the parts of Jamie Two she admired most in one soft hand. "May I?" she asked.

"May you, what?" he asked in a sleepy voice, and regarded her through slitted eyes.

"This."

Philippa squirmed on the bed, lowered her face, gently lifted the limp shaft to her lips.

"Oh, my God!" he gasped. "Yes! Yes, yes, yes!"

After a few torrid minutes, Philippa said, "Now I'm going to mount up, young sir, for a brisk gallop."

Which she did.

Cannons & Roses

Later, Jamie Two asked, "Shouldn't we marry before you have my baby?"

Philippa traced his lips with a finger. "I haven't been asked," she said in a husky voice.

"Will you marry me?"

"I haven't decided," Philippa told him. "Shall we canter now?"

"Hell, no," Jamie said.

"Too tired?" Philippa asked solicitously.

Jamie grinned. "No. I prefer to gallop."

There was a sultry, smoky look in Philippa's green eyes that Jamie had never seen before. "We'll be married, young sir," she said. "Now you mount up—I'm a bit tired." She sighed. "By the way, damned if I'll call my husband by such a silly name as Jamie Two."

Afterward, Philippa said, "I believe we've just made our daughter."

"I do, too," Jamie said. "What do we call her?"

"You say."

"Philippa?"

She smiled. "Thank you, Jamie."

DeWitt Scott swore. It was late and tomorrow would start at sunrise, but he couldn't sleep. He got up from his narrow bed in the smaller house behind the Great House.

"God damn it!"

Now you use the Lord's name in vain, he thought. *You who once wanted to be an ordained minister!*

DeWitt had come south from New York with a medical education. He'd planned to study disease that afflicted slaves but not their masters, and those illnesses endemic among whites, such as malaria, to which slaves weren't subject. His notes were gathering dust.

Cannons & Roses

Jeanette had hired him to be a compassionate overseer. DeWitt had tried to be. And he'd tried—very hard—not to fall in love with the mistress of Great Oaks.

Celeste had suggested *he* take a mistress.

DeWitt stripped off the shirt he slept in, to stand in a pool of moonlight, staring at the neat rows of cabins that were the quarters on Great Oaks. With a rueful expression, DeWitt regarded his swollen shaft of manhood.

"Time to go to Natchez-under-the-Hill," he said.

But DeWitt knew it would always be the same, when he chose a girl or woman for brief pleasure. He'd envision Jeanette's firm body.

DeWitt knew overseers usually had slatternly wives, or brought women back to the plantation for brief stays, and this practice was calmly overlooked by the owners and their wives. Or they took their pick in the slave quarters.

DeWitt wondered if Celeste's was good advice. He remembered Delray Bone's young black mistress with a flash of envy. But DeWitt knew he could never choose a mistress from Great Oaks. His firm control of the slaves depended more on the fact he didn't use their daughters or women than on his sparing them the whip.

Any one of the women he patronized at Natchez-under-the-Hill would be glad to return to Great Oaks with him.

Staring in the mirror, Celeste ran fingers through her cropped hair. She noted, with interest, the rise and fall of her pear-shaped breasts under the sheer fabric of her nightgown.

They really are nice, she decided.

Her mother had taken the bedroom on the other side of Spanish House, across the courtyard, opening off the ironwork-balustraded balcony.

The fountain was playing, and Celeste could hear the soothing patter of water through her opened windows. Stella would be asleep on a pallet, just inside Jeanette's door. Paul was in the small room, adjoining the kitchen, with its barred windows. Their cook was a free Negro woman who came in days.

"Damn you, Paul!" Celeste murmured.

I want a drink of water, Celeste thought.

A sweating ceramic jug of water hung near the wood stove in the kitchen.

Ignoring the wrap on a stool beside her bed, Celeste left her room, going barefooted down the stairs to the courtyard, then footing her way around the fountain toward the kitchen that, here, was a large room at the back of the house. There were only a few kitchens in New Orleans that weren't part of the house.

Shafts of moonlight dappled the courtyard's slate paving stones, and the warm night air was flower-scented. Celeste hadn't brought a candle from her room, but the kitchen, with its tantalizing food smells, was only half-dark in the moonlit night.

The brick floor cooled her feet.

Celeste found the dipper and sipped from it, staring through the open door into the darkness of Paul's room.

Was he asleep, or as restless as she was tonight? She heard the intimate creak of his rope bedstead, as Paul shifted his sleeping weight on the thin mattress.

So Paul was asleep.

Cannons & Roses

The dipper slipped from her hand and clattered on the brick floor of the kitchen.

Now Paul was awake, Celeste knew. She also realized shafting moonlight from the window behind her silhouetted her body, and she'd seem naked in the filmy nightgown, but Celeste didn't move off into the shadows.

She stooped to pick up the dipper. When she straightened, Paul's slim body was framed in the bedroom doorway. As she'd first seen him, Paul's only garment was cotton drawers. She couldn't see his face and he couldn't see hers.

"I came for a drink of water," Celeste said, in a low voice.

"I'm thirsty." Paul moved toward her. He reached for the dipper in her hand. "Thank you."

Their fingers had touched when Paul took the dipper.

Paul drank, then hung the dipper back on its hook. They stared into each other's eyes.

Celeste's breathing was shallow. She wondered if he noticed. "Paul?"

"Yes?"

"Will you follow me?"

"I shouldn't."

"It is late." Celeste spoke as if the hour was a valid reason Paul should.

He didn't answer, but followed her from the kitchen.

Celeste's bedroom was scented with her perfume and the faintly musky odor of her body, and the bedclothes were a tangle. Paul stood, his back to the door, as Celeste's nightgown shimmered to the floor. Her back was to him.

Cannons & Roses

Paul reached behind him and shot the bolt.

It is too late to go back now, he thought.

Paul had slept too long with haunting visions of a naked Celeste.

Celeste turned. With both hands, she raised her breasts—an appealing gesture—childlike, yet wanton.

The single candle in the room sputtered in a vagrant breath of night air.

Paul dropped his drawers, kicked them aside.

It was a matter of will now. Would she come to him, or would he go to her? Paul stood his ground. Celeste stepped carefully, moved toward him.

She raised her arms.

Paul gathered her to him, his strength driving a gasp from Celeste as his mouth sought and found hers.

Paul lifted Celeste easily, to carry her to the bed. A sweep of his hand, and the tangled bedclothes were heaped on the floor. He laid her out on the bed, as if she was a corpse, and Celeste didn't resist, but her eyes burned into his.

"You're a virgin?" he asked softly.

"Yes."

Paul leaned over to kiss the hollow between her breasts. His lips lingered there, tasting her sweetness, while a strong hand found Celeste between her thighs.

Paul joined her on the soft bed. "You'll be hurt," he whispered.

"By you, I want to be," Celeste whispered back.

Her breath was warm and sweet.

Neither spoke again.

Paul reined his passion as best he could, and Celeste offered herself willingly, eagerly. She caught her breath at the first sharp stab of pain. Now Paul couldn't hold back!

Cannons & Roses

There was more pain for Celeste, but somehow she relished it, eyes shut tight, tears squeezed from their corners, her mouth seeking Paul's.

Blood sang in Celeste's ears, and she gasped at each new, hard thrust, then involuntarily, crossing her ankles, with heels pressing the small of Paul's back, the girl helped him drive deeper within her.

In a spasm of pure sensual delight, Celeste's nerves exploded, at the moment Pal's warm release flooded her, and they fell apart, panting.

Celeste caught her breath first. "Was I all right?" she asked.

"That's a stupid question! You'd be the first to know if you weren't." Paul sighed. "Be assured you were *more* than all right."

"I'm a bit sore down there," Celeste confessed.

Paul raised on an elbow to study Celeste's shadowed face. "In Africa, when a woman is taken to bed on her wedding night, the strip of white cloth she wears at her loins is displayed the next morning as if it was some kind of flag. It flutters from a pole outside the nuptial hut. If it's stained, her relatives rejoice."

"If we made a flag from the sheet on this bed," Celeste told him in a dry voice, "I don't believe Mother would rejoice!"

"No," Paul said in a dark voice. "I'd better leave you."

"Not yet." Celeste's fingers gingerly explored between her thighs. "I'm not *too* sore, Paul." Her hand closed gently on his manhood. "He doesn't want you to leave," she whispered.

"He certainly doesn't," Paul told her.

"I think I love you," Celeste said. She clapped a hand to her mouth. "I shouldn't say that!"

Cannons & Roses

"If you mean it, you should," Paul told her, "because it changes things."

"Do you love me?"

"God help us both," Paul said, "I do."

"Do we have to talk so much right now?" Celeste asked.

"No."

Celeste turned over on the bed, and raised herself to her knees. "Be still," she whispered, when he started to move.

Paul obeyed. As she mounted him, his hands found her breasts, the stiff nipples tickling his palms.

"Oh, dear!" Celeste gasped, when she'd guided him in. "Bliss was right."

"Bliss?"

"Never mind!"

DeWitt tried to remember the name of the woman on the bed beside him. Ruth? Gladys? No. It was neither of those.

"What you thinking, honey?" She had a hoarse voice. She sat cross-legged, frankly studying the naked body of the man who'd bought her services for the night.

"I can't remember your name," DeWitt confessed.

"That bother you?" She laughed. "You ain't yet told me what your name is."

"DeWitt."

"That sounds like your real name."

"It is."

"The old dame downstairs named me Portia when I come here, God knows why. Out of some book, I reckon. She reads a lot when we ain't busy. But my real name is Alice. There. We're acquainted."

"Glad to meet you, Alice."

"Likewise. But you ain't paying me for a lot of conversation, and I always try to earn my money. How shall we do it this time?"

DeWitt studied the woman. He'd chosen her because she was new and fresh. Alice's hair really *was* that bright shade of red.

Alice preened, arching her back to thrust her breasts. She fingered her nipples. "Like me, honey?" she asked.

"You're a lot of woman," DeWitt said.

"You're a lot of man down where it counts," Alice complimented. "But we ain't getting anywhere. I got this girlfriend, Mabel. She ain't busy tonight, and she needs the money. Got a kid off somewhere. Let me get her to join us. All right?"

"Later maybe."

"Sure. Now let's you and me get on with it, De-Witt. Some girls fake it with a man, but I don't. I really like it! Oh, brother! How I like it!"

DeWitt dragged her down to him. Alice was the most willing sex partner he'd yet found.

She was clean, too.

Eyes closed, DeWitt pinned her wrists above her head, and it was Jeanette into whose body he was thrusting, thrusting, trying to punish her.

"I like a rough man!" Alice exclaimed. "Do it to me, Daddy!"

She wasn't faking.

I'm old enough to be her daddy, DeWitt thought.

He slowed the pace. Alice didn't seem to notice. Not at first, but she finally sensed that something was wrong, and stopped heaving.

"Something wrong?" she asked.

"No."

"Let's go, then, Daddy."

DeWitt left her and was on his feet beside the bed. "We'd better send for Mabel," he said.

"You're a real sport, Daddy."

"Call me that once more," DeWitt told Alice, "and I'll slap your mouth."

11

Jeanette was determined to save Spanish House from Ulric Bone. Celeste thought she was fanatical on the subject. But she considered it the last gift she'd receive from Jamie and was going to keep it at any sacrifice. Jeanette needed $10,000 to buy back Jamie's promissory note from Bone. Spanish House had been put up for security on the note.

Albert Grymes had sailed with Clarice. Paul was back at Great Oaks because DeWitt had sent for him. Celeste, Jeanette, and Stella stayed on in Spanish House. Celeste found herself at sword's points with her mother.

"We've seen every banker in New Orleans, Mother," Celeste told Jeanette. "Isn't it enough for you that Great Oaks and the Red River property are safe? Why do you need a town house? It's ridiculous!"

"Mind your own business," Jeanette said. "I can't

Cannons & Roses

believe Ulric Bone is the monster you say he is. I intend to ask him for an extension."

Celeste threw up her hands. "You don't know what you're doing! How did you get in touch with him?"

"I sent Stella with a message—how else?"

"When will you see him?" Celeste asked.

"Tomorrow. He's coming here."

"Can't you wait until Albert Grymes gets back? He can handle Bone. I don't know anyone else who can."

"I've sold some of my jewelry," Jeanette told her daughter. "I can offer Bone part of the money we owe, and I'm sure I can persuade him to wait for the rest." She smiled. "He won't refuse a woman—if I ask him right."

"Oh, I'm sure you'll try to charm the man. But you just don't know with whom you're dealing. Bone buys and sells women."

"Let me tell you something, Celeste," Jeanette lectured. "If I hadn't learned to take care of myself at an early age, you wouldn't be here. I've survived just about everything that can happen to a girl or woman. I don't intend to lie down while Ulric Bone steals Spanish House from me. I know his reputation. I can deal with him."

"Why don't you consult with DeWitt? After all, he's our overseer. Another thing, Mother, speaking of DeWitt. You must know the poor man is head over heels in love with you. Daddy's dead, and you need a man."

"Now you listen. . . !"

"Let me finish. I've seen you watching Stella's saucy little rump, and the girl is getting more insolent every day."

"What are you inferring?" Jeanette snapped.

"That you need a man. Louisiana isn't the Isle of Lesbos, you know. If not as your husband, take DeWitt as your lover. He's discreet."

Jeanette paced to the window that overlooked the street. She stood for a moment, her back to Celeste, clutching her elbows. When she turned back to her daughter, she said, "What do you know about lesbian love?"

Celeste flushed. "I read both English and French, you know. Those aren't all insipid books you and Father have collected at Great Oaks."

It was Jeanette's turn to blush. "You've mentioned Stella," she said. "She is insolent, I admit that. But she's also observant. You and Paul haven't been very discreet, dear. We'll have to sell him."

"No!"

"Paul's a nigra."

"Down here, yes, but he isn't really a slave. That was the business for me Albert Grymes had in Philadelphia—to establish that Paul's free."

"I see. But you told him not to make the inquiries."

"I wasn't thinking."

"Nor were you when you seduced Paul," Jeanette said. She paused, studying her daughter. "I worry about you. What will you do with your life?"

"I don't know yet."

"Do you love Paul?"

"Yes."

Jeanette shook her head. "That isn't good."

"Mother?"

"Yes?"

"What would you have done if father was part Negro? He was dark enough to have been," Celeste said. "Would you have married him?"

"It wouldn't have mattered to me if Jamie had been

Chinese and Eskimo, too! When you love a man as I did Jamie, nothing else matters. You'll find that out someday, if you're very lucky."

"I know what it is to love like that now," Celeste said in a quiet voice. "Paul has promised to take me north, maybe all the way to Canada."

For a moment, Jeanette was confused. "You've talked about this so soon?"

"Yes."

Ulric Bone had a plan, and it was fairly simple. Right now he wanted Paul and Celeste worse than he did Spanish House. When she sent a message by Stella, Jeanette played right into his hands. It was from Stella that Bone had learned of Celeste's and Paul's affair. No matter. She'd still be sold as a virgin.

A Chinese doctor from Hong Kong was in Bone's pay. By a simple if painful operation he could remedy that defect. Celeste would bring more than the aristocratic Cuban girl.

Only three trusted rich patrons would bid for the girl. It was understood that regardless of price, it was a rental, not an outright sale. Bone had stressed this condition.

"I have this luscious one ninety days," Don Ramon Sevilla said, "and I gladly give her back. You know my tastes." He grinned. "The last *puta* you sold me lasted but two weeks."

Bone knew Don Ramon's tastes well!

"I want her alive and sane."

"It will be so," Don Ramos said. "I am a gentleman of my word."

Gaston Domergue, the mulatto from Santo Domingo, was eager to get a virgin white woman. He readily agreed to Bone's terms. She'd be taken to sea on his next privateering expedition and personally delivered to Vincent Gambini, if that was agreeable.

"It is not," Bone said. "I will ship the girl and her nigger lover."

"She isn't virgin, then?" Domerque asked, with a raised eyebrow.

"The nigger is a girl," Bone lied when he realized his mistake.

"Good!" Domerque grinned. "That sort make better sport."

The third man invited to the exclusive auction was an American. Simon Browne was a respected citizen in St. Louis, a fur trader who'd lived among the Indians. When Simon went west, away from civilization, he became another man.

Celeste would be taken, Simon promised, to the next rendezvous with the Mountain Men, and passed from hand to hand freely.

"It is good for my business," Simon assured Bone. "She'll be delivered back, the worse for wear, of course, but that won't matter to you, will it?"

Ulric Bone had Paul under surveillance at Great Oaks. When his men had the word, he would be kidnapped, and delivered to Bayou House. DeWitt Scott would be convinced his assistant had run away.

Celeste, at Spanish House, would receive a message, purported to be from Paul, in hiding in New Orleans. She'd be seized when she went to him, and Bone was sure she would go.

Tomorrow Bone would play the gentleman with Jeanette. He would accept any money she offered and assure her they could arrive at easy terms to pay off the balance of the debt.

Maybe she would come to him as a friend when

Celeste disappeared. If she did, he would quickly convince her that her daughter and Paul had run away north.

Later he'd take Spanish House. Bone's ego was so great that he'd convinced himself that Jeanette McCoy might become his mistress.

Might? She wouldn't laugh at his deformity. Jeanette wouldn't pity him, either. Jeanette, he knew, was from Santo Domingo, a planter's wife, and probably one of those Frenchwomen who invited friends to see a slave punished.

Jeanette would share his depraved tastes.

Bone had very special *entertainment* for Celeste before she mounted the auction block. Whenever he whipped Vashti, and it was often, these days, Bone taunted the woman about Celeste. When he had the girl safe at Bayou House, the Amazons would have to be content with Paul.

Bone had promised Vashti that she could have Celeste to break her spirit. That would be something to watch and savor!

Bone licked his thin lips.

Bone wondered why Mercy hadn't learned her lesson the last time he disciplined her. One of her girls had passed the word that she was going to Governor Claiborne. The Amazons had her in The Room again and were waiting for his orders.

It was going to be a long night. Bone poured the dregs of the wine into his glass and drained it with a gulp.

The Amazons had been instructed not to wear Mercy out before he arrived to take over this final punishment. The girl who reported her would be rewarded. And one day, Bone was sure, would take her place on the table.

Women!

Bone touched all that was left of his manhood through the fabric of his tight pants. She hadn't made him a eunuch, but she had made certain he'd never again enjoy a woman as a man should.

Mercy would pay part of that woman's debt tonight. The alligators would have a fresh meal tomorrow.

Celeste had gone out before Ulric Bone kept his appointment at Spanish House with Jeanette. She couldn't stand the sight of him! When she came back, after Bone had gone, Jeanette was triumphant.

"Ulric Bone is no gentleman," Jeanette told Celeste. "And he's as ugly as frog's eyes on a mud fence, but he respects me as Jamie's widow. He'll wait as long as necessary for me to raise the rest of the money we owe him. I told you I could work this out."

"Do you trust him?" Celeste asked.

"The only man I ever really trusted was your father," Jeanette said. "But I have his word."

"I still say you should consult with DeWitt," Celeste told her.

There was a new softness in Jeanette's eyes. "DeWitt," she mused. "He's been very loyal all these years."

"You could do worse when you remarry," Celeste offered.

"I wasn't thinking of marriage just yet," Jeanette said. "Are you shocked?"

"I could say no, mother. But I'm a bit shocked, yes." Celeste laughed. "Who am I to judge?"

"I've wanted to ask," Jeanette said. "How do you really feel about Bliss and Richard?"

"I wish them only the best, but Richard is going to have his hands full—I'll tell you that."

"Bliss trapped Richard, didn't she?" Jeanette said.

Cannons & Roses

"Alicia Carroll knows more about how it happened than she's told me—I'm sure of that."

Celeste nodded. "Poor Richard is probably still wondering how she marched him to the altar, quickstep. He'll be better off if he doesn't find out. I love my sister, but she's a shameless little hussy when her mind's set on something."

Back at Great Oaks, Paul wanted to confide in DeWitt about the plight he found himself in. He sensed the man's compassion. Black children trailed DeWitt whenever he visited the quarters on the plantation, begging sweets, and DeWitt always had bulging pockets.

Like himself, DeWitt was a Northerner.

Paul's problem was how to get Celeste to Canada without any money. He knew the state of the plantation's finances. He and Celeste would have to buy transportation, whether they sailed from New Orleans, went up the Mississippi, or tried to reach Canada overland. And Paul had made up his mind about Canada.

In Philadelphia, Paul had regarded abolitionists with disdain. They were visionaries, but crabbed people, and, in his opinion, not very realistic.

President Monroe had the right idea, Paul was convinced. Liberia was the answer. For the Negro, that is. Paul didn't consider himself a Negro.

Like most Northerners, Paul had heard about the Underground Railroad. He hadn't confided to Celeste yet his new ambition to become a conductor. But he was certain she would throw in with him, and that they could raise enough money to ship ex-slaves back to Africa once they'd reached Canada.

Acting as an assistant overseer, Paul had become acquainted with some of the field hands, and had cautiously sounded them out regarding escape north. He

Cannons & Roses

was dumbfounded to discover that most were content with their brutish life! And only a few knew, by hearsay, that escape from slavery lay north. Most assumed that slavery was universal in the United States.

Only one man Paul had contacted, a bright Negro called Ben, had any real enthusiasm about escaping slavery. But Ben had been sold down the river from Tennessee, for trying to escape across the Mason-Dixon line.

"Them up there," Ben told him, "can see and smell freedom just across the river."

Paul was determined to carry the message in the border states. His flogging by Alexander Laffite, and admission that he was now a slave, rankled Paul. He felt he'd been cowardly. Paul was determined to erase that humiliating experience from his mind by proving his mettle along the Underground Railroad.

Paul's mother was a free Baltimore Negress. She'd never told him who his white father was. But she'd raised him strictly and insisted he get an education. Paul had gone to Philadelphia when his mother died. He was her only child.

Paul found Liberia was foreign, and much too African to suit his taste. But now, some day, Paul wanted to go back. The blacks there, he'd discovered, ranked lighter-skinned Negroes above them on the social scale. It was happening in Haiti (that had been Santo Domingo), too. He felt his future lay in Liberia, after he'd made himself a hero conducting slaves to freedom in Canada.

Protecting Celeste from Bone had been the only bright spot in his life since Paul was brought south. She loved him. She would love him more when she saw what he could do in striking a blow against slavery.

Paul didn't confide in DeWitt Scott, even when the

overseer hinted that, should Paul try to escape, any pursuit would be delayed.

DeWitt had talked with Paul enough to realize his story of once being free was probably true, but he couldn't talk with Celeste until she came back to Great Oaks. DeWitt had assured Paul, however, that the girl would keep her word.

"The only trouble is," DeWitt said, "that we need your services here badly. I want to discuss with Miss Jeanette letting you replace Delray Bone."

If his freedom was established, DeWitt advised Paul to stay south as a freed Negro. "You'll do better here than in the North," DeWitt said. "Unless you can pass up there," he added.

Paul intended to pass. It was integral to his plan. Traveling with a Canadian passport to visit the border states, he and Celeste would be able to move freely.

Word had reached Bone's agents that it was time to seize Paul. They were in the neighborhood of Great Oaks, posing as slave traders from North Carolina. One of the men actually was a slave trader.

Ulric Bone had made the brutal and simple plan these men would carry out. Rendered unconscious, bound and gagged, Paul would go south in a coffin. They had worked for Bone before—only this was the first time they would kidnap a man.

"Why do you reckon Bone wants the white nigger?" one asked.

His partner shrugged. "That ain't our business, Jeb. Pay's the same. That's all that matters, ain't it? How do we take him?"

12

*L*ater, Celeste decided that if she hadn't been awakened from a nap, and wasn't out of sorts with Stella, she would have thought twice. It was a stupid thing she did.

While Jeanette and Stella adjourned to Jeanette's bedroom across the courtyard from Celeste's to take an afternoon nap after lunch, Celeste usually adjourned to her room to read and write. But it had been a lunch of baked crayfish, deep-fried fresh oysters, during which Jeanette and Celeste shared a bottle of wine, a gift from Albert Grymes.

Celeste was too drowsy to either read or write, so she stretched out on her bed, fully clothed, and awakened only when Stella tapped on her door.

"Miss Celeste? You sleeping?"

"No, Stella, not now," she said crossly. "What do you want?"

"Some lady say she want to see you."

Celeste found her shoes and joined Stella on the balrony. To stay cool, the girl wore only a single garment, and that a shift barely covering her to the top of her thighs.

"You answered the door dressed like *that?*" Celeste asked.

"Yas'm. Miss Jeanette, she don't mind."

"Well, I do. Who is the lady?"

"Some trashy white lady with a big carriage."

"Look, Stella, you're not supposed to decide who is and who isn't trash—do you understand?"

"Yas'm. Miss Jeanette would want to know."

"All right, go back to my mother. I'll handle this," Celeste said.

"Yas'm."

Celeste blinked sleep out of her eyes going down the iron-grille stairway to the courtyard. The street door was closed but unbolted. That the woman, whoever she was, would wait in the street should have seemed strange, especially if she was a white woman. It did to Celeste later, but not at the time. A dressmaker soliciting business, perhaps?

Celeste opened the door. "Yes?"

Despite the heat, the woman was corseted and heavily veiled. The shades of her waiting carriage were drawn. The man on the box wasn't Negro.

"I've come from Paul," the woman said in a low voice, without lifting her veil.

"Paul?" Celeste asked, puzzled.

"Paul Wright. He's in the city, hiding at my place, and he's hurt badly."

"Paul should be at Great Oaks!"

"He's running away and needs your help." The woman opened the carriage door for Celeste. "Hurry! We may have been followed!"

Cannons & Roses

Celeste was in the carriage, the woman beside her.

"Where are we going?" Celeste asked.

"Never mind, dear." The woman clamped a pad soaked with chloroform over Celeste's nose and mouth, before the girl could react, and shifted her heavy body. Celeste was pinned in the seat, helpless.

The driver peered down from the box. "Got her, Maude?"

"Sleeping like a baby, Rafe," the woman said. "Pretty tidbit, ain't she?"

Rafe's whiskered face creased in a savage smile, and he smacked his lips. "Can't we have a bit of slap and tickle with her before she's delivered?"

"Not this one, Rafe," Maude said. "With Old Bone, she's personal, if you know what I mean."

Rafe sighed. "Only too well."

The woman had said not to give the envelope to Miss Jeanette until she woke up, and those were Miss Celeste's orders, so Stella laid it on the floor beside her pallet. In a moment, she was sleeping again. And dreaming of how coal-black Jackson was, compared to her brown skin, one of Stella's hands cupping herself between the thighs.

When Stella moaned in her sleep and turned on her side, the pallet beside the room door slid just enough to cover the envelope addressed to *Mother.*

Paul was naked, and in a damp stone cellar of some kind, arms outstretched as if he'd been crucified, wrists shackled to rings in the stone wall behind him.

Lifted from the coffin last night, bound and gagged, Paul's captors had handed him over to the grinning black women as if he were a package or a trussed fowl. They'd brought him here, taken his clothes, and shackled him to the wall.

It had taken two buckets of cold water to rouse Paul from his semiconscious state.

Déjà-vu!

The only thing to be said for this cellar was that it smelled less foul than between-decks on the slaver, the last time he'd been kidnapped.

It was a small cellar, reached through a trapdoor above. A dungeon, really, Paul realized. The women had pulled up the ladder when they left. Cool air flowed down from a small grille in the trapdoor, and it smelled of stagnant water. Paul shivered although he wasn't cold.

Those two women. They somehow reminded him of Vashti.

Where was this?

He shifted his bare feet and tugged at the wrist shackles. No chance of pulling either one loose. If it was possible, and he could get out of this dungeon without the ladder, where could a stark-naked man run?

These slavers know their business, Paul thought. *Strip a man naked to make him feel completely helpless and vulnerable!*

It was Ben who brought the message to Paul that sent him riding off in the night toward The Columns. Some white man, Ben said, had brought him the word that Miss Celeste was over there and needed to see him, alone, right away.

"You're not to tell anyone here, the man say," Ben told him. "She meet you at the old slave graveyard on this place. You know where?"

Cannons & Roses

"No."

Ben told him.

Paul saddled up the walking mare that DeWitt had assigned him.

Paul groaned. It was so damned obvious now! Celeste had sold him out. The bitch had taken her pleasure—given him her virginity!—and now he was on his way to some swamp camp and a shallow grave in the mud when his new master had worked him to death.

Every muscle ached, and thirst was a new torment. The iron shackles had already rubbed his wrists raw. Cramps tortured his legs. Each of the women, before she climbed the ladder from the dungeon, had fondled and squeezed Paul—rough caresses—and he remembered the prisoners he'd seen Dahomey women torture.

Three young Africans from a hostile tribe had been captured the day before and were tied to three stakes set in a row. Grinning women took turns squeezing, jerking, even biting, and what for the prisoners was at first a sort of pleasure, a new game, finally became terrible agony.

They'd begged the women to kill them.

These two women, Paul knew from their dialect, came from Dahomey.

But this wasn't Africa. Just the same, Paul shuddered, then cursed Celeste. Somehow, some way, Paul resolved, he was going to kill that woman!

Pure hate can lend strength. Paul knew he was going to need all the strength he could muster to survive this ordeal, so he concentrated on Celeste.

After a while, however, it didn't help. He couldn't put the way she'd stood in the moonlight out of his mind, and her whispered words, "Follow me."

She'd said it was late.

Paul stared down his naked body and was amazed. Betrayed, hurting, thirsty, thoughts of Celeste could still arouse him.

He wondered where she was and what she was thinking now.

Celeste wondered who had taken her clothes. Whoever it was had locked her into a small, bare room, with barred windows too high for her to peer out. There was a narrow bed, a chair and a table. On the table was a flickering lamp.

The bed was clean, and so was the room. There was a covered chamber pot in the corner. The room door was locked.

Celeste knew about white slavery. But that sort of thing only happened to poor white girls! Yet here she was. She'd been a stupid fool!

Paul. Was it possible *he* had betrayed her to the woman? For escape money? On the side of the bed, the sheets cool on her buttocks, Celeste ran fingers through her cropped hair and thought about that.

Yes, it was possible.

Because she wanted Paul so much, in a way she'd betrayed him when she asked Albert Grymes not to press inquiries in Philadelphia about his status. But that was before they'd been together.

If Paul had betrayed her, Celeste thought, he must really be desperate. She was certain, if it was only for those too-brief moments they'd had to share each other's body, that Paul loved her.

"Paul, change your mind," Celeste whispered. "If you've had me brought here, for whatever reason, come and get me."

Cannons & Roses

Celeste crawled between the cool, clean sheets. Her headache was better, but she was still slightly nauseated. And she was drowsy.

A tall black woman had undressed her, Celeste remembered now. She'd been too exhausted and sick to resist, and too bleary-eyed to recognize the woman if she saw her again, but something about her was familiar.

She remembered a strong-fingered caress, where only Paul had been. She tightened her thighs.

Celeste slept.

"You stupid girl!" Jeanette slapped Stella. In her other hand she had the note: *I've gone to Paul. Don't try to find me.* "Can't you do anything right?"

Tears stood in Stella's eyes, as she fingered the red marks on her brown cheek. "I sorry, Miss Jeanette. My head, it's no good sometimes."

"If you'd remembered to give me this right after Celeste left, so I could do something . . ." Jeanette stopped. *What could she have done then that she couldn't do now?* "It's all right, Stella, and I'm sorry I slapped you. Forgive me?"

Stella grinned through her tears. "It make you feel better, Miss Jeanette, slap me again." Stella offered her other cheek. "I just a dumb nigger."

"Oh, Stella!" Jeanette wept now. She gathered the girl to her, kissing her neck, then her face, and tasted the salt of Stella's tears. "Miss Celeste has run off with Paul, and there isn't a damn thing I dare do about it, tonight or any other time." She let the girl go. "Fetch us the decanter of peach brandy, Stella."

"Yas'm." Stella's smile was like a spring sunrise. "You undress yourself, Miss Jeanette, and Stella tuck you in. We's just two women all alone."

Cannons & Roses

"Stella?"

"Yas'm?"

"Hurry with that brandy, but don't drop the decanter."

"Stella sure won't, Miss Jeanette."

"And, Stella, you aren't dumb," Jeanette said, unbuttoning her dress.

"No'm, I sure ain't."

"You're insolent."

"Yes'm, I sure am." Stella took the dress that Jeanette handed her, folding it carefully.

"Do you love Jackson?" Jeanette asked.

"What he do to me, I sure love that," Stella confessed.

"I need a man, Stella," Jeanette said.

"Yas'm, Stella know that feeling."

"Neither of us has a man tonight, Stella."

"We sure don't, Miss Jeanette." Stella folded the rest of Jeanette's clothing as carefully as she'd folded the dress. "Can I look at you, real bold?"

"Please do." Jeanette turned before the girl. "Am I getting fat?" she asked.

"You sure ain't!"

Jeanette smiled. "You tell nice lies."

"Ain't no lie, Miss Jeanette."

"Hurry with that brandy."

"Yas'm, I sure will."

"I'm going to be your man tonight, Stella," Jeanette said. "A man tells a woman what he wants. Come back to me naked when you bring the brandy."

"Yas'm, I sure will." Stella no longer smiled. "I sure do that."

"Hurry, Stella."

While the girl was gone, Jeanette mused. It was

Cannons & Roses

Celeste who said Louisiana wasn't the Isle of Lesbos. She'd also said that Jeanette needed a man. Celeste was wrong on the first count, but so right on the second! In the meantime . . .

"No scars," Vashti muttered, to remind herself of what the white devil had ordered.

If there were any, he'd promised to do to Vashti what they'd done to that other white woman.

Vashti had grudging admiration for this one who'd sold her to the white devil. After fastening her wrists, and the wide leather belt around her waist that held her to the table, Vashti left her legs free so she could kick.

It was a game. Strike with the stiff leather crop between her legs. When she pressed her thighs together, flick a nipple with the end of the crop.

Vashti knew what that felt like! And the way the legs jerked apart, involuntarily. Vashti stung the open crotch with the swiftness of a snake. A strangled cry from Celeste, through clenched teeth, and it was her first.

That was no glancing blow!

Vashti admired the courage of this one. Sweat bathed her naked flesh, tears trickled from the corners of her eyes, but she cursed each new stroke with the crop. "Damn you, Vashti!" she gasped now.

No scars, he'd said.

Vashti trailed the tip of the crop through the hollow between Celeste's breasts, poked her navel, then slashed the mound at the base of her belly.

Too hard. She'd drawn blood.

Vashti didn't want to be hung by her heels, and have the white devil probe her as he'd done that other white woman before she died. A shudder of revulsion shook the woman.

With a cloth, Vashti wiped away the blood and found the wound wasn't too bad. It wouldn't leave a scar, but she'd have to be more careful.

An emotion she'd never felt before puzzled Vashti. It was her first experience with pity. She stared down at Celeste, slapping the palm of her callused hand with the crop.

Celeste licked her dry lips. "I'd like a drink of water, Vashti," she said in a hoarse voice.

There was water, in a jug. Vashti laid aside the crop and wet Celeste's lips.

"Thank you."

The jug set aside, the crop back in her hand, Vashti poked Celeste's knees so she'd open her thighs. It always amazed Vashti to find that white women were made the way she was down there. She'd never known that, assuming they were all horribly deformed in some way, and that's why they wore all those skirts.

"You like it when you hit me there, don't you, Vashti?" Celeste said.

Vashti tapped herself lightly between her black thighs and grinned.

Celeste thought that Vashti's shaved head gleamed like a black apple.

"Shall we change places?" Celeste said.

Vashti shook her head. She wished she were a man so she could mount this one. It was a strange new thought.

Vashti sighed. She wasn't a man, but she could explore Celeste, as she'd done after undressing her, with long fingers.

When she was thus gently entered, Celeste's eyes

closed. The first sob caught in her throat, but she spread her legs farther apart.

It surprised Vashti to discover that her intrusion wasn't unwelcome.

13

While one of the Dahomey women pushed chunks of bread dipped in rich gravy in Paul's mouth, and held a tin cup of wine mixed with water to his mouth so he could drink, her companion was hunkered at his feet. Her fingers dug his buttocks while she was busy with her lips and tongue. Paul couldn't see what she was doing, but he'd have to be dead not to know.

He was still shackled by his raw wrists. He was weak, but the gravy-soaked bread was putting some strength back in him.

The woman at his feet paused to tell the other, "We've made him a man again."

They couldn't know that Paul understood their dialect. He'd spent months in Dahomey.

"Careful with his manhood, sister," the one who had been feeding Paul said. "The white devil wants the woman Vashti has for herself right now to see when it is taken away."

They laughed.

Paul's heart lurched. Ulric Bone had him and Celeste, too!

Jeanette had been back at Great Oaks for a week, and she'd sent Stella to The Columns to help Alicia Carroll with house guests she was entertaining. She'd asked DeWitt to come to the house, with plantation business as the excuse, and given Robert and the other house servants a night they could spend in the quarters. It was Saturday night.

Robert patronized the field hands, but he looked the other way when delicacies were smuggled from the Great House larder (as Jeanette did), so he was a popular man, and Jeanette had ordered an extra rum ration for everyone on the plantation.

Stella had shared Jeanette's bed only that one night at Spanish House. There had been Bliss, the slave she grew up with, and Edith Radcliff, the woman she'd shared with Thomas, her second husband. But that was before Jamie claimed her.

With an inward smile, Jeanette remembered the voyage from China to the Sandwich Islands aboard Jamie's ship, when his man, Amos, couldn't navigate, and she'd kept Jamie too busy to worry about the ship's course. It was a wonder they'd arrived off Hawaii.

But Jamie was gone.

DeWitt was coming to the Great House. She wondered if he knew why. She'd given him enough reasons to guess since she'd been back. The need for a man's lust and strength was almost a sickness, Jeanette realized—or at least it was for her.

She wondered when she'd hear from Celeste and

Cannons & Roses

Paul? They must have had their escape well planned. She hadn't yet written Bliss and Richard, or Jamie Two.

There would always be a well of tears within her for Jamie, but she was glad there was no grave, only memory.

Jeanette was in the office, off the living room, primly at her desk.

It was a quiet, warm night outside, with hot and unblinking stars staring down. Jeanette could hear laughter and singing from the quarter. She hoped that Stella had managed to sneak off and meet Jackson.

Jeanette hadn't heard him enter the house, but DeWitt was framed in the doorway, freshly shaved. He was dressed in black pants, white shirt, and a black jacket. How tanned he was! When he'd first come to Great Oaks, DeWitt had sunburned fearfully.

Tanned and, yes, handsome. Blond hair, strong face, tall, slim hips, wide shoulders. Why hadn't she noticed before?

"Good evening, DeWitt."

Jeanette wore a proper negligee over her undergarments. When it was hot, she'd worked with him before dressed like this, and DeWitt in shirtsleeves, but she'd soaked half the afternoon in perfumed water.

DeWitt hadn't answered.

Jeanette wondered, *Does he have a mistress somewhere?*

Chilling thought!

"DeWitt . . ." Jeanette rose. "If you have something else to do tonight, we can work another time."

Two strides, and he'd taken her in his arms, lifted her easily.

DeWitt's mouth found Jeanette's. His demanding

kiss fanned her smoldering passion into a raging desire that consumed her last inhibitions.

"Take me!" she gasped, when she could. "On the couch, on the floor, anywhere, but take me!"

"Not here," DeWitt said.

Jeanette was prepared to face down memories of Jamie lingering in the bedroom they'd shared, but DeWitt wouldn't have her there either, so he carried her out into the night. He took her to his quarters, a place she'd never seen, and to his bed, freshly made.

"We'll undress you," he said. "I've never seen you naked."

His hands were strong, but gentle, and Jeanette's trembling hands tried to help DeWitt, but he wouldn't have it.

"Be still," he ordered. "Don't spoil this for me."

Jeanette didn't answer, but she lay still, and let him reveal her body, to feast his eyes on every detail of her nakedness.

He stroked each breast, and touched her gently, while Jeanette shut her eyes, and caught her underlip with her teeth.

DeWitt was finally naked, and beside her on the bed, staring down into a face that seemed swollen, somehow.

"Look at me," he said.

Jeanette's eyes opened.

"I've waited a very long time, Jeanette. Now I want *all* of you, and I won't settle for less."

She'd visioned DeWitt as an abject lover, thankful for crumbs, but it was she who was abject now, ready to beg if she had to.

As if he'd read her mind, DeWitt said, "You don't have to humiliate yourself."

"Do you want me to say I love you?" she asked.

"No. Not yet. I just want you to give yourself to a man, not a ghost."

"Try me," Jeanette said through stiff lips.

DeWitt had been gentle at first, but then, as Jeanette gave more and more of herself to him, he forgot gentleness, and demanded. Jeanette met each new demand with one of her own, her nerves finally singing like wires in a hurricane, and each new explosion of nerves overlapped the one before until she was exhausted before DeWitt.

She'd had to lay supine, finally, but still warmed enough by the heat of passion to meet his final surge with a mild one of her own.

And now they lay side by side, bodies touching, hands clasped, waiting to see who would speak first. Night air through an open window at the foot of the bed laved and cooled their bodies.

"An overseer has no social status," DeWitt said finally.

"Why tell me this?" Jeanette asked, surprised at his trend of thought.

"Because I love you," he said. "Because I can't ask you to be my wife."

Jeanette realized that DeWitt wasn't bitter, he was just stating a fact. "I don't like the word 'mistress.'"

"I don't, either," Jeanette admitted.

"We're lovers."

"Yes."

"That's enough for now, but I'll want more later," DeWitt told Jeanette. "I can be a very determined man."

Jeanette smiled. "You've just proven that, so far as I'm concerned."

She'd always considered DeWitt a bit too proper

and self-effacing, but what he said next shattered that illusion.

"You're better than two women in bed at once."

"Do I take that as a compliment?" Jeanette asked.

DeWitt grinned. "You can."

Jeanette stirred. "So that's why you go up to Natchez."

"No longer," DeWitt said.

"What if I tell you there won't be a next time?" Jeanette asked. "Will you go to Natchez?"

"Hell, no," DeWitt said. "I'm afraid you'll be raped."

"Try me," Jeanette said again.

"My pleasure."

"Don't forget mine, you beast."

Celeste wondered if this nightmare of pain and humiliation would ever stop. To all intents and purposes, she was Vashti's slave and plaything, with Bone often an avid voyeur, urging the black woman on. As yet she didn't know that she was to be sold. And she didn't know that Paul was in Bayou House.

She wondered vaguely why Bone hadn't raped her, until that night in The Room when Vashti mounted her with a cruel device strapped around her waist and accomplished what Bone hadn't.

Celeste shuddered. Was that last night, or the night before?

The sight of the coupling women carried Ulric Bone so far away that he finally exposed himself, and Celeste stared at a scarred, twisted, shrunken organ.

How had he fathered Delray!

She learned when he and Vashti forced her to service Bone with her mouth. *God,* she prayed, *not that again!*

Cannons & Roses

Vashti had left Celeste alone for a few minutes in the small room with the high windows. To stay sane, Celeste welcomed these brief absences of her keeper because she needed to gather her thoughts.

She'd stopped wondering about Bone's purpose in torturing her. She knew now he needed no sane reason. But the bizarre relationship she and Vashti had formed concerned Celeste.

In The Room, Vashti used the stiff riding crop or any one of the assortment of small whips, as Bone directed, but Celeste realized they didn't want to scar her body.

So Celeste guessed she was being spared for one of Bone's infamous auctions and hoped she'd pass into other hands soon. Nothing worse could happen, she thought, than what had already been done to her.

Vashti was cruel and merciless when Bone was there to watch, and seemed to enjoy what she was doing to Celeste. But when they were alone, together in this small room, Vashti was almost tender. But she was also insatiable. When Celeste realized this, she began to respond to the woman's rough caresses, mechanically at first, but now her ministering to Vashti brought a perverse pleasure.

What have I become? Celeste wondered.

"I'm just a naked female animal," Celeste told herself. "Bone's done this to me, with Vashti's help. Damn them both!"

Every muscle in her body was sore and stiff, and she was very tender between her thighs. Her breasts throbbed constantly from repeated whippings, and her backside burned for the same reason, but there would be no scars.

Pain of one kind or another had become Celeste's

constant companion. But damned if she'd let them break her! She had yet to beg, and could suffer now without screaming for relief.

It was dusk—she could tell by the faint light slanting in the high windows.

"Tomorrow night we've something special for you in the way of entertainment," Bone had gloated.

Then Celeste was too exhausted, and hurting too badly to care.

Now she did care, very much. Vashti would come for her soon. Maybe she'd be dead before morning. Never to see Paul again would be her only regret.

Tears stung her eyelids, but she dashed them away with the back of her hand.

Celeste still clung to the faint hope that somehow Paul would realize her plight, and come to save her from Bone.

That hope was all Celeste had.

For the past few days and nights, Paul had been well treated by the two women keepers. He was out of the cellar dungeon, in a room with a bed, and his wrists were scabbed without any sign of infection or blood poisoning.

The women brought good food now. *I'm being fattened up for the slaughter,* Paul thought wryly.

Last night he'd had to take each of his woman captors on the bed, while the other watched, and made lewd comments they now knew he understood. He'd managed. The women had then demonstrated their lesbian skills. That was a spectacle Paul wouldn't soon forget! He'd never patronized the sort of establishments in Philadelphia that catered to that vice.

When they weren't in the room with him, the women kept Paul shackled hand and foot to the bed, but were

Cannons & Roses

thoughtful enough to pad the iron circlets. As yet, he hadn't been confronted by Bone.

From the women he'd learned Celeste was alive, but that was all they would tell him. Paul knew that Bone planned to face them with each other soon.

He was so accustomed to his nakedness now that he wondered why uncomfortable clothes were necessary.

Paul had seen more than one African boy or man who'd been mutilated as prisoners of a rival tribe. Instead of being killed, they were sent back to their village, and soon became laughingstocks among their own tribesmen.

Bone would have to kill him first!

Ulric Bone had abandoned the idea of holding Paul hostage to make Celeste more docile.

He wanted to watch her tonight, and perhaps see her crumble into insanity while Paul was spread-eagled on the table. The woman in New York had mutilated him with a broken bottle. Bone had experimented with a rebellious slave who'd fallen into his hands. He'd forced an aphrodisiac down the man's throat.

Each new wound was salted to stanch the flow of blood. Scissors, heated properly, could be used, and the torture dragged out interminably with the aphrodisiac at work in the victim's blood.

Bone sent for the Amazons, and told them what to put in the wine Paul would be served with his supper.

From their whispering, Paul knew that the women anticipated some special treatment for him tonight, and had no trouble guessing what it might be. When the wine tasted bitter, he managed not to drink it.

Celeste drank the wine Vashti served her, despite

its bitter taste. She'd need all the strength she could muster to survive *this* night!

Bone was in The Room alone. Celeste would be shackled to the bare wall. Paul, of course, would be on the table.

Bone chuckled as he laid out the scissors and other torture instruments he planned to use. Celeste would be shackled hand and foot, against the wall, with her blood running hot. Paul would be on the table, as helplessly aroused as a man could get.

The white nigger, and his nigger-loving woman! Bone couldn't help clasping himself through the tight black pants he wore as his only garment.

Vashti would whip the girl before he went to work on Paul. He wanted the white nigger to watch that first.

Bone was mumbling obscenities to himself. He would finally have revenge for his missing hand and mutilated genitals, because he'd finally found the woman who'd done that. And he had the man who was with her that night.

He stripped off his tights. Let them both see what they'd done. His cruel face seemed to have a new inner glow.

Tonight he'd kill the woman who'd tortured him, and the man who'd laughed when he screamed, and tomorrow he'd be a whole man again. Saliva dripped from his chin. Bone didn't notice.

Women would want him. Perhaps he'd have another son, and this time the woman would enjoy conceiving, and not retch with revulsion when he'd finally finished.

How to kill the bitch Celeste? Hang her by the heels, as he'd done that bitch Mercy (who for a few moments, when he was driving that stake, he'd thought was the woman in the New York cellar)?

No. Mercy died too soon.

He'd think of something that could be prolonged for the rest of the night—perhaps for days.

14

The Amazons had spread-eagled Paul on the table under Bone's direction. They sensed as soon as Paul did that Ulric Bone had become a slavering madman, and hurried from The Room.

Bone's iron fist swung from its hook. Clad only in black tights, Bone resembled nothing so much as a medieval torturer, or executioner.

The Amazons had stretched Paul on his back.

Vashti brought Celeste.

"Oh, my God!" She staggered when she saw Paul.

Bone's was a cackling laugh, and Celeste realized, as Vashti fastened her wrists and ankles to iron rings in the bare wall, that she and Paul were at the mercy of a madman.

"Vashti, help us!" she pleaded.

Bone selected a whip. Arms crossed, Vashti watched him, ignoring Celeste and her plea.

Cannons & Roses

Paul spoke in her language. For the first time, Vashti seemed to recognize him.

Bone crooned obscenities as he chose a wicked whip of braided leather and shoved it at Vashti.

"Whip her, you African bitch!" he ordered.

Paul spoke to Vashti again, and she hesitated, the whip trailing on the floor.

Bone struck his mouth and tore Paul's lips.

Vashti examined the whip she'd been given and seemed confused. It was a weighted lash, designed to draw blood each stroke.

"No scars, you say," Vashti told Bone.

There was a faint flicker of hope in Celeste. But with a sweep of his arm, Bone knocked Vashti to the floor, and screaming his rage, snatched up the whip where it had fallen from her hand.

"I'm going to cut you to pieces!" he shrilled at Celeste. "See this?" He brandished the stub of his arm in her face. "You nailed my hand!"

Bone squared away and swung back his arm, but Paul shouted a command, and Vashti was up from the floor, behind Bone.

She'd grabbed his arm.

Bone lost the whip when he turned on Vashti. She ducked his rush with a nimbleness neither Celeste nor Paul would have guessed she had, and Bone staggered against the table, falling across Paul's legs.

Vashti had the whip.

Bone recovered his balance, swung around, and caught the first blow squarely in his face. It smashed his nose and blinded him.

Howling, Bone covered his face with his arms.

Vashti went to work on his body. Both Paul and Celeste winced involuntarily as each new cut with the whip spattered blood on them and the mirrors.

Cannons & Roses

It was a scene from hell!

Vashti followed Bone until he was cornered, snatching back the whip when he tried to grasp it. His face was a bloody mask. White ribs gleamed through the blood coating his chest. His eyes were gone from their sockets.

Bone sank to his knees, blubbering, arms over his head, and Vashti paused to admire her handiwork, a grim smile on her face.

Paul ordered her to stop.

Vashti shook her head. She made a noose with the bloody lash, slipped it over Bone's head, and jerked him back on his heels. Staring at his bloody face, Vashti garroted him.

Celeste had fainted.

Vashti was familiar enough with Bayou House to find the three of them clothing, without encountering the Amazons. She assured Paul that those two were the only others in the house that night.

Out in the night, they followed the winding road to the highway between New Orleans and Lake Pontchartrain.

They paused to rest.

Paul sat with an arm around Celeste. Vashti watched them, but she was disinterested. Killing Bone had temporarily slaked her fierce nature. She sat on her heels.

She would mutter under her breath, smile, mutter again, as if she were lost in the past, reliving some pleasant incident.

"Albert Grymes isn't in New Orleans," Celeste said, "but we must reach his young partner."

It was the first coherent sentence either she or Paul had spoken since escaping The Room and Bayou House.

Cannons & Roses

"Vashti has killed a white man," Paul said.

"I know, but Raoul Arcenaux will help us with the authorities. Listen to me!" she exclaimed. "Ulric Bone kidnaps us, tortures us, was going to kill us, and we're worried because Vashti killed him? That's ridiculous!"

The rest of the night, they walked single file along the highway, toward New Orleans. As soon as it was daylight, they hailed a farmer taking fruit and vegetables to the French Market.

Paul managed to force the street door to Spanish House.

Raoul Arcenaux listened to their story with growing alarm.

"My partner has been to the governor about Bone," he said when Paul and Celeste had finished, "and he left me instructions to confer with the district attorney about the man and his organization. But it looks as if Vashti has rid us of the verminous scum."

"What do we do about Vashti?" Celeste asked.

Raoul had been considering this problem while their story spilled out and had arrived at a solution he thought Albert Grymes would approve.

"Take her upriver to Great Oaks. We don't want to go to the authorities for a number of good reasons." Raoul ticked them off on his fingers. "She's killed a white man. Both of you are witnesses to the crime. No matter the provocation, it remains a crime, I regret to say. Then there's your reputation, Miss Celeste." Raoul turned to Paul. "My partner will inquire into your status when he reaches Philadelphia."

"Are you sure?" Celeste asked with a sinking feeling of guilt.

"I'm sure," Raoul told her. "He spoke with me about it just before he embarked. With the proper

Cannons & Roses

affidavits, and with the cooperation of Miss Celeste and her mother, we'll establish your legal status, Paul, but until then you can't testify in open court about Bone, even though he's dead."

"Your laws down here are interesting," Paul said bitterly.

"We have as many refugees here from Santo Domingo as they have in Charleston," Raoul told him. "Our Black Codes are harsh because we live on a sleeping volcano. They are necessary, believe me. Just a few years ago, there was a plot. Only a slave maid's reluctance to kill the white children she was caring for gave it away."

"How many *nigras* paid for plotting to escape slavery?" Paul asked.

"Nine of the ringleaders, I believe. They were hanged at landings along the river to set an example. Quite a few were flogged, of course."

"Of course," Paul said.

Raoul regarded him. "In strict confidence, Paul," he said, "I think slavery is the doom of the south. My family owns no slaves and never has. But if there's a general uprising, we'll be slaughtered with the goats. What is your opinion?" he asked Celeste.

"A nigra woman wet-nursed me," she said. "We treat our slaves well. I think they're better off here than they'd be in Africa." She couldn't read the expression on Paul's face. "How can we exist without slaves?"

Raoul shrugged. "You've asked a good question. I don't know the answer."

Raoul offered to arrange passage for them and Vashti on the mail boat going upriver the next day.

"Would you be so kind?" Celeste asked the lawyer.

Cannons & Roses

* * *

Back at Spanish House, sitting with Paul on a stone bench near the fountain, Celeste meant to discuss plans for going to Canada. She knew they couldn't stay in the south, regardless of what Albert Grymes might find in Philadelphia. How they'd get there, or live when they did, Celeste didn't know, but after what they'd suffered, she was more determined than ever to have Paul on any terms.

But there was a sudden stirring in her loins she couldn't understand. After what she'd endured for the past week, at the hands of Bone, and as a sort of love slave to Vashti, Celeste knew her sexuality should be exhausted. Yet it wasn't.

She suddenly wanted Paul, and she wanted him now.

Celeste was fevered with sex. "Paul, I have to have you," she blurted.

He was startled. "Now?"

"If you don't take me, I'll go to Vashti." It wasn't an idle threat. Celeste involuntarily pressed a hand hard against her sex, through the skirt and petticoat she wore. "Damn you, Paul, I'm begging! I can't help it."

I'm insane, she thought. *This is how it is to be crazy with desire.*

Paul sensed what was wrong with Celeste, but he didn't tell her because the naked lust reflected in her eyes was arousing him.

He could do *anything* with this woman! "Take her," a voice inside him whispered. "Use her."

Paul swept her up in his arms, carried her to the balcony, kicked open the bedroom door. He dumped Celeste on the bed. She had stripped before he was naked.

Paul fell on Celeste, forcing her thighs apart, and entered with a savage lunge that jolted a cry from her lips, but her ankles locked in the small of his back. His hands covered her breasts, nails digging the soft flesh, as Paul was caught up in her dizzying passion that couldn't be denied.

With Celeste, one swift climax overlapped the next until she'd lost count and rode the crest, grinding her pelvis against Paul's.

When he had spent, she wouldn't let him leave her. Paul found himself swelling and rising again. Celeste had inflamed him with her wanton abandon.

Her eyes were wide open, and staring, but she no longer saw Paul. Her face was contorted, ugly and swollen with passion that couldn't be slaked.

"Enough," Paul said finally and escaped Celeste. But with strength he'd never guessed she had, she pinned his shoulders to the bed, and was astride his chest.

Head thrown back, Celeste rocked there, making animal sounds. Her nails tore at his shoulders. Spasms shook her body and trembled her pointed breasts. Then, with a final shudder, it was over.

Celeste was on the bed beside him, face buried on her arms. She sobbed with relief. Paul rose on an elbow to stroke her back and follow the soft curve of her buttocks.

"You're all right now," he whispered. "You're all right. Sleep."

Celeste stopped panting between sobs and hiccuped. "I'm sorry, Paul. I don't understand."

"Bone must have drugged you with an aphrodisiac, as he tried to do to me," Paul explained.

She turned her face to him.

Celeste's lashes were still damp with tears, and there were dark smudges under her eyes. She reminded Paul of a wistful child who had been naughty, but now repents. "Have I hurt you?"

Paul patted her rump. "You've bloodied my shoulders, but it doesn't matter." Paul rose to draw a sheet up over her body and stooped to kiss the nape of her neck. "Sleep. When you wake up, I'll tell you how much I love you."

"You love me." Celeste spoke as if she couldn't quite believe what Paul had just said.

In moments her even breathing told Paul that Celeste was sleeping.

After he'd dressed, Paul settled in a chair to watch Celeste sleep.

Canada. Paul wondered if it was true that there was little racial prejudice up there. He'd heard there wasn't, but people thought Philadelphia was free of race prejudice. It wasn't.

His body was overcome with an enervating lassitude, but not his mind.

Liberia. The American Colonization Society could send him there again. They wouldn't send Celeste out with him—he was sure of that—but she could join him in Liberia.

"I'm thirty, and she's little more than a child," Paul told himself.

Celeste slept with wrists crossed on her chest, lips slightly parted. To Paul she was a dark child-angel. Tears welled in his eyes. She had given him all of herself impulsively, ridden across the color bar with no backward glance. He felt guilt that he'd never confess. He should have known in his heart that Celeste would never betray him.

Cannons & Roses

Sometime during the past week's ordeal, and without Paul's being conscious of it, the whole thrust of his ambition had changed direction. He saw now that retreat to Canada was the coward's way out. He knew that he had neither the courage nor the nerve to be a conductor on the Underground Railroad.

Celeste stirred in her sleep, and the sheet slipped down to expose her breasts. Paul thought of snow and cherries before he gently covered them again.

Back in Liberia, Paul could strike a blow at slavery more severe than moving a few runaways to sanctuary in Canada. Strike at the slave pens and slave traders. Dry up the source of fresh black ivory.

Would Celeste come with him to Liberia? He knew that the new Red River plantation would someday belong to Celeste (and her husband), and that she was a child of the south, raised in its traditions.

Paul confessed to himself that he envied the indolent life of the planters, with their endless supply of slave labor. He was honest enough to acknowledge that, in their position, he would be selfish enough to resist any change from the status quo.

But he never could attain the position of the rich white planters. They called themselves the southern "race," and in a sense they were right. Yet, like the Bourbon kings, they never learned anything, and they never forgot.

Paul remembered something DeWitt Scott had told him. DeWitt was another northerner come south, so Paul respected his opinions.

"Slavery is so morally wrong," DeWitt had said, "that these southern aristocrats will be severely punished for their belief that it is right. They bolster their wrong belief with the Bible, and *believe* that God ordained slavery. It isn't hypocrisy, I'm convinced. Do you suppose those Hebrews who worshiped the golden calf were hypocrites?"

"No more than the worshipers of Baal," Paul had said.

"Exactly," DeWitt told him.

Dusk was creeping into the room. The door to the balcony was ajar, and Paul realized, with a start, that neither of them had thought to bolt and close it. He wondered where Vashti was now, and where she had been?

With a shudder, he remembered the virago who had whipped and strangled Ulric Bone. He remembered her telling him, with relish, how she'd impaled a rival queen on a sharpened pole and carried her triumphantly through the village, before setting the pole in the ground.

Vashti was delighted that her rival survived from sundown to sunup, impaled on that pole while they roasted her alive in a circle of fire. And the woman had been served up, half-raw, to Vashti and her women.

Vashti had saved his life, and Celeste's, yet Paul knew she might one day kill them as casually as she'd slain Bone. He wondered if she had ever felt a twinge of pity. Paul thought not.

Celeste spoke his name in her sleep. He put a hand on her forehead and found it cool.

Celeste turned over, and regarded him with eyes unblurred by sleep. "Hello, Paul."

He stooped to kiss her. "Are you hungry?"

"Very."

"I'll bring you something to eat."

Paul was startled to find Raoul Arcenaux on the

Cannons & Roses

stone bench in the courtyard. "I wouldn't have waited, but it's a matter of importance," Raoul said. "I sent the servant to find Miss Celeste."

Raoul's voice was guarded, but not hostile.

15

*P*aul waited, wondering what Vashti had seen. Raoul's smile was amused. "The servant, Vashti—isn't that her name?"

"Yes. She doesn't have much English yet."

"*Mon ami,* a certain most delightful activity can be reported without words, yes?"

Paul nodded gravely.

"Miss Celeste's reputation is safe with me," Raoul said. "Cold-blooded Americans might consider it a *mésalliance*. As a Creole, I do not."

"What was important enough to bring you here?" Paul asked.

"Ah, that." Raoul hesitated, then said, "In the night, Bayou House was destroyed by fire. Is there something I haven't been told?"

"No, there isn't," Paul told him. "We set no fire."

"You would have been justified, but no matter. A charred corpse was found, identified by the missing hand as Ulric Bone." Raoul crossed himself. "You say two women were also in the house?"

"Yes. Have they been found?" Paul asked.

"No. It is thought they murdered their master, and fled to the swamps. No effort will be made to bring them to justice. We are rid of what might have been a troublesome problem."

Paul sagged with relief.

Vashti sulked in the room off the kitchen that Paul had occupied. Her first impulse had been to tear Paul off the white bitch, and strangle her with bare hands, but Vashti was cunning enough to resist it.

In her village, what to do about such a rival was a simple matter. She remembered a certain anthill. She'd had the last woman who tried to steal her man staked out on this hill, and then anointed her nipples and woman parts with wild honey. Vashti had stirred the hill with a spear and invited her other woman attendants to see the woman writhe and hear her screams. It had been very amusing.

Too bad she didn't know of an anthill here. But there were other painful ways to kill a rival. Poison was too merciful.

Vashti sat on the floor, in a corner of the room, cross-legged and bare to the waist so she could finger and admire her scarred breasts. She was proud of each scar. They proved her courage.

But how to kill the white bitch? Vashti envisioned Celeste's slender neck between her muscular thighs. She'd killed at least a dozen captive men and women with those thighs. It delighted her girl and woman attendants when the victim was a healthy boy or man because slow strangulation permitted them to take turns satisfying themselves.

Cannons & Roses

Once her man had used a woman she was strangling that way. He'd reported it was most satisfying, and she wondered if Paul might participate when she killed Celeste.

Jeanette was reconciled and had told DeWitt that as soon as Celeste and Paul reached a safe place in the north, her daughter would write.

"What we must do," she said, "is sell the Red River plantation and send the money to them. After all, it is Celeste's heritage."

Now that Celeste was gone, Jeanette regretted the clashes she'd had with her headstrong oldest daughter, and finally knew the cause. She hadn't wanted to share any part of Jamie with Celeste. Yet she was more his daughter, in disposition as well as coloring, than she was Jeanette's.

So when the mail boat brought Celeste, Paul, and Vashti to the landing it was a shock. "Where have you two been?" was the first question she asked.

"I'll tell you later, Mother," Celeste said in a tired voice. "Right now I need to sleep the clock around twice, and so does Paul."

He's taken her, Jeanette thought. *They have slept together more than once.*

Jeanette's thought was reflected in her manner and face for Celeste to read. "Maybe we'd better talk now," she said.

"Yes. Come to my room." Jeanette was over the first shock. She said to DeWitt, "You will question Paul."

"Paul doesn't owe anyone answers," Celeste told her mother. "He's saved my life, and I'm setting him free."

"We'll have to talk about that," Jeanette said. "Paul

Cannons & Roses

belongs to Great Oaks. Colonel Carroll will have to be informed, as will Bliss and Richard."

"You've forgotten that Paul was a gift to me, Mother."

"She's right," DeWitt said quietly. "The bill of sale is in her name, Miss Jeanette."

Paul listened to this discussion of his future with a wooden expression. It didn't change when Celeste gave him a warm smile.

DeWitt looked from one to the other. "I'd like to hear whatever you see fit to tell me, Paul," he said in a quiet voice. "We can talk in the office."

Upstairs, in Jeanette's room, Celeste sat in a chair, while her mother thoughtfully arranged the jars of cosmetics on her dressing table, and then rearranged them.

"I love Paul," Celeste said finally.

Jeanette didn't reply.

"I know we must leave the south, Mother."

"Where will you go?" Jeanette asked.

"I don't know yet. Paul and I have been in hell."

"Tell me about it," Jeanette said, still toying with the jars on her dresser.

Celeste spoke to her mother's back. "Ulric Bone used me as bait to kidnap Paul, and Paul to kidnap me. We were his prisoners for a week. Vashti killed Bone, Mother. She did it for Paul, not me."

Jeanette spun around. "Ulric Bone is *dead?*"

Celeste nodded. "Bayou House burned. The note entailing Spanish House burned with it, Raoul Arcenaux thinks. So you have your gift from my father."

Jeanette let out a long-held breath. "Thank God! You were right, I never should have tried to do business with Bone. Maybe I should listen to you more often."

Celeste studied her mother. There was a flush in her cheeks, and something about her eyes, as well as the way she held her mouth, was different. Celeste was almost sure that Jeanette had taken her advice about DeWitt Scott.

"Paul told me on the boat coming up from New Orleans that he wants to make a new start in Liberia," Celeste said. "I'll need money to join him there. Can we sell the Red River plantation?"

"I don't know. I'll have to consult with Colonel Carroll."

"Ply the old reprobate with peach brandy, and you can wrap him around your little finger, Mother, and you know it," Celeste said, laughing. "Let him pinch your bottom. He enjoyed doing that to Bliss and me every time Alicia Carroll looked the other way."

Jeanette tried to keep a stern face. "We are kin to the Carrolls now, Celeste."

"I should watch my tongue," Celeste said in a resigned voice. "Sorry, Mother."

Jeanette started to laugh. It was infectious. Before they could catch their breath, both were dabbing at the tears in their eyes.

"You little vixen," Jeanette said. "You don't miss much, do you?"

"Not if I can help it. Do you suppose Richard has Bliss pregnant by this time? If he hasn't, it won't be for not trying, I'm sure."

Jeanette frowned. "It's not Bliss I worry about," she said. "Your father had friends in Lexington. A Miss Leighton, whoever she may be, has written that Jamie Two is involved with an older woman in Richmond—some rich widow. A Philippa Randolph."

"That's a good name," Celeste said.

"But the woman is years older than he is!"

Cannons & Roses

"So?"

"I don't know that I like Jamie Two having an affair with a woman old enough to be his mother," Jeanette said. "What if there should be a child?"

"Jamie Two would make an honest woman of her."

"That's why I'm afraid."

"Don't be," Celeste said. "June and January marriages work, you know."

"When the bride is younger, yes. Girls need an older and experienced man to initiate them into the rites of womanhood. But it's different with young men —you'll have to admit that."

"I don't admit it," Celeste said.

Jeanette wondered if she'd ever understand this daughter. "I want you to visit Jamie," she said.

"When?"

"Very soon. Before this affair gets out of hand."

"All right," Celeste told her mother. "I'll begin packing."

Celeste would go to New Orleans first and arrange Paul's freedom with Raoul Arcenaux, or Albert Grymes when he came back. She'd take Paul with her, and they'd stay at Spanish House.

Celeste was convinced that Paul could pass.

She, too, could pass, as another young man, and they'd be brothers on the ship. There was no question of going overland.

It was their chance to break clean with the past.

"I should be suspicious," Jeanette said.

"Why?"

"You're too willing to make the journey."

"I'm an obedient daughter, Mother."

"You are a conniving little hussy."

* * *

166

Cannons & Roses

Slaves in Virginia and the border states were an item of commerce in the Deep South. To furnish the necessary labor required by cotton planters since Whitney's gin was invented in the late 1700s, slave owners in Tennessee, Kentucky, and Virginia enjoyed tidy profits from selling slaves farther south.

Until the cultivation of cotton became economical, the slave population and its rapid increase had been a worrisome thing in these states. But now it was so profitable to sell prime field hands for $1,500 to $1,700, that there were slave breeding farms.

Experienced in breeding fine horses, it was a simple step to breeding men and women who could stand the rigors of gang labor. A slave owner might have only two or three stud males. He'd breed them to a dozen or so young females.

Most owners supervised the mating of their studs just as if they were breeding horses, and not human beings. They rationalized that the black man and woman were a subhuman species.

And there was more profit in such enterprises than in horse breeding.

A slave breeder named Wainwright lost his best male studs when one ran off, another was killed by a jealous fellow slave, and the third man castrated himself with a rusty knife.

"Damned fool nigger," Wainwright said. "He didn't cotton to covering his own daughter."

Wainwright had decided that inbreeding might produce superior stock in some instances.

Wainwright had come Deep South with an idea. Buy prime nigras, male and female, those who'd been able to survive in the Deep South climate, and at the hardest labor. Ship them back to Virginia and his farm.

Cannons & Roses

Take his pick, then sell off the rest to other breeding-farm owners.

Wainwright had toured the plantations, especially those making new ground along the Red River. He'd marched a coffle of thirty men and sixteen girls and women to the slave pens of New Orleans. There he'd arranged to have them shipped on the sloop *Good Friend* to Norfolk, where he'd meet the ship and take delivery of his human merchandise.

Herman Wainwright expected to make a small fortune.

He'd chosen the *Good Friend* because a New Orleans shipping agent told him she was formerly in the slave trade and had the necessary accommodations to chain men and women between-decks in the conventional spoon fashion.

Herman rode out of New Orleans well pleased with himself. Next year he'd have enough money to send his only child—a daughter—to that fine new academy for young ladies in Richmond.

Herman Wainwright loved his daughter, as he did his wife.

In selecting his new slave stock, Herman had made one mistake. He'd bought the man Jason from Delray Bone. Jason had been a common seaman, kidnapped, like Paul, and Delray knew a troublemaker when he saw one. He was relieved to be rid of Jason.

Jason was a stocky man, with broad shoulders, a bull's neck, a bullet head with a flat nose, and swollen Negro lips. Herman sized him up as an idiot. But the best gang-labor slaves were those with muscles and not too much mind, so he bought Jason when Delray Bone set a bargain price.

Herman Wainwright was pleased with this purchase.

He paid only $500 for Jason. He anticipated six times that amount in stud fees. But he'd have to be careful. The size of the man's male organ precluded Herman from using him to cover young girls.

Cabot Andrews, captain of the *Good Friend,* was a former slaver. He'd made a fortune in the three-corner trade: slaves for sugar, sugar for rum, rum for more slaves. He'd survived two mutinies in the Middle Passage. A churchgoing man, Cabot gave up slaving when law prohibited further importations from Africa's west coast. The *Good Friend* coasted between New Orleans and Boston.

Cabot's wife, Minerva, and their fourteen-year-old daughter always sailed with him. Jessie Wainwright was a slender girl, with a sweet church-choir voice.

Herman Wainwright was promised safe and sound delivery of his purchases.

One thing Delray had forgotten to tell Herman Wainwright.

Jason Smith had a mind like a steel trap.

Neighbors thought a young man and his body servant had moved into Spanish House. Celeste enjoyed the freedom of men's clothes. Loose-fitting jackets disguised her breasts, and she'd obtained a codpiece, so popular with English gentlemen, to complete her masquerade.

She and Paul were to remember their weeks in Spanish House as a honeymoon.

Papers proving Paul was a free Negro finally reached Raoul Arcenaux. Paul went before a district judge and was declared free. That night Celeste told him that she planned to go to Liberia with him.

"When I've seen my brother, we can arrange passage from New York or Philadelphia," she said. "Mother is selling the Red River plantation, so we'll have enough money for a while."

As yet they hadn't discussed marriage.

They had talked about Liberia. Paul planned to recruit a force of free Negroes and raid the slave pens down the west coast of Africa, striking, as he said, at the heart of slavery. He expected to have at least the tacit approval of the Liberian government. Slaves freed by these raids could return to their native villages or become citizens of Liberia.

Celeste had her doubts. "You can get yourself killed," she told Paul. "Why can't you teach, as you did before?"

Paul planned to teach, but only as a cover for his other activities. Celeste thought, once they reached Liberia, she could talk him out of trying to raid the slave pens.

She booked passage to Norfolk, aboard the *Good Friend*.

While in the pens, waiting to be taken aboard the *Good Friend,* Jason Smith recruited his mutineers. Once they'd rounded Florida and were reaching up the coast for Norfolk, Jason planned to catch the captain and crew off-guard and seize the ship. He was confident he could navigate well enough to reach Nassau and the British.

From there, with replenished supplies, they would sail to Liberia.

Jason cautioned his new recruits that no one should be killed. Captain, crew, and passengers would be put ashore at Nassau.

"We kill anyone," he cautioned, "and they'll hang us for piracy."

Cannons & Roses

Among Jason's recruits was a towering Negro named Bill. Whip-scarred and branded, Bill was determined to rid himself of Jason at an early opportunity and take over as leader.

An all-consuming hatred of whites had kept Bill alive.

16

*P*hilippa Randolph was pregnant. It was embarrassing and damned inconvenient, coming this early in her relationship with Jamie McCoy, despite her boast that she wanted to bear his child. By tacit consent, neither had spoken of marriage again. Jamie would have to drop out of Washington College if they were married.

Philippa toyed with the idea of taking her problem to Mrs. Brady, but decided against that course of action. Being with child at this point might be inconvenient, but Philippa wanted the child. She wanted it with a fierceness she'd never felt before. She set about making plans.

It didn't occur to Philippa to confide in Jamie. The boy was completely besotted with her and would try to rush her into marriage, regardless of the consequences. No, the thing to do was go off somewhere, bear the child, then return to Richmond and pass it

Cannons & Roses

off as someone else's. It would be time enough to tell Jamie then.

Maybe he'd still want to marry her, and maybe he wouldn't. It was a risk she was willing to take. What she'd started as an exercise in sexuality had become love on her part, but Philippa didn't think Jamie was in a position yet to know his own mind.

There were Randolphs in Boston—a branch of the family had settled there when they came from England and had gone into shipping. She'd go there from Richmond for a long visit, and to have her child.

With her mind made up, Philippa sat at the desk in her bedroom, and wrote Jamie a letter. It was a warm and friendly letter, thanking him for his attention to an older woman, and hoping they could see each other again when she returned from her extended business trip to Boston.

Philippa wrote a second letter, this one to her brother Chester, and explained that she contemplated investing some of her fortune in the Randolph Shipping Lines. With her tracks covered, Philippa closed the town house in Richmond and went to Norfolk accompanied by her Irish maid. They would sail from there.

The first ship they could take would be the *Good Friend*. It was a few days overdue, the shipping agent told Philippa, but he thought she would find the accommodations on board quite satisfactory.

Philippa paid him for two first-class passages.

Philippa's letter stunned Jamie. He sat in his dormitory room and for the first time in his life got drunk. When Chester Randolph couldn't get the whisky jug away from Jamie, he sat down with Jamie and got as drunk as his young friend.

Cannons & Roses

When his tongue got loose enough, Jamie poured out his love for Philippa.

"You mean, you and she. . . ? " Chester was having trouble with his own tongue.

"We did," Jamie muttered.

Neither could remember exactly how one thing led to another, and what happened to the eternal friendship they'd sworn earlier in the evening, but dawn found them staggering from the dormitory, pistols in hand.

Neither could stand up without the support of the other, which posed a problem when they reached the drill field, where they planned to settle this affair of honor.

"You seduced my sister," Chester muttered. "Must have satisfaction."

"Love your sister," Jamie muttered back. "You're a rotten brother. I love your sister, see?"

"Never mind. You"—Chester was having trouble with "seduce."—"You . . . you're a cad!"

"What's that?" Jamie wanted to know.

"Don't exactly know," Chester admitted.

"Cad." Jamie had become fond of the word.

They circled, holding onto each other, then sank to the damp ground in a tight embrace.

"Cad," Jamie said.

"Cad," Chester repeated.

"Lost my damn pistol," Jamie told Chester.

"Here. Take mine."

"You're a good friend."

"The best."

Jamie lay back, the pistol on his chest, and went to sleep.

Chester, owl-eyed, regarded his roommate for a few minutes, sitting cross-legged, then took back his pistol and uncocked it, before Jamie had a chance to blow off his head.

Stretching out, with his head on Jamie's stomach, Chester went to sleep.

Professor Thomas J. Jackson found them that way the next morning. Sucking a lemon, he regarding the two young men. Finally he nudged them both with the toe of his boot.

Jackson had noticed the pistols lying in the dew-wet grass.

"Who won the duel?" Jackson asked.

It was the only humorous remark either Chester or Jamie had ever heard Old Jack make, and it was the last they'd ever hear from him.

Jackson stood there, raising first one arm, and then the other, still sucking his lemon.

No wonder most of the cadets think he's crazy, Jamie thought. Then: *Sure as hell he'll expel us!*

As a professor of military science, Jackson was a stickler for strict observance of rules and regulations.

"Get cleaned up and we'll forget this," Jackson said, and surprised them for the second time that morning.

Sitting in class that day, with a roaring headache, and a queasy stomach, Jamie considered himself a damned fool. Philippa had wanted him, so she'd taken him. Now it was all over. She'd probably find a dozen new lovers in Boston!

"And she's welcome to them," Jamie tried to tell himself.

But he knew, when he was no longer hung over, that it wouldn't be quite that easy to crowd Philippa out of his life.

She'd helped him prove, once and for all, that he was a normal male who could lust for a woman, and not another man.

Cannons & Roses

Celeste had been right!

After rounding Florida's keys, the *Good Friend*, sailed into the teeth of a full gale. Captain Andrews ordered all hands on deck to take in sail and heave the ship to, riding out the storm, a sea anchor holding her stern to the wind.

Mountainous seas coursed over her, sweeping two seamen away, and she began to take water. All her boats were smashed to splinters and swept away.

Paul and Celeste braced themselves in their bunk. Water sloshed on the floor of their stateroom. There was no way they could tell what might be happening on deck.

It was cold. Both of them were thoroughly wet, because a sea had poured in before Paul could screw the port shut.

Captain Andrews decided to rig a storm jib. Those few feet of wet canvas would pull the *Good Friend* enough to have steerage.

The dark, wet hell it would be between-decks, where naked men and women were chained, preyed on his conscience. If the *Good Friend* was lost, they'd go down with her, without any chance of escape.

He intended to save his ship. But fear alone can kill, he well knew. He'd seen slaves die in the Middle Passage because they were chained and helpless in a storm such as this one.

"Mr. Masters," he told his mate, "take two men and unchain our between-decks cargo. Put the able-bodied at the pumps."

"Aye, sir."

"Then get on with rigging the storm jib."

"Aye, aye, sir."

His wife and daughter would be praying.

Cabot Andrews was too busy to pray, but he hoped God was listening to Minerva and Jessie. He was going to need all the help he could get to save the *Good Friend*.

"Don't you dare sink under me!" he told his ship, and cocked his head to better hear the creaking timbers.

Andrews and the *Good Friend* had been together more years than he liked to remember. She was getting old, as he was.

This is the last time we go out together, old girl, he thought.

He was too old to ride out a gale like this one. It drained a man. Andrews knew he didn't have what it takes any longer. Two good seaman already gone. He and he alone was responsible for all the other souls on board, and that included the nigras.

Poor devils!

Unlike the others, Vashti wasn't chained by a neck ring to the sides of the ship, and stretched out on the wide shelves. Paul and Celeste had insisted that she not be. But she was confined to the between-decks area.

When the *Good Friend* first bucked into the gale, Vashti had been frightened. This was no longer so. She was African, with the fatalism inherent in Africans.

She remembered her village, where the girls and women went to the river for water every day, and always at the same place. The crocodiles knew that place well, but the village women and girls never varied their routine.

Everyone knew that if a woman was meant to be dragged under by a crocodile, it would happen, regardless of what she did.

If Vashti was meant to drown, there was nothing she could do about it.

Each lurch and pitch of the ship half-strangled the slaves on the shelves. Vashti moved up and down the aisle between the shelves, trying to ease their agony and soothe their fear.

Masters and two seaman were releasing the slaves, coming down the aisle toward her. Jason Smith was one of the first released.

Celeste was miserably seasick. "I wish this damned thing would sink!" she wailed to Paul. "Why didn't we think of another way to reach Virginia?"

Paul's own stomach had begun to churn, but he patted Celeste's head. "Just hang on," he said. "The ship's seaworthy, and Cabot Andrews is a good man."

"I wish *I* were seaworthy," Celeste said. "I didn't know anyone could be this sick. Why aren't you seasick?"

"I have my sea legs," Paul told her, but then the ship rose on a particularly steep wave and lurched down into its trough.

Paul just managed to reach the bucket before he lost everything he'd eaten.

When he'd finished retching, Celeste said, "Now I feel a little better."

With the men slaves helping with the pumps, the water level in the hull was reduced, and the *Good Friend* was no longer in danger of foundering. With most of the crew on deck, Jason Smith found the arms locker. It contained half a dozen old-fashioned rifles and two pistols. He broke each rifle over his knee before arming himself with the pistols, first making sure they were loaded.

The gale was blowing itself out, and Cabot Andrews

Cannons & Roses

was on the quarterdeck, with the crew putting on enough sail to get underway again.

Minerva Andrews and her daughter were locked in their cabin with Vashti and two other slave women. Jason had cautioned Vashti that neither was to be so much as touched.

Jason found Captain Andrews. One pistol was thrust into the belt of the trousers he'd stolen from the empty forecastle, and the other was in his hand.

"Get off this deck and below where you belong," Andrews blustered. He reached to take the pistol in Jason's hand. "I'll have you flogged!"

Jason stepped back and pointed the pistol at Andrew's head. "We got your women. We taking this ship, captain."

The man at the helm, wide-eyed, stared over his shoulder.

Andrews sensed the determination in this black man. "What's your name?" he asked.

Jason told him, adding, "I can sail this ship. I been many times to sea, captain. You don't take us to Nassau, we take her there."

"You say my wife and daughter are safe?"

"Go below. You see. Women are guarding them."

"You think the British will set you free?"

"They do it," Jason said. "Many times I been to Nassau."

Cabot Andrews was bone-tired. It had been a mistake to have anything more to do with slaving, and he'd shipped this cargo of slaves against his better judgment. But the cargo was insured.

"We'll set a course for Nassau, but there is to be no violence," he advised Jason.

"No violence," Jason agreed.

Cannons & Roses

When the *Good Friend* was on a new course that would take her to Nassau, Jason conducted Andrews below and to his cabin. Vashti stepped aside so they could enter.

He found his wife and daughter huddled together on one of the bunks. Minerva's arms were around Jessie, and the girl was crying.

"What is happening, Cabot?" Minerva asked over Jessie's head.

As he knew she would be, Minerva was icy calm.

"There has been a mutiny. I'm still in command, but we're changing course."

"Where will we go?" Minerva asked and patted Jessie's shoulder. "Hush, dear."

"Nassau."

Minerva stared at Jason. "You will see that my husband comes to no harm," she said.

"We hurt nobody," Jason promised.

Celeste and Paul didn't discover the ship had changed hands until they came on deck the next morning. Jason was on the quarterdeck with Captain Andrews, and except for the captain, there wasn't a white man in sight. Bill was at the helm.

"We're on a different course," Paul told Celeste. "Wait here amidships. I'll talk to the captain."

"What's going on?" Celeste asked.

"It looks as if the slaves have seized the ship," he said.

He looked around for blood on the deck, but found none.

Celeste was chilled with apprehension. "Be careful."

Paul promised that he would be.

With a sour expression on his face, Captain Andrews referred Paul's questions to Jason.

180

Cannons & Roses

"Where is the crew?" Paul asked.

Jason grinned. "Between-decks. Under guard. You and your brother be safe, white man. We reach for Nassau."

"His wife and daughter?" Paul asked, nodding toward Captain Andrews.

"They be safe. Your slave, Vashti, be guarding them."

"My brother and I will take over that chore," Paul said in a cool voice. "I'll have that pistol you have in your belt, please."

Jason shook his head. "No."

Paul studied Jason for a minute, trying to assess his character. He beckoned Jason out of Captain Andrews's hearing. "You've done well to secure this ship without bloodshed, Jason," he said, "but you're going to need help before you make Nassau. I've just escaped slavery. I was kidnapped in Philadelphia and brought south."

Jason scowled. "You be white."

"I'm not," Paul said. "My mother was mulatto."

"Your brother be white." Jason pointed at Celeste who was watching them from amidships. "Why is that?"

"My former master," Paul explained. "We are good friends. We were sailing for Norfolk to get a ship that will take us down to Liberia."

Jason's face brightened, and he handed over the pistol to Paul. "You got passage there."

"I thought we might have," Paul said, and went to rejoin Celeste.

When he'd explained the situation, they went to relieve Vashti.

"She probably has Mrs. Andrews and her daughter terrorized by this time," he said.

17

When she'd donned men's clothing, Celeste took the name of James. It was by this name that Paul introduced her to Minerva and Jessie Andrews. He'd ordered Vashti between-decks to help guard the captive crewmen. Paul introduced himself as Mr. Wright.

"Are you and your brother part of this plot to steal my husband's ship, Mr. Wright?" Minerva asked. She was a large, spare woman, with severe features, and graying hair drawn to a bun at the nape of her neck. "When we reach Nassau, the blacks will be free, but the British will never let you take the *Good Friend*."

"I know that, but the slaves don't as yet," Paul said. "My brother and I aren't part of this plot, Mrs. Andrews. Your husband is cooperating, and at this point we are, too. We don't want bloodshed."

Jessie was a pretty if pale girl, with brown hair and dark eyes. She still huddled on the bunk.

"That woman you just sent away—is she your slave?" Mrs. Andrews asked. "She was forward with Jessie. You should have her whipped."

"You may have noticed her scars," Paul said. "I think Vashti has been whipped enough, don't you?"

Mrs. Andrews sighed.

"She really didn't hurt me," Jessie said.

"All of them are poor dumb brutes," Mrs. Andrews told Paul and Celeste.

"James will stay here with you." Paul handed Celeste the pistol. "You won't be harmed in any way, and you have my word."

"Thank you, Mr. Wright," Minerva Andrews said.

Paul told Captain Andrews that his brother was guarding his wife and daughter. The man heaved a sigh of relief. "I mark the big female nigger as a rogue," he said. "I've seen her kind before."

"She's a Mandingo," Paul said.

Captain Andrews nodded. "I know that tribe well. It's hard to tame the brutes. I was once in the slave trade," he confided to Paul, "but maybe you've guessed that."

Paul nodded. "I've seen the between-decks."

"Mine was always a clean ship, and we exercised the nigras every day during fair weather. I seldom lost more than a dozen in the Middle Passage, and some of them were suicides. Africa!" He sighed. "It gets into a man's blood, Mr. Wright. But I'm a law-abiding man, and always have been."

Jason was listening to this conversation. "Your men don't be chained in the between-decks, as you chained us," he said, and spit over the rail.

Captain Andrews drew himself up. "My seamen aren't niggers, and they obey my orders."

Cannons & Roses

Jason snatched the pistol from his belt. Then he thought better of it. He contented himself with a backhanded slap that sent Captain Andrews staggering.

Clenching his hands, Captain Andrews licked at the trickle of blood from the corner of his mouth. "I'll have the skin off your back for that," he threatened.

Paul stepped between the two men. "I'd suggest we watch our tongues, Captain Andrews."

The angry flush faded from Captain Andrews's leathery face. "My apology," he said to Jason stiffly.

Jason's grin showed broken teeth. "Make you feel better, call me nigger," he said.

Bill was in charge between-decks. With half a dozen men at his back, field hands chosen by Wainwright for their height and strength, he felt brave enough to insult the captive seamen. They were demoralized by their captain's orders not to resist the Negroes, and, except for the mate, Masters, were cowed. They sat on the shelves while Bill paced the aisle.

Masters sat in a forward corner, hugging his knees, and swearing to himself at Andrews. The man must be senile as well as a coward!

"You not smart now, white man," Bill jeered at one crewman. "Look at you down here." He slapped the man's bare feet. "Just like a dumb nigger."

The man drew his feet up, managing a weak grin.

Bill turned on an older man. "You too old to enjoy a woman, I say," he jeered. "That right, white man?"

"I ain't that old yet," the man said.

"That what you say." Bill's eye fell on the stripling cabin boy, just ten. "Bet an old man like you like to bugger that child." He grabbed an ankle and jerked the older seaman off the shelf. "Get off them pants. I hold the child for you."

Cannons & Roses

Vashti, from a shelf at the opposite end of the between-decks from Masters, had been watching Bill with interest.

Bill ripped down the seaman's pants, and made a grab for the cabin boy.

"Mr. Masters!" The boy's was a shrill cry for help.

Masters wasn't an iron-fisted bucko mate—he wouldn't have been aboard the *Good Friend* under Captain Andrews if he had been—but he was a husky Salem man, and had been in a few brawls. He came off the shelf with a bound, hooked an arm around Bill's neck, tripped him to the deck, and delivered a kick to his head.

In a moment, between-decks was the scene of a frantic brawl. Neither slaves nor seamen had any weapons but their hands and feet.

There were fifteen crewmen and only six slaves, not counting Vashti, but in the sweltering half-darkness it was an even fight. Hardened by field work, and Deep South heat, each Negro was capable of handling two or three of the seamen.

Despite a kick in the head, Bill grappled to his feet, and flung Masters half the length of the hold. Masters jerked loose one of the chains used to secure slaves.

"Stand clear!" he shouted, flailing with the chain, and advancing on Bill.

He'd cleared the aisle. Brawling slaves and seamen, jumped on the shelves, as Masters's chain hissed through the air.

Masters had forgotten that Vashti was behind him, but when she jumped into the aisle, someone shouted, "Behind, mate!"

She'd meant to grab the chain from Masters's hands and beat him with it, but the mate whirled and caught her full in the face.

Cannons & Roses

Bill had found his own chain.

Vashti was down, writhing, arms covering her face. Animal sounds bubbled from her throat through smashed teeth and gums.

Masters and Bill stood their ground, neither man wanting to advance against a flailing chain. At that moment, the hatch was jerked open, and Paul peered down into the hold. He came down the ladder, pistol in hand. Seamen tumbled over each other trying to get behind him.

"Out of my way." Paul ordered Masters.

Masters looked around, saw the weapon, and obeyed.

"Drop it," he ordered Bill.

Bill threw the chain at Paul. Flinching away from the whirling chain, Paul's finger tightened on the trigger of the pistol. The heavy ball shattered Bill's breastbone and dropped him to the deck, dead.

"Get him out of here, and up on deck!" Paul ordered the seamen.

Paul found Masters kneeling beside Vashti, who was unconscious now, trying to pull her arms away from her battered face. The mate was deathly pale. His jaw muscles were working.

Vashti's face was a bloody gargoyle's mask, embedded with splinters of skull. Paul was reminded of Ulric Bone.

"No way to help her," Masters said through clenched teeth.

Paul stripped off his shirt and handed the pistol to Masters. He daubed at Vashti's ruined face, but he saw that the end of the chain had penetrated the side of her head. Gray matter oozed from the wound.

Death rattled in Vashti's throat.

Paul took back his pistol.

Cannons & Roses

He ordered the slaves to bring her on deck, but first he wrapped his shirt around her head.

Jason Smith came amidships. Masters reported what had happened below, and Jason took it in, his ebony face expressionless.

The white seamen were standing around the deck, with curious glances at the slaves working the ship, waiting for some kind of order from Captain Andrews.

"Jason, let me talk with the captain," Paul said. "I'll try to get you and the others safe passage to Nassau. I think we've shed enough black blood."

Paul and Andrews went below to the captain's cabin. He left Jason the job of getting Bill and Vashti over the side. As soon as they reached the cabin, Paul realized that Minerva and Jessie had seen through Celeste's disguise. The three were chatting like three women.

Minerva's arch glance and Jessie's giggle made him wonder how much Celeste had told them.

"They know we're eloping, Paul," Celeste said.

"James is not a boy," Minerva told her puzzled husband. "They're to be married."

"Because they took the ship without killing, I think we should proceed to Nassau," Paul said. "You'll be considered a hero by the British there. Celeste and I will back whatever story you tell your owners."

"I own this ship," Captain Andrews said.

"Then it's a simple matter," Paul told him. "Work the ship with your own crew, but reach for Nassau."

Andrews wanted back full control of his ship and crew. And there was guilt in the man, left over from his voyages as a slaver. He'd never become completely callous to the plight of the men, women, and children the *Good Friend* carried into a life of slavery.

Jessie had abolitionist leanings, and Minerva was more and more inclined to listen to her daughter.

"We reach for Nassau and freedom for these black brutes we have on board," Captain Andrews said. "You have my word."

"Good." Paul shook his hand. "I still have some influence with the American Colonization Society. I may be able to get them to charter your ship to carry those now on board, and others, to Liberia. You've said you miss Africa."

"That I do," Captain Andrews agreed.

When they were alone, Paul told Celeste how Vashti had died. She listened quietly, but when he was finished, Celeste found she could cry for the black woman.

Paul was touched. "Vashti was dangerous, especially to you," he said. "You've told me only a few of the things she did to you in Bayou House, but I should think you'd hate her."

Celeste dashed at her tears with the back of her hand. "Don't try to understand me, or any other woman," she cautioned.

British officials in Nassau were correct in their handling of the *Good Friend* affair. The mutinous slaves stood trial in an admiralty court and were granted asylum, but were sentenced to a year of hard labor on the island's roads. This sentence, except for a month, was then suspended.

Captain Andrews and his crew were then commended for their handling of the mutiny.

"You, sir, have shown compassion that is quite unusual on the part of an American captain, engaged in the nefarious activity of transporting slaves," the judge in his robes and powdered wig said.

The American consul lodged a formal complaint with the court, claiming that the court had seized legiti-

Cannons & Roses

mate cargo belonging to a citizen of the United States, but it was a formality.

William Rankin, the consul, hailed from Indiana, and two of his brothers were active in the branch of the Underground Railroad that ran through that state. He'd gone to Congress as a representative of a border district along the Ohio River where slavery was anathema. Privately he congratulated Captain Andrews on his decision.

A week after the *Good Friend* made port, the ship sailed for Norfolk. Paul promised Jason Smith he would keep his word and try to obtain financial help for the *Good Friend* Negroes from the American Colonization Society.

"I'll see you in Liberia," Paul told Jason before they parted.

Jamie learned that Philippa Randolph and her maid were waiting for a ship at Norfolk to take them to Boston. As a member of the cadet corps, he went to Professor Jackson for permission to take a leave of absence from the college.

"Sir, I have most important personal business in Norfolk," he said, stiffly at attention. "I must go there within the week."

Jackson looked up from his daily reading of the Bible. "What sort of personal business is this, Cadet McCoy?"

"That, sir, I cannot divulge."

"I see." Jackson marked his place in the bible with a bony forefinger. "I trust it has something to do with the disgraceful condition I found you and Cadet Randolph in the other morning?"

Jamie flushed. "Yes, sir."

Jacskon opened his Bible and resumed reading. "At

ease," he ordered Jamie. Jackson followed the lines with a finger, and his lips moved silently.

Jamie waited.

After minutes, Jackson said, without looking up, "Permission granted."

"Thank you, sir!" Jamie turned on his heel to go.

"My regards to Miss Philippa Randolph," Jackson said.

Philippa was restless. Waiting had never been an easy thing for her to do, and word had come that the *Good Friend* had left Nassau, but wouldn't reach Norfolk for another three days.

Maura, Philippa's Irish maid, watched her mistress pace their small hotel room, kicking at her long skirt every time she turned.

Maura O'Houlihan had sore eyes this morning from altering the waistband of that skirt and three others last night. She knew from the laundry that the mistress had missed a period, and very regular she always was.

"So the mistress has one in the oven," Maura told herself. "Praises be!"

Maura hoped it would be a wee colleen, not a bawling brat of a boy. She'd left seven older brothers to come to America, and back in Donegal she hoped they'd stay.

It's probably that handsome cadet with an Irish name, Maura thought.

"You'll be wearing yourself out, Miss Philippa," Maura said, "and you can walk from Kerry to Dublin, but it won't bring the ship sooner."

Philippa paused in her pacing to regard the girl. "I've been an utter damned fool, Maura," she confessed. "I wrote a letter I shouldn't have. Now I don't know what to do about it."

Maura looked at her hands, folded in the lap of her skirt. "You could be writing another."

Philippa shook her head. "Damned if I will. There's been no answer to the first one."

"A woman sometimes must carry her pride in a pocket, my old grandmother used to say," Maura told Philippa. "The wee one will need a father when she comes."

Philippa resumed her pacing.

This is one hell of a time to find yourself heels over appetite in love, she thought.

Jamie was saddle-sore, mud-spattered, and hungry. He'd been in the saddle two days and a night. And he hadn't known there were so many boardinghouses and small hotels in the port city of Norfolk.

Damn Philippa! He'd ridden out of Lexington in the best Sir Walter Scott tradition: determined to win back his lady love, overcoming all odds, and slaying a few dragons, if that was necessary. Now, more than anything else, he wanted a hot breakfast and a place to sleep.

Just down the muddy street was the Colonial Arms. It had only a small, discreet sign, and Jamie hadn't noticed it when he set out on his quest. Now he dismounted and wrapped the reins around the hitching bar. He patted the sweaty neck of his tired horse, stamped some of the mud off his boots, and strode into the lobby.

The smell of ham and gravy, frying potatoes, and bacon drew him toward the open doors of the dining room with a watering mouth.

"Young man!" It was the elderly woman behind the desk. "You can't go in there."

Jamie turned, went to the desk, and asked, "Why not? Isn't this a public house?"

"Your clothes." The woman fastidiously wrinkled her nose. "And you smell like a horse." She took pity.

"Go around to the kitchen entrance, and you'll be served there."

"Do you have a Miss Philippa Randolph of Richmond as a guest?" Jamie asked.

"Why, yes, young man, we do," the woman said. "Young man! You can't go upstairs dressed like that!"

Taking the stairs two and three at a time, Jamie didn't hear her.

18

A bleary-eyed man answered Jamie's first knock, trailing suspenders and scratching his beard. "Who the hell are you?" he asked.

"My mistake. Sorry."

A high-pitched woman's voice said, "Just a minute," behind the next door.

"Never mind, ma'am."

Jamie's hand was poised to rap on the third door when it was thrown open. "What the devil is all this racket?" Philippa demanded to know. Her eyes widened. "Jamie!"

"It's me." He spoke meekly, suddenly realizing how much he needed a shave, and finally aware that he did smell of horse—a well-lathered horse at that. "I wanted to see you before you sail for Boston."

Maura was making cooing noises in the background.

Relief and welcome were written on Philippa's expressive face. Everything was all right. She held and squeezed Jamie's blistered hands. Her breathing was uneven. "Oh, my love."

Maura sidled past them. "I'm thinking I'll have my breakfast, Miss Philippa."

Neither Jamie nor Philippa heard the girl.

"You can't sail for Boston," Jamie said.

"I have to."

"Why? What's so important about Boston just now?" Jamie asked. "Are you trying to run away from us?"

Philippa touched a finger to his chapped lips. "No, my love. I'm going to have our baby, and you can't marry me because you'll be expelled from college. I know how much that means to you."

For a moment, Jamie was stunned.

Philippa laughed. Taking a hand, she pressed it to her stomach. "She's in there, Jamie."

Jamie had regained his composure. "We'll be married today. Damn college! I love you, woman."

"Can you be sure?" Philippa asked. "You're so young, Jamie, and I'm thirty. Your family will never approve. And you need an education."

"We're getting married," Jamie said grimly.

Over her astonishment at his sudden presence, Philippa's mind was racing. "I don't know anybody here in Norfolk, and you don't, either, do you?"

"No."

"So we'll be married." There was a happy lilt in Philippa's voice. "I'll go to Boston to have our child, you'll return to school, and no one need be any wiser. I'll bring her back to Richmond as . . . as a child of a poor relative, father deceased . . . no, the mother —that would be better. I'll find an excuse to sell my Richmond home and move to Lexington, or maybe Winchester." Philippa nodded to herself. "Winchester wouldn't be so obvious, and I own property there—a dear little house."

"I've never had my future planned so quickly," Jamie said.

Philippa was concerned. "Have I offended your masculine pride?"

Jamie laughed. "Hell, no. How long does it take your Irish girl to eat breakfast?"

"Maura knows I'm pregnant and probably suspects you're our baby's father. She'll eat well this morning," Philippa said, and there was a sultry look in her eyes. "Kiss me."

Jamie was hungry for Philippa. He folded her softness and warmth against himself until she knew he was fully aroused. His hands explored her bodice and found her breasts. He groaned.

"God!" he muttered into the sweetness of her hair. "I want you!"

"Then take me, damn it," Philippa breathed.

"I need to bathe."

"No. Not this time. I can't wait."

Jamie hesitated. "Is it all right, with you pregnant? I don't know much about women."

"I'm not that pregnant yet," Philippa said. "It will be very much all right, love."

With his child growing in Philippa's womb, Jamie discovered there was a new depth to their passion, and with it, tenderness that he'd never felt before. By giving herself, Philippa had taken Jamie.

She'd go to Boston. She'd bring back their child. She'd come to Winchester.

Philippa was security. Whatever she planned, that's the way it would be. Jamie was content.

* * *

Cannons & Roses

"We'll arrive in Norfolk by tomorrow morning if this following wind holds," Paul told Celeste aboard the *Good Friend*. "I don't intend to go ashore."

"Where will you go?"

"Captain Andrews has promised to carry me on to Philadelphia. I have to get in touch with the society, and arrange passage for the men and women back in Nassau on to Liberia." Paul kissed Celeste. "And make arrangements to go down there myself."

"What about us?" Celeste asked.

"You need time to think. If you were mulatto, or even octoroon . . . it would be better."

"What are you trying to tell me?"

"West Africa is another world. It's going to be a hard life, and would be for anyone, but as a white woman in an all-black culture, you'll have problems."

"There wouldn't be any problems for me if we went to Canada," Celeste said.

"There still would be some," Paul told her.

Celeste was thoughtful. "You're determined to go to Africa, aren't you?"

"Yes, I am. I was nobody in Philadelphia. In the South, I was subhuman. Celeste, I want to be *somebody!* In Liberia, I'll have that chance." Paul's voice hardened. "And I want to hit the slave trade where it hurts."

"You begin to sound like a fanatic, Paul," Celeste told him.

"I've become one," he acknowledged.

Celeste took a deep breath. "I'll be your woman, Paul. I won't be your wife. If you want me enough, we'll go to Liberia, but I'll go as your woman. That way we'll never be tied to each other by anything but our love. And it is *our* love, isn't it?"

"Yes."

Celeste smiled. "That's settled, then."

But later, after they'd made love aboard the *Good Friend* for the last time, Celeste realized that nothing was settled. When Celeste lay in his arms, there was no past, no future, either, only the present. She craved his lovemaking as if it were a powerful drug. She loved his light brown body, contrasted to the ivory whiteness of her own.

Celeste knew she would go with him to Liberia, or follow him there. But she'd begun to sense that Paul might be an interlude in her otherwise well-ordered life.

Celeste wondered what women wore in Liberia. If anything.

Once the Red River plantation was sold, she'd have money of her own. She'd probably miss the lazy life on Great Oaks. But her mother had DeWitt and didn't need a daughter at home. Anyway, Bliss and Richard could look after Jeanette.

Bliss and Richard were in a suite at Jefferson House in Washington. There had been a short trip to New York, and another to Boston, but they'd kept the Jefferson suite. Washington, Congress, and the White House fascinated Richard. He left Bliss increasingly to her own devices while he sat for hours in the House gallery, or watched the Senate in session.

He was determined to return to Washington as an elected representative from Louisiana. When they first arrived in Washington, Bliss and Richard had been invited to a reception at the home on E Street of Senator Russell Barnes, their Louisiana representative in the Senate. The stately senator, with his leonine head and shock of white hair, befriended Richard.

Cannons & Roses

His younger wife, Mary Kay, sought the company of Bliss.

Mary Kay was the only daughter of Frank Sellers, a wealthy New Orleans cotton broker, and widower with a fine town house just a block from Spanish House.

With the knowledge of his daughter, Frank Sellers kept an octoroon mistress in a small but neat house behind the levee, and had two children by her, a boy and a girl. Sellers money had helped Russell Barnes gain his seat, and this was his second term. He planned to retire to his plantation near Iberville before the next election, to breed and raise horses.

Frank saw a political comer in Richard. Mary Kay found Bliss a relief from the boredom that being a senator's wife entailed.

"Honey, I have to keep a sweet smile on my face while Russell pontificates at these Washington parties and receptions," she told Bliss. They were in the Carroll suite at Jefferson House, sipping peach brandy. "It's deadly. Women fawn all over him, and Russell loves it. Power," she mused, holding her glass up to the light, "is a powerful aphrodisiac for any man. Do I shock you?"

Mary Kay was neither beautiful nor pretty. Her mouth was a shade too wide, her hair a muddy brown. She carried her small-breasted body well, but there was a breadth at the hips her dressmaker couldn't entirely disguise. Mary Kay's eyes were pale blue.

"No." Bliss laughed. "Richard has been bitten by the political bug, and I don't think he'll ever recover, so I'd better learn all I can about Washington. Russell loves you, doesn't he?"

"I think so." Mary Kay sighed. "When he remembers I'm alive between committee meetings, that is."

"This is supposed to be our honeymoon," Bliss

Cannons & Roses

said, "but sometimes I think Richard has forgotten. I sit here alone day after day." Bliss was exaggerating, and she knew it, but Mary Kay was impressed. "Are you left alone much of the time?" she asked.

"Too much of the time."

"More brandy?"

"Please." Mary Kay laughed. "I do believe I'm getting drunk."

Getting up, Bliss poured Mary Kay's brandy, and in doing so, brushed her breasts with an elbow. "Oh, excuse me."

Bliss had heard that women sometimes made love to each other, and was shocked, but now she was becoming curious. Was this discussion of neglect a subtle invitation from Mary Kay?

"I'm so small, there's no harm," Mary Kay said, and laughed. "But Russell likes mine small, or so he's told me."

Bliss still stood beside Mary Kay's chair, the decanter in her hand.

"I really am a mess, or so my dressmaker tells me," Mary Kay rattled on nervously, "but we all can't have as luscious a body as yours, can we, now?"

Bliss set the decanter aside, but didn't answer.

"Is it as hot as I think it is in here?" Mary Kay asked, fanning herself with a handkerchief. "I'm about to perish!"

Bliss let a hand fall on Mary Kay's thin shoulder. She could feel the heat of the woman's body through the fabric, and it excited her.

At her touch, Mary Kay looked up, and the hand holding the brandy glass trembled. The naked appeal in her pale blue eyes was unmistakable.

Bliss leaned over and kissed the part in Mary Kay's hair. "Let's be comfortable."

199

Cannons & Roses

Humming under her breath, and moving about the room, her eyes pointedly avoiding Mary Kay's, Bliss began to undress.

She made sure the door was locked and bolted.

When Bliss was down to only a thin shift, Mary Kay asked, "Do you intend to take off *all* your clothes?"

"If you'll join me," Bliss said, and sank to her knees facing Mary Kay's chair.

She lifted the shift over her head, and laid it aside, rewarded by the other woman's quick intake of breath.

"You're beautiful!"

Bliss crossed her arms to hide her breasts, bent her head, and said meekly, "Thank you."

Squirming in the chair, Mary Kay fumbled at buttons.

"Let me help," Bliss said.

When they were both naked and stretched on the bed, Bliss discovered Mary Kay, unlike herself, was no novitiate. She quickly took command, with her hands, her lips, and her tongue, her only reward at first the ripples of erotic pleasure she could make Bliss feel.

But Bliss was a willing pupil. "Teach me," she begged Mary Kay. "Tell me what you want."

Mary Kay was delighted and quickly initiated Bliss into the various rites of lesbianism. And with another woman, Bliss was discovering secrets of her own body that she'd never guessed.

I wish Richard were here. This daring thought was followed by another. *If I handle him right, and I know how, he can be next time—or the time after that.*

But not with the wife of Senator Barnes. There would be other women and other times, Bliss knew.

Cannons & Roses

She felt no guilt whatsoever about this new dimension of sensual pleasure. It was her beautiful body, wasn't it? She'd do with it as she pleased.

What she would have given to know about this when she was, say, twelve or thirteen!

The germ of an idea was planted. Bliss didn't know when, or where, or how she'd accomplish the seduction, but she knew this idea would bear fruit.

Mary Kay's body really was unlovely, poor thing.

Bliss closed her eyes, supinely accepting the other woman's ministrations, and pictured herself in bed with a lovely, willing girl-child.

Colonel Carroll, in his cups, quarreled with the overseer at The Columns, and ordered the dour New Englander off the plantation. Sober, he decided that firing Thaddeus Ward wasn't too bad a mistake.

With the McCoy Red River plantation up for sale, Delray Bone would soon be looking for a job. Discipline was too slack at The Columns, what with Ward warming his bed with a different wench every other night. That equaled a good slave increase, but interfered with the strictness Colonel Carroll considered necessary.

A strong-handed nigger driver like Delray Bone was what he needed. Colonel Carroll set out to hire him before someone else did.

Word had reached Delray only yesterday that his father was dead. Delray didn't know who his mother had been. Ulric had brought him from Five Points to New Orleans when he was only two.

Ulric had boarded Delray with one sleazy family after another, until he was old enough to run errands for various madams and learned to pimp. Tired of this

Cannons & Roses

existence, Delray attached himself to a plantation owner who patronized the current madam for whom Delray was working, and quickly learned the trade of nigger-driving.

Delray liked the work and the chance it gave him to become a respectable planter himself one day, so he had no interest in the various enterprises Ulric Bone had managed. Let the jackals fight over them. Delray was proud of his accomplishments here on the Red River. He'd proved, left almost entirely on his own, what he could do.

Widow McCoy, as he thought of her now, had become an obsession with Delray. He'd convinced himself she needed him in the fields as well as in her bed at Great Oaks. Scott was a soft fool! If Widow McCoy didn't fire him first, Delray would find a way to be rid of Scott.

Murder? Not if he could help it. That was too dangerous. Delray had seen men hanged. He didn't want to end his days kicking at the end of a rope.

If it should come down to murder, however, well, that couldn't be helped. Nothing could stand between him, the Widow McCoy, and Great Oaks. Not for very long, anyway.

So when Colonel Carroll rode up the Red River, and approached Delray about driving the niggers on The Columns, he considered that Fate was on his side.

"You've got your man, colonel," he said. "Let me show you what I've done here."

When they'd ridden over the fields, and cleared new ground, Colonel Carroll was properly impressed.

They shook hands. "You'll have to whip my niggers into shape," Colonel Carroll warned Delray. "They've had it too soft lately, the reason I fired Ward's ass off my place." He'd noticed the girl Delray kept in his cabin. "Get yourself some kind of white woman when you come to The Columns, will you, Bone?" Colonel Carroll asked. "Keeping a nigra wench doesn't help morale on a place like mine, and my wife wouldn't approve."

"Sure, colonel, a white slut it will be." Bone grinned. "I'll drag her by the hair down from Natchez."

19

Before she went ashore, Paul assured Celeste that he'd be waiting for her in Philadelphia. From there they might have to go to Boston before shipping out for Liberia. "Much of the society's money comes from rich Bostonian abolitionists," Paul told her.

Celeste thought a week in Lexington and Richmond would be enough time to learn what her brother was up to. In the letter she'd dispatch to Jeanette she'd outline her plan to go to Liberia with Paul.

Celeste's baggage was being lifted into a dray by a ruddy-faced Irishman.

Celeste had abandoned her masculine disguise when she disembarked from the *Good Friend,* and the drayman admired her figure before he asked where she would be staying.

"I don't know," Celeste said. "Do you have a suggestion? I've never been here before."

The drayman cocked his derby to scratch his head.

"Quality like you, miss, should stop at the Colonial Arms," he said. "Carousing sailors ain't allowed on the premises, the food ain't bad, and the beds are soft."

"That sounds all right," Celeste said. "You can take me there." It was an effort in skirts, but she joined him on the driver's seat.

The drayman was dumbfounded. "There's proper carriages, begging your pardon, miss."

Celeste smiled at him. "Do you mind? I'm starved and anxious to sample one of those soft beds after weeks at sea."

"Mind?" The drayman laughed. "I'll be the envy of Norfolk."

"Blarney," Celeste said.

Norfolk streets were as muddy as those in New Orleans, but there was bustle in the salt-scented air that Celeste found invigorating, and she noticed that even Negroes here moved with a quicker step and more purpose. After weeks at sea, even just the smell of dry land was pleasing to Celeste.

Confinement aboard a ship seemed to Celeste how it must be to live in prison, seeing the same people day after day until you're tired of their faces, and the sound of their voices. Coming ashore was like being set free.

And for the moment she was glad to be out of Paul's presence, and on her own again.

The drayman had asked a question.

"I'm sorry," Celeste said. "There's so much to see and feel, I didn't hear what you've asked me."

"I've been wondering where you're from," the drayman said.

"A plantation up the river from Baton Rouge, a place named Great Oaks," Celeste told him.

"Baton Rouge." The drayman wrinkled his forehead. "Ain't that Louisiana?"

"Yes, it is."

"The river would be the Mississippi?"

"Yes. We sometimes call it 'Big Muddy,'" Celeste said.

The drayman laughed. "Tell me," he said then. "Are there crocodiles in your Big Muddy?"

"No, only alligators, and as you can see, at least one of them sacrificed his skin so I can have luggage."

"A lovely end for such a brute!"

Celeste laughed. "I doubt the alligator would agree. What part of Ireland do you come from?" Celeste asked.

"The stews of Dublin, and that was eleven years ago tomorrow. I came over indentured to pay for my passage, and seven years it took me to get free in this lovely land." The drayman shook his head sorrowfully. "It's a proper crime the way indentured Irish are treated in your land."

"Were you mistreated?" Celeste asked.

"The man who bought me papers rented me out to dig muck in the swamps, because it was building a road they were, and prime niggers cost too much to risk them doing such dirty work. Good St. Patrick's snakes must have all swum here! Of the Irish gang, only me and two others survived the snakes and the fever."

"You're free now, aren't you?" Celeste asked.

"That I be, and own this rig. It's better here than Dublin. There if the drink don't get a man, and he dodges the bloody British hangman, he'll starve at an early age. Here we are."

The drayman pulled up at the entrance of the Colonial Arms. Celeste slid down to the wooden side-

Cannons & Roses

walk before he could come around to help her, and was reaching for her bags.

"Here, now, that ain't ladylike," the drayman scolded. "Bad enough you should arrive in my company. Independent sort, aren't you?"

"I try to be," Celeste told him.

Maura hustled out of the hotel. "My mistress needs to go to the docks," she told the drayman. "It's the *Good Friend* that will take us to Boston, and safely, I hope." She crossed herself. "Are you for hire?"

"I am," the drayman said. "Paddy O'Rourke is me name. You and your mistress ain't from here, are you?"

"No, we've come from Richmond. She's a Randolph," Maura said proudly. "Miss Philippa Randolph."

"Now, that *is* quality," the drayman said.

"Where is your mistress?" Celeste asked.

"With her young man this minute."

"Who would that be?" Celeste said.

Maura flushed. "Are you acquainted with Miss Randolph?"

"Not yet," Celeste said, "but if her young man is named McCoy, I will be soon."

"It is McCoy," Maura acknowledged. "Jamie McCoy."

"He's my brother. What is he doing over here?"

Jamie stepped out on the sidewalk just in time to hear Celeste's question. Surprise at finding her here in Norfolk was quickly followed by anger.

"For God's sake, what are you doing here, sister?" he demanded to know. "Spying on me?"

Philippa joined him. "Jamie." She put a hand on his arm. "You must be Celeste," Philippa said. Her smile was warm. "Jamie has spoken of you often."

Philippa turned to Maura. "You will go with our luggage to the ship, dear. We have at least an hour before she sails. You can tell the captain that I'll be along."

Celeste was impressed with Philippa's calm poise in this embarrassing situation, and wondered if she could carry it off so well in Philippa's shoes.

Jamie was standing on one foot, and then the other, cracking his knuckles.

The drayman had taken Celeste's bags into the hotel.

"I believe I would like another cup of tea, Jamie, or perhaps something a bit stronger. You must be tired after your journey," Philippa said to Celeste. "Won't you join us?"

"Certainly," Celeste replied. "That is, unless my brother objects. I don't believe he's exactly delighted to see me here."

Philippa laughed. "He'll recover from his shock."

Jamie finally grinned and kissed Celeste's cheek. "How the devil did you get here?" he asked.

"On the same ship Philippa is taking to Boston," Celeste told him. "Small world, isn't it? If you'll forgive the cliché."

"Sometimes too small," Jamie said. "But it is good to see you, sister."

They'd found a quiet table in the dining room, and Jamie had ordered rum punches. Philippa remained in command of the situation.

"Your brother came to see me off to Boston," Philippa told Celeste. "It was quite a surprise, as you may well imagine. But a most welcome surprise." She looked at Jamie, sipping his rum punch, and didn't try to disguise the way she felt toward him. "You see, I love your brother," Philippa told Celeste.

Cannons & Roses

"I love Philippa." There was a hint of defiance in Jamie's voice.

"In that case, why aren't you going with her to Boston?" Celeste asked Jamie. "Or are you?"

"No," Jamie said.

"I won't let him," Philippa told Celeste. "He must finish his education. By the way, we were quietly married yesterday."

"Oh?" Celeste raised her eyebrows. "Then my best wishes are in order. Mother is going to be more surprised than pleased, I imagine, but that's neither here nor there if you two love each other."

"Mother is going to be a grandmother," Jamie told his sister.

Philippa flushed slightly but met Celeste's eyes. "Our marriage will be a secret until Jamie graduates." She outlined their plan to keep it so. "Don't you think we're doing the right thing?" she asked. "It goes against my grain to be secretive, but in this case . . ." Philippa shrugged. "I don't believe it can be helped."

"I'm not going back to Great Oaks," Celeste said. "Do you remember Paul, Jamie?"

"What about Paul?" Jamie asked.

"He came here with me on the *Good Friend*. I'm to join him later in Philadelphia. I believe we'll be going down to Liberia," Celeste said.

"For God's sweet sake!" Jamie exploded. "Paul is a nigger!"

Philippa's expression showed only interest.

"I believe a man with some color best describes Paul," Celeste said coolly. "He's saved my life, and we love each other, as you and Philippa do. Mother knows, Jamie, if you're thinking she doesn't."

"Paul is still aboard the *Good Friend*?" Philippa asked.

"Yes. He'll sail with you as far as Philadelphia. I want you to meet him."

Jamie was trying to adjust to the idea of his sister and Paul being lovers. Philippa patted his hand. "You're married to a woman almost old enough to be your mother," she reminded him. "And our child will have a drop or two of nigra blood, you know."

"What do you mean?" Jamie asked.

Philippa smiled. "I've shocked him," she told Celeste. "I have it on good authority that nearly every Virginia slave-owning family isn't as lily-white as it claims to be."

Philippa glanced at the small watch pinned to her blouse. "Jamie, will you see me to the ship?"

Jeanette and DeWitt had an easy, if clandestine, relationship. Jeanette sold Stella to the owner of her lover, Jackson, and began grooming a pretty child from the quarter to become her body servant. She gave this child a new name, Emma, and promoted her mother from the fields to kitchen helper.

Jeanette was discovering there was a masterful streak in DeWitt that she'd never suspected. Now that they were lovers, he wouldn't set foot in Great House—even on business. When they came together, it was always in the overseer's house, and then because it was she who went to DeWitt.

Bliss and Richard were expected back from their honeymoon soon. Jeanette was glad they would be staying at The Columns.

She'd heard from Celeste. The Randolph woman was in Boston for an extended stay, and Jamie was in Lexington. Celeste didn't say how she'd managed that separation, and Jeanette didn't intend to ask. She had written that Philippa Randolph was a lovely and cultured woman.

In his bed last night with DeWitt, Jeanette had discussed the other part of Celeste's rather long letter.

"It's obvious that Celeste loves Paul, DeWitt," she said, raised on an elbow to watch his face in the candle-lit half-darkness. "But she doesn't mention marriage. Maybe it's better they don't marry. What do you think?"

"I think Celeste is old for her years, and a lot wiser than we credit her with being," DeWitt told Jeanette. He brushed a lock of hair away from her forehead. "You worry too much."

"I do worry about Alicia Carroll," Jeanette said. "I've told her Celeste is away on a long visit with some of Jamie's relatives, but she's suspicious."

"Why not tell her the truth?" DeWitt said.

"Celeste may come back here. And, after all, Alicia is mother-in-law to Bliss. She might take such information out on Bliss and Richard."

DeWitt grinned and touched the tip of Jeanette's nose with his forefinger. "Don't you think Bliss can manage one slightly dotty mother-in-law? She had no trouble marrying into that family."

"That's true," Jeanette admitted. "All right, if she ever asks, I'll tell Alicia that Celeste is going down to Liberia with Paul. Her reaction to this piece of news should be interesting."

"It will be," DeWitt said. "On the other hand, with Delray Bone nigger-driving over at The Columns, now that your Red River acreage is sold, Alicia Carroll may have her hands too full to question you about anything."

"What do you think about that?" Jeanette asked.

Cannons & Roses

"I haven't made up my mind yet. Things in the quarter have been bad over there. He did a good job for you, although I don't approve of his methods. Delray can't help it that Ulric Bone was his father."

"Have you seen young Bone lately?"

"Yesterday. He rode over for a visit."

"Oh? Why didn't you mention this to me?"

"I am. Now. I've been pretty busy in the fields lately, you may have noticed."

"I've noticed," Jeanette said. "When our crop is in, I'm going to spend some time in New Orleans, at Spanish House." She hesitated. "Can we manage for you to join me there?"

DeWitt caught his hands behind his neck and studied the ceiling of his bedroom. "I've saved enough money to set myself up as a cotton broker, Jeanette. You and Colonel Carroll plan to join Great Oaks to The Columns, and that's a good plan."

"You thought so when we three discussed it," Jeanette said. "How long have you been planning to quit Great Oaks?"

"Since the night we first came together. I want to marry you, but on my terms. I've told you that."

"When?"

DeWitt ignored her sharp question. "One overseer with nigra help can follow the work-gangs on both plantations. You don't have to rattle around in the great house with its memories. Give it to Bliss and Richard."

"And come live with you in *my* New Orleans town house?" Jeanette asked.

"As my wife, yes," DeWitt said. He hadn't missed the sarcasm implicit in her question. "But only if you agree. You can sell that place, and we'll make a fresh start."

Cannons & Roses

"What do you do in bed with *two* women?" Jeanette asked.

"What?"

"It was a simple question, DeWitt."

"For some reason I don't understand, I believe you're trying to get a rise out of me," DeWitt said. "You can't be jealous."

"Can't I, DeWitt? You don't know a thing about women!"

"What's getting into you?" DeWitt asked. "If you don't want to remarry, just say so."

"And you'll have me on any terms?"

"No."

Jeanette was off the bed to flaunt her nakedness. "I'm a good whore, aren't I? You should know after all your trips up to Natchez and those brothels under the hill."

"Stop this," DeWitt ordered.

"Am I disgusting you? If I'm not, it isn't because I'm not trying."

"You're being a child," he scolded.

"Oh?" For a moment, Jeanette hated herself for provoking DeWitt this way, but she slapped his face. "Treat me like a child, then."

"What do you mean?"

"You well know what I mean!"

DeWitt's eyes narrowed. "I think I do."

"Well?"

He sat on the edge of the bed. "Come here."

"Why?"

"I want you across my knees."

"Then put me there!"

He grabbed a slender wrist.

"Don't hurt my arm!" Jeanette laid herself across his thighs, face down.

DeWitt smacked the right cheek of her ivory backside. Red finger-marks immediately showed. He struck the other cheek, harder.

"Yes!" Jeanette gasped.

20

Jeanette didn't ask for mercy until DeWitt's callused hand had turned her ivory buttocks blood-red. Then he discovered her sexual demands were nearly insatiable. But she'd stimulated him enough to meet them.

When they were finally exhausted, and DeWitt sat propped up with pillows, Jeanette's head in his lap, she said, "Thank you."

She was a composed woman again.

DeWitt bent to kiss her. It was a lingering kiss, and he savored the sweetness of her mouth. "I think I'd like a drink," he said.

"Let me get it for you," Jeanette said.

DeWitt's eyes fixed on the flaming red of her flanks as she padded from the room, not bothering to don a wrap. Jeanette came back with two tumblers of brandy. She handed him one tumbler, then sat on the edge of the bed to sip from the other, eyes modestly

Cannons & Roses

downcast. DeWitt was reminded of a child who had been naughty, and is now ashamed.

She sat gingerly, he noticed.

"If you think I should, I'll deed Great Oaks to Bliss and Richard," Jeanette said, after a while. "You're right—there are too many memories here. I can't live in the past." She hesitated. "Do you still want to marry me?"

"More than ever," DeWitt said.

"Don't you think I'm depraved, wanting . . . that?"

"No."

Jeanette smiled. "Thank you for understanding."

"I don't believe that I do," DeWitt said, "but it doesn't matter."

Jeanette finished her brandy. "You've said we'll make a good profit this season. I want to use some of that money to help you get started as a cotton broker."

"No," DeWitt said flatly.

"Why not? We could marry sooner."

"Pride," DeWitt told her. "As I've said, I want you on my own terms."

Jeanette's reply was a helpless shrug. "So be it then."

Paul was discouraged. He'd been in Philadelphia a week, during which he'd spoken three times with the local secretary of the American Colonization Society. William Oosterban was a placid Pennsylvania Dutchman on his mother's side, and his father had come from Sweden. Oosterban was a Quaker.

"These coloreds you describe, Mr. Wright, aren't the type of settlers we send to Liberia these days," Oosterban had finally told him. "They are free and are safe in British Nassau. My associates and I think that is enough."

"These people aren't murderers," Paul protested.

Cannons & Roses

"Jason Smith took the ship without shedding a drop of blood. He insisted on that. Both of those killed afterward were slaves. I've told you how Masters killed the woman defending himself, and, as you know, I shot the man."

Oosterban nodded. "You've explained that incident. See here, Mr. Wright. Our funds are limited—strictly limited—and it costs a great deal to ship a single Negro to the colony, much less the numbers you've mentioned."

"I gave my word," Paul said.

"You shouldn't have done that without first consulting us," Oosterban told Paul smugly.

Boston was becoming a hotbed of abolitionism, Paul was told.

"As you know, our society is more conservative," Oosterban said. "Abolish slavery? Yes. But over a long period of time, with slave owners compensated, as the English may do in the West Indies. Otherwise, our country will split along north and south lines, and I assure you this is a real danger."

"You believe the abolitionists are wrong?"

"I believe they are trying for too radical a solution. They're zealots. The more they rant and rave here in the north, the more slave owners become disaffected with any rational plan to abolish slavery in our generation, and probably the next."

"My cause is hopeless?" Paul asked.

"I haven't said that. I've written letters of introduction to interested people in Boston, most of them active in the abolitionist movement. I hope you can find help up there."

Celeste had written that she'd arrive tomorrow. Her money had brought him up to Philadelphia, but what she'd given him was nearly gone. His rented room in

Cannons & Roses

a poor section of the city was grimy, with a lumpy bed. Paul wondered where they could stay together and how they were going to reach Boston.

Paul was still quietly determined to keep his word to Jason Smith and to find his future in Liberia. Celeste was right—he was becoming fanatic. His aversion to every form of slavery was whetted to a cutting edge, and he had to strike someway at the foundations of the institution.

Celeste didn't care to marry him. Paul found secret relief in this fact, yet his desire for Celeste was unchecked. He wanted the way she looked at him, and spoke when they were together, as much as he wanted the warmth and excitement of her soft body.

They'd survived a great deal together.

The woman and her Irish maid on the ship had known that he and Celeste were intimate, Paul was sure of that, but it hadn't seemed to matter to Philippa Randolph. There had been no confidences, but Paul realized that she was the older woman in Jamie McCoy's life.

Jamie McCoy had chosen well, Paul decided.

Paul had mentioned to Philippa Randolph that he might come to Boston on his way to Liberia, and she had given him the address of the relatives where she would be staying. It was a Beacon Hill address.

"Please visit if you and Celeste come to Boston," Philippa had told him. "The Boston Randolphs are in shipping of one sort or another. I don't know them well, but they might be willing to help."

His future—and Celeste's, if she stayed with him—was murky just now. In his heart Paul found he couldn't blame Celeste if she turned back, but he hoped and prayed that she wouldn't.

* * *

Cannons & Roses

Celeste had spent a week in Lexington, in a boardinghouse near Washington College, boarding with a family named Boyd. Their youngest, Belle, had captured Celeste. A tumble of blond curls, and blue eyes with lashes that shadowed her cheeks, delicate features belied by the three-year-old's sturdy little body. Celeste hoped that Jamie and Philippa's child would only be half as beautiful.

But there was more to little Belle than beauty. Spirit was one word for it. Mischief danced in those blue eyes, and bright intelligence.

If Celeste was captured, Belle was fascinated by this beautiful young woman, and she shadowed her footsteps whenever she could.

"Please don't let our Belle bother you," the girl's mother told Celeste. "I've never seen her so much taken. She told me the other night that she wants to be just like you when she grows up."

"Bother me?" Celeste said. "Belle is a delight. And I usually don't care too much about children," Celeste confided. "But Belle makes me look forward to having one of my own."

Jamie introduced Celeste to all his professors. The one who impressed her the least was moody Thomas Jackson. In her presence he was so shy it made her uncomfortable. Each of Jamie's professors invited her to have tea in their homes, except Professor Jackson.

To Celeste, Jamie seemed overly impressed with Old Jack. She asked him why.

"The man may be the genius you say he is when it comes to military science," Celeste said, "but, Jamie, I don't think he has enough common sense to come in out of the rain."

"Most of his students would agree with you," Jamie said. "Me, I like the man. So does Chester Randolph."

Cannons & Roses

"Well, I could be wrong," Celeste admitted. "But he doesn't impress me as being overly smart."

Jamie didn't tell her about the dueling incident. By mutual consent, they didn't discuss Philippa and her situation, either. Nor did Jamie mention Paul again.

Looking back, Celeste would remember that week in Lexington as her first opportunity to know her younger brother, without the domineering presence of Bliss. They became good friends.

The Cumberland and Blue Ridge mountains that guarded the Shenandoah Valley from either side were a constant reminder to Celeste of the flatness of Louisiana. She wondered if there would be mountains in Liberia. She hoped there would be.

Before Celeste left Lexington, to ride the new railroad to Washington, Baltimore, Wilmington, and, finally, Philadelphia, Mrs. Boyd packed her a basket of food and fruit.

"You'll have a terrible journey," the woman warned her. "Don't wear anything you care about. It will be soot, sparks, and ashes all the way."

Jamie was nervous when he saw her off on the train. "I've thought about you and Paul," he confessed.

"Oh? What have you decided?" Celeste said.

"How sweet twin sister Bliss ever hooked Richard Carroll, I'll never know, and I'll probably be better off if I don't find out," Jamie said. Celeste laughed. "I thought you'd marry him, and Mother did, too. Since you didn't, I'm sorry that I called Paul a nigger."

It was the best apology Jamie could manage, Celeste knew. "Thank you," she said.

"You're going to him now, aren't you?"

"Yes. I love Paul, Jamie."

"Then what, Celeste?"

"We'll probably go to Liberia together," Celeste said. "Paul's been there before. We'll be working for the American Colonization Society."

"Aren't you afraid of cannibals?" Jamie asked.

"I wouldn't make much of a meal. Paul says that Africans like their women fat," Celeste told him.

Jamie smacked his lips. "You'd be delicious, I imagine."

Jamie had put his sister on the train at Winchester. She'd telegraphed Richard and Bliss, who were still in Washington, and they met her at the station. Her train to Baltimore, Wilmington, and Philadelphia wouldn't leave until the next morning.

Celeste mentioned Paul to neither Bliss nor Richard, explaining her presence by saying that her mother had suggested a trip north. Jamie hadn't been in touch with Bliss, or if he had, he hadn't confided in Bliss about Philippa. Celeste described her visit with Jamie in Lexington, but avoided any mention of the purpose of that visit as suggested by Jeanette.

To Celeste's surprise, she discovered that Great Oaks on the plantation would be where Bliss and Richard took up residence when they returned from their honeymoon. For the first time, she learned that Jeanette planned to live at Spanish House in New Orleans.

Senator Russell Barnes and his wife, Mary Kay, insisted that Celeste, as well as Bliss and Richard, take supper with them before she departed for Philadelphia.

"Your brother-in-law has a fine future in national politics," Senator Barnes told Celeste. "He's the land- and slave-owning caliber of man we need here in

Cannons & Roses

Washington. These damned Yankee abolitionists are stirring public opinion in the North. Garrison is the worst!"

"Please don't start on Mr. Garrison tonight, Russell," Mary Kay begged. "My husband has quite violent opinions on the subject of abolition," she confided to Celeste.

Senator Barnes was flushed with wine. "The man has had the brass to try to use the United States mail to subvert our southern institutions," he said. "By God, our southern race is still strong enough in the Senate and House to put a stop to that sort of treason."

"I've never thought of us in the south as a different race," Celeste said.

"Ah, but we most certainly are," Senator Barnes said. "The northerners have become what we would call, in Louisiana, a general mixtry. Unlimited immigration is a natural crime!"

"Who would we get to work in the swamps if it wasn't for the Irish?" Celeste asked. "I also understand they built most of the Erie Canal."

"You have a point," Senator Barnes acknowledged. "And our Germans along the German Coast of the Mississippi are good, frugal Americans. But you'll find the north swarming with foreigners these days, Miss McCoy."

"What he says is true," Richard acknowledged. "In New York it's particularly bad. In some parts of that city, you don't hear a word of English."

"How do you feel about the American Colonization Society?" Celeste asked Senator Barnes.

"Liberia is a good dumping ground for free nigras," Senator Barnes told her. "The brutes are a plague in the north. Ship every living son of them to Liberia,

Cannons & Roses

I say. The British have a colony of them in Sierra Leone—did you know that?"

"No, sir, I didn't," Celeste said.

"Wilberforce, I understand, had a lot to do with that. He and John Wesley, the Methodist. A pair of nigger lovers, those two. They point with pride to Haiti." Senator Barnes chuckled bitterly. "The damned nigger ruler there—Christophe, or Henry I, as he calls himself these days—is worse than the French planters. I have that on good authority."

"Can we change the subject, Russell?" Mary Kay asked.

"In a moment," Senator Barnes said. "West Indian slavery, and our southern institution, are vastly different. Our nigras are domesticated and generally treated well. Those poor African devils imported to Jamaica and the other British-held islands are treated worse than dogs. I can understand why Parliament is deluged by petitions to emancipate them, compensating their owners, of course. Mark my words, it is going to happen. A good thing, I say. But, for their own sake, we of the southern race will fight, if necessary, to protect our loyal darkies from the damned abolition movement, and rabble-rousers like Garrison."

"Enough, Russell," Mary Kay said.

"Yes, dear."

Paul was on the platform when Celeste's train pulled into the Philadelphia station. Coming from Washington, Celeste had tried to analyze her feelings toward Paul.

Their backgrounds had nothing in common. But their physical attraction for each other had been overpowering. Celeste blushed when she remembered how overtly she'd seduced him at Spanish House. Yet she couldn't forget the sweet pain of his first penetration. Or the small-boned symmetry of his brown body, his touch, the way his teeth clenched and the pupils of his eyes became pinpoints when he spent in her womb.

"I'm a wanton bitch," she told herself.

And she felt a creeping warmth in her loins, the nearer she came to Paul again.

Off the train, she went into his arms. "My God, but I've missed you, darling!"

Paul's arms tightened. *Damn all these curious people,* she thought.

Celeste liked having her breasts crushed against his chest.

It wasn't hard for her to realize that Paul wanted her as much as she did him.

There's no way men can hide their sexual excitement, she thought. *No way at all.*

Paul caressed her short-cropped hair. His mouth found Celeste's again. "Have I missed *you!*" he said when that kiss was finished.

"I have money," Celeste said. "Where can we stay?"

Paul kissed her again. "I've got a rented room," he said, "but it isn't fancy."

"I don't care," Celeste told him. "Take me somewhere or I'll rape you here."

Paul's was a dreary room, Celeste thought, and smelled of stale boiled cabbage. It was baking hot, too. And there was a babble of traffic from the street outside. But naked and together again, nothing else mattered.

God! How much she wanted Paul!

Sweat-slippery, gasping, they writhed on the lumpy bed, and there was a new, more savage drive to Paul's lovemaking. Celeste rose to meet these new demands. Her nerves exploded time and time again, until she lost count.

Someone was begging for more. Celeste was startled to realize *she* was making those sounds! Then, deep inside, she was bathed by a surge of warmth from Paul's loins, and he fell aside, panting.

Celeste clasped her breasts until she had her breath back. "I think we've just made a baby," she said.

Paul didn't answer. He was asleep.

21

Christopher Randolph was forty, a widower with no children. Of the Boston Randolphs, made wealthy since the American Revolution by Randolph Shipping Lines, Christopher was the only Randolph who had ever been to sea. He'd served before the mast when he was a youngster, had his master's ticket before he was twenty-two, and retired from the sea at thirty-eight after his wife died during a China voyage.

Christopher lived alone except for a free Negro body servant in the spacious Colonial house his grandfather built in 1778. From an office on Milk Street, he commanded the seven ships that comprised the Randolph Shipping Lines fleet. Two Randolph ships were in the Far Eastern trade. Three were on the West Indies run, and one, the *Jane Marie,* coasted West Africa, selling rum and trade goods outward bound from Boston, and bringing palm oil, ivory, as well as miscellaneous cargo back to American ports.

Cannons & Roses

The *Jane Marie,* named after Christopher's dead wife (she'd been a Lodge before their marriage), had been Christopher Randolph's last command. Currently she was skippered by Thaddeus Baker of Salem. Baker was fifty-five, and, according to his crew, tough as an old boot. To survive in the African trade he had to be.

When Philippa Randolph wrote to Jane Marie that she was coming to Boston for a long visit, Christopher realized that his Richmond cousin wasn't aware of his wife's death. Christopher's knowledge of the Virginia Randolphs was as vague and sketchy as their knowledge of the Boston Randolphs.

He arranged for a lady's maid, had a room prepared for his southern cousin, and awaited the arrival of the *Good Friend* in Boston Harbor. At one time Christopher had served aboard her on a slaving voyage.

That single experience in the Middle Passage had seared him for life. It had taken the *Good Friend* a stormy thirteen weeks to raise Cuba instead of the normal four or five. Although 600 slaves had been shipped, only 460 survived the voyage—a satisfactory average, Christopher was told, considering time at sea.

The stench of that voyage still lingered in his nostrils, and the horrors of it haunted his sleep. Christopher was the prime mover in the fledgling Boston Anti-Slavery Society, so his emotions about receiving Philippa Randolph were somewhat mixed.

What if she arrived with an entourage of slaves?

As the *Good Friend* rounded Cape Cod to reach for Boston Harbor in Massachusetts Bay, moving cautiously through light fog with double lookouts posted forward, Philippa Randolph was nervous. She wondered if Jane Marie Randolph had received her letter.

Cannons & Roses

In the easygoing southern planter society, months-long visits weren't unusual, but in New England? For one of the few times in her life, Philippa wasn't sure of herself. She wished now that she and Maura had gotten off the ship in New York. She could have gone full term, and had her child there, with no one the wiser.

"I've been a dithering idiot!" she told herself. "If Jane Marie and that husband of hers finds out my real reason for coming to Boston, they'll ride me out of town on a rail, or burn me at the stake."

Philippa decided that she wouldn't confide in Jane Marie or her husband. She and Maura would stay a few weeks, then return to New York, or perhaps Philadelphia.

Philippa was sure that with Maura's help, and a competent midwife or doctor, she could manage the ordeal of childbearing alone.

She damned herself for falling in love with a man so young that he was still in college. Yet her fierce need to have this child hadn't changed.

"We have to go on to Boston," Paul told Celeste. He showed her Oosterban's letter of introduction to Christopher Randolph. "Isn't he the cousin Philippa Randolph is going to visit?"

"Yes, he is. We can go to him for help, but not money, Paul. Philippa is family now."

"It's the Boston Anti-Slavery Society that will help us," Paul said. "Christopher Randolph heads it. Oosterban says he's the man to get things done."

Celeste had received a $5,000 bank draft from Jeanette, after the sale of the Red River property.

"If we can't get any help in Boston," she said, "we'll use my money to charter a ship and hire a crew."

"Do you really believe in what I'm trying to do?" Paul asked.

"Do you want an honest answer?"

"Please."

"I don't know what I believe about slavery," Celeste said. "How will we southern people survive without servants and field hands?"

"Northern farmers make out."

"But they don't raise cotton, tobacco, and sugar cane," Celeste told him. "I've seen the books at Great Oaks, and you have, too. By the time we house, feed, and clothe slaves, there's nothing left for wages."

"Hell! If you'd pay wages, the blacks could take care of themselves, as wage earners do up here."

"Now, Paul, do you really believe *that*? Take Vashti as an example. I doubt she knew what money is." Celeste waved aside the protest he was going to make. "All right. I want to be with you. Isn't that enough? Damn it, Paul. Give me time. I was born into the southern way of life, and a nigra was my wet-nurse."

"That you want to be with me in Liberia is enough," Paul said. "I only hope that you won't regret it."

Vincent Gambini's fort and barracoons were located at Gambia on the Senegal Coast of West Africa, just above Guinea, Sierra Leone, and Liberia. It was a stone structure built by the Portughese a hundred years ago, located on a narrow point of land at the mouth of the Gambia River. It was built to be defensible from the sea, the river, and the land.

Dungeons beneath the fort were used to store the more valuable slaves obtained from upriver tribes, and brought down in canoes. A stockade within the fort itself served to store less important stock.

Ulric Bone had picked the right man to become a

successful slave trader. With trade goods, Gambini had ventured into the interior, bribing upriver chiefs and kings to bring him their captives, furnishing a chosen few with firearms and ammunition so they could war more successfully on neighboring tribes.

Years as a pirate helped him deal with the slaver captains and their crews.

Men like Captain Andrews were a thing of the past along the Slave Coast. With British and American ships patrolling the coast, trying to stop the traffic in fresh slaves to be smuggled ashore in the West Indies or the United States, the scum of the sea had taken over the trade. The stews of Liverpool furnished crews for the British slave smugglers. Crimps in New Orleans, Charleston, Baltimore, and New York crewed American ships in the illicit trade.

Fifty percent mortality wasn't unusual among these slaver crews. Once ashore in Africa, yellow fever and malaria took their toll, as well as the crude native alcohol and fermented beer. Hogsheads of rum were saved to deal with the natives. This rum was cut with water and adulterated with red pepper and tobacco to make it more palatable to African taste.

Mutinies of slaves in the Middle Passage weren't uncommon, but were rarely successful, because most of these slavers had a swivel gun aft that commanded the forward deck. Loaded with grapeshot, by slaughtering a few dozen rampaging slaves, the slaver captains usually saved their ship. But in the process they lost some of their crew.

Gambini was smart enough to furnish all the shore entertainment slaver captains and crews could handle. A portion of the trade rum he purchased was set aside for these captains and seamen. From each new batch of slaves delivered to Gambini, he chose a few women,

Cannons & Roses

girls, and stripling boys to be used at will by his visitors.

A young virgin girl was Gambini's gift to each slaver captain who came ashore at Gambia. If he wanted to take her to sea with him, Gambini offered a bargain price. So he'd stolen trade from Abidjan on the Ivory Coast, Conakry in Guinea and Accra, a trading post formerly supplied with stock by the fierce upcountry Ashanti. Now the Ashanti dealt almost exclusively with Gambini.

Gambini had bribed Damongo, the Ashanti king, with a mulatto prostitute kidnapped from Liberia. After he'd used her, Damongo rented her out to minor chieftains, and had accumulated a small fortune in gold and ivory.

The woman was now dead. Damongo wanted a replacement. But this time, Damongo said, he wanted a full-blooded white woman. White flesh was a novelty among the Ashanti. Only a few had ever seen a white woman, much less lain with one. Damongo was getting more insistent each time he brought fresh slaves to Gambia.

There were a few white missionaries and teachers in Liberia, but kidnapping one of them to give to Damongo would be too dangerous.

Gambini's fortress was safe from native attack, but he had no illusions about what would happen if a determined American or British shore party attacked, backed up by their ship's guns. Gambini didn't want to find himself kicking at the end of a rope strung from a ship's yardarm.

Gambini had a problem.

Philippa recognized her cousin the moment she saw Christopher Randolph on India Wharf, waiting for

Cannons & Roses

the *Good Friend* to tie up. He was tall and spare, with a weather-beaten face, and the Randolph beak of a nose. He was dressed plainly in black, but the expensive cut of his clothes was unmistakable.

Christopher raised a hand in greeting, and Philippa realized he'd recognized her. But where was his wife? Maura hugged the rail at her side.

"That's what I'd say was a distinguished gentleman, Miss Philippa," she said.

Christopher raised his hat. A wide white streak ran from his high forehead through his black hair. On the wharf, he took her bags, and Maura's, himself.

"Welcome to Boston, cousin." There was no nasal twang to his deep voice. "Was it a pleasant voyage?"

"Most pleasant, Cousin Christopher. Maura and I seem to be good sailors. Neither of us was seasick," Philippa said. "How is your wife?"

They'd reached his carriage. The Negro was stowing their bags. Christopher finally answered.

"She died on a China voyage two years ago," he said. "We buried her at sea."

Christopher spoke quietly, objectively, as if Jane Marie's death affected someone else, but Philippa sensed the deep well of grief in the man.

"I took the liberty of opening your letter to Jane Marie," Christopher went on, while Philippa was trying to think what she should say. "There was time to reply, but I wanted your visit for selfish reasons. I hope you're not too disappointed."

"Oh, no, Christopher. But I'm terribly sorry about your wife. Myself, I've lost two husbands."

"We have that in common, then, besides the Randolph name." Christopher's was a grim smile. "It can be a lonely life, can't it?" His hand touched the white streak in his hair. "It will be my pleasure to have a woman in my home once again, although I see you've brought your own maid. Can you use two?"

"Would you like company, Maura?" Philippa asked.

The girl wrinkled her forehead. "Would she be Irish?"

"Do you know?" Christopher said solemnly. "I didn't think to ask when she came for an interview, but Kitty O'Reilly doesn't sound like a Dutch name, now, does it?"

Maura laughed. "That it does not, and you've a bit of a brogue yourself, Mr. Randolph."

"We'll soon have as many Irish in Boston," Christopher said, "as they have in all of Ireland. They're welcome yeast in the dour New England dough."

"You're being very kind to me, Christopher," Philippa said.

"I spent so many years at sea, I don't have many friends here in Boston," Christopher confessed, "and for the past two years I've avoided those I do have. I mentioned selfish reasons for welcoming you, Philippa. I'd like you to be my hostess, if you're so inclined. It's time that I got on with the business of living."

Tears stung Philippa's eyelids.

"I'm afraid we won't agree on what is becoming a burning issue," Christopher went on, "but I hope that won't interfere with friendship."

"The issue is slavery, of course," Philippa said. "Your William Lloyd Garrison's vituperation is quite familiar to southern ears."

"Garrison!" Christopher dismissed him with a wave of his hand. "There's a crackpot. Like so many abolitionists, he's confusing sin and slavery. I'm active in the Boston Anti-Slavery Society, but if the Garrisonites infest it, they can look for someone else."

Cannons & Roses

"I don't own slaves," Philippa said. "The other Virginia Randolphs do, of course. They have for many generations. I don't believe slavery will interfere with our becoming friends, Christopher."

Christopher grinned. "We won't let it."

"What does your society do?" Philippa asked.

"For one thing, we support the American Colonization Society with its Liberian experiment. And we're most interested in stamping out the slave trade at its source. After that, we want to encourage southern slave owners to educate, and, over a period of time, release their slaves. Does that sound reasonable?"

"Reasonable, yes," Philippa said. "Practical? No. We Southerners are too set in our ways, and too damned unreasonable on the subject. But don't listen to me. Mine is only one woman's opinion."

"An intelligent woman's opinion," Christopher said.

Philippa smiled. "Thank you, sir."

"Here we are," Christopher told her.

The house, made of granite quarried in Vermont, had been built to last for centuries. White shutters relieved the granite grayness, and a century-old oak tree shadowed and shaded the entrance.

"It's said that both the British, and later General Washington, held strategy conferences under that tree," Christopher told Philippa and Maura. He laughed. "But then there's scarcely an old tree in Boston that wasn't the site of an important war conference. I can understand how the British lost the war, if their commanders spent all their time standing around in the shade. But if we Americans were doing the same thing, I can't understand how we won!"

It was a week later that Celeste and Paul arrived in Boston. From the station, they went directly to the

Cannons & Roses

Randolph Shipping Lines office on Milk Street to present Oosterban's letter of introduction.

Christopher was now familiar with Philippa's situation. She'd found it impossible not to deal honestly with her cousin.

"That settles it," Christopher had said. "You and Maura will stay here in Boston until the baby is born. I won't have it any other way."

Christopher also knew from Philippa about Paul and Celeste.

He came from his office to meet them with the letter of introduction in his hand. After shaking hands with Paul, Christopher turned to Celeste.

"I hear we're now related by marriage," he said. For the first time he really saw Celeste. She was tired from the journey, and her clothing was rumpled. There was a smudge of soot on her cheek.

My God! he thought. *Where has she been until now?*

"I believe we are," Celeste said.

Paul was uncomfortable. "We've come begging, as you've probably guessed from William Oosterban's letter," he said, and wished Christopher would stop looking at Celeste like that.

Celeste seemed to be unaware of Christopher's scrutiny. Later Paul would remember the solemn ticking of a grandfather clock in that quiet outer office of Randolph Shipping Lines.

"I'm sorry," Christopher finally said. "I didn't mean to stare," he told Celeste, "but you suddenly reminded me of someone I once knew." Jane Marie's hair had been auburn, and her eyes green. There was very little physical resemblance. Just the same . . .

Christopher turned to Paul. "Begging?"

"Yes."

"I've had another letter from our mutual friend,"

Cannons & Roses

Christopher said. "My ship, the *Jane Marie*, sails for Africa in a few weeks. She'll take on passengers at Nassau under your direction, Mr. Wright. In the meantime, you'll be my guests."

22

*T*haddeus Baker went to sea from Salem as a cabin boy aboard a whaler. In middle age he still had the erect carriage and quick step of that youngster who spent three years whaling, and came back to Salem a man.

He was a wiry, medium-built man, with a tanned face that was a maze of wrinkles, and a permanent squint from looking at too many sea miles of sun-dappled water. He was a teetotaler, and a leading light in the Boston Temperance Society when he was ashore.

Baker subscribed to the *Liberator* and considered Garrison second only to the Angel Gabriel. Besides the *Liberator,* his only other reading was the Bible, and the Old Testament was his gospel, an angry Jehovah his God.

He preached to his crew every Sunday in a high-pitched, ranting voice, promising hellfire and damnation. Thaddeus modestly considered himself a slightly

Cannons & Roses

lesser prophet than Moses, and his crew willful Israelites who needed a touch of rope-end, from time to time, to correct their sinful ways.

He couldn't abide a Negro near him, or even aboard his ship. "They're the benighted sons of Ham," he told his wispy wife, "and stink to the high heaven because they're soaked in Sin."

Thaddeus despised black skins, but hated southern slave owners with equal fervor (he'd never been south of the Mason-Dixon line). He believed in phrenology, cold-water therapy and was a vegetarian, converted by Mrs. Baker shortly after they were married.

Thaddeus wore a matted beard to protect his chest, on the advice of a doctor he'd once seen, and remarkably resembled an Old Testament prophet.

Thaddeus suspected Paul was part nigger. The McCoy girl was a slave-owning southern bitch if he wasn't mistaken. He assumed they were married. Christopher Randolph had ordered him to sail with them to Nassau, then Monrovia, Liberia's port.

He would have to ship niggers in Nassau and deliver them in Monrovia.

"You don't have to like it, Thad, but that's the way it has to be," Christopher Randolph had told him, after issuing his orders.

Owner's orders were second only to God's so far as Thaddeus was concerned. His world was the *Jane Marie*. His owners proposed, Thaddeus disposed, and he would as soon question the orders of an owner as he would a direct order from God.

"Thy will be done," he told Christopher.

When Jonah was ordered to Nineveh, he'd at first rebelled, until a big fish swallowed him, and God withered the gourd under which he'd sought shade.

Thaddeus resolved he wouldn't be another Jonah!

Cannons & Roses

"Welcome aboard," he said when Celeste and Paul came up the gangplank at India Wharf.

The *Jane Marie* was a roomy but trim three-masted and square-rigged schooner built in Nova Scotia for privateer service during the War of 1812. Thaddeus assigned Paul and Celeste to the ample owner's stateroom aft. The cabin boy, Tom Bixby, would serve their meals, and take care of their other needs.

On course for Nassau, Thaddeus put it out of his mind that Celeste and Paul were aboard.

From Nassau, with additional passengers aboard, Thaddeus would set a course for Liverpool, there to load a cargo of trade goods before coasting down to Africa, and passing Madeira, then the Canary Islands, before raising a landfall at Gambia. Half of the good New England rum aboard was consigned to Vincent Gambini.

Gambini always paid in gold bars and ivory, cash on the barrelhead, and invited Thaddeus ashore. As yet, he'd never accepted the Italian's invitation. Nor did he let his crew sample Gambini's fleshpots. The only shore leave they got on an African voyage was at Freetown in Sierra Leone. But this trip Thaddeus decided he'd also let them ashore at Monrovia, when they reached Liberia.

Abidjan, Conakry, and Accra would be his other ports of call—slave ports every one. Profit for his owners and himself lulled Thaddeus Baker's conscience. Contributing half of his bonus from each voyage to the Boston Anti-Slavery Society salved it.

"What do you think of our good captain?" Celeste asked Paul when the *Jane Marie* was underway, and they'd settled into their cabin stateroom. "That beard is a bit terrifying."

Cannons & Roses

Paul stripped off his shirt and reached for a towel. Muggy summer heat had swamped Boston, and they'd had to wait on India Wharf before they embarked. Paul's shirt was soaked with sweat.

"Randolph claims he's a competent skipper," Paul said, toweling himself down. He handed Celeste the towel, and turned his whip-scarred back. "I'd guess he knows I'm touched with the tarbrush, and that you're a southern belle, but he has his orders."

Celeste dabbed at Paul's back with the towel.

"I don't like our Captain Baker," she said.

"Beggars can't choose," Paul told her. "From what I've seen so far, he runs a taut ship. We'll be only three or four weeks at sea, with luck."

Celeste had enjoyed their stay at Christopher Randolph's Beacon Hill home, with a chance to become better acquainted with Philippa Randolph, but the sound of water rushing along the ship's hull, and the sense of movement, exhilarated her. There was magic in the name "Africa."

She was also content to be alone with Paul again. They'd slept apart at Randolph's. It was only midmorning, but she wanted to make love.

Paul reached for a fresh shirt. "More like five or six weeks at sea," Paul decided. The American Colonization Society was sending books and medicine to Liberia with Celeste and Paul. "Plenty of time for me to brush up before teaching again."

They'd be living at Careysburg just south of Monrovia.

"You'll like Africa," Paul assured Celeste.

She captured his fresh shirt.

Paul looked at her, questioning.

"Clothes are a bore," she told him.

240

Paul grinned. "At a time like this, I agree," he said. "Let me get rid of yours."

Celeste turned her back. "Hurry with the damned buttons."

"A southern lady doesn't swear," Paul teased.

"A southern belle does," Celeste assured him.

Paul kissed, then nibbled the nape of her neck.

"Paul?"

"What?" His voice was sleepy.

"I'm glad Bone didn't do to you what he had in mind," Celeste told him.

"So am I."

"It's a very good thing little girls don't know how much they'll want a man someday," Celeste said. "If they knew, they wouldn't wait."

Paul's even breathing told Celeste he was asleep.

Celeste couldn't share Paul's lassitude. She slipped his shirt over her head and found it reached the middle of her thighs. She moved to the open port to drink in fresh salt air, and watch gulls soar and swoop in the wake of the ship.

The *Jane Marie* slipped past a close-hauled fishing trawler coming off the Newfoundland banks, loaded down with cod. Knives sparkled in the morning sun as the crew cleaned their last catch, and ribbons of fish blood, turned dark green by the salt water, trailed the vessel like shimmering scarves.

A man waved, and Celeste waved back. Another blew her a kiss.

Gulls wheeled away from the *Jane Marie*'s wake, screeching their excitement, to follow in the fishing vessel's wake.

Elbow on the rim of the port, chin resting in her

Cannons & Roses

hand, Celeste reviewed the past weeks in Boston. She'd been very much aware of Christopher Randolph's close scrutiny when they met on India Wharf. Was it possible she'd reminded him of his dead wife?

Christopher hadn't pursued the subject. As a matter of fact, he avoided it. He never looked directly at her again.

Celeste wondered if he'd taken a mistress. It was with some envy that Celeste remembered Philippa Randolph's still enjoying Christopher's hospitality. Celeste wasn't pregnant—a period had told her that while she was in Boston. It was a relief.

At the same time, Philippa glowed, carrying Jamie's child. She was old to be carrying her first child, as the Boston doctor that Christopher called had pointed out. He'd warned there might be serious complications.

Philippa hadn't seemed to mind. "There can be worse things than dying," she'd confided to Celeste.

"Name one," Celeste answered with a shudder.

"For a woman to live out her life without ever being completely fulfilled," Philippa said. "That's a tragedy I've narrowly escaped."

Paul's hand raised the shirt, then followed the soft curve of Celeste's flanks. "Very, very nice," he gloated. "Come back to bed?"

"Now just why should I do that, kind sir?" she pouted. "I've already been ravished once this morning."

Paul turned her to face him and ran his hands up under the shirt to cover her breasts.

"Let's storm your gates of Venus once again, kind lady," he urged. "Standing, if you will. An interesting position, you'll find."

"I'm a willing pupil," Celeste confessed.

Cannons & Roses

Afterward, Celeste admitted it *was* interesting, if somewhat uncomfortable.

The *Jane Marie* bucked the heaving swells off Cape Hatteras, clawing her way into unfavorable winds with reefed sails. Clear of the meeting ocean currents off Hatteras, a stiff following wind blew into a gale, and a mainsail was carried away.

When the mood was on him, Captain Baker was a driver. He crowded canvas on the *Jane Marie* until she protested by starting a seam. With men at the pumps, Captain Baker put in at Charleston, sliding past Fort Sumter, for minor repairs, and new canvas.

The ship was laid up two days there.

Celeste and Paul found that city still crowded with French refugees who were lucky enough to escape the bloodbath on Santo Domingo. Many were penniless and relied on charity. Some years ago, a few had been enticed to return to what was now Haiti, only to become victims of a second massacre.

Versed in French since she was a child, Celeste conversed freely with some of these people.

A Monsieur Antoine Tointeau had been one of the richest planters on Santo Domingo, but was reduced to tutoring the children of Charleston in French. When he learned that Jeanette had been a DuBois in Port-au-Prince, he invited Celeste to a Sunday evening salon in the shabby home of a Madame Grimaux.

It was a sobering experience. Her mother had seldom mentioned the hardships she and her slave, Bliss, suffered escaping from Santo Domingo. But now, from each person with whom she conversed for more than a minute or two, Celeste was treated to a report of horrors.

Cannons & Roses

She heard how more than six hundred men, women, and children had been shot in batches, and stacked like cordwood in the main square of Cap Haïtien. There were tales of rape and torture, whites burned alive, children carried on spears.

"You will see, mademoiselle, this same thing happen here," Antoine Tointeau told Celeste, "unless these abolitionists are dealt with by your government. Napoleon could have handled them."

"According to Mother," Celeste said, "he wasn't able to do much on Santo Domingo."

"Ah, that was a different matter. It was the climate. Soldiers died as if they were flies."

All were disdainful of Haiti and its black governing class.

"They're all vicious and savage black monkeys," one elderly French woman told Celeste. "Can you just imagine, they ape the British with fine carriages, and even hire governesses for their black brats, while their people starve. Some, I've heard, get so hungry they butcher and eat their own children!"

Most of these refugees clung to the forlorn hope that France would someday reconquer the western half of Hispaniola. Then they could return to their homes and their estates.

"We Santo Domingans only visit here," a palsied old man told Celeste. "It's the nigras who will send for us."

Paul wasn't invited to the salon. When Celeste rejoined him aboard the *Jane Marie* (they would sail for Africa on the morning tide), she was beginning to have second thoughts about Liberia.

"I've pictured the country as sort of a tropical paradise," she told Paul. "But from what I've heard tonight about Haiti, I'm wondering what it will be like, living in a country governed by ignorant former slaves. I'm becoming afraid, Paul."

"It isn't paradise," Paul admitted, "but the appointed white governors are usually compassionate men, and no one is starving."

When they arrived in Nassau, they discovered that Jason had escaped that island with a dozen picked followers. They'd stolen a fishing boat, but instead of trying the Middle Passage to Liberia, they'd sailed for the north coast of Jamaica to join the Maroons in the Cockpit Mountain area of that island.

Emancipation of all slaves on the islands comprising the British West Indies was supposed to be enacted by Parliament any day. There were rumors that when that came to pass, the Maroons and freed slaves would take over Jamaica and drive out the whites.

The few mutineers still at Nassau had found menial jobs of one kind or another and were no longer interested in trying to make a new life in Liberia.

Captain Baker was disgusted at having been taken out of his way, and wrote a blistering letter to that effect to Christopher Randolph.

Paul was philosophical—and secretly relieved that he wouldn't be responsible for other passengers aboard the *Jane Marie*.

Damongo was seated on his symbol of Ashanti royalty, a stool studded with diamonds and encrusted with gold. Naked except for a breechclout, and a rusty black derby contributed by Gambini during his last visit, Damongo's wrists and ankles were circled with raw gold nuggets. A necklace of nuggets was around his neck, and he drank palm wine from the gold-mounted skull of an enemy king he'd conquered and slain.

Cannons & Roses

Damongo was tall, even for an Ashanti, with a regal carriage when he walked, which was seldom. He usually traveled in a hammock borne by his women. His ebony features were more Arabic than Negroid. His black flesh glistened with palm oil.

Warriors just returned from a successful raid into Dahomey territory squatted in a half-circle behind Damongo's stool-throne, resting on their spears. The spears were crusted with dried blood.

Damongo's harem numbered 150 or 170 women—he could never remember which. Ashanti villages in his realm sent girls and women to him as a matter of tribute. Some he kept, some he parceled out to his more loyal followers.

The fiercest and cruelest of his women served as warriors, fighting alongside the men. Their reward was the right to torture to death any prisoners taken, above the number Damongo needed for trade.

A hundred men, women, boys, and girls were penned in the village and would be marched toward Gambia in a few days. Damongo owed Vincent Gambini 75 prime slaves. With luck, fewer than 25 would die along the jungle trail. Damongo would drive a hard bargain for any above the 75 he owed.

Four women, six men, five boys, and three young girls were fastened to stakes, evenly spaced, facing Damongo and his warriors. Eighteen victims. It was just after sunrise, and the entertainment hadn't yet started. Damongo had appointed the eighteen Amazons who'd most distinguished themselves in Dahomey to torture these Dahomey prisoners.

The rest of his women were clustered behind the warriors, except for the one fanning him with a palm leaf, and the two kneeling girls, one on either side of his stool. They were there to retire with Damongo for a

Cannons & Roses

few minutes whenever the antics of his Amazons, and the sight of their naked, writhing victims, aroused him enough to require their erotic services.

The spectacle about to begin would last at least until sunset, Damongo hoped. The Amazon whose victim lasted longest and suffered the most would be rewarded handsomely. They stood in a group apart, clutching their sharpened knives, with various torture instruments of their own making dangling from cords around their waists, eyes on Damongo's scepter.

This scepter was the whitened and now gold-inlaid shinbone of the mulatto woman who'd increased his fortune—until he decided, one night when he was drunker than usual, to find out how her flesh would taste.

Torture sweetened the flesh of humans, as well as of animals, the Ashanti believed, so they'd taken pains with the mulatto. She'd been flayed. She had tasted differently, but the feast wasn't a complete success. Some of his warriors claimed she wasn't salty enough.

Damongo regretted eating her now and resolved he wouldn't be so foolish again when Gambini delivered the white woman he'd promised.

The Amazons were getting restive.

Damongo raised his scepter. With delighted shouts, they raced toward their victims.

PART TWO

1

As soon as the *Jane Marie* swung at anchor a quarter of a mile in the roadstead from the Gambia fort of Vincent Gambini, a broad, flat-bottomed canoe put out from the beach in front of the gloomy fort. Once the canoe was launched through the surf, a dozen blacks swung their paddles in perfect unison, and wet blades winked in the African sun. A white man was sprawled in the stern sheets.

Some of the *Jane Marie*'s crew perched in the rigging; other crewmen lounged forward and amidships to watch the canoe approach. When they came on deck, Celeste and Paul noticed that Captain Baker had armed his crew. He stood amidships, waiting to greet the white man. Celeste and Paul watched the scene from the quarterdeck.

An offshore breeze was riffling the calm water. For the first time, it brought to Celeste the smell of Africa. Rich with the blended scent of flowers, jungle foliage, and rich soil, it also carried a whiff of decay. The town of Gambia was a cluster of mud huts, thatched with palm fronds, with pigs, chickens, and naked black children crowding the narrow dirt streets.

Paul pointed out a slender-waisted sloop with a sharply raked prow, and three masts, that was anchored off their port quarter. "There's a slaver," Paul told her. "Built for speed to outrun any British or American ship on patrol."

She was painted a glistening black. "Look at her closely and you'll notice the air grilles amidships," Paul said. "They ventilate the slave deck and hold. And the swivel gun mounted aft to sweep the decks, if necessary, also marks her as a slaver."

"She doesn't show any flag," Celeste said.

Paul laughed bitterly. "At least a dozen of different nationalities will be in her flag locker," he explained. "American, British, French, Dutch, Spanish, and Portuguese, with false papers for each. She's American, if pursued by a British frigate, and British if one of our ships overtakes her, and so on. Would you believe that small ship will have five or six hundred men, women and children stifling in her hold when she lifts anchor?"

"No. It looks too small."

"They're packed naked and spoon-fashion, and chained like the slaves aboard the *Good Friend*. A few women and girls are available to the crew, of course. The wind is shifting," Paul said. "You'll get the stink of her soon."

"What about . . . well, sanitary conditions?" Celeste asked.

"There aren't any for the slaves. Once or twice a day, they're hosed down. In good weather, they're taken on deck for half an hour, or an hour, and made to dance. A slaver carries a double crew. They ring the dancers to keep any of them from plunging over the side. Still, a dozen or so will commit suicide every voyage. Those paddlers out there are Krus," Paul said. "A canoe like that, manned by Krus, is used to ferry slaves out to the slaver."

Paul explained that, of all the African tribes, only Krus were impossible to enslave.

"Why is that?" Celeste asked.

"Pride. They'll curl up and die for no good reason, or be obstinate until they're flogged to death—or set free. This is why most of the slave traders use them as guards and canoemen. Slaver captains have the cute habit of shanghaiing canoemen to fill out a cargo. If they're Krus, however, the trader doesn't have to worry."

The canoe with the white man in the stern had come within hailing distance of the *Jane Marie*. Captain Baker raised his hailing horn. "You there, Gambini. You know my rules. Only you come aboard. Tell your canoemen to sheer off, once you're on my deck, or, by God, I'll sink 'em!"

Both Celeste and Paul stiffened at the name "Gambini." They stared at each other, and Celeste's hand leaped to her throat. "The man who murdered my father?" she wondered.

Paul studied the man in the stern sheets of the canoe for a moment, then nodded grimly. "That's the man, all right."

"What do we do?" Celeste asked. Panic squeezed her heart. "He'll kill us both."

"We do nothing now but keep out of sight," Paul said. Then: "No. Gambini has seen me only once or twice, and both times I was stripped. I'm going to get permission to go ashore."

"No, Paul! Why? That's crazy dangerous."

"I want to map the inside of that fort in my head," Paul explained. "I owe Gambini for kidnapping me into slavery and killing your father, not to mention trying to rape you. I've told you I intend to strike at slavery where it counts. When I'm ready, I'll start with Vincent Gambini."

Gambini and Captain Baker were below in the captain's cabin.

"If you're going ashore here, I am, too," Celeste said determinedly.

It was Paul's turn to say no.

"I'll go with you as another man," Celeste insisted. "We can do it. But what's our excuse for going into the fort?"

"I've thought of one," Paul said. From the crew he'd learned how Gambini entertained the crews of slavers. Men aboard the *Jane Marie* were bitter that Captain Baker forbade them such an orgy while swinging at anchor off Gambia. "I'll have a chat with Captain Baker."

"How long will we be here?" Celeste asked.

"Two days at least. Captain Baker won't allow any canoeman aboard his ship, and he's wise. It's not unknown for slave traders to seize a ship for themselves. So our crew will be lightering rum casks and other trade goods ashore. I'll persuade him to put me in charge of the detail."

It would be a simple step beyond that duty, Paul thought, to get himself invited to one of the nightly orgies, and while it was in progress, explore the fort.

"What about me?" Celeste asked. Curiosity was beginning to gnaw her. She wanted to see, firsthand, this aspect of the slave trade. "It will be less chancy if there are two of us."

"No," Paul said.

"Yes, damn it," Celeste told him. "We're in this together. God knows, after what I've experienced at Bone's Bayou House, I'm no shrinking violet. I'll carry a weapon, and so will you."

Paul was undecided. She pressed. "Paul, while you're off exploring, I can cover for you. You need me, and I've as much reason as you have to want to bring Gambini down. I want to see that man dead!"

"You're a fierce one, aren't you?" Paul said.

"You can believe me. Remember, I saw Gambini kill my father. Let me talk to Captain Baker."

"What will you tell him?" Paul asked.

"As much as I need to tell him, and no more."

"How much did Christopher Randolph tell you about Paul and me, Captain Baker?" Celeste asked.

She was alone with him in his cabin. It was the evening of their arrival off Gambia. Rum casks, cases of rifles, and other trade goods were being taken from the ship's hold, to be stacked on the desk. The lightering ashore would begin in the morning.

When Celeste asked to speak with him in private, Captain Baker had ordered Tom Bixby to bring them supper. They'd finished eating.

"Miss McCoy, isn't it?" Captain Baker said.

"It is," Celeste admitted. "Paul and I aren't lovers," she lied. "Captain Baker, I think I can confide in you, since you're a member in good standing of the Boston Anti-Slavery Society."

"My orders are to take you and Paul to Monrovia," Captain Baker said.

"Yes, that's right, but we are . . . well, on a secret mission." Celeste hoped her conspiratorial air was convincing. She lowered her voice. "Disguised as a young man, I need to get ashore with Paul Wright. You can help us."

Captain Baker listened intently.

"Appoint Paul to supervise the lightering of cargo ashore tomorrow," she said. "He will manage an invitation to Vincent Gambini's quarters tomorrow night, and I will go ashore with him then. This is all we ask."

"What is your mission?" Captain Baker asked.

"Our government will move against these slave traders, and soon," Celeste lied again. "They need to know about this fort."

Captain Baker frowned. "Randolph mentioned nothing about this."

"He had his orders not to do so," Celeste said. Her eyes shifted around the cabin, as if seeking an interloper. Finding none, she confided: "I can tell you this much. We've made sure that you're a man who can be trusted."

Captain Baker had swallowed her tale whole. "I'll have Wright in charge of the lightering tomorrow," he said. "Miss McCoy, I admire your courage."

"Thank you, sir." Celeste assumed her most modest air. "I'm as dedicated to our cause as you are to this fine ship."

"I've misjudged you and Wright."

"You were meant to do so," Celeste confided.

"Tell me this," Captain Baker said. "Isn't your, er, partner part Negro?"

"No," Celeste lied for the third time.

"How in hell did you draw the wool over his eyes?" Paul asked. They were together in their bunk and had just made love.

Cannons & Roses

"I missed my calling," Celeste said. "I should have been an actress, and played boys' parts on the stage. Maybe I will go on the stage," Celeste said.

"We're playing a dangerous game," Paul warned her.

"Listen, Paul." Celeste raised on an elbow and looked down into his face. "I didn't come to Africa with you to twiddle my thumbs. We're together in whatever you plan to do here, and you might as well get used to the idea."

Paul traced the line of her jaw with a finger.

"I have to tell you something," Paul said.

"I'm listening."

"I don't want to love you—it just complicates my life—but I can't help myself. Why aren't you my brother, or sister?"

"Because what we do together would be very wicked," Celeste told him. "Don't you think that you've complicated my life, for God's sake? Right now I could be at Great Oaks fighting off suitors." Her fingertips were straying down his naked body, and Paul stiffened. "Lie still."

She found his limp manhood and squeezed gently. Celeste shifted her position on the bunk. "Just relax now," she said.

His member was hardening in her soft palm. "I don't want you chasing girls and women ashore," Celeste told him.

"My dear God!" Paul sighed.

Blood still sang in his ears, and his pulse was pounding. The vision of Celeste finally astride him, nails digging his chest, as she took her erotic pleasure and gave him his, was still bright in his mind.

"Are you praying, dear?" she asked smugly.

Cannons & Roses

"No, but I guess we both should be," Paul said. "Tomorrow night our heads will be in the lion's mouth."

"Gambini is no lion," Celeste said, with scorn. "A jackal describes him best, I'd say. But we don't have to do this thing, Paul."

"We're going to do it, just the same," Paul said. "I am, anyway. I couldn't live with myself if I didn't. Scum like Gambini shouldn't share the same earth and breathe the same air as men like your father. I didn't know Jamie McCoy, but DeWitt Scott did, and he's told me what a man he was. Would your father have left Gambini alone?"

"No, he would not," Celeste said. "But you're my lover, not my father." She kissed Paul, and it was a lingering kiss. "Thankfully," Celeste breathed.

"You're a witch!"

Celeste smiled. "Of course I am. Are you just finding that out?"

"I've suspected," Paul said. "A good witch can go far in superstitious Africa."

"I'm glad to hear that. Your Africa fascinates me. Will Liberia be like Gambia?"

"The climate there is more healthy," Paul said. "That's why the Colonization Society chose that part of the west coast. Back in the 1700s, a British explorer —I've forgotten his name—had a farewell supper here in Gambia with nine white men. When he returned a year later, all nine were in that graveyard near the fort. Malaria, yellow fever, smallpox, and God only knows what else, had taken them all."

"Paul, if you're trying to frighten me, you can stop —because you have."

Their plan to get into the fort had worked. The slaver in the roadstead would be loaded tomorrow, so

Cannons & Roses

most of her crew had come ashore for one last night of dissipation before sailing out into the Middle Passage. The slaver captain had joined his men, his virgin girl gift safely stowed in his cabin to be ravished at sea.

The slaver captain called Jones—whatever his real name was—slouched in a corner of the square room just off the entrance to the fort. He was a swarthy man, a hunchback with a cast in one eye.

Celeste, fitted out as a seaman from the *Jane Marie*, wearing a pea jacket, stood beside Paul at the opposite side of the room.

The slaver's crew were the most villainous lot either Celeste or Paul had ever seen.

Bearded or unshaven, all of them were staggering drunk on uncut rum. Six women, six girls, and half a dozen stripling boys were locked into the room with the drunken slavers. All were naked, of course. Most were as drunk as the slaver crew—even the girls and the boys.

The slaver captain, Celeste, and Paul were the only voyeurs. Gambini had a woman pinned to the floor. Celeste and Paul had seen him rape her. Now it amused Gambini, who'd captured her wrists with one hand, to prick her nipples and breasts with a sheath knife, laughing each time she cried out. A circle of seamen from the slaver egged him on. Gambini, stark naked, was astride her belly.

Two seamen had one of the boys. They had him on his knees. One was thrusting, cruelly, between his buttocks, while the other man had the boy's shaven head between his hands, forcing him between his legs.

Celeste found herself swallowing revulsion, yet unable to look away from the orgiastic frenzy all around her.

Cannons & Roses

Paul touched her shoulder. "Nobody's watching us," he whispered. "I'm going to look around."

Celeste licked dry lips, unable to look away from Gambini and the woman he was torturing. "Be careful," she whispered.

Paul was gone.

The woman's black breasts were laced with trickles of blood. She'd stopped crying out. The whites of her eyes contrasted with her ebony skin and the bright red of her gaping mouth.

Gambini's face was a cruel mask. Two slaver seamen grabbed her ankles and spread her thighs. When two others had pinned her wrists, Gambini got off the woman, his blood-stained knife in his hand.

"Mother of God!" Celeste had guessed what he would do to her next.

The woman and Gambini were the focus of everyone's attention.

On his knees, between her splayed legs, Gambini pricked with the knife point, taking his time, intent on his work.

"Spread her more," he ordered.

The grinning seamen holding her ankles pushed her heels until they dented her buttocks, then pinned her knees to the stone floor.

Gambini wiped the knife blade on her heaving belly.

Then, slowly, he began working the broad blade of the knife up into the woman, grinning as he did so, oblivious to the rush of blood coating his hand and wrist. Finally, with a hard thrust, he buried the knife in her to the hilt. The agonized woman screamed.

Celeste screamed, her knees buckled, and she fainted.

2

Gambini's cruel act had partially sobered the slaver crew, and their whole attention focused on the dying woman. Only Captain Jones had seen Celeste faint and slump to the stone floor. He crossed to her quickly, as the terror-stricken black women, boys, and girls rushed the room's doors. When they'd burst through the doors, Kru guards in the passage outside the room drove them back with whips.

When Celeste's head cleared, she found Jones on his knees beside her, one hand thrust inside her man's shirt, the hunchback's other hand fumbling with the belt of her trousers. His face was twisted in a wicked grin.

"You sure ain't no cabin *boy,* missy." Fetid breath bathed her face. "You sure ain't, and that's a fact!"

Celeste jerked her knees up, and grabbed the wrist of the hand that was fondling her breasts. "Please!"

"Touchy, eh?" Jones chuckled. "Don't you fret,

missy," he whispered. "Captain Jones ain't one to mind your business."

While the woman Gambini had violated with his knife writhed in a widening pool of her own blood, Gambini and the half-drunk seamen joined the melee at the doors, using their fists.

Jones was helping Celeste to her feet when Paul fought his way into the room to reach her side. A glance at the dying woman told him all he needed to know.

"Let's get out of here!" he said.

"Bucko, that there's a purely fine idea," Jones told Paul. "My stomach ain't as strong as she used to be."

Jones took command of their escape, knocking down a frenzied Kru who tried to stop them.

They reached the beach through a narrow, winding passageway that took them past the dim dungeons where Gambini kept his prime human stock. Behind bars, each was crowded with men or women, all naked. Celeste would never forget the whites of their eyes in the darkness, and the fact no one made a sound.

On the beach, while Paul and Jones were launching the ship's small boat that had brought them ashore, Celeste sucked the warm salt air into her lungs and prayed that sometime she'd be able to forget the horror she'd just witnessed. But she knew it would always be there in her memory, with the sight of the Mandingo gelded and emasculated with a whip, Vashti cutting Ulric Bone to death, and what Paul had told her about the way Vashti herself died.

Paul scooped her up in his arms, and waded out to dump her into the boat. He and Jones manned the oars. As they approached the black slaver, for the first time Celeste breathed the awful stench of the ship. It smelled of human excrement, sweat, blood, and death.

Cannons & Roses

Jones noticed the expression on her face and laughed. "The smell of the trade, missy," he said. "After this voyage, we burn her, fine ship that she is."

Back aboard the *Jane Marie,* Paul told Celeste, "That fort can be taken by only a few brave men. We can't storm it—that would be suicide—but Jones just gave me the key."

The passageway through the dungeons was the open back door to Gambini's fort.

"We'll come ashore on a night like this one, when everyone is drunk," Paul said. "We'll break slaves out of those dungeons and arm them. Before Gambini sobers up, we'll have his fort."

"I have to bathe, Paul," Celeste said. "I feel as if I'll *never* be clean again!"

Paul poured her a tumbler of brandy. "While you drink that," he said, "I'll wake up Tom and have him bring us hot water from the galley. Get out of those clothes."

Celeste and Paul never discovered how Vincent Gambini learned who they were. Perhaps it was her resemblance to Jamie McCoy, linked with their quick escape, that jogged his memory when he'd sobered up. Celeste and Paul learned that he had recognized them the next day, when he came aboard the *Jane Marie* to settle his account with Captain Baker.

Celeste didn't know Gambini was aboard and was alone on the forward deck, watching the crew prepare to lift anchor.

"Ah, Miss McCoy."

Celeste whirled around to find herself face to face with the grinning Italian. "So we meet again," he said. "The long arm of coincidence, no?" He snatched her hand to his lips, laughing when she pulled away from him. "I play the gentleman today, Miss McCoy. But we'll meet again, here in Africa, I assure you."

Celeste's back was to the rail. For the first time, she knew how a snake can charm a bird. She couldn't avoid Gambini's black eyes.

"Didn't you enjoy my little entertainment last night?" he asked. "You did come to my party."

Celeste licked dry lips. Where was Paul?

"Your nigger lover is with the captain," Gambini said. "Well, until we meet again, and may it be soon. I have a most impatient client."

"Stay away from me," Celeste said, finally finding her voice.

"Because of you, it was strongly suggested that I leave Louisiana and come here, Miss McCoy," Gambini said. "You owe me for that, and Gambini always collects his debts."

Mocking Celeste with a salute, Gambini turned on his heel. He was over the side before Paul joined Celeste. She told him what had taken place between her and Gambini.

"That man scares me to death!" she said. "I have a feeling I never should have come to Africa."

Robert Leatherman, an officer of the American Colonization Society, and an ordained Methodist minister, met their ship when it docked in Monrovia's harbor. Paul had been under Reverend Leatherman's direction when he served the society in Liberia previously. News about their arrival had come on a faster ship.

It was Christopher Randolph's idea to explain their traveling together, although unmarried, by saying that Celeste was a missionary. Reverend Leatherman hadn't been hoodwinked. He was among the first to come out

Cannons & Roses

to Liberia from England. His African years had mellowed Robert Leatherman's ideas about morality.

"Well, Paul, welcome back," Reverend Leatherman beamed, shaking both of Paul's hands. "And this is Miss McCoy?"

"Yes, sir," Celeste said.

Reverend Leatherman was a stocky man, shorter than both Paul and Celeste, with a round face creased with laugh-wrinkles. Bald as an egg, he wore a full reddish beard, over which bright blue eyes danced, but missed nothing. He was a bachelor.

"You two are not married, I take it?" he asked in a mild voice.

"No, sir, we're not," Paul said.

"I have a post for you and Miss McCoy in Ganta, just over the Cavalla River from the Ivory Coast," Reverend Leatherman said. "Careytown, Paul, is too tame for a man with your experience. I've promised the town folk a married couple to set up their new school and church."

Celeste blushed.

"You're not previously married?" Reverend Leatherman asked Celeste.

"No, sir."

"You, Paul?"

"No."

Reverend Leatherman rubbed his palms together and beamed. "Very good. Shall we take care of that matter immediately? A matter of government policy," he apologized. "We whites must set a good example."

Celeste and Paul exchanged glances. He nodded. She turned back to Reverend Leatherman, saying, "Will you please marry us?"

She and Paul were starting a new life, in a new land, and it somehow was appropriate they should be married, Celeste thought. She hoped that he felt the same way.

Reverend Leatherman married them in a chapel just a block from the wharf, with a handsome Negro woman who cleaned the chapel standing in as a witness.

Celeste remembered the quiet wedding of Bliss and Richard as she held Paul's hand in the hot chapel, with perspiration trickling between her shoulder blades, and down her back. The high-pitched voice of a woman in the street outside the chapel, calling, "Chicken, here, buy 'em cheap," intruded on the service.

The Negro cleaning woman stared off into space, her face blank.

"Now you may kiss the bride," Reverend Leatherman said finally, and Paul gathered Celeste into his arms.

For the first time, she realized her cheeks were wet with tears. Her lips were salty when they kissed.

The kiss finished, Paul held her by the shoulders, staring into her eyes.

"Are you sorry?" Paul was concerned.

"No!" It was too sharp a denial. "No, Paul," she said, in a calmer voice. "I cry at other people's weddings—why can't I cry at my own?"

"No reason," Paul said, grinning. "Damn that woman hawking chickens."

They stayed with Reverend Leatherman for two days before starting for their station at Ganta. Near a bend in the Cavalla River, Ganta was bordered by Guinea on the north, the Ivory Coast to the south. It had once been an important junction on the slave route between these two tribal areas.

Cannons & Roses

Peanuts and cocoa were the crops Liberian farmers were trying to grow.

"Coffles of slaves are still taken through Ganta—at night, of course—and the people there have asked Monrovia to stop this traffic," Reverend Leatherman told Celeste and Paul. "A Liberian child or two has been kidnapped."

The main slave route, Reverend Leatherman told them, now passed between the river and Mount Nimba just west of the river.

"Your people there are mostly from Canada," he told Celeste and Paul. "They are a sturdy crowd, but they need leadership. You're empowered to form a Liberian militia to deal with the slave traders, but I don't believe you'll run into much trouble. Black and white traders are a villainous lot, but most don't want trouble from a country backed by the United States."

There was a mulatto doctor, Samuel Corey, in Ganta. "You'll find him a most remarkable man," Reverend Leatherman told them. "He's one of the few slaves that ever escaped north from the deep south, and for years was a conductor on the Underground Railroad, and a somewhat foolhardy one, if I'm to believe what I've been told."

The upper Ashanti country bordered the Ivory coast on the south. "An Ashanti king, Damongo, trades with a man named Gambini," Reverend Leatherman told them. "He's the worst offender at routing his slave coffles through Ganta. Damongo used to do his trading in Accra, which is much more convenient, but Gambini now gets his custom. I've heard some rather ugly rumors why, but I won't bother you with them."

Paul showed Celeste the Liberian capital. In comparison with slovenly Gambia, Monrovia was remarkably clean for an African city, with neat rows of houses and wide streets. Palm trees lined the paved streets and shaded the houses.

Liberians, Celeste discovered, were all shades of color, from jet-black Africans to mulattoes nearly as white as Paul. Upcountry people, here in the city to sell produce, were a barefoot and bare-breasted minority, women carrying their babies in a back sling. Liberian city-dwellers were well dressed, for the most part, and usually lighter complexioned. With some amusement, Celeste noticed that the black country people treated them with the deference a slave showed his master and mistress.

"We in the south aren't the only ones with a color caste system," she told Paul.

Paul didn't say it, and Celeste didn't know if he really knew it, but she sensed one reason Paul was in Liberia was this respect accorded his light skin.

"Boston and Philadelphia abolitionists claim that Liberia is merely a dumping ground for the free northern and Canadian Negroes," Paul told her. "I'm not convinced they're wrong. You saw how welcome immigration of the *Jane Marie* mutineers was when I contacted the Colonization Society."

Aboard ship, Celeste had read some of the books and pamphlets Paul was bringing out.

"What do you think Mr. Garrison means when he rants and raves about immediate abolition?" Celeste asked Paul. "One abolitionist—I think it was the Reverend Parker, or it might have been Gerrit Smith—writes that if all the slaves but one die exterminating all the southern slave owners, it would be a good thing in the eyes of God. Do you believe that?"

"No, and you don't have to ask," Paul said. "I'm

not that fanatic. I'm not sure, however, that Garrison isn't."

"I know," Celeste said. "It seems to me what he really wants is abolition of the southern states. He doesn't love Negro slaves so much as he hates us southerners."

It wasn't possible for them to reach Ganta by going up the Cavalla River, because a few miles back from the coast of West Africa the land rises sharply to a plateau. Nearly every African river pours off this shelf in roaring falls and cascades.

"This geologic feature," Reverend Leatherman pointed out, "is God's way of keeping Europeans out of the interior for so long."

Coastal West African tribes were accustomed to European gin and American rum, as well as firearms with which to slaughter each other more efficiently, long before men like Mungo Park penetrated the heart of West Africa.

While more or less isolated from their lowland neighbors, tribes like the Ashanta and Dahomey had traded only with the few enterprising Arabs who came so far west. A trickle of criminals, debtors, and war captives were sold these Arab traders, but it was so far back across Africa, and so many died en route, that it wasn't a profitable trade.

But when they discovered an insatiable demand for slaves a relatively few miles east, along the coast, the Ashanti and Dahomey began raiding the more docile lowland tribes for huge coffles of slaves to be sold at profits they'd never realized from the shrewd Arabs.

And they soon made it clear, by slaughtering any white traders who tried to collect their own slaves, that the slave trade was their monopoly.

Cannons & Roses

"If Reverend Leatherman is right, and God designed West Africa to keep white men out of the interior, it seems to me He didn't do a good enough job," Celeste told Paul. "They got in there just in time to populate the West Indies and United States with slaves."

The white American interim governor of Liberia, Roberts, invited Celeste and Paul for tea at his official residence before they started for Ganta. They found him a genial, comfortable man, dedicated to his task of shaping Liberia into a true democracy, modeled on the United States.

Roberts congratulated them on their marriage and thanked them for coming to Liberia. "This is no longer an experiment," he assured them. "Liberia is a viable democracy and will prove to the world that the Negro, given the opportunity, can govern himself as well as any other people, and better than most."

Roberts assured Paul that the Liberian government was behind whatever he thought necessary to stamp out the Ashanti and Dahomey funneling of slave coffles through Liberian territory.

"One day," Roberts boasted, "we'll be strong enough to stamp out this horror. A few patrol ships won't do it. We've got to hit Gambia, Abidijan, and Accra, and raze the barracoons."

Paul and Celeste exchanged glances when they'd heard Roberts make this statement.

"Sir, I have some ideas along that line," Paul ventured. Without going into detail, he related his own experience to Roberts, and then said, "So you can see why I want to strike back."

"You say Vincent Gambini had you kidnapped?" Roberts asked.

"I can't be sure about that," Paul said, "but it was

Gambini who sold me into slavery. I want to put him out of the trade."

Roberts thoughtfully stroked his chin. "When you get to Ganta," he said, "talk with Doc Sam Corey. You two will get along just fine. Should you and he strike upon a feasible plan to close down Gambini's fort, don't inform me officially."

"No, sir, I won't," Paul said.

"Sam and I are old friends," Roberts said. "It was from my grandfather that he escaped north. Trust him with your life."

3

Dr. Samuel Corey's skin was the color of rich chocolate. He was a slight man at fifty-five, and walked with a limp, hitching along the right leg that was shorter than his left. He'd broken his leg as a child, and it hadn't been set properly.

In repose, his Negroid features and cap of gray hair, made him the sort any southerner would address as "Uncle." Only when he was amused or excited did his face light up. When that happened, he was ageless. And it was only then that his native intelligence shone through.

Dr. Samuel escaped from the Roberts plantation, The Halcyon, when, as near as he could reckon, he was twenty-one, born of a slave mother, and fathered by an unknown white man. Mrs. Roberts, however, suspected the Jewish peddler who called on plantations in the Houma area of Louisiana. Simon Levine was a spindling little man, with compassion for slaves and their owners alike.

Taken into the big house a few years after he was injured, and his young mother had died from yellow fever, Dr. Samuel was made a pet by the Robertses, and their sons and daughters. He was assigned only light chores. The other pampered house niggers liked the always cheerful boy with a limp, too. So he was the last slave on the plantation anyone—black or white—thought would become a runaway.

It was Aunt Beulah, the plantation seamstress, who told Dr. Samuel there was a place where Negroes weren't born and died slaves.

"That's a place called North, boy," Aunt Beulah told him, when he pressed for details.

"Where's this North?" he asked.

"Don't rightly know," she told him. "Just heard."

The plantation blacksmith, Jethro, pointed out the North Star to the boy.

"That Mr. Simon, the Jew man, he tell me North that way somewhere, Samuel," Jethro said, "but pay no mind. Heaven that way, too, but you got to die to get there."

Born into captivity, most animals prosper and breed, and if released from their cages, become frantic to return. But there are rare exceptions. Samuel was an exception.

He stole a side of bacon from the smokehouse and began limping in the direction of the North Star, or the Drinking Gourd, as it was known to the slaves.

Certain slaves often ran away, to enjoy a few days or even a month hiding in the swamps, only to return from their vacation, take their whipping, and go back to work. Matt Roberts was a more enlightened man than his neighbors. Runaways who returned and said they were sorry were seldom punished, except for being deprived of certain privileges for a stated length of time.

Massa Roberts was surprised when Dr. Samuel disappeared, but he posted no notices and didn't inform the slave catchers. After three months, it was assumed he'd had a fatal accident in the nearby swamp.

The Roberts family felt as badly about Samuel as they did when Fancy, Governor Roberts's pony, broke his leg and had to be destroyed.

Many times during the next year young Samuel yearned for the comfort he'd escaped. He traveled by night and hid and slept by day, unless the skies were cloudy. Then he huddled in a canebrake, or in a deserted barn, if he was lucky, and waited to see the North Star again.

"If there had been a Southern Star, I think I would have turned back," he said, years later.

He learned to snare rabbits, mice, and rats, sometimes forced to bolt them down raw. He stole raw corn. Once he killed and ate a mongrel dog that had taken up with him. For the rest of his life, Dr. Samuel would regret that necessity.

By the time he reached the Ohio River, Samuel had learned that freedom was somewhere on the opposite bank. But how to cross? He couldn't swim. He didn't know how to make a raft. For a week, sick and fevered, Samuel hid and stared across at Indiana.

It was a bitter winter.

"The Red Sea parted for the Israelites," he was to say. "God's miracle for me was a hard freeze."

On Christmas Day the river froze over.

Samuel crossed.

Cannons & Roses

Dr. Judd Corey found the shivering young Negro trying to steal his setting hen Christmas night.

Judd and Mary Corey were strong pro-slavery people. Their neighbors, the Browns, were practicing Quakers. Dr. Judd hitched up his horse, Mary wrapped a blanket around Samuel, and he was delivered to the Browns.

"Can't somehow turn this boy back," Dr. Corey told the Browns. "He's come too far."

Samuel had found his surname.

Because of Samuel, the Browns became one of the first underground railroad stations in southern Indiana. Passed from one Quaker family to another, Samuel finally reached Canada. He was employed as a porter at the University of Montreal medical school. Other free Negroes taught him to read and write.

Admitted to the school on a provisional basis (a professor wanted to prove that Negroes weren't educable), Dr. Samuel astounded his professors by graduating at the head of his class.

But no one needed the services of a Negro physician, even in liberal Canada.

Dr. Samuel returned to the Browns. Disguised as an old woman, he acted as a midwife on Tennessee plantations, passing himself as a free Negro. Knowing he was suspected of soliciting slaves to run north, but not of being a man, Dr. Samuel went to the planter who was most suspicious. He convinced Dred Small that he was just a poor nigger woman, trying to keep body and soul together, putting on a performance that would have shamed Sarah Bernhardt.

He then proceeded to lead the entire Small labor force across the river to freedom, as a final gesture of defiance, and conducted them all to Canada without losing a man, woman, or child.

Cannons & Roses

With his underground railroad usefulness at an end, Dr. Samuel applied to the American Colonization Society and was sent to Liberia to cope with a problem that threatened to halt free Negro migration.

The immigration house in Monrovia was Dr. Samuel's solution. Here immigrants, under his supervision, lived their first months in Liberia and adjusted to the change in climate. The mortality rate among new settlers was soon cut in half.

Dr. Samuel Corey chose Ganta when ill health forced him to retire. Sandwiched between Guinea and the Ivory Coast country, this poor village, convenient to slave traffic, was where Dr. Samuel planned to strike one more blow against slavery.

But he needed help.

Perhaps Paul Wright would be the strong right hand. It was unfortunate, Dr. Samuel thought, that Paul should be bringing a wife to Ganta, but that couldn't be changed.

From Monrovia up into the hills to Ganta was a nine-day journey for Celeste and Paul because they chose to make it on horseback, with Paul's case of books and their other belongings loaded on pack mules. There was little jungle, to Celeste's surprise, and the days were no hotter than summer in Louisiana, with much cooler nights.

Farms they passed looked prosperous, and the people seemed contented, with some even rich. Most of the towns were as neat and clean as Monrovia.

Ganta was on a steep slope above the river, with a church and a one-room schoolhouse side by side. Their houses, like most of the others, was built with thick mud walls, a thatched roof, and was divided into only two rooms. Dr. Samuel's bungalow, the church,

Cannons & Roses

and the schoolhouse were the only wood-frame buildings in Ganta.

Stretching down the slope to the river, outside the town of Ganta, were straggling mud-wattle huts. Naked black children, goats, and chickens roamed this Sosoo village. In Liberia, the Sosoo, a gentle and placid people, found a haven from the warlike Ashanti and fierce Dahomey. For their labor in the fields they were paid in trade goods.

While Celeste and Paul were moving in, Dr. Samuel paid them a call. He walked with an intricately carved ebony cane.

"Welcome to Ganta," he greeted them, shaking hands with both Paul and Celeste, before settling into one of the lashed bamboo chairs. Chin on the knob of his cane, he regarded them a moment. "You're a younger woman than I expected up here," he told Celeste. "You've chosen a beautiful bride," Dr. Samuel complimented Paul, before a coughing fit wracked his slight body.

A Sosoo woman had been appointed to cook for them, and a Sosoo girl would do their house chores. There was a cook shack in back of the house where food would be prepared over a wood fire, with a lean-to behind it where the woman and girl would sleep.

"We have forty-seven school-age children here in the village," Dr. Samuel told them, "and some of our adults will attend."

"I've been commissioned to form a militia unit," Paul told Dr. Samuel. "Monrovia has promised guns and ammunition. But I have no military training," he confessed. "I'm going to need any help you can give me."

"You will have it," Dr. Samuel assured him.

* * *

Cannons & Roses

Drum telegraph spread the word through Ashanti country that a young white woman had arrived in Ganta, and Damonga began to plan a raid. Gambini had three slavers coming to Gambia and had informed Damongo that he would pay premium prices for a thousand prime slaves. Damongo's barracoons were nearly empty.

The Sosoo village at Ganta had tempted Damongo before, but his chiefs advised against raiding into Liberia. Damongo had drained his barracoons because his uncle had died recently. As was customary with the Ashanti, fifty captives had been tortured before they were buried alive with Damongo's dead uncle.

The funeral had been three months ago. Every day since, at least one man or woman had been sacrificed, to carry word to the uncle that Damongo was paying him all proper respect.

The pyramid of human heads outside his village, stinking in the tropical sun, was higher than it had ever been before.

But only a few dozen men, women, and children languished in his barracoons. There were captives to be had at Ganta, and a white woman, also. It was too much of a temptation. He sent word through Ashanti country for his chiefs to gather and bring their best warriors.

Sailing as a privateer and sometime pirate for Jean Laffite, Vincent Gambini had learned the value of spies ashore in important ports. His spy in Monrovia was assistant to the port director. From this man, Gambini learned the movements of American patrol vessels that made Monrovia their home port on the Slave Coast.

As a good spy should, this free Negro, who'd been

278

Canadian-born, also passed along any information he thought Gambini might use, whether it concerned ship movements or not. In an indirect way, he'd been responsible for the mulatto prostitute Gambini had presented to Damongo.

The spy sent a routine report that Celeste and Paul had gone upcountry to Ganta.

Gambini saw a unique opportunity to ingratiate himself with Damongo and gain revenge against Celeste. His Kru canoemen, salted with a few of the desperate white men ashore in Gambia, could make a respectable raiding party, with the proper leadership. The Sosoo village, as well as Ganta itself, would yield a fine assortment of slaves for his Spanish and American slavers due to arrive within the month.

After this raid, if it was successful, Gambini knew the Americans—probably with the British—would hit his fort. But when they reacted, he planned to be on the high seas aboard the American brig *Aeronautica*. The last two trips she'd made to his fort, Gambini had kept an eye on this trim ship. This time the American captain was going to meet a fatal accident, along with his mate.

Gambini was tired of being a landlubber.

Fifty of the free Negro farmers, and their sons, enlisted in the Ganta militia Paul and Dr. Samuel were forming. Monrovia was slow in sending enough guns and ammunitions, and uniforms were out of the question. The militia drilled with native spears.

Until the Ganta militia was armed, Dr. Samuel wasn't going to unfold his plan for disrupting Ashanti and Dahomey slave traffic.

Paul still cherished his plan to take Gambini's fort

Cannons & Roses

by surprise, and destroy it and him. But until he was more sure of his free Negro militia, Paul didn't intend to share his plan with Dr. Samuel.

Celeste was homesick for the first time in her life, and completely miserable. Surrounded by Negroes, she felt as if she were the last white woman on earth. The Sosoo cook and house girl didn't help matters. The woman's idea of cooking was to boil everything—meat, rice, potatoes, vegetables—and all in the same iron pot.

Celeste wondered if the Sosoo girl had ever used water to bathe. She was certain that she'd never been introduced to a bar of soap. When Celeste tried to force the girl into taking a bath, the cook flew into a rage. Celeste had just enough grasp of Nigger-English to understand a bath for the girl broke a tribal taboo. She would bathe only when it was time for her to marry.

Except for sweeping out the dirt floor of the mud house, the girl was useless. She stood all day in a corner of the house and stared off into space.

"I'm sorry, but you can't fire either one," Dr. Samuel told Celeste when she asked. "It would disgrace them with the tribal elders."

With teaching school and training his militia Paul didn't have much time for his new wife. When she complained about the cook and the girl, Paul said, "You've been spoiled, Celeste. You've had a slave at your beck and call since you could toddle."

"When I want a lecture from you, I'll ask for one!" Celeste flared at him. "You've brought me out to the end of nowhere, without a white face in sight, and you expect me to like it. Well, I don't."

Paul was tired. "You came out here of your own

Cannons & Roses

free will," he said, then asked, "Isn't my face white enough for you?"

Celeste realized she was about to cry. "Yes, yes, it is. Damn it, Paul! What's happening to us? I've become a shrew!"

"Come here." Paul was slouched in one of their rickety chairs.

Celeste slid onto his lap, arms around his neck, her eyes closed, waiting for his kiss.

The chair collapsed, dumping them on the dirt floor. After a startled moment, Celeste began to laugh, and Paul joined her. She'd landed on top of him and wouldn't move so he could get up. Their laughing wrestling match on the floor of the room aroused them both, but when Paul tried to take her, Celeste resisted.

Paul was no longer a tired man.

They wrestled and rolled all over the floor, knocking over chairs, neither speaking; and the more Celeste stubbornly resisted him, the more Paul wanted her. She matched her strength against his and knew she couldn't win this battle, nor did she want to prevail.

She wanted to be raped.

"I give up," she gasped finally.

Paul drove into her savagely, still pinning her wrists to the floor, his swollen face inches from Celeste's so he could see the flicker of pain in her eyes.

"That's *good!*" Celeste's mouth found his.

Paul had lifted Celeste's limp body from the floor, and carried her to the bed. "Are you all right?" he asked.

Celeste sighed. "Never better." Her eyes were closed. "I'll have my breath back in a minute. Have you ever raped a woman before?"

"No."

"You do it very well."

"Is that a compliment?"

Celeste opened her eyes to stare up into his face. "If the shoe fits," she told him, "you'd better wear it."

Paul grinned. "I think we were about to have a quarrel."

"Is that so?" Celeste said. "I don't remember." She caressed the line of his jaw. "I can think of a much better way to spend this night."

4

Ashanti warriors treasured their trade muskets and gunpowder for the noise they made. Traders wrapped musket barrels with wire to prevent an explosion that would tear off an Ashanti head, but warriors still were able to ram enough black powder in their muskets to explode the weapons. The Ashanti never considered carrying an unreliable musket into battle and despised tribes that did.

Six- or seven-foot spears, and knives resembling the Malay kris, were weapons enough for any Ashanti male warrior, or one of Damongo's Amazon women. Men carried a long, narrow shield. The women didn't bother.

Warfare was a centuries-old Ashanti art.

Damongo's dead uncle had schooled him in the art. Killing your enemy was a pleasure an Ashanti could enjoy only up to a point, his uncle taught his nephew. The object of warfare was to take captives and booty.

Cannons & Roses

A typical Ashanti raid on a village saw the warriors sweep in first, after the village was ringed with Ashanti to prevent escape. When their work was finished, and it usually was, quickly, the Ashanti women were the second wave. Their job was to butcher the wounded, but, more important, collect captives.

Selected captives for them to torture and butcher would slake their blood thirst.

One precept Damongo's uncle stressed: Never divide your forces. Strike one village—and only one village—at a time. So Ganta and the Sosoo village between the town and the river presented a problem. Damongo wanted the white woman. He also wanted all the Sosoo he could get to sell to Vincent Gambini.

Against the advice of his chiefs, Damongo divided his warriors into two parties for the dawn assault on Ganta and the Sosoo village. He also violated another of his uncle's rules. Damongo decided to lead the party assaulting Ganta himself. Traditionally, once an attack was launched, Ashanti kings and chiefs gambled or otherwise diverted themselves. Reports from runners were received with a careless shrug. It was considered bad form or an insult to the warriors to show any anxiety about the outcome.

Dawn was the traditional hour for an Ashanti attack.

Vincent Gambini had recruited three men as desperate as himself, and as ruthless, to raid the Sosoo village, and in the confusion kidnap Celeste after he'd killed Paul. Gambini was an expert at sea warfare. Ship handling, grappling, and boarding were his forte.

He'd trekked forty-two of his Kru canoemen within striking distance of Ganta and the Sosoo village. The Kru were armed with cutlasses and pistols. Formidable warriors in their own right, when properly led, the Kru were a match for the Ashanti. Against unorganized free Negroes, and the peaceful Sosoo, they would have no trouble carrying the night.

Gambini had decided on a night attack. They would sweep through Ganta from the east, and he would capture Celeste to present to Damongo (when he'd finished with her). Since he was leaving Africa, a gift to Damongo was no longer necessary, but Gambini thought it a fitting revenge.

The Winchester Arms Company was experimenting with a repeating rifle, using brass cartridges. The American Colonization Society, chronically short of money, bought two cases of the experimental rifles at a bargain price. They were shipped to Governor Roberts in Monrovia.

Deviled by Paul's urgent requests, Governor Roberts sent these rifles up to Ganta, promising more suitable weapons for Paul's militia as soon as it was possible.

There were five rifles in each case.

Paul kept one, issued one to Dr. Samuel, and stored the rest, with ammunition for them, in the schoolhouse.

Gambini's base camp was across a river ford from Liberia, a mile above Ganta and the Sosoo village. Damongo's Ashanti were grouped on the Liberian side of the river, half a mile below Ganta and the village. Moonrise was at eleven that night.

In the late afternoon, the sun set into gathering storm clouds west of the river.

A few minutes before sunset, torrents of rain drenched the Kru and the Ashanti, and turned the river into a boiling flow of high water. It was impossible for Gambini's Kru to ford until a few minutes before dawn.

Damongo's Ashanti considered the sudden storm a bad omen.

The evening before, Paul had been disturbed and restive. For no good reason, he'd been depressed and irritable all that day. He'd planned to issue the remaining eight rifles to his best militiamen, but the storm prevented that. The next day would be soon enough, but getting ready for bed, Paul had the feeling there was something important he should have done.

Celeste was in bed. She was tired and yawning. Paul was sitting across the room, working the action of his new Winchester.

"Are you going to play with that all night?" she asked.

Paul looked up. "No."

There was a crack of thunder and the rush of rain.

"Is something bothering you?" Celeste asked. She had to raise her voice. "I hate it here when it rains!"

Paul laid aside the rifle. He remembered a question he'd meant to ask Celeste. "Why did you visit Dr. Samuel today?"

Celeste's mood changed. Paul sensed she was gloating inwardly. "A small matter, Paul."

"Are you sick or feverish?"

"No."

He came over to sit on the side of the bed. In a ruffled nightgown, with ribbons at her throat, Celeste reminded him of a child with a secret, and a sudden rush of affection made him take her in his arms. Her head was against his chest.

"I love you," Paul said.

"I know." Celeste's voice was muffled. "I can hear your heart saying that."

Paul's hand found her heartbeat. The sweet scent of her hair was in his nostrils. Paul kissed the top of her head.

"All right," he said. "Tell me."

"Tell you what?" Celeste teased.

"You know something I don't."

"I know many things you don't. I'm a woman. Remember?"

"That fact is hard to forget," Paul said.

Celeste sat up, and brushed hair away from her face. "We're going to have a baby. You'll be a father. Dr. Samuel says I'm two months with child."

Paul's was a radiant grin. "Hey! Will it be a boy or a girl?"

"How should I know, stupid?" Celeste laughed. "If I follow my mother, it could be both. Dr. Samuel says that's entirely possible."

The Baltimore chapter of the American Colonization Society had sent Ganta the bell that hung in the church steeple. Except on Sunday, it was to be rung only in case of an emergency. Up early the next morning, because absorbing Celeste's news had made it a night of fitful sleep for Paul, he decided to call together his men and issue the rifles.

The disturbed and restive mood of the day before was still with Paul.

The hot morning sun drew tendrils of steam from the wet ground as Paul strode toward the church. On his way, he met Dr. Samuel. The mulatto was carrying his new Winchester rifle as he limped along.

"Hunting elephants today, doctor?" Paul asked with a grin.

"No. Tigers." Dr. Samuel grinned back. "From your step this morning, I judge that Celeste told you the news."

"That she did," Paul admitted.

"Congratulations."

"Thank you. Is she going to be all right?"

Dr. Samuel nodded. "She's a strong young woman."

By dawn the river was fordable, and Gambini's Kru came across, but they were grumbling.

"Mate, these buggers ain't in a good fighting mood," Gambini's Cockney lieutenant told him on the Ganta side of the river. He was a wizened little man with a black patch where his right eye should have been, and only the stub of a left arm. "We can't hit the village and town for an hour yet. I ain't so sure, myself, we don't get ambushed."

Gambini jabbed the Cockney with the barrel of his pistol. "You yellow limey bastard! We do it. Back down now and I'll blow your guts."

"Now, guv'nor, don't get your dander up," the Cockney whined.

Gambini uncocked his pistol and thrust it back into the red sash around his waist. "I want Abullo and Cuffee with me. When you hear my first shot, you and the others hit the village."

"Aye." The Cockney touched his forelock. He grinned. "Randy for the white bitch, ain't you? Bet your tool is rock-hard right now."

The church bell pealed, and both men cocked their heads to listen. "This ain't Sunday, is it?" the Cockney asked. "Bow bells, that sound reminds me."

"It's not Sunday." Gambini listened for urgency in the pealing bell and heard none. "Get on with it," he ordered.

"Aye, guv'nor." The Cockney touched his forelock again.

Gambini was a fool, he decided. He had no intention of leading the Kru attack on the village. Not with them niggers smelling Ashanti. Cut the black buggers loose, get back across the river, and dust out for Gambia. That's the ticket.

Finished ringing the bell, Paul sat on the church steps, waiting for his militia to assemble. He studied the Sosoo village, and the river beyond it.

Smoke from morning cook fires rose straight up into the morning air, and he could hear the chatter of children. The river was a band of silver under the early morning sun. Across the river, Mount Nimba's five-thousand-foot crest wore a necklace of fleecy clouds.

Paul decided that building some sort of stockade to protect the Sosoo village would be a good project for his militia. So many docile Sosoo in one place might be a temptation that some tribal king, hungry for slaves, couldn't resist.

Damongo had had to convince his subchiefs once again that splitting the attacking force was the best way to accomplish their objective. Each man was promised a free turn with the white woman, while she was still fresh and strong. Damongo didn't like the idea—he wanted all the gold he could get from his men for using Celeste—but his generous offer assured their cooperation.

The Ashanti divided. The pealing church bell meant nothing to them. Moving to the attack, both men and women were aroused to a fever pitch. Mouths were dry, throats tight. A skirmish line moved silently through high elephant grass toward the village, while Damongo led his force of a dozen warriors up a steep path toward Ganta.

The mop-up force of Amazon women giggled and laughed as they sharpened spears and knives.

Gambini and his two picked Kru had reached the outskirts of Ganta. The town was awake, so sudden surprise was out of the question, but Gambini's reckless streak curbed any second thoughts.

The Cockney was right about one thing: the thought of Celeste at his mercy had Gambini aroused. He cocked the pistol, and raised it to fire.

Paul had distributed the rifles. Most of the militiamen were returning to their chores in Ganta, but several were discussing with Paul what sort of stockade to erect around the Sosoo village. Only one of the remaining few was a rifleman.

They heard the crack of a pistol.

"What was that?" Paul asked, and knew the answer before anyone could answer.

The Ashanti swept out of the elephant grass, and across a plowed field, shouting their high-pitched war cry, and brandishing spears.

Women in the village screamed and snatched for their children. Sosoo men cried the alarm and ducked into their wattle huts, most of them to cower and hide, but a few emerged with clubs and knives.

The leaderless Kru tribesmen, crouched and waiting on the opposite side of the village, were first astonished when the Ashanti attacked on their own signal, but the war cry of their traditional enemy galvanized them into action. Screaming hate, they rushed into the village from the opposite side.

Paul grabbed back the rifle he'd just issued. "Ring the bell!" he ordered.

Paul raced toward the village. None of the men with whom he'd been talking followed. After a frozen moment, one man jumped inside the church to tug at the bell rope, sounding a frantic alarm. The others tore off, each in the direction of his own home.

Paul skidded to a halt on a knoll just outside the Sosoo village. Kru and Ashanti were locked into a swirling melee, fighting with spears and knives, and a few Krus using clubbed muskets. Sosoo were fleeing in every direction.

Damongo's Amazons were running to join the fray. When they did, Paul realized, the outnumbered Kru were finished.

The pistol shot from the town!

Paul spun around and raced off in the direction from which he'd come.

Celeste started when the pistol cracked. Windows of the mud-walled house were narrow slits, designed that way by early settlers when they built the house. It could be used as a fort. Unable to see anything through these slit windows, she stepped outside.

While she stared in the direction from which she thought the pistol shot had come, the Ashanti war cry split the morning silence. Celeste spun around.

"My God!" A hand jumped to her throat.

Others were coming out into the narrow street.

Paul was Celeste's first thought. He'd gone to the church. But his new rifle was just inside the door to her house, and he'd told her it was loaded. Jamie McCoy had taught Celeste to use firearms when she was a child. He had taken her to hunt rabbits.

Take the rifle. Find Paul!

But she hesitated, spellbound by the clash of Kru and Ashanti in the middle of the Sosoo village. It had all the unreality of a play, as Kru and Ashanti impaled each other on their war spears, and krislike knives twinkled in the bright morning sun.

That moment of hesitation cost her dearly. When she turned, she blundered into the arms of Vincent Gambini, flanked by a pair of the most evil-looking naked Negroes Celeste had ever seen. Too stunned to struggle, Celeste went limp. She'd never forget the sweat-smell of Gambini.

Gambini rushed her back through the open doorway, into the house, accidentally kicking the rifle away from the wall.

"Got you, you McCoy bitch!" Gambini glosted, and wrenched her to her knees by the grip on her hair.

Celeste heard the Italian's surprised yelp.

Scrambling away, when his hand released her hair, she turned, still on her hands and knees, and saw Gambini clutching at the broad spear blade that was protruding from his rib cage. Gambini's eyes rolled up. His knees buckled. He went down, still surprised, hands clenching the spear blade that had impaled him.

It was like a nightmare sequence. Where Gambini had been, Damongo stood, his naked black body glistening with palm oil, the bizarre face-tattooing making him a demon.

Celeste scrambled for the rifle.

In the street, outside, Damongo's Ashanti were butchering the two Kru who'd come with Gambini. For a moment, Damongo diverted his attention from the white woman who was his prey.

It was enough.

Celeste had the rifle, and at point-blank range, she

jerked the trigger. The heavy slug knocked Damongo back against the wall.

She levered a new shell into the firing chamber. Her second shot doubled the Ashanti king over, and he pitched forward on his face.

Still on her knees, Celeste glimpsed a second man bursting through the doorway into her home, and she swung the rifle, jacking in a fresh cartridge, and squeezed the trigger.

It was close quarters, but she had no chance to aim. Celeste should have missed, but she didn't. The third bullet struck Paul in the middle of his forehead.

5

From the increasing amounts of blood he was coughing up, Dr. Samuel Corey knew his days were numbered, but death didn't frighten him. The militia strike against Damongo and the Ashanti would never take place, Dr. Samuel knew, and it was just as well.

Dr. Samuel had implicit trust in God. He saw the finger of God in the pitched battle between the Kru and Ashanti, a circumstance that permitted the militia to rally nine rifles, under his leadership, and drive the Ashanti, when they were victorious over the Kru, to the river.

Pinned on the riverbank, it became a battle without quarter, the worst defeat in Ashanti history. The few wounded who tried to swim the river were dragged under by gathering crocodiles.

By nature, Dr. Samuel wasn't a bloodthirsty man. His God was a deity of mercy and kindness, but Dr.

Cannons & Roses

Samuel felt the slaughter of the Ashanti men and women were justified. Word would spread to the Dahomey and other warlike tribes ringing Liberia. There would be no more slave raids into Liberia.

Dr. Samuel thought that what work God had chosen him to do was nearly finished. But Celeste and her grief were heavy on his heart. It was three weeks since Paul had been laid to rest. His dry-eyed wife hadn't left her house since, and had refused to see him, or anyone else. Dr. Samuel was afraid for her sanity.

Today, Dr. Samuel resolved, the widow was going to see him, if he had to batter down her door. He knelt and prayed for the gift of understanding, and the strength to break through the wall Celeste was building around herself, then picked up his ebony cane and limped through the town to her house.

The stupid house girl opened the door when he rapped on it with his cane.

"White missy no see no one," the thick-tongued Sosoo girl said.

Dr. Samuel waved her aside with his cane.

He found Celeste in bed, although it was the middle of the morning, staring up at the roof, hands clutching the thin blanket to her breast. She was pale and hollow-eyed, and for a moment didn't seem to remember who he was.

Without a word, Dr. Samuel sat on the edge of the bed to take her pulse.

Celeste turned her face to the wall.

Peeling down the blanket, he explored her abdomen with gentle fingers. When he'd covered Celeste again, Dr. Samuel asked, "Do you believe in God?"

He gently turned her face so she had to meet his eyes. "Only Paul's body is dead. Mine will be, too, and very soon, but my soul will join Paul's, and both of us will watch to see what you do with the life Paul placed in your womb." He brushed hair away from her sweaty forehead. "We're not supposed to understand God's plan, Celeste. We are supposed to have faith that there is one."

Celeste reached a hand toward him, and Dr. Samuel took it.

"Time for you to go home," he said, "but, first, you must weep, not for Paul, but for yourself."

"I can't," Celeste said in a husky voice.

"You can."

"No."

"Yes." His own eyes filled with tears.

A sob caught in Celeste's throat.

Dr. Samuel gathered her in his arms and was shocked at her lightness. "Cry."

"Oh, God!"

He patted her back. It was as if this gentle touch had touched a trigger somewhere within Celeste. She was wracked with sobs that seemed to tear her apart, and cried out, beat Dr. Samuel's chest with her fists. He tightened his arms around Celeste's shuddering body.

When Dr. Samuel laid her back on the bed, Celeste was limp, with her emotional self washed clean. At that moment, there was a stirring in her womb. Wide-eyed, Celeste stared up at Dr. Samuel.

"My baby moved!"

He smiled. "They sometimes will do that, you know. Now let's get you bathed and dressed so you can begin to pack. Paul's ashamed of the way you've tried to give up."

"I can bathe myself," Celeste said.

"Good." Dr. Samuel rubbed his palms together. "I'll

get that lazy girl to bring water and a towel. Then you're coming to my place for a decent meal."

Celeste wasn't sad to leave Liberia aboard the British mail ship, *S. S. Calypso*. She was a steam and sail packet returning from India, crowded with soldiers going home on leave, and East India Company pensioners. The *Calypso*'s maiden voyage was to the British West Indies, hence her name.

Dr. Samuel saw her off in Monrovia. Celeste had formed a close and warm friendship with the mulatto since Paul's death. In a series of quiet discussions with Celeste, Dr. Samuel had opened up a new vista regarding slavery.

"White slave owners are as much captive as the souls they own," he'd told her. "They're warders of people sentenced to a lifetime of labor, guilty of nothing but being born black."

He readily acknowledged that Liberia wasn't the answer after emancipation. Dr. Samuel had little use for the abolitionists.

"They're sowing seeds of an ugly hatred that is going to cause bloodshed someday," he prophesied. "Governor Roberts and I have talked about this, and we agree. Left alone, slavery will vanish in a few generations, and the southern white man will take credit, but a number of northern zealots want a cause to fret you Southerners who own slaves. They have it in slavery."

"You seem to have more wisdom than any other man I've ever met," Celeste told Dr. Samuel. "I wish you could deliver my child."

Aboard ship, Celeste had time to be alone with herself, and a chance to consider her future now that Paul was gone. From Liverpool, she would take a ship to Boston. With luck and a swift passage, she would arrive in Boston Harbor just before Philippa bore Jamie's child.

In Liberia she'd had one letter from Jamie, and another from her mother, who was planning to marry DeWitt Scott.

Jamie had managed a trip to Boston. He was awed with the experience of becoming a father and was convinced the baby would be a son.

Influenced by Professor Jackson, Jamie had decided on a military career, and through Senator Russell Barnes, would obtain an appointment to the military academy at West Point as soon as he graduated from Washington College.

Jeanette wrote: *Remember Delray Bone? He became the overseer at The Columns after your Red River property was sold. A Natchez woman who was living with him shot young Bone to death last week because he trifled with a nigra wench.*

After their marriage, she and DeWitt would live in Spanish House. Bliss and Richard were at Great Oaks.

Albert Grymes had astounded New Orleans by marrying his octoroon.

Colonel Carroll was terminally ill. *It's a wasting disease,* Jeanette wrote. *The man lives in terrible pain that no amount of peach brandy or laudanum helps much. Alicia Carroll is a much stronger woman than any of us suspected. Under her management, The Columns is prospering.*

Richard Carroll was going to run for Congress.

Bliss and Richard make a most handsome couple, Jeanette wrote, *but I worry about them. Bliss wraps him about her little finger. As her mother, I shouldn't say this, but your sister flirts.*

The last word had been underlined three times.

When you and Paul come home, Jeanette wrote, *and you will, stay with DeWitt and me.*

Celeste still smiled when she remembered the postscript to her mother's letter.

Damn! I'm getting rheumatism! And if I plucked out all the gray hair, I'd be bald! DeWitt is getting an old woman.

The word *old* was underlined three times.

Home to Celeste was Boston, Christopher, and Philippa. Great Oaks was where Bliss and Richard lived. Spanish House would be the residence of Jeanette and DeWitt. Celeste was determined not to return to Louisiana. She hoped that she and Philippa could live together, with their children, in the Winchester house Philippa Randolph had mentioned.

Christopher Randolph's understanding of herself and Paul had set him on a pedestal in Celeste's mind. He'd lost a woman he loved; now she'd lost the man she'd loved. Celeste wanted to see him again, as much as she wanted to meet Philippa a second time.

Each day aboard the *Calypso* was another day farther away from Liberia, and, yes, Paul. Celeste could remember him now without tears.

But never without longing! She had shuddering nightmares about the body she'd loved so much now in a grave.

Celeste remembered every detail and nuance of the last time they'd been together. She'd worn mourning black when she came aboard the *Calypso,* with a veil. But each night at sea, in her small cabin, Celeste stripped to study her body in the small mirror, as best she could, lifting her breasts to the mirror, as she'd done to Paul.

Tears would come. But Celeste was too young, too

resilient, to believe there would never be another man to taste her lips and thrust into her.

"Nuns," she told herself, "are made of stronger flesh than mine."

Celeste was learning, also, that men considered a widow, no matter how recently widowed, fair game. The purser, a friend of Dr. Samuel, had hinted plainly enough he was willing to "*console*" her for the length of the voyage. (He had a wife and children in Aberdeen, she knew.) And the handsome first officer, Peter French, with his cap of curly brown hair, and sunburned face, had been more explicit.

On the moon-drenched boat deck, pointing out different stars, his arm had crept around her waist. A hand came up to cup a breast.

"You need a man," he whispered in her ear.

"I have one," she whispered back, removing his exploring hand.

"You're not a widow?"

"Oh, yes, I'm a widow all right," Celeste said, "but my man is in here." She placed a hand on her still-unswollen belly. "Would you like to feel his heartbeat?"

Peter French beat a hasty retreat.

Dr. Philip Ross had just finished examining Philippa Randolph. *It's a welcome change,* he thought. *I'm sick and tired of women so goddamned modest I have to fumble around through sixteen petticoats!*

"Maybe we can manage a normal delivery when you've come full term, Miss Randolph," he said, then corrected himself. "I'm sorry. Mrs. McCoy."

Philippa perched on the edge of his examination table, comfortable in her slip. "Tell me the truth, doctor," Philippa said. "I'm small, aren't I? And a bit

Cannons & Roses

old to be having my first child. I want to know my chances."

"It's going to be a hard delivery."

Philippa's eyes didn't flicker. "So?"

"There are ways . . ."

"To abort my baby?" Philippa laughed. "No, thank you, doctor."

"It's going to be difficult," he warned her.

"Just being a woman is difficult," Philippa said. "May I have my dress?"

Philippa's mother had died after bearing her brother. Whatever face she showed the doctor, Philippa was honest enough to admit to herself that she was frightened. Death had no appeal whatsoever to her, but the fierce desire to bear Jamie's baby was unabated.

She was tired of her swollen, clumsy body, and anxious to have childbirth over with.

Philippa and Christopher Randolph had an easy relationship. It was as if they had always known each other. The other Boston Randolphs were scandalized with their living situation, but knew Christopher too well to say anything to him about it. When provoked, he could be very difficult. The Randolphs hadn't forgotten the uncle he threw out of his office, bodily, into Milk Street, or the cousin who'd had to swim ashore from his ship.

Celeste had written Christopher from Monrovia before she embarked. She had been scant with any details about Paul's death, but asked sanctuary so she could bear his child.

Philippa looked forward to Celeste's company during her confinement.

Christopher Randolph was eager for Celeste to arrive.

* * *

Cannons & Roses

Under both sail and steam, the *Scotsman* was trying to establish a new record for the Liverpool-Boston run, but it wasn't a smooth crossing of the North Atlantic. The ship pitched, strained, and tossed, battering passengers and crew alike, but Captain Angus Bull was a dogged Scot. He wanted to prove what his new Clyde-built ship could do.

Celeste had kept to her cabin as long as she could stand being confined. The *Scotsman* was plowing the first reasonably calm sea off the Newfoundland fishing banks the ship had encountered since clearing Liverpool's harbor. It was evening with a misty fog. Celeste decided to take a turn or two on deck.

Captain Bull had ordered full speed ahead. The whole ship shook and quivered to the tempo of the slashing paddle wheels. She was dressed in full sail to catch the light air.

At the stern, Celeste paused to watch the churning, twin wakes of water stirred up by the paddle wheels. Off to starboard, a number of lights were winking and bobbing.

"What are those?" she asked the crewman standing lookout.

"Them be fishing smacks, ma'am," he said with a thick Yorkshire accent. "Fish for cod, they do. Last time across, Captain Bull scattered the like of them like they was quail." He chuckled. "The air, she turned blue. Yankee cussing is something to hear, but not if you're a lady."

Celeste laughed. "I hope I'm a lady, but I've heard fancy swearing. My father was a ship's captain."

"Aye? And who did he sail for?"

"Himself. He was a privateer in the West Indies when he met my mother," Celeste said.

The seaman sighed. "Those were good days. These blasted teakettles ruin life at sea."

"They get us there faster," Celeste said.

As she started forward, the Yorkshireman said, "Watch that you step lively, ma'am."

"I will," Celeste promised. "Good night."

"Good night, ma'am."

The fresh salt air felt good on her face. She drank it in with deep breaths.

"Fog's thickening, sir," the starboard lookout on the flying bridge sang out.

"Reduce speed?" the first officer asked Captain Bull.

Angus Bull knocked ashes from his pipe and stowed it in a pocket. "Mr. Gillespie, when I want your advice, I'll be asking for it," the captain growled, then stepped to the engine-room speaking tube. "Mr. McAdams, half ahead now."

The first officer hid a grin.

Celeste rounded the corner from the side deck just in time to see the three-masted schooner's rigging dead ahead, and to hear the forward lookouts yell, "Ship ahead! Collision course!"

Bells rang.

Celeste was too fascinated by the spectacle of mast and sails to brace herself. She heard the grinding crash as the *Scotsman* rent the schooner *Emily* nearly in half, just before the *Scotsman* shook herself like a wounded thing. She was smashed back against a steel bulkhead as if someone had hit her with a fist.

On the deck, helpless, Celeste saw the three masts felled by the collision. Trailing tattered sails and snakes of rigging, the middle mast crashed on the *Scotsman*'s forward deck, and Celeste was smothered by wet canvas. She started to struggle free.

It was no use. A yardarm across her stomach was pinning her to the deck. There was a quick, tentative cramp inside Celeste.

I'm going to miscarry! she thought.

6

Angus Bull's nephew from Glasgow, Rory McDonald, was the ship's doctor, and this was his first Atlantic crossing. One seaman on lookout duty had been lost over the side, and his mate had suffered a broken leg. By keeping way on his ship, thrusting its prow into the schooner, Captain Bull kept the schooner afloat until most of her crew were brought aboard the *Scotsman*. Five seamen and the schooner's cabin boy were killed or drowned in the grinding crash.

Celeste lay buried by canvas, and pinned to the steel deck, only half-conscious most of the time, until the damage-control party found her the next morning. She was carried on a litter to the ship's infirmary.

Doctor McDonald had just finished his first amputation. White-faced and trembling, he'd just downed a full tumbler of smoky scotch whisky when they carried Celeste in.

"She's the little lady the first officer shined to," one

Cannons & Roses

burly seaman told Dr. McDonald. "The wee lass has bled something fierce."

Out from under the yardarm and smothering wet canvas, Celeste was fully conscious. She saw the doctor's pale, freckled face looking down at her, the empty whisky glass still in his hand. She sensed the fear and frustration in the young man.

"Doctor."

The seamen who'd brought her were gone.

"Yes?"

"I'm sorry, but I was going to have a child, and now I think I've lost it," Celeste said. Her smile was weak, but it was warm. "I'm a nuisance, aren't I?"

"That you are not, lass." Dr. McDonald took a deep breath. "When I've washed my hands, we'll see about you and the bairn."

"I'll be obliged," Celeste said, and closed her eyes. Nothing of Paul was left now.

When the *Scotsman* docked at India Wharf, Celeste was brought ashore on a litter. She was pale and weak, but without fever, and there would be no infection.

"Oh, my God, what's happened to you?" Philippa asked.

"I lost my baby." Celeste was matter-of-fact. "Hello, Christopher." Dr. McDonald had accompanied Celeste ashore. "This is my sister-in-law, Philippa McCoy, and her cousin, Christopher Randolph, doctor," she said, then told them, "Dr. McDonald saved my life."

"You've a plucky lass here," Dr. McDonald said. "I did what I could in my bumbling way, but she needs a better man now."

"She'll have the best in Boston," Christopher promised.

* * *

Cannons & Roses

Dr. Philip Ross complimented Dr. McDonald's emergency surgery, but told Celeste, "It's very unlikely you'll be able to bear another child. I'm sorry to have to tell you this, especially a healthy young woman like yourself."

Celeste laid back against the pillows. The doctor was watching her closely. There was some weakness yet from loss of blood, but cared for and coddled by Philippa and the two Irish maids, she was gaining strength every day. Dreams of being buried alive under wet canvas had begun to fade.

Paul was dead. His child had never lived. There wouldn't be another child.

I should be crushed, Celeste thought.

She wasn't.

"Somehow that doesn't seem too important," she told the doctor. "There must be something else for me to do with my life."

"You certainly take this well." Dr. Ross was perplexed, because he'd expected a sobbing, stricken woman. "I wish I had more female patients like you, Mrs. Wright."

"Thank you," Celeste said. "But if you had, there wouldn't be many babies to deliver, would there?"

Dr. Ross chuckled. "Maybe that would be a blessing in disguise."

"Don't you like babies?" Celeste asked.

"I'd like them better without fretful mothers," Dr. Ross confessed.

Celeste laughed. "Or frantic fathers?"

"Them, too."

"I'm afraid you have one of those on the way here," Celeste told him. "My brother Jamie is coming to Boston next week. Philippa wrote him that she is about due."

307

Cannons & Roses

* * *

Philippa went into labor at ten o'clock on a Friday morning, and Dr. Ross was in attendance half an hour later. Jamie wouldn't arrive until Sunday morning. Celeste was on her feet and determined to help Dr. Ross deliver Philippa's child.

"It's strange," she told Christopher. "I keep thinking of this baby as Philippa's, yet I'm sure my brother had something to do with the matter."

It was late Friday afternoon. She and Christopher were having tea and sandwiches while Maura and Kitty O'Reilly spelled Celeste. Dr. Ross had gone out on another call, but promised to be back within the hour.

"I'm certain he did," Christopher said with a chuckle. He regarded Celeste over the rim of his teacup. Placing the cup back in its saucer, he said, "Jane Marie would have said something like that."

"You really loved her, didn't you?"

"Yes. You remind me of her, you know." A hand strayed to the white streak in his hair. "I don't know what it is about you, though. In most ways, you're entirely different."

"She was a woman, and so am I. Maybe that's it."

"Maybe." Christopher grinned. "What do you think we'll have upstairs, a boy or a girl?"

"Philippa is sure it will be a girl."

"Has she told Dr. Ross?"

"I don't know, but I suppose she has."

Maura was in the doorway to the small sitting room at the front of the Beacon Hill house. "Ma'am, can you come? Miss Philippa is asking for you."

Celeste followed the girl upstairs.

"Maura, Kitty, leave us alone," Philippa ordered. She motioned Celeste to the straight-backed chair near the bed.

Cannons & Roses

"Are the pains worse?" Celeste asked. With a damp towel, she wiped beads of perspiration from Philippa's forehead. "Dr. Ross will be back soon."

"They're worse," Philippa said, "but that's not what worries me right now." She reached for Celeste's hand. "Did you know I never had a sister?"

"No." Celeste patted her hand.

"I never did, only brothers. Celeste, Jamie won't be here before this baby is born." Philippa closed her eyes, and Celeste was alarmed by the waxen pallor of her face. "I want you to tell him something for me."

"I will, of course," Celeste said, "but why can't you tell him yourself? He'll be here the day after tomorrow."

"I have this feeling I may not be," Philippa said. "I tell myself that's foolish, that I'm only having my first baby, but the feeling won't go away."

"Philippa . . ." Celeste paused. Something about the other woman's resignation stifled the protest she'd been about to make. "What is it you want me to tell my brother?" Celeste asked quietly.

"Two things. That I've loved him with all my heart, and he's not to feel blame." Philippa's face contorted, and she moaned. "That hurt!" she said, when she had her breath.

"I'm sorry."

"Not your fault," Philippa said through clenched teeth.

The first hard labor pain passed.

"Celeste, if anything happens, will you raise my daughter?" Philippa asked.

"Damn, you're *going* to make it!"

"Surely. Of course I am." Philippa's was a tired, strained smile. "But for now, humor an older woman. Will you?"

"Of course I will."

"That's good." She closed her eyes and squeezed Celeste's hand. "I feel better now."

A summer storm had been building all day Friday. The air over Boston was still and muggy. No breeze off the North Atlantic cooled the city, and everyone noticed the strong smell of stale fish.

Bathed in perspiration, Philippa fought agonies of pain, hands clenched.

"Damn!" Dr. Ross whispered to Celeste. "It's going to be a breech birth."

"What's that?" she asked.

"Rear end first, instead of the head. I can't seem to turn the rascal."

"Your hands are too big."

Dr. Ross looked at her small hands. "I wonder."

"Tell me how, and I can try," Celeste said.

"We've nothing to lose," Dr. Ross said. "The child will be strangled by the cord if it's not turned. Wash in carbolic acid."

By the time Celeste managed to turn the child in Philippa's womb, the woman was unconscious, but her body kept trying, and the baby came headfirst, to be laid in Celeste's arms while Dr. Ross tried to save Philippa.

It was no use. Just as the thunderstorm broke, Philippa died, without regaining consciousness.

Celeste took the child, wrapped in a towel, to Maura, Kitty, and Christopher.

"We have a girl," she said in a dull voice.

"Philippa?" Christopher asked.

Celeste shook her head.

BOOK II
Philippa Randolph

PART ONE

1

*I*t was Sunday morning and a fine clear day after the storm when Christopher's man drove Celeste to the railroad station to meet Jamie. Church bells pealed. The streets of Boston were empty except for men, women and children in their Sunday best. She worried about baby Philippa, left in the care of Maura and Kitty. It was the first time she'd been beyond the range of the child's cry.

"Do you want me to meet the train with you?" Christopher had asked at breakfast.

"I don't think so," Celeste had told him. "It will be better if I meet him alone. After all, he's my brother."

Christopher shrugged. "If that's the way you want it."

Under its tan, his face was pale, and there was weariness in his eyes because he hadn't slept since Philippa's death. While Celeste and the Irish girls minded the baby, Christopher had kept vigil in the parlor with her mother's body.

Christopher wondered why she looked so much younger in death than she had in life.

His patient free Negro, Amos Cinque, a refugee from Santo Domingo who had been a small slaveholder there, had shaved Christopher that morning and offered brandy.

"It is hard to meet death," Amos told him, "but more difficult, sometimes, to face another's grief."

Christopher seldom took a drink before dinner, but as he toyed with the food on his plate, he was glad he had this morning. Jane Marie had been pregnant when she died.

"How will you tell Jamie?" he asked Celeste.

"I'll just tell him," she said.

In the carriage that Sunday morning, as she neared the station, Celeste wished that Christopher was with her. She'd been too involved with the baby to give much thought to her brother. She'd been at Philippa's bedside when she died, with her own hands feeling death's coldness creep from the hands and feet up the arms and legs.

It had been a quiet death. Just a few moments before oblivion (but only for her body, Celeste thought), Philippa's eyes had cleared, and she spoke to someone in a clear voice.

"Yes, I'm coming, I'll hurry," she'd said.

Someone other than the doctor and herself had been in that room with Philippa in her dying moments—Celeste was convinced of that. God? Celeste thought not. Perhaps Philippa's mother, or her father.

No one spoke to God in such a matter-of-fact voice. They were at the station.

Cannons & Roses

"I will wait here with the carriage," Amos said. "It is better you meet your brother alone."

"Yes, I think so," Celeste said, but wished Amos would come to the train with her.

There weren't many people in the gloomy South Station that smelled of smoke, cinders and stale food. The travelers who were there put Celeste in mind of lost souls waiting in a vacant corner of hell.

"Damn!" Celeste said to herself. "How can I tell him?"

The train was chugging in, and fresh soft coal smoke stung Celeste's eyes, so she seemed to be crying when Jamie rushed off the train.

"Hey, sister!" He hadn't noticed her tears, or thought they were gladness because he had come. Jamie's was a rib-straining embrace. "Has the baby come yet?"

"Yes, she has."

Jamie offered a handkerchief. "So it is a girl, after all. How could Philippa be sure?" He had his bag on his shoulder, and an arm around Celeste. "We'll name her Philippa, of course. Is there a carriage?"

"The carriage is that way."

"Let's get there, then, and stop dragging your feet. I'm going to get my appointment. Professor Jackson says it may be possible for me to bring my wife and baby to The Point."

Jamie was sweeping her through the station.

"These last few months have been hell with Philippa up here." Celeste wondered what had happened to Jamie's shyness and reserve. Celeste hadn't been in touch with Jamie, Bliss, or Jeanette since returning from Liberia. "What happened to your nigger . . . to Paul?" Jamie asked. "Is he here in Boston?"

They were on the sidewalk outside the station.

315

Cannons & Roses

"No, Paul is not," Celeste said. "Paul was killed in Liberia. I'm alone."

"Oh, say, that's bad." Jamie sounded relieved. He wasn't going to ask how it happened, Celeste was relieved to discover. With a disapproving glance at Celeste, Amos had taken Jamie's bag. "Why are we waiting here?"

Jamie's seeming indifference about Paul's death armed Celeste. "Jamie, there's something you have to know. The baby is just fine. But . . ." She hesitated. "I don't know how to say this."

Jamie had gone dead quiet. He licked his lips, but he wasn't going to help his sister.

"Philippa died when she was born."

Jamie didn't move. His face was blank of any expression. Celeste was reminded of the blankness of Paul's face at the moment the bullet slammed into his brain.

Now I've killed Jamie, she thought, with a rush of panic. *As surely as if I'd shot him.*

Steel shoes clanked on the brick pavement as the restless horse shifted his feet.

Celeste reached to touch Jamie, but he jerked away from her, turning his back.

Celeste waited.

When Jamie turned back, he asked, "Where is she?"

"At Christopher's, in the parlor. He's been sitting up with her. The funeral will be tomorrow."

Jamie had only heard the first sentence. He was in the carriage. "Hurry," he told Amos.

Amos swung down to help Celeste into the carriage, then mounted the box again, and tickled the horse with the buggy whip.

* * *

Cannons & Roses

After her withdrawal when Paul was killed, with its deep-seated feeling of guilt, Celeste should have been able to understand Jamie's reaction to the fact Philippa was dead. But she didn't.

Barely acknowledging Celeste's introduction of Christopher, Jamie locked himself in the parlor with Philippa's body. He remained there alone all day.

"He hasn't asked to see his daughter yet?" Celeste asked Christopher that Sunday afternoon. "I don't understand."

"Your brother needs time. When he's ready to face the child, he'll ask," Christopher said. He hoped he was right.

Christopher was wrong. When Jamie finally came from his vigil in the parlor, he was haggard but determined. He found Celeste holding the baby.

"I'm going away on the first train tomorrow," Jamie told his sister, without a glance at the child. "You tell Christopher. I don't want to talk with anyone."

"Jamie." Celeste offered him the baby.

"No." His voice was a rasp.

When Jamie turned to leave, Celeste asked, "Where are you going? You haven't had anything to eat."

Jamie gave her a disgusted look. She heard the street door close behind him. When the baby was tucked in, Celeste found Christopher in the parlor again.

"I'm worried about my brother," she said. "He won't even look at his child."

There were dark smudges under Christopher's eyes, and his hand trembled slightly when he poured Celeste a brandy.

"What do you expect so soon?" he asked her. "The baby killed his wife—or at least that's the way he sees it now. My wife died because she was pregnant."

"I didn't know that. I thought it was some sort of disease."

"We were on the Indian Ocean, and it was too hot and stuffy for her in our cabin," Christopher said. "She was three months with child, and very sick mornings. A heavy sea was running, but she came on deck, against my orders, for a breath of air. A seventh wave swept over the waist of the ship, and she was gone."

"A seventh wave?"

"Your father would have known what I mean. For some reason, every seventh wave is usually bigger than the six before it. Or the one after it."

"I'm sorry about your wife," Celeste said, still puzzled. "But I don't understand why Jamie rejects Philippa's child."

"He blames the baby—and himself—because she's dead. I can't say it more plainly than that."

"No, I guess you can't," Celeste said.

"How do you plan to care for the baby?" Christopher asked. "By the way, I haven't been able to discuss Philippa's will with you yet. Did you know she's left you her house in Winchester?"

"No. Why would she do that?"

"It was a codicil, when she first thought she might not live. A place for you to take her child to be near her father, I suppose."

"I just don't know what to do or say."

Christopher regarded Celeste steadily, and she noticed his eyes were slightly bloodshot. "You and the baby can stay on here as long as you like. After all, she is kin to me."

Celeste shook her head. "It wouldn't be right. What would all your relatives think?"

"No worse than they think right now, but I hold the Randolph purse strings. At best they'll credit me with hiring a beautiful young governess for my cousin's child." Christopher smiled and poured himself and Celeste another brandy. "They will all rally in North Church tomorrow. What do you say?"

"Let me think about it, Christopher."

"You don't want to take the baby to Winchester to be near Jamie, not right now. Stay on. We'll see how it works. You'll need the help of Maura and Kitty. And you're not too well fixed for money."

"Now, how would you know that?" Celeste asked, nettled. "My financial affairs aren't your business."

"Not yet," Christopher admitted.

Celeste stood beside the casket to stare down into Philippa's composed, so young-looking face, as if the answer was there, while Christopher waited.

She sensed now that Jamie wouldn't soon accept young Philippa—if he ever did. Someday he might marry again, but that wouldn't be soon. Even then Jamie's wife might not want another woman's child. Celeste was sure that she wouldn't. Jamie was embarked on a military career, and would soon be at West Point. And after that?

Most important, from the moment her hands touched Philippa, still struggling to be born in her mother's womb, something began to happen inside herself. She suspected, then, and knew afterward, the first time she held the squirming, warm little body in her arms, that Philippa would be *her* child.

Despite Philippa's generosity, Winchester was out of the question. She'd be stranded in the Shenandoah Valley with little money and a child to raise. Could she take Philippa to Great Oaks, or perhaps Spanish House?

The answer was no. Bliss and Richard were at Great Oaks, Jeanette and DeWitt, by this time, at Spanish

Cannons & Roses

House in New Orleans. Neither couple needed a third wheel—especially one with a small child.

Philippa would be the only child given her to raise. Philippa would need a father. Christopher wasn't just being kind.

I'm being cold-blooded, Celeste admitted to herself.

She knew, despite his efforts to conceal his feelings, that she had a strong attraction for Christopher Randolph. Celeste liked the man well enough, and knew his kindness, also feeling that she should have some sort of mutual attraction toward him, but there wasn't any.

That part of me must have died with Paul.

She heard Christopher set his empty glass on the metal tray. It was a beautifully chased silver tray made by Paul Revere.

"Well?" Christopher said.

"I'll stay on."

"Good. Another brandy?"

"No, thank you, Christopher. It's time to feed the baby."

"Don't worry about your brother."

It was sometime in the early morning. Jamie didn't know the time because he'd forgotten to wind his watch —a gift from Philippa when they married. It was a beautiful gold antique watch some Randolph had brought from England. Jamie would lay it away, never to wind it again.

Star points flickered out on the dark, flowing water.

Jamie wouldn't—couldn't—attend her funeral tomorrow. Philippa would understand. She'd hated funerals.

Philippa was past tense now, Jamie realized. Philippa had liked to ride. Philippa had liked champagne laced

Cannons & Roses

with brandy. Philippa had liked to make love in the morning.

"God!" Jamie pressed fists to his temples.

Maybe she wouldn't have died if he'd been there by her side, where he was supposed to be. Too late now. The creature they'd made together had killed Philippa. It wasn't fair. God had made a mistake.

"Damn you!" Jamie shouted toward the sky.

Birds startled from their perch in the nearest tree chirped, then were still.

Jamie could get up, wade out into the Charles, and find peace under the water, but Philippa wouldn't like that.

He couldn't return to Lexington and Washington College. Too many memories of his happiness with Philippa.

West Point? To hell with it! Philippa wouldn't be there.

Chester had received a letter recently from a friend who'd migrated to Texas. His friend had urged Chester to join him and help throw the Mexicans out of what should belong to the United States.

We've got to have this Texas place for the South, Chester's friend had written.

Why not? Texas would be a new beginning. He and Philippa had never discussed the Texas question.

His mind made up, Jamie started to find his way back to the Beacon Hill house. On his way, a discouraged woman with a bedraggled feather in her hat accosted Jamie.

"Want my company?" she asked, with a painted smile.

"How much?" Jamie asked.

"You talk funny," the woman said. "You one of them southern *gentlemen?*"

Cannons & Roses

"I'm from the south," Jamie said shortly, wondering why he'd paused. And why he'd asked the question.

God knows, he didn't want her!

"You sleep with your niggers?" She was tipsy.

"No."

Arms outstretched, she turned before him. "You name your price, gentleman."

"Here." Jamie pressed a ten-dollar gold piece in her hand.

The woman stared at it, bit the coin, then it disappeared down her cleavage. "My place ain't too far."

Jamie brushed past her. "Go there, then. It's late."

"Ain't I good enough for you?" The prostitute was shrilly angry.

"No," Jamie said, over his shoulder.

"You goddamn, lousy, southern puke!" she screamed.

Jamie spun around, and raised a hand.

The woman fled, the sound of her heels echoing in the empty street.

Jamie wondered why he'd given her the gold piece, until he realized he'd done it because a murderous wrath had begun to stir inside him.

With Philippa dead, a woman like that one had no right to be alive, and walking the street.

2

*B*ecause tomorrow would be Philippa's first birthday, Celeste had given both Maura and Kitty a day off to attend the Roxbury Fair with their suitors, the O'Grady boys, recently arrived in Boston from Ireland. Christopher had released Maura from the last three years of her indenture, and she was as free as Kitty to marry whom she pleased, and work wherever it pleased her. But both Maura and Kitty had become attached to Celeste.

"Miss Celeste, now, she's a breath of spring back in our Emerald Isle, when the mood is on her," Maura claimed. "And a banshee when it ain't."

To Christopher's amusement, both girls tried to copy Celeste's mannerisms and the casual way she dressed.

Petted and spoiled by the Irish girls, within a year Philippa would have become a sturdy little tyrant, and spoiled brat, if it hadn't been for Celeste's mothering. Christopher had to leave the room to hide his laughter when Celeste and Philippa locked horns, as he put it. In temperament they were alike, both headstrong and quick to anger, only to regret their anger just as quickly.

"Who would ever know Philippa isn't Miss Celeste's own babe?" Kitty said to Maura once. "They's as alike as peas in a pod."

It was true. Philippa had Celeste's hair, black as coal, and the same crystal-clear blue eyes. But her bone structure and height at one year promised a woman as tall as her mother.

With the Irish girls out of the Beacon Street house, Celeste had the kitchen to herself to bake a chocolate cake for Philippa's birthday party. In the past year, she'd become a remarkably good cook, considering her plantation upbringing.

Christopher would be in from the maiden voyage of the Randolph steam packet, the S. S. *Jefferson,* on tomorrow's tide, in time for Philippa's party. Celeste hummed to herself as she worked and listened for Philippa who was down for her nap.

It had been a good year, this first for Celeste in Boston. She'd needed sanctuary for herself and her niece, and Christopher had offered it. But Celeste had soon abandoned any cold-blooded plan to marry him so Philippa would have a father. That was too crass.

While she beat the batter for her cake, Celeste marveled at how much the past twelve months had healed the emotional state she was in when she debarked at India Wharf. She had Christopher to thank for this. He wanted her, and Celeste knew it, but he'd never so much as touched her.

Christopher knew Celeste needed time to rebuild the

shattered walls of her inner strength, and restore her emotions. He didn't remark that she was sublimating her sensuality with love and care for the baby. At this point in Celeste's life, and after the ordeals she'd endured, Christopher thought this was right and fitting.

She was young. She would heal fast.

Their arrangement had shocked the proper Randolphs at first, but they'd come to accept Celeste as a widowed aunt, solely interested in the welfare of her niece. Celeste had dressed and conducted herself to heighten this illusion, and always referred to Christopher in public as "Mr. Randolph." She sat demurely in a separate pew whenever they attended North Church on Sunday morning.

Christopher had been at sea for the past six weeks. Before he made the decision to take command of the new Randolph flagship, they'd had an easy comradeship, based on their mutual interest in the baby, which was temporarily satisfactory, but both knew it couldn't last.

There was too much physical attraction between them. For Christopher, it had begun the moment they met. His kindness, consideration, sense of humor, and innate strength had wooed Celeste from a morass of self-pity. Because of the desire quickening within her that she was not yet ready to acknowledge, Celeste was glad when he went back to sea.

But the interval of his voyage had given Celeste the chance she needed to sort out her feelings, as Christopher had known it would. She was young. She was healthy. Celeste needed a man, but not any man.

Christopher was quietly confident that Celeste would recognize the need within herself for him while he was absent.

Celeste's cake was in the wood-stove oven. She tiptoed from the kitchen to the front hall, and up the stairs to the small sewing room Christopher had let her fit out to be Philippa's nursery. The child was curled up with a small fist pressed to her mouth, and frowning as if it was necessary to concentrate upon sleeping. Celeste covered her with the light blanket she'd kicked to the foot of the crib.

Philippa smiled in her sleep, made a satisfied sound, and turned over. She raised a bare foot to push the blanket back where Celeste had found it. With a sigh, she began to snore lightly.

Jamie had been off somewhere in Texas since his daughter was born. His rejection of Philippa had shocked Celeste at first, but by this time she was used to the idea. Would he find another woman he could love as he had Philippa Randolph? Celeste was doubtful.

The interlude in her life spent with Paul seemed dream-stuff now, and more so with the passage of additional time. She had begun to wonder if there had been more to their mutual attraction than sex.

In fairness to herself, Celeste thought there must have been, that she'd given herself to Paul in love, but Liberia and the subsequent loss of Paul's child had curtained off that part of her life.

Here in Boston was the beginning of Celeste's future, and she knew, now, that Christopher Randolph was a linchpin in that future.

Icing Philippa's cake, Celeste hummed to herself, and then broke off, laughing.

Maura had come back for something while Kitty and the O'Grady boys waited outside in a carriage they'd hired for the occasion.

Cannons & Roses

"Would that be the wedding march you're humming to yourself, Miss Celeste?" Maura asked from the kitchen doorway. Her face was flushed, and her eyes dancing with mischief. "Aren't you the forward colleen!"

"And what are you doing back here on your day off?" Celeste made a shooing motion with her hands. "Scat! I'd like a little privacy, if you please."

The S. S. *Jefferson*'s maiden voyage to Havana and other West Indies ports had been an unqualified success.

Donald McKay was the naval architect who'd designed and built her according to Christopher's specifications, and under protest when the keel was first laid in New York.

"Sail's the thing," McKay had told Christopher. "For the next fifty years, anyway."

McKay, who'd recently migrated to New York from Nova Scotia, had his first clippers on the ways for the China trade. These slender and graceful ships, with their sharply raked prows and immense spreads of canvas, were his dream of the future.

"More cargo space below decks, and better passenger accommodations—that's what I need in this ship, McKay," Christopher told him. "These seagoing greyhounds you're building are fine for rushing tea back from the Orient, but I need a bread-and-butter ship. Another thing. Within twenty years, your sailing ships will be as extinct as the dodo. Do you want to make a little wager?"

"Nay." McKay scowled. "There's a canny feeling in my Scots bones you could be right."

Christopher was certain that he knew the future of steam. He'd staked his reputation and the financial security of Randolph Shipping Lines on it, and it looked as if he'd won. The *Jefferson* was rigged for sail—depending entirely on steam just yet would be foolish—but she was built around the engine below decks, as the English had begun to build their ships. A single large paddle wheel astern drove her instead of a pair amidships. She had an extra-wide beam, and a bluff, sturdy hull.

No thing of beauty, the *Jefferson*. But she'd carried manufactured goods to the islands and was bringing back raw sugar for rum. The profit from this first voyage, Christopher knew, would settle the minds of his more timid stockholders. It had been a tooth-and-nail fight to get her built and launched. Stubborn bullheadedness on Christopher's part had won that battle.

Now that she was in trade, the *Jefferson* was going to win the war for him, so he could phase out sail and bring in steam. In his cabin, on the drawing board, were designs for a ship without masts for sails, and driven by a pair of giant screws instead of the conventional paddle wheels.

Christopher grinned to himself, anticipating McKay's remarks when he showed him those designs.

On the bridge, with the first streak of daylight just showing along the eastern horizon, Christopher braced against the slight roll of the ship as she rounded Cape Cod and listened to the muffled beat of her steam engine. She was making a good ten knots without so much as a handkerchief to catch wind. Christopher planned to take her into Boston Harbor with bare masts.

Would Celeste bring the baby and meet him at India Wharf? Christopher hoped she'd missed him as much as he'd missed her.

"We're going to have to talk about us," he muttered to himself.

"Aye, sir?" the helmsman asked, over his shoulder.

"Steady as she goes, man."

"Aye, sir."

It must be all this sea air, Christopher thought. *I'm as randy for Celeste as a billygoat.*

A year was a long time to wait for any woman, but Celeste was worth it.

Celeste had taken Philippa into her own bed, and the child was cuddled against her back as she watched dawn break through the open window of her bedroom. The fresh morning air streaming in that window was a heady wine.

Celeste had slept fitfully. Nearly every sleeping moment had been plagued with erotic dreams. Christopher was a key figure in all those dreams!

Philippa's feet found the small of her back, and pushed.

"So you'd kick me out of my own bed, you little vixen?" Celeste whispered. "Well, off you go to your crib."

She scooped the child into her arms and kissed the top of her head. "Happy birthday."

When Philippa was tucked in, Celeste paused outside the nursery, at the head of the stairs whose polished length disappeared into the downstairs darkness. She debated a visit to the kitchen for an early snack, but decided against it. Instead she went along the hall to Christopher's bedroom and pushed open the door.

Morning light showed her his bed that she'd never seen, a broad ship's bunk with drawers beneath it, flush against the far wall. She moved on into the room,

Brussels carpet tickling her bare feet. Celeste sniffed the subtle smell of Christopher when she threw open a wardrobe door, to bury her face in the sleeve of his jacket.

Celeste tried the bed. Hands clasped at the nape of her neck, she stared up at the ceiling. She was amused.

What if he found me here?

His dressing gown was neatly folded over the back of a chair. Getting up, Celeste ducked out of her nightgown, dropping it on the floor, and shrugged into Christopher's dressing gown. It was big enough for two of her!

A sharp, yelping cry from Philippa, down the hall, and Celeste pulled up the robe to race to the nursery and crib.

Philippa was on the floor, beside the crib, more angry than hurt. Celeste snatched her up.

"Me fall!" Philippa sobbed.

"Sure you did." Celeste held her close. "How did you manage?"

The child sniffled. She settled her head between Celeste's neck and shoulder, to chew on her fist. "Me fall." Her voice was contented, and sleepy now.

Celeste took Philippa back to bed with her.

It was Kitty's turn that morning to bring up Celeste's breakfast tray, and she found her asleep, with Philippa in her arms, both of them enmeshed in Christopher's dressing gown.

She stifled a giggle and backed out of the room. Downstairs, she found Maura yawning in the kitchen.

"Faith, Maura, if I was to tell you, would you believe Miss Celeste and the wee one are asleep in one of Mr. Christopher's robes, and her with not a stitch on?"

Maura patted another yawn. "I'm thinking that Sean O'Grady has your head in a whirl."

Kitty raised her hand. "I swear it, on the Blessed Mother."

When Christopher came down the gangplank, Celeste's heart felt as if it had turned over, and the hustle and bustle of docking, with its calls and oaths of stevedores, faded. She was standing back in the shadow of a warehouse, alone and uncertain. Christopher had seen her.

Without smiling or even raising a hand, he came toward her, weaving through the hurrying people. His was patient but determined progress, and then Christopher was before Celeste and took both of her hands.

"I've missed you," he said.

She waited, but Christopher didn't draw her to him, so it was Celeste who disengaged her hands, only to raise them to his sunburned cheeks, and draw his face to her own.

What she'd meant to be a brief kiss became something else when his arms crushed her body to his, and his mouth covered hers.

Celeste stumbled, but his body pressed hers against the wall of the warehouse, and his arms locked her tighter.

Then she was free. Involuntarily, a hand jumped to cover her mouth, and Celeste's eyes widened.

Christopher grinned in the lopsided way Celeste remembered so well, but he said, as if nothing had happened, "How's my Philippa?"

Celeste had to catch her breath before she could answer. "Sassy," she said.

His eyes appraised Celeste. "I like your dress."

"It's new, thank you."

"I'll send for my sea bag later." He was escorting her toward the carriage, but Celeste felt as if she was walking a foot off the ground.

Amos Cinque greeted them with a wide grin when they reached the carriage. "Welcome ashore, captain."

"Glad to see you again, you rascal," Christopher said. He tossed the man a package.

"What's this?"

"Shawl for your wife, bless her, earrings for your daughters, some special Havana tobacco for you."

When they were moving, Celeste teased, "Didn't you bring Philippa and me anything?"

"There's a doll or two in my sea bag for Philippa," Christopher said. He reached in the pocket of his jacket and handed a small package to Celeste. "For you."

Her fingers trembled as she tugged at the ribbons and paper.

Whistling softly, Christopher stared around at the streets of Boston.

Nestled in Celeste's hand was a chain made of tiny gold links that suspended a gold cross crusted with small diamonds. She sucked in her breath. The workmanship was superb!

"Christopher, this must be worth a fortune!"

"Here." He took the gold chain and deftly fastened the clip, his fingers brushing the nape of her neck. This time his lips just brushed Celeste's. "Wear it in good health."

3

Philippa had spent her first birthday climbing all over Christopher, when she wasn't playing with the Carib Indian dolls he'd brought from the island of St. Thomas. She'd gone to bed limp and exhausted, but only after Christopher consented to tuck her in, and tell her a bedtime story.

Maura no longer lived in at the Beacon Hill house. She and Kitty shared a room at Mrs. Buckley's Boardinghouse for Young Women. Although she wasn't Irish herself, some of Mrs. Buckley's best friends were, so she accepted Irish roomers, but only if they were Bible-reading young women of good character.

Mrs. Buckley justified having Papists in her house.

"My girls and I gather for Bible readings every morning," she told her friends. "They hear from me how a truly Christian woman can think for herself, without running to some rheumy old priest. So I'm doing missionary work with the heathens in our midst."

But Mrs. Buckley was strict about what she called "Idolatry." No pictures of Jesus, Mary, the Mother of God, or crucifixes were permitted to decorate *her* rooms.

Maura and Kitty retaliated against this stricture by lighting a candle for Mrs. Buckley whenever they sneaked off to early mass.

"Just wait until St. Peter tells her about all them candles we lit!" Kitty crowed. "The good woman will have crying fits."

With Philippa finally asleep, Christopher joined Celeste in the parlor. It was a cool evening, so she'd lit the fire Kitty had laid, and set out a carafe of the peach brandy Jeanette and DeWitt had recently sent.

She'd let down her hair, and gotten out of her tight-fitting new dress, bought for the occasion. She was wearing a brocaded silk dressing gown over her undergarments, with a stiff collar in the Elizabethan style. Kitty, who was adept with the needle, had helped Celeste make the gown while Christopher was gone.

Christopher found Celeste thoughtfully poking at the fire. "Is she asleep?" she asked.

"Finally." He grinned. "I believe she'll stay that way, too. A teaspoon of good rum never hurt any child."

"You should be ashamed of yourself!" Celeste laughed. She put aside the brass poker and settled on the couch.

From the doorway, Christopher watched Celeste pour two crystal tumblers of peach brandy. "I thought we might enjoy a southern drink tonight," she told him.

"Mind if I smoke?" he asked.

"Yes."

Christopher paused, a Havana cigar halfway to his mouth, and cocked a surprised eyebrow.

Celeste laughed. "Teasing," she said. "You live here, remember?" She struck a match and rose to light his cigar. "Hmm. Smells good."

"Do you want one?"

"I don't think so."

They were sparring, and both of them knew it, because that impassioned kiss on India Wharf had paced them all day to this first moment alone.

They toasted each other with the peach brandy. Then, before she could refill the glasses, Christopher set her tumbler, and his, on the mantlepiece.

Celeste was on the couch.

Christopher leaned an elbow on the mantle. "Look, I'm pretty damned direct, Celeste. It's a bad habit, I guess, but I'm too old to change. I want you tonight, tomorrow night, and every night, so long as we both shall live. The yes or no is up to you, but don't say 'maybe'." He paced the room as if it was the bridge, or a quarterdeck. "I'm older than I should be for your husband. You can't bear me children. Did you know I knew that?"

"I've thought Philippa might have told you before she died."

"She did. She also told me something else."

"What was that?"

Christopher stopped pacing. He reached for Celeste's hands and raised her from the couch. "She said I'd be a fool if I ever let you get away."

Celeste smiled. "Bless Philippa."

"I'm many things, but no fool."

"Who said you were?" Celeste asked in a quiet voice. "Can I say something?"

Cannons & Roses

Christopher's was a wry grin. "Permission to speak granted, madam."

She put her hand over his mouth. "Be quiet." When she removed her hand from his lips, she replaced it with her lips, and pressed the length of her body against his, arms locked around his neck.

"Celeste . . ."

"I said, 'be quiet,'" Celeste told him. "You can carry me upstairs, and I think it should be your room. I left my nightgown there."

"I know." Christopher lifted her. "I found it this morning."

"I thought you might."

"Vixen!"

"Hush."

Celeste helped him out of his clothes before she started to remove her own. In the flickering candlelight, with her back to the bed, Celeste took her time. But her heart was pounding, and blood sang in her ears.

A glance over her shoulder, when she was finally naked, told her Christopher was as fully aroused as a man could be.

She was ready, too. It was as if warm, sweet honey flowed in her loins instead of blood.

I'm too thin, she thought.

She turned to face Christopher on the bed, and was rewarded by his quick intake of breath. She touched her breasts, and went to him.

Christopher sensed her readiness and took immediate command, entering with gentleness, but then driving deep.

Celeste's was an involuntary cry of gladness. Lashed

Cannons & Roses

by sensuality she'd thought would never be with her again, Celeste writhed from one climax to another, and after that, still one more.

They fell apart.

"Thank you," Celeste said.

Christopher heaved a sigh. "You're welcome."

"I wonder now why we waited so long," she said in a dreamy voice. She raised on an elbow to look down into his face. "But what are we going to do about the fact I can't bear you a son?"

Christopher caught his hands behind his neck. "We have a daughter. It's enough. She will be raised as a Randolph, since Jamie has relinquished his parental responsibilities."

"Will it always be?"

"Yes."

Celeste had another thought. "Should I become only your mistress, Christopher, you could marry some healthy woman to have you a son."

"That's nonsense," Christopher said in a sharp tone of voice. "You're going to be my dutiful wife."

"Dutiful? I've always wondered exactly what that means," Celeste told him.

Christopher grinned. "You've just been very dutiful, and considerate of my ugly masculine needs."

"So *that's* what it means," Celeste said, as if she'd just made a discovery. "My great-aunt Sarah! I didn't know I wasn't supposed to enjoy what we just did. Six weeks is a long time to be at sea. I need to practice, too, if I'm to be a good wife."

Christopher grinned. "You are what my great-aunts would call a shameless hussy."

"I know." Celeste rose on an elbow, and was serious. "In a minute I think I'm going to cry because

Philippa and I love you so much. I'll make you a good wife, Christopher, and that promise comes from my heart."

He touched her breast. "Let me feel it beat."

Celeste covered his hand with her own. "It beats for you, my love."

After a few moments, Christopher's hand strayed down Celeste's body. Celeste turned to him on the bed. "Wait. I'm feeling very dutiful."

"What do you have in mind?" Christopher asked.

"You'll find it interesting."

"Oh, yes." Guessing her intention, his fingers explored the soft, sweet mass of her hair, and he lay back.

Celeste and Christopher, from his room, watched a blood-red dawn. "If I was at sea," he said, "I'd be watching the glass."

"Why?"

"Red sky at night, sailor's delight, red in the morning, sailor take warning."

Celeste reached for her nightgown. "I'd better get to Philippa, and then my room," she said. "Kitty and Maura will be here soon."

Dressing gown and undergarments over her arm, Celeste left Christopher's room just in time to meet Maura in the hall, on her way to the nursery.

"Good morning, Miss Celeste." The girl's face flushed, and she looked away. "I was thinking maybe the baby is awake."

Celeste hoped she wasn't blushing, too.

"Christopher thinks we may have a storm today," Celeste said, and immediately wondered: *Why am I saying a stupid thing like that?*

Her sense of humor got the upper hand. "What you

think happened here last night . . . well, it did," she told the girl, "so you can look at me now."

Maura giggled, with imps of mischief dancing in her eyes. "Praise the Holy Mother you don't have to see Father McCully in the confession booth next Friday, Miss Celeste. Faith, and if it weren't for that nosy old man . . ." Maura's hand jumped to her mouth. "And would you listen to my mother's daughter prattling?"

Celeste laughed. "I think the good priest would understand—Christopher and me, I mean. We're to be married."

Maura crossed herself. "It's them candles Kitty and me lit for you and himself. It's a hearty breakfast you and him will be wanting?"

"Yes, please. And, Maura?"

"Yes, Miss Celeste?"

"Serve us in himself's room. Bring Philippa's oatmeal on the same tray, will you?"

His plans for the slave uprising the first day of July were nearly complete, and Denmark Vesey found it increasingly hard to be servile with his white customers. His small carpenter shop near the waterfront in Charleston, a shop from which he could see Fort Sumter, was crowded with fine cabinetwork for the best Charleston families.

Denmark's real first name was Telemaque, but only fellow refugees from Santo Domingo called him that any longer. To local slaves and whites, he was Denmark.

Vesey spoke good English and excellent French. Under the floor of his shop was a horde of literature trumpeting Freedom, Brotherhood, and Equality, as well as accounts of the slaughter of whites on Santo Domingo.

Toussaint 'LOuverture was his idol. The man was dead now—one reason Denmark had to flee Santo Domingo (Henri I had set a price on his head)—but Denmark still wrote secretly to friends on the island, the western half of which they now called Haiti.

Denmark dreamed of an alliance with Haiti when South Carolina, after the bloodletting, was a new Negro republic. But first the slaughter of all white men, women and children. July 1 most of the prominent planters would be gone to northern resorts for a cool summer vacation.

That would be the time to strike. In a secret room behind his carpenter shop were pikes made at the blacksmith shop around the corner. With them Denmark's picked local free Negroes would storm the arsenal and seize arms.

Denmark had worked three years to put together his plot, and it involved nearly every free Negro in the state, as well as dozens of carefully selected slaves.

It was June 10. Everything and everyone involved in Denmark's plot was ready to strike. Once Denmark had achieved his goal, he was certain black troops would pour over from Haiti to help him and his loyal followers drive off any counterattack the United States might make.

In the meantime, he had the cabinet to finish for Mrs. Charles Rodney, the woman whose husband was in command of the arsenal. Denmark himself had promised to kill Mrs. Rodney and her three young children. Denmark had insisted that she and her family would be his prey, because she'd been kind to him. There would be torture, rape, and looting before everything was under his control. It couldn't be helped. But Mrs. Rodney and her beautiful children would die at his hand, and mercifully.

As he polished the rosewood panels of her cabinet, Denmark debated the kindest way to kill Mrs. Rodney. Cut her throat? Break her neck? Shoot her?

Poison? On Santo Domingo he'd rid himself of a rival that way, but the man had died a horrible death, so Denmark ruled out poison for Mrs. Rodney and her children. She'd been too good to him the last time he was taken with the fever.

A hulking, whip-scarred dock worker, a half-witted giant, would be his right hand man July 1. Rufus was dog-loyal to him, and had the muscular arms and big hands for it, so Denmark decided he would be delegated Mrs. Rodney's execution.

First, however, he'd assure Mrs. Rodney the children would be under his protection. Time enough to cut their throats when she was dead.

The rosewood panels were showing a high sheen as he rubbed banana oil into them. Denmark would deliver the cabinet personally, so he could study the interior of the Rodney home. He stood back for a moment, hands on his hips, to study his workmanship. This, he decided, was the most superb cabinet work he'd ever done. With its mother-of-pearl inlaid panels, it was Denmark Vesey's masterpiece.

It would be handed down through the Rodney family for generations, he dreamed, and one day would be a museum piece, to be pointed out by succeeding generations.

"That's a Vesey piece, you know, created during his Charleston period."

Denmark's daydream came to a grinding halt.

Cannons & Roses

Rodney would be killed at the arsenal, Mrs. Rodney and her children in their home. Well, he'd work tonight so it would be finished tomorrow.

Denmark wanted Mrs. Rodney to enjoy his masterpiece during the last few weeks of her life. It would repay her for the soup and fruits she sent by a slave the last time he was ill.

Denmark Vesey believed in paying his debts.

Celeste and Christopher decided to be married quietly in the Beacon Hill house, then ship out for New Orleans on the Randolph barkentine *Revere*. It was sailing in ballast to take on cargo at New York, Philadelphia, Baltimore, and Charleston, returning to Boston with refined sugar.

"I'll take over her command, and we can take Philippa with you, if you like," Christopher told Celeste. "We'll be ashore in New Orleans long enough to visit your mother and her new husband, as well as Great Oaks. Will you like that?"

"I'll love it," Celeste said. "You've made Boston a lovely home for Philippa and me, but I have been a little homesick for the South."

Jamie McCoy arrived in Texas after the Alamo had fallen, and Santa Ana had massacred 300 Texans at Goliad. He was in time to enlist with General Sam Houston, and rose in the ranks from private to lieutenant by the time wily Old Sam lured Santa Ana into the slaughter pen at San Jacinto.

Old Jack had taught him tactics well. Commanding a company of bearded and wild-eyed cavalry, men who'd learned to ride chasing steers in the brakes, Jamie and his men cut a column of Santa Ana's cav-

Cannons & Roses

alry into bloody bits before they rode down a battery and sabered the Mexican gunners.

General Sam promoted Jamie to colonel on the battlefield while they were still burying the dead. But back in Austin, Jamie found himself a cavalry colonel without a command. Once the Mexican danger had passed, his company melted away like butter in an August sun.

Virgil Loring's letters had brought Jamie to the fight for Texas independence. They'd been schoolmates at Washington College, but Loring fled Virginia after he got a Lexington girl in the family way, then severely wounded her brother in a duel.

Loring had been Jamie's adjutant at the Battle of San Jacinto, and saved his life with a quick pistol shot. Bearded, with a flowing moustache, Loring wore his taffy-colored hair in two Indian braids, and always went armed with a bowie knife, two Navy Colts, with a Sharps rifle within easy reach.

In Austin, Loring told Jamie, "That British guy, Hugh Forbes, is trying to find men to go up to Kansas. Somebody named Brown is enlisting fighting men."

4

Hugh Forbes, the second son of a wealthy Leeds draper, graduated from Sandhurst with honors, and then bought a captain's commission in the Coldstream Guards. A bad streak of gambling luck made him resign his commission and leave England to seek his fortune in South America. Hugh trained troops and planned strategy in half a dozen revolutions, always working for the highest bidder, before he migrated to Texas during her war of independence from Mexico.

Since he'd been instrumental in shaping up Santa Ana's crack regiments, Hugh was a valuable addition to Sam Houston's staff. The rest of his life he'd take personal credit for the triumph at San Jacinto.

When Houston's volunteer army scattered, Hugh was stranded with Virgil Loring and Jamie McCoy in Austin. Hugh's drinking partner one night, at the Alamo Saloon, was John Brown, Jr., who was in Texas on a scouting and recruiting expedition for his father, the man everyone who knew him called Old Man Brown.

"Dad's at Osawatomie right now putting together a Free Soil rifle company to fight Jim Lane's Missouri pukes," Junior confided after a few drinks. "We get money from eastern emigrant societies—all the money we need to kill off them ruffians from the western hills of Missouri. We need a man like you to whip us in shape."

"My services come high," Hugh warned.

Junior fished a roll of greenbacks from the pocket of his shirt. "Name your price and we strike a bargain."

"I say! What sort of chaps will I have to work with? These Texans are superb fighting men, but they never heard of military discipline."

"All sorts," Junior admitted. "But you can depend on it—my father will keep them in line. Have a deal?"

"I'll ride up there and talk with your father," Hugh said. "No offense, but I do business only at the top. Policy of mine, you know."

"Suits me," Junior said. "Any recruits you take to Osawatomie, there's a twenty-five-dollar bonus in it for you."

"I'll remember that," Hugh promised.

For the next few drinks, Hugh regaled Junior in his clipped British accent with details of the funeral Santa Ana staged for his severed arm and the Mexican dictator's way with boys and girls. As Hugh anticipated, Junior finally asked for the best local whorehouse.

"We'll go to Sally's, and you'll be my guest," Hugh said.

Junior had heard of Sally's famous glass floor, and eagerly accepted Hugh's invitation.

There was a ball and reception room on the second

Cannons & Roses

floor of *Sally's Parlor House, High Class Gents Only.* The floor of this room was clear glass sections. That floor was the ceiling of the bar below.

The evening dresses for Sally's girls, it was said, came from Paris. It was forbidden for a girl to wear anything beneath the flounced skirt of her dress.

Instead of the conventional parade, Sally always assembled her girls upstairs, while the prospective customers sat below, drinking and craning their necks. The girls played at billiards, danced together, or gathered in giggling groups while they waited to be chosen for the night. (It was strictly an all-night establishment.)

"Rather an unusual way to choose a bed companion," Hugh remarked in his best patronizing tone, "but a man isn't distracted by a pretty face."

Sally selected her girls carefully for all shades of coloring, from a flaming redhead to a sultry black-haired beauty from below the border. There were blondes, redheads, brunettes, and Sally bragged about the natural coloring of her girls.

When a drinker decided on his companion, he got a number from the bartender and went upstairs to claim her. Bedrooms were on the third floor. No Negresses or mulattoes were allowed on the premises.

Hugh Forbes got a percentage of every dollar a customer he brought spent with Sally. The next morning, Junior paid their bill. He never could figure out how that happened, or how Hugh could enjoy *three* women at the same time.

While Junior disported himself with Elena, the Mexican, Hugh won $123 playing stud poker with Sally. He also graciously accepted $100 from Junior to pay his way to Osawatomie.

Cannons & Roses

Later that day, Virgil, Jamie, and Hugh rode out of Austin, bound for Kansas.

Hugh Forbes conveniently didn't mention to either Virgil Loring or Jamie McCoy that abolitionist money was backing John Brown. It would be time enough when he'd collected his bounty money for bringing them up to Osawatomie. Hugh thought Virgil would probably join Brown's Osawatomie Rifles, despite his southern heritage. He'd known other men like Virgil.

Killing was the thing with them. It became even more important than money.

About Jamie McCoy, Hugh wasn't sure. Jamie was a moody one. He drank very little and didn't gamble at all. But fired up, as he'd been the day of San Jacinto, Hugh wrote Jamie McCoy down as a holy terror. Men loved Jamie, Hugh realized, and would follow him to hell.

What Jamie did about women was a puzzle to Hugh. He didn't patronize whorehouses and would blush if spoken to by a saloon girl. But he didn't seem to have Santa Ana's weakness for boys and girls. Jamie didn't smoke, chew tobacco, or indulge in opium, as Santa Ana had. Tired of bust-skull whisky, some Texans chewed peyote, a habit learned from the Indians, but Jamie didn't indulge himself in that direction, either.

Hugh's conscience was clear when he invited Jamie to join him and Virgil for a jaunt to Kansas. If Jamie didn't want to fight for the abolitionists, he'd be welcome in the proslavery ranks.

Christopher chose Caleb Stott to be his first officer aboard the barkentine *Revere*. While he was nominally captain for the voyage, Christopher planned to spend most of his time at sea with his new wife and his niece. Caleb was a terse Maine man, from Ogunquit. He was a quarter-blood Indian.

A leather-faced, scowling small man, for years Caleb had sailed from Charleston, coasting Florida and the keys, as well as reaching every port in the Gulf of Mexico.

After this voyage, Caleb would retire to his rocky farm in Maine. For this voyage, Christopher needed his knowledge of Gulf waters, and paid a bonus to get it.

A playpen was constructed on the forward deck for Philippa, and Maura would make the voyage to look after the youngster.

Christopher planned to enjoy his honeymoon with Celeste.

The *Revere* weighed anchor June 1. She was due to reach Charleston late that month to pick up cargo that would be waiting on the docks.

The Kansas-Nebraska Bill was approved by Congress. Missouri had come into the Union as a slave state, and abolitionists didn't intend to lose Kansas to the proslave south. Her status would be decided by popular vote before she was admitted to the Union.

William H. Seward delivered one of his more vitriolic speeches.

"Come on then, gentlemen of the slave states, since there is no escaping your challenge, I accept it in behalf of the cause of freedom. We will engage in competition for the virgin soil of Kansas, and God give victory to the side which is stronger in numbers as it is in right."

The Massachusetts Emigrant Aid Society decided

to furnish each settler going west to Kansas a new Sharps rifle, as well as seed and resettlement money. Randolph money was behind this society, and Christopher opposed the rifles, but William Lloyd Garrison had his way, with Christopher off on a honeymoon.

The society was also financing Old John Brown. Men like Emerson and Thoreau considered him a prophet straight out of the Old Testament, God's strong right arm. His raid into western Missouri, during which he and his seven sons killed a slave owner, liberating the man's twelve slaves, was the mark of distinction Brown had needed.

The slaves were led to Canada. Their owner's horses and cattle were sold by Brown in Kansas. In Leavenworth, Atchison, and Lawrence, Old John Brown was a conquering hero. In Topeka and Wyandotte the proslavery settlers branded him a horse thief.

In Osawatomie, Old John Brown flogged his youngest son with a leather strap until the blood ran because the boy had raped the slave owner's wife before they left her half-crazed, and bleeding, beside her husband's dead body.

A shipment of a hundred new Henry rifles were on the docks in Charleston, waiting for the *Revere*. Consigned to New Orleans, a wrong bill of lading had delivered them to the United States Arsenal in that South Carolina city. Charles Rodney had chosen Randolph Shipping Lines to deliver these rifles because he and Christopher had graduated from Harvard in the same class.

Jane Marie had been Charles Rodney's second cousin.

The Randolph shipping agent in Charleston had also

Cannons & Roses

arranged for the *Revere* to carry a second cargo of paper to New Orleans, so the *Revere* would have to lay in port a week waiting for this shipment.

"You three will stay ashore with Eunice and me," Major Charles Rodney told Christopher and Celeste. "My three girls are going to be delighted with the baby."

While the adults talked, Philippa had been peeking out from behind Celeste's skirt, playing the shy child, but she understood "baby."

"No baby," she corrected Charles. "Girl now."

"And so you are, darling," he said with a chuckle.

Philippa made a face at him and stuck out her tongue, trusting that Celeste wouldn't take exception here in public.

Philippa was wrong. A swat to her backside nearly lifted her off the ground. "We'll have none of that, young lady!"

Eunice Rodney had been a Hampton before her marriage, and her dowry was a fine old house on Broad Street built before the American Revolution.

The Rodney children were six, eight, and ten; Lucinda, Lucy, and Lucille. All three had their young mother's blond hair, and delicate coloring, with the Hampton fine bone structure. Charles had been right; they were delighted to have Philippa visiting, and vied with each other to watch after the child.

Behind the Rodney house was a walled formal garden where Eunice served afternoon tea. The children were playing hide-and-seek. Eunice's maid, a pretty brown-skinned girl, came to pick up the tea things.

"The man Vesey, he come, bring your new cabinet," the girl told Eunice Rodney. "Another man, he wait to see Mrs. Randolph, too."

Cannons & Roses

"Is Denmark waiting to see me?" Eunice asked. "You should have told me the minute he arrived."

"He say not to," the girl told Eunice. "Other man, he say he your captain, very important," she said to Celeste.

Celeste was impressed with the bearing and dignity of Denmark Vesey, when Eunice introduced him. "This is a genius with wood," Eunice complimented. "Santo Domingo's loss has been Charleston's gain.'

Denmark bowed. "You are too kind, madam." He went to supervise the men bringing Eunice's new cabinet into the house.

All this time, Caleb Stott had stood in the background, nervously twirling his cap as he eyed Denmark Vesey.

"What is it, Caleb?" Celeste asked. The man's manner puzzled her. "Has something happened?"

"Begging your pardon, ma'am, but we need to speak alone," Caleb said to Eunice.

Eunice was slightly taken aback, but she rallied to say, "Of course, how thoughtless of me. I really must see that Denmark places my cabinet properly."

"Now that," Celeste said, when she was alone with Caleb in the drawing room off the front hall, "wasn't very polite. What in the world can be so important that you can't mention it in front of Mrs. Rodney? I am a guest in her home."

Caleb ignored the reprimand. "I'll speak bluntly. From a slave on the docks I've just heard an alarming story, and it concerns Mrs. Rodney, as well as her children. May we sit down?"

"Of course."

They sat in chairs facing each other.

"I've sailed from Charleston many times in the past," Caleb began. "Christopher Randolph suspects

Cannons & Roses

I've smuggled runaways aboard his ships, but he doesn't know and has never asked."

"Just a minute," Celeste said. "Don't bring any information to me that I can't share with my husband. Are you in trouble of some kind?"

"Mrs. Randolph, damn it! Hold your horses. To understand the seriousness of what I'm about to tell you, I have to go back to Rufus. I took two of his children out of the harbor in my flag locker, some years ago. They were about to be sold south. So the man, dimwitted though he may be, holds me in some regard. He's told me there's a plot afoot to kill Mrs. Rodney and her children. He trusted me with this information."

"Are you serious?" Celeste asked.

"Never more so, and listen to this. That was Denmark Vesey who was here a minute ago, wasn't it?"

"Yes. Is he concerned?" Celeste wasn't as shocked as Caleb expected she would be, because rumors of slave rebellions, and the murder of their masters and mistresses, were always rampant in the south since the Santo Domingo holocaust. There was little real truth in any of them. "It's hard for me to believe that."

"Is he the Vesey who's a refugee from Santo Domingo?" Caleb asked.

"Yes, he is. The refugee community here thinks highly of him. I understand he's the finest cabinetmaker here in Charleston."

"He's the man, then," Caleb said. "Rufus is too simpleminded to make up the tale he's just told me. On the first of July there's to be a general uprising all over South Carolina, led mainly by free Negroes, but the slaves are disaffected, too. Vesey is the ringleader, and has been planning this thing for years. Rufus came to me because he's supposed to kill Mrs. Rodney."

Cannons & Roses

"Oh, my God!" Celeste breathed. It was a nightmare about to come true.

"I couldn't reach Christopher at the arsenal, so I came here," Caleb said. "Now, Mrs. Randolph, I want your word of honor."

"Yes?"

"I want you to swear the authorities never know how I came by this information. Rufus is a dead man if they find out. Don't even tell your husabnd."

"But the man planned cold-blooded murder!"

"No. Vesey planned it. Rufus was to be his cat's-paw. Do I have your word?"

"You have it, Caleb," Celeste said.

Caleb slapped his cap on his head. "I'll be off to the ship. You know the date?"

"Yes. Today is the twenty-eighth of June."

Celeste sent a messenger to Christopher at the arsenal. She decided not to alarm Eunice until she'd talked with her husband. Christopher came back with the messenger, slightly out of breath.

"We'll talk in the garden," Celeste told him.

"Your expression tells me this is serious," Christopher said.

"I believe it is."

They found a bench at the far end of the garden from the house.

In as few words as possible, Celeste told Christopher what she'd just learned from Caleb.

"Where did he get this information?" Christopher asked. He'd paled slightly. "Coming from the north, Charles had been nervous about something like this happening. We spoke of it just this morning."

"I can't tell you that," Celeste said, "and Caleb won't, either. He's trusted me."

"I see." Christopher chewed his lip. "Caleb and I will have to go to the authorities right away. Where is he?"

"He told me he was going back to the ship."

"Don't breathe a word to Eunice about this," Christopher said. "Time enough for her to know if it turns out to be true."

"Damn it, Christopher, I'm not stupid!" Celeste said. "Give me credit."

Grinning, he raised her chin. "Do you love me?"

"You know how much."

"Some people would call that stupid," he said. "Take care until I get back."

5

Caleb and Christopher went directly to Governor George Hampton with their information. The governor heard them out with an expressionless face. When the men were announced, his secretary had placed on his desk a confidential file on Caleb Stott, and the Randolph Shipping Lines.

Governor Hampton was the principal slave owner in South Carolina, and one of the few prominent men who could afford to deal in slaves. Most slave traders were despised by the plantation owners they served.

"How did you two gentlemen come by this information, may I ask?" Governor Hampton said. "You're making a most damaging accusation about a respected man of color. I've known Denmark Vesey for years and would trust him with my life."

Anger flushed Caleb's face. "Damned if you get the name of my informer, sir, but search Vesey's shop. If the literature and pikes aren't there, *then* you can call me a liar."

Governor Hampton lifted the confidential file, and weighed it on his hand. "I am trying to guess your new game, sir." Hampton's voice had a cutting edge. "A year ago it was stealing nigras from their proper owners. You lied then, when my patrol searched your ship. Why am I to believe you now?"

Caleb clenched his teeth.

"Do you have proof for that accusation, sir?" Christopher asked in a quiet voice.

"No. If I had, your man would be under our courthouse, in a dungeon, and your ship would have been auctioned by the State of South Carolina." Governor Hampton was urbane. "We'll look into these charges, gentlemen."

"I'd advise you to do that speedily," Christopher said. "I have a wife and child in your city."

"Thank you for coming to me." Governor Hampton smiled. "You northerners can't seem to understand how satisfied with their lot our slaves are."

Christopher's voice turned ice-cold. "You are a damned fool, sir. Your rotten labor system is just about to explode in your face while you sit here twiddling your thumbs. Tell me: how safe do you think your family is right now? If Major Rodney is so high on their list, as governor, you and your family must be higher. I intend to question Vesey, and right now, unless you take immediate action."

"You can't take the law in your own hands, even if Vesey is a man of color. I won't have it."

"Then you'd better act, because if you don't, I surely will."

Caleb and Christopher stormed out of Governor Hampton's presence.

Governor Hampton slapped the bell on his desk to call his secretary. "Jarvis, go get him, and bring me Colonel Roberts." Jerome Roberts was commander of the Charleston militia. "I don't give a damn what he's doing."

"Yes, sir," the young man bustled from the office.

From a desk drawer, Governor Hampton took out a cut-glass carafe, and poured himself a drink. He downed the bourbon in one long swallow, wiped his mouth with the back of his hand, got up and strapped on his pistol belt.

Hands behind his back, he stared from the window at the busy Charleston open-air market while he waited for Colonel Roberts.

"So those whispers I've been hearing are right!" he muttered to himself. He slapped a fist into his palm.

The latest report in the Randolph-Stott file mentioned an earnest conversation between the dockworker, Rufus, and Captain Stott. He knew Rufus well. It was Governor Hampton who had to refund the price of his son and daughter, and Rufus bore the scars of his anger, but the dimwitted nigger had told him nothing.

Could Vesey be involved?

Governor Hampton decided that was entirely possible.

"You sent for me, sir?" Colonel Roberts saluted.

"Yes. Take a party of men to Denmark Vesey's shop. Tear the place apart."

"Yes, sir, but what am I trying to find?"

"Pikes."

Young Roberts was incredulous. "Pikes?"

"Those things the French used to carry aristocratic heads through the streets of Paris. Pikes. Also inflammatory literature. And, Roberts?"

"Yes, sir?"

Cannons & Roses

"How many of your young men are still here in Charleston?"

"Not too many, sir. You know how it is at this time of year."

"Depending on what you find at Vesey's, I may declare martial law," Governor Hampton said. "If I do, we'll have to call up every able-bodied man in South Carolina. We may have very serious business on our hands."

Denmark Vesey had planned his secret room, and the hiding place under the floor of his shop, well. The entrance to the room was concealed by boards so cleverly mortised with the wall boards that an inexperienced eye couldn't find the joining.

His lathe straddled the trapdoor in the shop floor and seemed to be solidly bolted to the thick floorboards. Colonel Roberts left his party of five young men loitering in the street and went in to question Denmark alone. Colonel Roberts's father had always spoken highly of Vesey.

"Good evening, Denmark," he greeted Vesey.

"Good evening to you, young sir." Vesey looked up from his planing. "May I be of service?"

Roberts scratched his head, a quizzical expression on his face. "I don't know. Mind if I look around?"

"Be free to do so." Vesey picked up his plane.

Vesey slept in a room behind his shop, and there was a small courtyard behind this room. The room door was open, so feeling foolish, Roberts went into it, at loss where to start his search.

George Hampton has a wild hair up his rear end this time, Roberts thought. *Funny about that. The tough old boy is hard to panic.*

There was a table beside Vesey's unmade bed, with

a Bible on it, and a folded newspaper. Roberts idly picked up the newspaper and shook it out. He was staring at a recent issue of Garrison's rabid *Liberator*. It was a criminal offense for Vesey to have it in his possession!

Colonel Roberts strode out and slapped the paper down in front of Vesey. "You're under arrest."

Vesey's eyes met Roberts's and didn't flicker away. He spit a quick sentence in French.

"What did you just say?" Roberts asked.

"I said, monsieur, that you are the son of a pig," Vesey told Roberts in a calm voice, "and that your mother, and sisters, too, are whores."

"I am not much amused, Mr. Vesey," Roberts said, and stamped the heel of his riding boot on the soft pine floor of the shop. "Pikes?" he asked.

Vesey smiled. "Assuredly, *mon ami*. Good steel pikes."

Roberts shook his head. "Well, I'll be damned."

"Excellent weapons when you have no other," Vesey told him.

"Nice for carrying heads around on the point, I suppose," Roberts said.

"Ah, yes. Very good for that." Vesey smiled. "But I believe you were arresting me."

Governor Hampton had declared immediate martial law all over South Carolina, and North Carolina towns were in a panic, too. As darkness fell, mobs had begun to form in Charleston, as the narrow escape of the white population spread like wildfire.

Colonel Roberts could muster only forty-six militiamen. They were ordered to ring the courthouse. A list of Vesey's followers had been found in his secret room. Police were picking up these free Negroes as quickly as they could. Governor Hampton didn't want the courthouse stormed by a mob as prisoners were crowded into the basement dungeons dating from the 1600s.

Denmark Vesey asked to see the governor.

George Hampton was curious about the man, and as he began to grasp the full extent of his plot, convinced that outside abolitionist help had come from the north.

"Bring him up," he told the jailor. "Have you got that dock nigger named Rufus?"

"No, sir. He's vanished."

"Tell the police to keep looking."

When Denmark Vesey was brought to the governor's office, he was chained hand and foot, but didn't seem to be harmed. Governor Hampton laid a pistol on his desk, and ordered Vesey unchained.

"I've sent for wine," Governor Hampton said. "Sit down over there."

"*Merci, monsieur.*"

"We'll speak English."

"As you wish."

There was a long pause while the two men studied each other. Governor Hampton couldn't help admiring the aloof coolness of this man who'd planned to kill him and every other white person in South Carolina.

Hampton's secretary brought two bottles of the governor's best Bordeaux. Hampton poured a sip of wine into his glass, then filled Vesey's before topping his own.

Vesey sensed the quick intelligence behind that bland, ruddy face, and warmed to Governor Hampton.

Vesey spoke first. "You are going to ask me, a man of color with some standing here in Charleston, and a man of property, why. Is this not so?"

Cannons & Roses

Governor Hampton glanced at a slip of paper on his desk. "You're worth eight thousand dollars free and clear, I understand."

Vesey nodded. "This is so."

Governor Hampton hooked an arm over the back of his chair. "You've guessed right. I would like to know why."

"I can say it in one word. Power."

Governor Hampton didn't blink.

"Do you understand?"

Governor Hampton's eyes narrowed. "I think I do. Tell me, Vesey, do you think it would have happened? You're going to take a lot of free niggers to the gallows with you, and the ones we don't hang will be banished. Was it worth the risk?"

"You were born to power, monsieur. I was not. What would you risk to keep your power, if it were threatened?"

"Everything I have and everyone I know." The bald frankness of his answer astounded Governor Hampton, but he let it stand. He was talking to a dead man.

"Ah, you see?" He held out his hands. "With these I am an artist when working with wood. But it is not enough. Telemaque Vesey would have more, and so I gambled."

Governor Hampton nodded. "You gambled, and you've lost. In a way, I admire you, but that won't stop me seeing you hang. Who in the north put you up to this plotting against people who befriended you when you fled Santo Domingo?"

Vesey sipped his wine. "You have an excellent cellar, Governor Hampton. Not as good as my own, but then you are American, not French."

"Answer my question."

"It was my plot and mine alone, but I doubt you'll

believe that of a man touched by the tarbrush, as you Americans say. I am a nigger, no? Therefore I am stupid." Vesey smiled but malice glittered in his dark eyes. "When you're dead and rotting, sir, I will be remembered long after you're forgotten. This is a sort of power—don't you agree?"

"Your own people will spit on your name."

"No. I will be remembered as a martyr."

Governor Hampton struck the bell on his desk. "Take this man back," he told the jailers. "No torture, do you understand? Finish your wine," he said to Vesey.

"Thank you, sir."

When Vesey was gone, Governor Hampton stared at the liver spots on the backs of his hands, and felt old for the first time in his life. There would be an investigation—an attempt to find some link between Vesey and the abolitionists—but now Hampton doubted there was one.

So long as men enslaved other men, there would always be men like Denmark Vesey, Governor Hampton realized.

Word of Vesey's plot spread like wildfire through Charleston. It quickly reached the plantations, and from one end of South Carolina to the other, slaves were locked up. Slave patrols scoured the roads, and any slave caught without a signed pass was shot or hanged.

Governor Hampton issued an order calling for the arrest of every free Negro in Charleston. For a week the city shuddered with fear.

Charles Rodney took his family to Fort Moultrie, across the harbor entrance from Fort Sumter, while Celeste and Christopher retreated to the *Revere* with

Cannons & Roses

Philippa. Captain Stott took the ship to a safer anchorage at the mouth of the Ashley River. Mobs were roaming Charleston streets, convinced that northern abolitionists were behind the plot. There was danger they would board the *Revere* and set the ship on fire.

Rufus was aboard, hidden in a forward hold. He'd come to Caleb Stott shaking with fear.

"I couldn't feed the poor beggar to the wolves," Caleb explained to Christopher. "Maybe we'd better forget the paper cargo and clear this harbor."

"No. We'll wait the rioting out," Christopher said. "I won't give Governor Hampton satisfaction."

The *Revere* swung at anchor a hundred yards off the Middleton Place Gardens. The third night after Vesey's arrest, Caleb Stott called Christopher on deck and handed him a spyglass.

A mob of a dozen men had captured a young free Negro and his mulatto girl-wife. They'd been stripped, and tied to opposite sides of the same tree trunk, and their captors took turns wielding the whip.

The mob had built a fire to illuminate their activity.

The crew of the ship drifted on deck, drawn by the shouts of the mob, and screams of the young man and his wife.

The bosun came to Christopher. "Goddamn it, sir, can't we lower a boat and put a party ashore?"

Ceelste had come on deck. "Do it," she urged Christopher. She covered her ears to shut out some of the girl's shrill screams.

Their tormentors had thrown aside the whip and were jabbing her with brands from the fire. They'd untied her husband, suspended him from a tree branch by his ankles, and were coating him with tar.

"They're going to burn him alive," Caleb Stott said.

"Sir?" the bosun urged.

"As you were," Christopher snapped at the young bosun. "Nobody leaves this ship tonight."

"You can't stand here and let them torture those two!" Celeste said. "What sort of man are you?"

"I'm your husband," Christopher snapped. "Get below and mind Philippa."

The man's screams drowned those of his young wife—the mob had fired the tar.

Sobbing, Celeste obeyed Christopher. When she was gone, he crossed the ship and retched over the side.

An offshore breeze brought the smell of burning tar and human flesh.

Christopher rejoined Caleb Stott. "Get the ship ready to sail on the morning tide," he ordered. "I've seen enough of this part of the south."

Old John Brown and his sons shared adjoining farms along Osawatomie Creek, and he ruled them and their wives as if he were an Old Testament patriarch. To heighten that illusion he'd grown a white beard that covered his chest and disguised his cruel, knife-slit mouth.

Pale blue eyes with yellow irises and madness behind them stared at a world he despised. He had a plan in the back of his mind to change it. Brown genuinely loved the Negro race. That love was the only soft spot in the case-hardened man. He saw himself as a modern Moses and Africans as his Israelites, a chosen people he would lead to freedom.

A remote valley he'd once visited, high in the Blue Ridge mountains of Virginia, would be their Promised Land.

Kansas was God's testing place for him, John Brown was convinced. It was all part of God's plan. Like

Cannons & Roses

Moses, he lingered in a foreign land, waiting to be called. When the time was ripe, there would be a burning bush.

More often lately he dreamed of blood and saw it while awake in dappled leaf shadows on the ground, or in the water of Osawatomie Creek when the moon was full.

Pounding headaches just before the voice of God spoke to Old John Brown were his cross. He suffered them philosophically these days.

6

When the *Revere* was at sea, and Celeste could look back at the Charleston experience, she realized how much Boston had changed her point of view on slavery. She despised William Lloyd Garrison. Christopher had entertained him at dinner one evening, and the mild-looking little man had harped all that evening on the Sin of Slavery.

Full-bodied hate screamed at his readers from the columns of the *Liberator,* but personally he was a dreary, almost colorless man. His high-pitched voice droned and droned, speaking the same inflammatory words he wrote, but from his mouth they became a tired and repetitious litany.

"How can you stand that man?" Celeste asked Christopher while they were undressing for bed. "He makes my head ache."

"You have to listen to what he says, not how he says it," Christopher told her.

Cannons & Roses

"Can you believe the little worm wanted to read the bumps on my head?"

Christopher laughed. "Most of these abolitionists are what I call Cause People," Christopher said. "They go in for anything new and unconventional. Garrison also believes water will cure anything, if you drink enough of it. Phrenology has become sort of a hobby with him."

As much as she despised Garrison, however, Celeste was impressed with the ex-slave, Frederick Douglass, when Christopher took her to Mechanics Hall to hear him speak about slavery. With his heavy-set figure, intelligent face, and haystack of white hair, in the rostrum he put the ranting abolitionists to shame.

Douglass spoke calmly of the economics of slavery and its stultifying effect on both slave and master. He avoided Sin. He stressed education of his race as its final salvation.

Christopher introduced Celeste to Douglass after his speech. She found herself *shaking hands* with the Negro.

His face had crinkled in a smile. "No, madam, my blackness doesn't rub off," he'd said. "Are you not a southern lady?"

"I am . . . I was," Celeste admitted.

"Strange as it may seem, I have always admired southern womanhood," Frederick Douglass said. "You ladies have the gift of kindness."

In Douglass, Celeste had seen what, with education, and the will to get it, a Negro could become. For the first time, she'd had to ponder whether Negroes were or were not as educable as white people. Before Douglass, it had been a foregone conclusion with her that they weren't, that African blood related them closer to the apes than was the case with the white race.

Cannons & Roses

Douglass had almost convinced her that she was wrong.

The flogging of Vashti and the Mandingo man, to entertain a crowd, had shocked Celeste, but it wasn't the shattering experience of seeing the lynching of the young free Negro and his wife. Being a victim of Ulric Bone, and at the mercy of Vashti, had taught her about willfully caused pain.

That, she now realized, was another thing. The mob who'd burned the man and poked flaming brands at the most vulnerable parts of the girl's naked body acted out of hate, spawned by fear.

Bone was insane. Vashti, too. But those were normal white men ashore in the park, torturing to death a pair who couldn't have harmed them or their families. They were *southern* white men. Most of them, Celeste guessed, had wives and families.

Celeste had been raised to believe that slavery was a normal fact of life in the south, a necessity for both blacks and whites. It was, Celeste had believed, as unchanging as the man-and-woman relationship.

But a year in Boston had opened her mind more than Liberia ever could have.

Philippa had become the pet of the *Revere*'s small crew. One or two off-watch seamen were always forward, playing with her, or offering treats from the galley. The child, Celeste decided, was a born courtesan. She charmed the men, remembering each man's name, and playing up to him as if he were her favorite. She was being carried all over the ship by one or another crewman as much as she was in her playpen.

"I'm going to have a fine time getting that one unspoiled when we reach New Orleans!" Celeste told Christopher. "She thinks she's the Queen of Sheba."

Cannons & Roses

Christopher was amused. "Would you have her less of a charmer?"

"Not until she gets old enough to compete with me, I wouldn't," Celeste confessed.

Once clear of Charleston's harbor, and on the high seas, Rufus was permitted on deck. He was a shambling black giant of a man, missing an ear (it was cropped when he was caught stealing), an R burned into his sloping forehead, for Runaway, and his torso was a mass of whipping scars. Rufus had a cast in one eye, and yellow fanglike teeth. Altogether, Rufus was the ugliest and most evil-looking man Celeste had ever seen. He frightened her.

When she glanced forward one morning and saw him sitting on the deck with Philippa in his lap, Celeste turned cold. A man who was capable of murdering Eunice Rodney, and perhaps her girls, had Philippa! Celeste hurried forward, looking around for help, but there was none.

When she stooped to snatch up Philippa, the child clasped both small arms around the slave's neck and wouldn't let go.

"No!" Philippa said.

The big man's good eye focused on Celeste. His arms protected the child. "No hurt her."

"Let me have her, Rufus." Celeste managed a calm voice.

"No, missy." Philippa's small fingers were exploring the furrowed R branded in the middle of his forehead. "No hurt her."

Christopher had come on deck, and was coming forward to see what the fuss was about.

"He won't let me have her," Celeste told her husband.

Cannons & Roses

"Come on, doll." Christopher reached out for Philippa.

"No." She slapped at his hands. "Stay Rufus."

"No hurt her," Rufus told Christopher.

Hands on his hips, Chirstopher regarded the pair. Philippa was now exploring the scar where the man's ear had been, while Rufus's sausagelike fingers stroked her hair.

"No hurt you," he told Philippa.

She squirmed in his arms, seized one of those fingers with both small hands, examined it, then poked it in her mouth to find the sore spot where she was cutting a tooth. With a contented sigh, she stared up at Celeste and Christopher.

Christopher restrained Celeste from reaching for the child again.

"You have a new friend, Rufus," he told the slave. "Don't let her swallow that finger."

Rufus grinned. "No hurt her."

Christopher drew Celeste away from the pair. "He cared enough for his children to get them out of Charleston," he said. "It won't hurt if he gets some comfort from our Philippa."

"I'm afraid of him, Christopher," Celeste said.

"I'll keep an eye on them," Christopher promised.

For the rest of the voyage, when she was on deck, Rufus was the girl's constant companion, walking beside him while she held onto a thumb (he had to slant his broad shoulders to keep from lifting her off the deck), or riding on his back.

The patience of Rufus with the child was infinite. Philippa seemed to find in the dullard Negro a childlike quality that appealed to her. She wouldn't come from Rufus to Celeste. Only Christopher could take her from his charge.

Cannons & Roses

For Rufus, Philippa snubbed the other men aboard whom she'd so carefully courted.

"That nigra has a way," Caleb told Christopher. "We can't dump him in New Orleans, God knows. What do you think we should do?"

"I'll talk with Celeste about buying him," Christopher said, "and don't look at me like that. I'll arrange the sale through Governor Hampton before we clear New Orleans. He's a trader and owes us something."

"Won't it be awkward to own a slave back in Boston?" Caleb asked.

"When we get back, I'll free him and keep him as a servant. We owe Rufus, you know."

"So do the good people of South Carolina," Caleb said in a dry voice.

It took a tedious three days for the *Revere*, with a river pilot aboard, to navigate the 90 miles of river below New Orleans. Over some stretches of the river, Captain Stott had to order the longboat lowered, and his crew to man the oars.

Celeste was fascinated when they passed Chalmette Plantation, where the Battle of New Orleans was fought, and bragged to Christopher about the part her father and the Baratarians had played in that battle.

"He was personally commended, and decorated by Andrew Jackson," she said. "I wish you could have known my father. You would have liked him, and he would have liked you."

"I'm sorry I didn't have the pleasure," Christopher told her. "He must have been quite a man."

"He was," Celeste said, "but you measure up to him in every way. I've been a lucky woman."

* * *

Cannons & Roses

As the *Revere* worked up the river toward New Orleans, Christopher was having second thoughts about this deep south voyage. The Crescent City had never been a port of call for him, but he knew its reputation.

"They got the blackest niggers there you've ever seen, and some nearly white," a mate had told him. "You buy your wench from her ma, if she's light-skinned, and get your money's worth—believe me."

The easygoing Spanish-French Creoles impressed American sailors with their courteous manners, but few sailors he'd ever spoken with had much use for the raftmen, Kentuckians and Tennesseans who came down the river, sold their merchandise and rafts for lumber, returning home up the Natchez Trace when their money was gone.

"Them is half-horse, half-alligator," a sailor had told Christopher. "Both halves are pure dirt-eman. Killing each other is their idea of fun."

But it wasn't taking Celeste and Philippa ashore in New Orleans that had begun to worry Christopher. He was bringing his new wife home. She might decide she wanted to stay on at Great Oaks with Philippa, or in New Orleans with her mother. Christopher knew well enough that Celeste had a strong mind, and was stubborn. She'd mentioned a few times during the past year that she felt out of place and out of step in Boston.

The state legislature was meeting in Baton Rouge, so Bliss was alone at Great Oaks, and in a dangerous mood. Richard Carroll was becoming increasingly immersed in state politics, with his eye on the House or Senate in Washington, and his first step in that direction was a seat in the state legislature. When he wasn't

Cannons & Roses

in Baton Rouge on state business, he was visiting important planters around the state, getting support for his national political ambitions. Bliss encouraged Richard in this direction.

Politics bored Bliss, but she wanted the social life of Washington. Senator Barnes was getting ready to retire, and he was determined that Richard Carroll should succeed him. The senator and Mary Kay often visited Great Oaks.

Bliss had avoided sex with Mary Kay since their brief encounter in Washington. There had been ample opportunity when Mary Kay visited Great Oaks, but it amused Bliss to tantalize the older woman. She permitted just enough touching and sly caresses to keep Mary Kay's desire at a fever pitch.

This week Senator Barnes was in Washington. Richard was in Baton Rouge. Bliss had invited Mary Kay to spend the week with her. But there was a string to this invitation.

Bliss insisted Mary Kay bring her young niece. Alice Sue Richardson had caught her eye when she and Richard visited Senator Barnes and Mary Kay last Christmas. Thirteen, and more mature than she had any right to be, with taffy-colored hair, and a peaches-and-cream complexion, Alice Sue was Mary Kay's ward. Bliss sensed a boldness in the girl she wanted to cultivate.

Bliss didn't have to put it into words. Mary Kay knew exactly why she would have to bring Alice Sue to Great Oaks, and hated herself for agreeing to do so. She'd been very careful to conceal her lesbian leanings from the young girl. The vision of the three of them, naked together, repulsed Mary Kay, but attracted her at the same time.

Mary Kay realized that she'd reached a point where Bliss controlled her.

Mary Kay and her husband no longer slept together. And she stayed in Louisiana when he was in Washington. She was certain he had a mistress somewhere, and she no longer cared. Bliss as she'd been in Washington was always in Mary Kay's mind, and in her dreams. She had no desire for any other woman.

"I've become her slave," Mary Kay admitted to herself. "She could beat me if she wanted to, and I'd kiss her hands."

Mary Kay was drinking more than she ever had before.

Bliss was certain she could seduce Alice Sue Richardson. All it would take is a little careful planning. The girl was ripe for sex, so why let her fall into the hands of some randy young stud? She'd initiate the girl carefully. She could teach things no man could. Alice Sue would be grateful.

Bliss had established Mary Kay as her procurer, hinting they would share the girl. The woman would have to have her crumbs, but once the bribe was paid, that was it. Mary Kay would be dismissed. Bliss had nothing but contempt for her.

Mary Kay and Alice Sue would arrive in the morning.

Celeste hadn't written either Jeanette or Bliss that she had remarried, and in fact hadn't been in touch since a short note to Jeanette after Philippa's death.

They knew Paul was dead. They knew she would stay on in Boston to care for Jamie's daughter. Neither Bliss nor Jeanette knew anything else about her affairs. Celeste hadn't been truthful with Christopher.

Cannons & Roses

"You've certainly written your mother and sister that we're coming, haven't you?" he asked at the supper table a week before they embarked.

"Would I neglect to do something like that?" she'd countered.

Not a lie, but certainly not the whole truth.

It was a dismal, muggy night, with pouring rain, when the *Revere* finally anchored out in the river off the New Orleans levee and wharf. By torchlight, files of sweating Negroes carried cotton bales up the gangplanks of steamboats tied to the wharf. Until some of them departed upriver, the *Revere* would have to swing at anchor out in the stream.

This close to her mother, Celeste suddenly wanted to see her, bringing Christopher.

At supper they'd agreed morning was the reasonable time to go ashore and find Spanish House, but when they went to their cabin after supper, Celeste changed her mind.

Maura had been too seasick most of the voyage to be much help with Philippa, but now the ship was still, the Irish girl felt much better.

"Listen, Christopher, I want to surprise my mother," Celeste said. "Let's leave Maura to look after Philippa and go ashore. We've been cooped up on this ship too damned long."

Christopher always winced slightly when Celeste swore, but never said anything, so she delighted in shocking his Boston propriety every so often.

Christopher had just taken off his shirt and was tugging at his boots.

"Hell!" He looked up. A boot in one hand, he stared at Celeste. "You didn't write her, did you?"

Celeste shook her head.

"Or your sister?"

"No. Come on, Christopher."

Christopher shrugged his bare shoulders, and reached for his shirt. "Women!" he muttered, then grinned at Celeste. "I surely hope your mother will be glad to see her oldest daughter, and DeWitt Scott doesn't have in mind what I had until a minute ago. You're not very predictable. Did you know that?"

"I try not to be," Celeste said. "You wouldn't want a predictable wife."

"Women and ships, they're the same," Christopher said. "Any skipper who thinks he knows his ship's moods is a damned fool. I guess that's why a ship is a she."

"Are you going to get that boot on?"

Christopher turned the boot in his hand. "On one condition."

"Oh?"

"That you be a dutiful wife and pull your husband's boots off when we finally get to bed tonight. If we do," he added.

7

*I*t was early in the evening when Celeste and Christopher were put ashore, and the wharf and levee should have been crowded despite the drizzling rain but they weren't. Only the stevedores loading cotton on the steamboats were in sight, singing dirgelike songs with indistinguishable words as they worked.

"Something is wrong," Celeste told Christopher.

"It isn't very likely," he said, looking around. "The pilot mentioned yellow fever. He said he was going back downriver as fast as he could."

"You should have told me," Celeste said. "Have you had it?"

"No."

"I had a slight case when I was a child, so I'm immune, but you aren't, Christopher."

"So?"

"Let me go to Mother. You can wait for me back aboard the ship."

Cannons & Roses

"No, thank you," Christopher said. "I've seen the disease in the tropics, but never caught it."

"I don't want you sick."

"I won't be," Christopher assured her.

The only carriage they could find for hire was a dilapidated affair with a ragged Negro driver who looked as discouraged as his bony horse.

"Do you know Spanish House?" Celeste asked.

The driver took off his cap to scratch his grizzled head. "That belong Massa Scott?"

Celeste nodded, drawing her shawl tighter around her shoulders. "That's right. Will you take us there?"

"I disremember exactly where it is," the driver said.

Celeste fished for a coin in her purse, and handed it up to the driver. "Does that help your memory?"

"Sho 'nuff." The driver pocketed the coin and grinned.

Smudge fires were burning all over the city, and filled the wet air with stifling smoke. With a fare, their driver had cheered up considerably, and whistled as his horse slogged through the fetlock-deep mud of the street.

The absence of people on the streets, and other wagons and carriages, was uncanny, and Celeste found herself shivering. Christopher put his arm around her shoulder.

On nearly every corner a fire smothered with wet leaves, or trash, was being solemnly tended by a scarecrow Negro. Passing one corner, they saw a Negro swing a dead cat by the tail and toss it on his fire.

Celeste choked on the rancid smoke.

"Them fires, they's to smother Old Man Fever," their driver said, over his shoulder, and cackled with laughter. "Old Yellowjack, he think that dumb, just go on killin', and killin'. Lordy!"

378

"You don't seem to be afraid of it," Christopher said.

"I ain't," the driver said. "Got me a ju-ju bag from that Marie Laveau herself. Old Yellowjack, he don't want this child. Nossuh. Had me a lemon-color wife, though, and Old Yellowjack, he come for her. That last time he come here."

"I'm sorry to hear it," Christopher said.

The driver shrugged. "No way to help it. If she gone, she gone."

A long flatbed wagon turned into the street ahead of them, and came in their direction, pulled by two horses. Two men were on the box, and a third Negro pumped through the street mud, following the wagon and ringing a bell.

"Here come that dead wagon." Their driver pulled his horse over to the curb, and took off his battered straw hat.

"My dear God!" Celeste breathed, and clamped a handkerchief over her nose and mouth.

Corpses were stacked on the bed of the wagon as if they were cordwood, some naked, others in nightgowns. There were two stacks of men, women, and children; one white, the other black.

"Old Yellowjack, he kill so many, they got to use same wagon now. White and colored folks ride together to the graveyard."

The flatbed wagon passed, but its stench of death lingered. Christopher had covered his nose and mouth with a handkerchief.

"Christ!" he said. "They must be burying them in trenches."

"Yassuh," the driver said. "One for white folks, another for us."

When they were moving again, Celeste said, "I hope

Mother and DeWitt got up the river to Great Oaks before the epidemic got this bad."

"Is there a chance they might have?" Christopher asked.

Celeste nodded. "Jeanette is scared speechless of illness."

They passed the Grymes & Arcenaux law office, and Celeste told Christopher he should see Albert Grymes about buying Rufus from his Charleston owner.

"He handled all my father's legal business," she explained, "and kept Spanish House for Mother after my father was killed."

They were concerned about Governor Hampton's demanding the extradition of Rufus for the part he'd played—or been about to play—in the Denmark Vesey plot. Thirty-five Negroes, including Vesey, had already been hanged in Charleston, and thirty-seven others banished to West Indian slavery. That, as Christopher told Celeste, was equivalent to a slow death.

No one would guess how many had been shot out of hand, or lynched.

They'd arrived at Spanish House.

Celeste expected that the street door in the wall would be locked and bolted, and wondered how they could arouse a servant, but they found it thrown wide open, spilling a shaft of yellow light into the street. Beside the door, in a neat row were three corpses: a white woman tinged yellow by the disease, a Negro woman, and a young boy.

Each was wrapped in a sheet, wrists crossed at their breasts, pennies weighting their eyes.

Christopher paid the driver.

Here is death with some dignity, Celeste thought, staring at the corpses. The women couldn't have been more than twenty, the boy scarcely more than a child.

Cannons & Roses

As if he'd been waiting for them, DeWitt was framed in the courtyard doorway. "Do you bring more sick?" he asked Christopher.

Celeste spoke up. "No, DeWitt, it's me, Celeste. Where is Mother?"

DeWitt Scott was unshaven, hollow-eyed, and haggard. It took him a moment to focus his eyes on Celeste. Finally recognizing her, he heaved a deep sigh. "She's inside, caring for the sickest." His glance at Christopher was disinterested. "Come in."

They followed him into the courtyard.

Except for Jeanette, kneeling beside the fountain, and wringing out a sheet, the paved courtyard was deserted, but yellow lamplight from every room in the house spilled into it.

Jeanette saw them, rose wearily from her knees, and came to meet them, the wet sheet trailing from her hand. Jeanette's face was drawn, her eyes red-rimmed, and gray streaked her hair, but Celeste had never seen her mother more beautiful.

"My darling." Jeanette dropped the sheet to embrace Celeste. "So you've finally come." She held Celeste's arms to study her face. Jeanette nodded, as if satisfied with what she'd found there. "And who is this?" she asked, turning to Christopher."

"My husband, Mama." It was the first time Celeste had called Jeanette anything but "Mother" since she was a small child. "Christopher Randolph."

Jeanette embraced him, and kissed Christopher's cheek. "Welcome to Spanish House."

"We're a hospital these days," DeWitt told them. A tall, stooped Negro woman had come to Jeanette to ask a question. "It's been like this a week now, if I count the days right."

Jeanette had stooped, and picked up the sheet. Her

arm was around the Negro woman's bent shoulders, as they walked toward the fountains, and she spoke to her earnestly.

"This is no proper welcome," DeWitt apologized, "but as you can see . . ."

"Help is needed," Christopher said. He glanced at Celeste. "Maybe you . . . I forgot. You've had the fever. I was going to say we could send you back to the ship."

"No." Celeste crossed to her mother, and took the wet sheet from her hands. "I'll do this. What else, you'll have to tell me."

Christopher was going off with DeWitt.

It was a week before an unseasonable cold wave swept down from the north, flushed the streets and the stagnant swamps surrounding New Orleans with icy rain and sleet. There was a freeze after the rain and sleet. Old Yellowjack, as the Negro driver had called him, was driven to his knees, then finally prostrated, and the survivors of this latest epidemic could draw breath without drinking in acrid or rancid smudge smoke.

Body trenches on the outskirts of the city cemeteries were filled, and flowers planted over them. The flood of sick through the doorway to Spanish House became a trickle, then dried up.

The rooms emptied and pallets were burned. The women volunteer nurses, most of whom were free Negroes, went their separate ways.

"The way we got into this," DeWitt told Celeste and Christopher, "was a Negro family's putting their sick out on the sidewalk to die. We were bound for a boat that would take us to Great Oaks and out of the epidemic, but Jeanette couldn't stand it. She made me bundle those children into the carriage, and we came back to set up sort of a hospital. After that, the flood!"

They were at the dining-room table, having their first decent meal in days. Jeanette was sound asleep at the foot of the table, her cheek on her hand.

Celeste's hands were raw. Her head throbbed and her back ached. She doubted her legs would have held her up much longer. For the past week, days and nights merging into one another, Celeste had washed excrement-soiled sheets and bodies. Children had died in her arms. She'd helped lay out the dead.

"Are you all right?" Christopher asked from across the table.

Celeste's smile was tired, but her face was peaceful. "Yes, very much all right," she said. "I'll never be afraid of death again."

Rufus had brought medicines and hot food from the ship and stayed to help DeWitt and Christopher lay out the dead between journeys through the deserted New Orleans streets.

"I doubt yellow fever is contagious from one person to another," DeWitt said to Christopher. "If it was, we certainly would have caught it, and Jeanette, too. Did you know that none of the nigras tending the smudge fires caught it?"

"I didn't know that," Christopher said.

"Or any of the handlers of the dead, for that matter. Strange, don't you think?"

Christopher nodded.

"Nearly all first-generation Africans are immune to the disease."

Jeanette's face slipped off the palm of her hand,

and she jerked awake. "Celeste, what of Jamie's child?" she said. "You and Christopher brought her, didn't you? I don't remember if you told me."

"Yes, she came with us," Celeste said. "Maura has cared for her aboard the *Revere*."

"We haven't heard from Jamie."

"I haven't either," Celeste said.

"I wish he'd write and let us know he's alive out there in Texas. DeWitt, can we all go up to Great Oaks?" Jeanette asked.

"I can't, but you should. Now that things will be normal again, I'll have to attend to business."

"How shall we go upriver?" Jeanette asked Celeste and Christopher.

"Aboard my ship," Christopher said. "We can start tomorrow. Caleb believes the bark has a shallow enough draft to sail up to Great Oaks, given a good pilot."

"I can recommend a man," DeWitt said.

The unexpected arrival of her mother, Celeste, Philippa, and Christopher tore the web Bliss was weaving around Mary Kay Barnes and Alice Sue Richardson. Worse, Richard was coming up from Baton Rouge because the legislature had adjourned early. But she played the role of southern plantation hostess to the hilt.

And she played up to Christopher while Celeste was busy keeping Philippa out of mischief. Mary Kay, with no children of her own, fell in love with the child. Alice Sue was left pretty much to her own devices.

Jeanette rested. She'd always been closer to Bliss than Celeste when the girls were at home, but after the past week, and seeing Celeste's love for Philippa, as well as her husband, Jeanette found she admired Celeste much more than she did Bliss.

Celeste had compassion and depth Bliss would never realize.

Richard Carroll was as handsome as ever, and gracious to his guests, but Jeanette realized politics was his lifeblood and always would be. He accepted Bliss as an excellent hostess, and, in his way, Jeanette supposed, loved her. But it wasn't the way Christopher loved Celeste.

Bliss could glitter like a diamond, and she was as hard under the soft surface as that gem. Celeste reminded Jeanette of a rich ruby.

She wondered what the friendship between Bliss and Mary Kay Barnes fed upon. And she was amused to see that Christopher saw through the cute game with him Bliss was trying to play. Celeste had done well to marry that man!

After dinner, over coffee, port, and cigars, Richard discussed the growing division between the northern and southern states with Christopher. It was his first opportunity to meet with an antislavery supporter from Boston, and he made the most of it.

"Sir, the institution of slavery benefits both the servant and master," he said. "You people don't understand this. A northern millhand has no security. His employer abandons him when he's sick or too old to work. Essentially, he's a slave, without the benefits our servants have."

"He's never whipped," Christopher said.

Richard chuckled. "You've been reading the *Liberator*. That, sir, is a slander!"

"We've just come from Charleston," Christopher said in a mild voice. "We saw a black man and woman whipped and burned to death. Celeste and I had something to do with discovering the Vesey plot. I can't speak for my wife, but I think slavery is dead wrong."

"Your opinion, sir," Richard said. "I respect it. I think your northern handling of Irish and German immigrants is immoral and hypocritical. Am I wrong?"

"I'll duck that question on the basis that I'm a seafaring man," Christopher said. "I'm not a merchant or textile factory owner, but some of the Randolphs have interests in that direction. They do their best to maintain a modest profit and improve the lot of their workers. Education is the answer here."

"What do you suppose would happen in the south if we let our slaves learn to read and write?" Richard Carroll asked.

"Your Negroes might better appreciate all the benefits of being enslaved," Christopher said.

Richard missed the sarcasm. "We'd have a hundred Denmark Veseys. No southern girl or woman would be safe from rape, or worse. You Yankees just don't understand the African mind."

"I don't think we understand the southern mind very well," Christopher said. "From what I know about Kansas and Nebraska territory, it's farm rather than plantation country, yet you want them to come in as slave states, despite the Missouri Compromise."

"We've got to be free to take our slaves anywhere in the United States, sir. The government must protect our property, and unless it does, we southern people will go a separate way—have no doubt about that. Make this point with your northern abolitionist friends. They are tampering with a powder keg, sir."

"I'm not sure any longer the abolitionists are my friends," Christopher said. "But I will spread the word in New England."

"You're not an abolitionist? You come from Boston."

"Yes," Christopher said. "The city where Garrison was dragged through the streets at the end of a rope. We do a lot of business with the south. Some of our merchants don't want you buying from England."

"You may force us to do just that, sir."

Jamie McCoy, Hugh Forbes, and Virgil Loring were camped near the Brown farm on Osawatomie Creek.

"Old Man Brown is crazy!" Jamie said.

Hugh chuckled. "So was Oliver Cromwell, or so a lot of Englishmen thought. He's got the cash—and the weapons."

8

Jamie scuffed the fire's embers with his boot. "Are you joining him, Hugh?"

Forbes nodded. "Why not? He needs my services, and they're for sale."

"What about you, Virg?"

"I'll help him play soldier."

"You'd throw in with the Free Soilers?" Jamie asked, incredulous. "You're as southern as I am, Virg."

Virgil shook his head. "No longer. I'm a Texan and like a good fight, regardless of what it's about."

"Well, this is where we split," Jamie told the men. "I'm riding out for Atchison in the morning."

"Watch yourself going through Lawrence," Forbes advised. "That's a Free Soil stronghold. They just might arrange a rope party for you."

"I understand they've made a fort out of the hotel there," Virgil told Jamie. "We've got us a nice little war brewing here."

Cannons & Roses

"Looks as if," Jamie agreed gloomily. "I don't know yet whether I want any part of it."

"Chap named Jim Lane is the man to see if you decide you're a slavery man," Forbes said. "A somewhat bloodthirsty gent, according to Old Brown, but then, as you say, John the Prophet may be a little touched in the head himself."

Jamie couldn't avoid riding past the ramshackle farmhouse with its sun-warped outbuildings where the Brown sons, their wives, and Brown's second wife lived under the thumb of the old man. During the past few days, Jamie had been amazed to see grown men and women obeying the old man as if he were God.

It's almost as if he has them hypnotized, Jamie thought.

Old Brown was at the gate, sucking on a raw egg. Straw from the hen's nest he'd raided was tangled in his patriarchal white beard.

Stuck in his belt were a pair of pistols—which wasn't unusual in Kansas, Jamie had discovered. Nearly every man went armed to the teeth, even more so than Texans. But in Brown's free hand was a razor-sharp navy cutlass. With it the old man was absentmindedly slicing the heads from daisies.

Pale blue eyes studied Jamie when he rode up. "You're up early to be about the Lord's work, I see." Brown's voice had a deep, resonant timbre. "McCoy, isn't it?"

Jamie pulled up his horse. "Yes, sir."

"A true steel blade, this one," Brown said, showing Jamie the cutlass. "One of a dozen from my admirers in New England. The Sin of Slavery must be washed out in blood."

Jamie's hand uneasily found the butt of his Navy Colt. Brown ignored this nervous movement to say,

"There will be close-order drill for my Osawatomie Rifles this afternoon. Time is short before we must smite the Philistines, as it is God's order we must. Smite them we shall, hip and thigh. Blood!" Brown's eyes gleamed and gloated. "It will wash our southern brothers clean of their sin."

Jamie felt his blood rising, and he tightened his grip on the revolver.

There was Old Man Brown, reaching for another stolen egg in the pocket of his overalls, the cutlass in his other hand. Draw and fire. Nearly point-blank range.

Jamie's mouth was dry and tasted of brass.

Kill him here, kill him now!

The thought was almost a sharply spoken command, but Jamie's body went slack, and his hand fell away from the revolver.

"I'm riding on, Brown," Jamie said, but he turned his horse.

To hell with Atchison, to hell with Jim Lane, to hell with Kansas!

Jamie McCoy was going home. He needed time to rest, to think, yes, and to see Philippa's daughter. She'd been increasingly on his mind lately. Her mother's death was a wound that would never completely heal, and there hadn't been another woman since Philippa, but she dead, and he alive, they still shared the child.

Jamie kicked his horse into a trot, and began to whistle. Now he was glad that he hadn't shot down Old Man Brown.

He wondered if Celeste was being a good mother to Philippa. Thank God that Paul was no longer part of her life!

From what he'd seen and learned in Kansas, now

would be a good time to resume the military career he'd once planned. From Great Oaks, Jamie decided he'd go east and join the army or marines. It would be a real pleasure to see Old Jack again. Jamie had heard that he now taught at Virginia Military Institute in Lexington, a new school modeled on West Point.

He put Old John Brown out of his mind.

It was a hot afternoon, with the sun beating down from a cloudless sky, but thunderheads had begun to tower across the river. They reminded Mary Kay of billowing castles. Jeanette, Celeste, and Christopher, as well as Alice Sue, were resting in their rooms after a midday dinner of chicken and rice.

Mary Kay was restless. She'd seen Bliss wander out to the summerhouse, and now followed along the path. Mary Kay was certain that Bliss knew she would come. She'd fortified herself with peach brandy and felt a little dizzy in the sun, despite her bonnet.

Bliss had played a teasing game the past few days. She was clever, Mary Kay decided. No doubt about that. A flirt. But Bliss didn't yet know the plan Mary Kay had worked out for them and their love.

She and Russell were practically separated now. Richard Carroll was seldom at Great Oaks, and Bliss couldn't love him! Why shouldn't Bliss come to live with her and Alice Sue?

She'd wait on them both, hand and foot.

Mary Kay had reached the summerhouse. She tapped on the door. "Bliss?"

"Who is it?"

Bliss was cross. She shouldn't have kept her waiting so long. "It's your Mary Kay."

Bliss threw open the door. "Is anything wrong? I thought you'd be in your room for a nap."

Cannons & Roses

"Nothing is wrong." Mary Kay stepped inside, closing the door behind her. "I knew you expected me, but I waited awhile for the others to settle down."

Bliss frowned. "You waited?"

Mary Kay stepped closer. She could smell the sweet warmth of Bliss. "Yes. So we could be all alone this afternoon, because I've made some plans for us."

Bliss had been brooding and was still in a dark mood. "You mean the picnic tomorrow? I thought that was settled this morning. I've already ordered the food."

"Bliss, listen to me. I love you. I want you. There isn't anything I won't do so we can have each other. It can be all the time like it was with us in Washington. Better, really, because I've waited so long, and love you so much."

Bliss was shocked out of her thoughtless, pouting lethargy, and snatched back her hands when Mary Kay tried to seize them.

This woman is crazy!

"You don't know what you're talking about, and I think you're drunk," Bliss accused. "Please leave me alone."

"I'm not drunk!"

Bliss backed away.

"You'll come and live with me and Alice Sue," Mary Kay said. "I'll be your servant—even your slave —do anything you want me to do. We'll be so happy!"

Bliss was frightened. Convinced Mary Kay had become unbalanced, she tried tact. "Look, Mary Kay, right now a lot is on my mind, and it *is* a very hot day." There was a distant roll of thunder across the river. "We'd better talk later, don't you think?"

"No." Mary Kay's face set in stubborn, ugly lines.

Cannons & Roses

Bliss shivered. "Storms get on my nerves, and this isn't my best time of month."

"Don't you love me, Bliss?"

Bliss smiled. "We're good friends, Mary Kay."

"Friends?" Mary Kay's voice was harsh.

"Yes. I like you." *I was a fool to ever invite her to Great Oaks,* Bliss thought. *Now she'll go to Celeste or Mother—worse yet, Richard!*

Richard had returned to Baton Rouge for the day, but would be back that evening.

"Mary Kay, I think Alice Sue is homesick," Bliss said. "Shouldn't you leave later this afternoon for your home? It must be very dull for her here. I'll come for a visit as soon as I possibly can."

Mary Kay stared at Bliss.

"Please leave me alone now," Bliss said.

The full force of the storm was about to break. Mary Kay balanced on the stool in her room at Great Oaks, kicking off her shoes. She was still dizzy from the brandy, the heat, and fleeing the summerhouse.

Alice Sue had seen her and wondered why Aunt Mary Kay was in such a hurry. Philippa saw her, too. The child was up from her nap while Celeste and Christopher still dozed on the four-poster bed. Philippa saw a bird on the tree outside their window, and forgot the hurrying woman.

There was a loud clap of thunder. Philippa scooted under the bed and held her ears.

The drapery cord was stout enough, but Mary Kay wondered if the drapery fixture would hold her weight. Her balance on the stool was precarious.

Bliss had seduced her in Washington, and they'd had a golden and purple afternoon together. Since then, Bliss had promised, promised, promised. There had been no one else with Mary Kay since then. She knew she was the first with Bliss.

Bliss had never loved her!

"Bitch!"

She'd make her sorry for the rest of her life.

But what about my life?

Mary Kay was suddenly sober, and remembered Russell, Alice Sue, and how good coffee tasted in the morning, and how sweetly birds sang, and the rain! She loved the rain.

Drops spattered the window of her room.

Thunder crashed.

Mary Kay involuntarily started. The stool collapsed. She was hanging by her neck! Hands fought to find the cord. They found it.

The fixture tore out of the wall. There was a sudden jerk. The sound of her neck breaking echoed in the bedroom.

Rain drenched Great Oaks.

It was Alice Sue with Philippa in tow who found her dead aunt.

"God! Why would she do a thing like that? And *here,* of all places!" Bliss said.

Russell Barnes was there. Richard, too. Celeste and Jeanette clasped hands. Alice Sue was caring for Philippa upstairs.

In a corner of the parlor, Christopher crossed his arms on his chest, clasped his elbows, listened, and waited.

Bliss was storming the room where Mary Kay would be laid out as soon as her body was bathed and dressed. House servants were seeing to that. Russell Barnes would take her home tomorrow.

Cannons & Roses

"I don't understand!" Bliss said.

"My wife has been depressed," Russell Barnes offered. His face was ravaged with grief.

I'm looking at a man who will soon be as dead as his wife, Christopher thought.

He and Celeste exchanged glances. Christopher nodded. They knew.

"Do you realize that Mrs. Barnes has a crush on our Bliss?" Celeste had asked him just last night. "It's as obvious as the nose on your face."

When he'd raised a skeptical eyebrow, Celeste said, "Damn it, Christopher. Don't be superior. I know my sister, and she's no winged angel. Women do bed women, you know."

He doubted that Bliss and Mary Kay had ever been intimate, but he couldn't help noticing the way Mary Kay's eyes followed every move Bliss made.

"Be quiet, Bliss," Jeanette said.

Richard led her from the parlor, an arm around her waist. There was the murmur of their voices in the hallway.

Jeanette spoke up. "We've had a most unfortunate accident here. Dr. Spenser agrees. The children, well, I'll speak with them. Senator Barnes?"

"Yes?" His head snapped up, but his cheeks glistened with tears.

"You have my word, and that of my daughters, that your wife fell in her room during this afternoon's thunderstorm and broke her neck. We're truly sorry."

"Thank you." Russell Barnes buried his face in his hands.

"Christopher?" Jeanette said.

He snapped alert.

"We'll all attend the funeral," she told him. "Gossip

is the bane of the plantation south, and you'll be questioned as our family's Yankee."

"I'm forewarned," Christopher said. "The way I see it, sir," he said to Senator Barnes, "it *was* an accidental death, and I'd swear to that under oath. Your wife was too lovely a person to take her own life."

Jamie arrived at Great Oaks the day of the funeral to find the plantation deserted except for the servants and field hands. The overseer who'd replaced the dead Delray Bone was a Mr. McAlpin from Vermont, a dour individual. He was in Natchez after supplies.

Buck, a handsome mulatto, was McAlpin's driver, and the hands were in the field that afternoon.

New majordomo in the great house was Seth, too crippled by rheumatism to work in the fields any longer, a long-nosed, hunched man. Seth didn't recognize the man who'd dismounted in the portico and was beating dust from his clothes.

"Nobody here, sir. Only us niggers. They gone to do some burying, sir."

"What's your name?" Jamie asked.

"Seth, sir, and it please you."

Seth was afraid of this sunburned stranger, with his worn boots, and way of squinting when he looked at you. Yet something was familiar about him.

"You be a friend this family, sir?"

Jamie's hand found the butt of his revolver, and Seth took a quick step back.

"Hold it, Seth." Jamie threw up both hands. "Just a reflex."

"Yes, sir, yes, sir!"

Jamie grinned. When he did, and the amusement in his eyes was warm, not scoffing, Seth was no longer afraid.

"Seth, don't be so damned service with me, will you?" Jamie said. "I think I remember you. Didn't you have Martha for a wife?"

"Mr. Jamie!"

"You can bet." Jamie slapped the man's shoulder and saw him wince. "Rheumatism?"

"The swamp misery, sir."

"Sorry, Seth. By the way, who died?"

"Wife of Massa Barnes, the senator man. She here to visit, and fall, break her neck."

"God, that's too bad." Jamie couldn't place any Barnes. "Can you rustle me a good hot bath, and I left some decent clothes here."

"Yes, sir, Massa Jamie, and you be wanting hot food, something to drink. You too thin, sir."

Jamie chuckled. "You'll fatten me up. Cut down a ham in the smokehouse. I'm sick of beefsteak so tough you can use it to sole your boots. And peach brandy, if we've got it. Have you ever tried skull-bust redeye, Seth?"

"No, sir, Massa Jamie, no, sir. Seth don't drink these days."

"Good." Jamie grinned. "How about that bath? I'm filthy as a timber wolf, and just about that hungry. By the way, how's Mother?"

"She here to visit, with Massa Scott. Miss Celeste, her husband, and their baby, too."

"Their baby?"

Seth bobbed his head. "The child named Philippa. She cute, that one, Massa Jamie."

"I'll wager she is," Jamie said, and Seth wondered about the faraway look in his eyes.

In fresh linen, shined boots, and a frock coat, Jamie drifted from the house to the quarter to watch the hands come in from the fields. They came—men, women and children—in a straggling file. Buck followed on a tall, black horse, a coiled whip in his hands.

Jamie remembered Buck and some of the slaves. All eyes turned in his direction as they passed, and a few faces lit with recognition, but no one spoke.

No one was singing.

When DeWitt was overseer, Jamie thought, *they always came in singing.*

Buck drew up, and saluted with the whip. "Massa Jamie, I do believe."

"You're our driver now?" Jamie asked.

"Yassuh."

He pointed to the whip. "Use that much, Buck?"

"Only when they lazy. Nigger understand the whip."

"You've got some pregnant girls and women working the fields."

"Yassuh. Mr. McAlpin's order, suh."

"I see." Jamie licked his lips. "Good evening, Buck."

PART TWO

1

Widowed Maura O'Grady left Philippa Randolph that night with foreboding—the feeling someone had just walked on her grave—but for the life of her, Maura couldn't trace the cause. What eighteen-year-old girl wouldn't be a bit wan and nervous on the eve of her wedding, and to a man as important as Mr. Philip Morley, soon to be the senator from Massachusetts?

In her small room off the kitchen of the Randolph Beacon Hill house, Maura stirred the embers in the fireplace grate, found a shawl, and waited for the teakettle to boil.

"She's the spitting image of her mother, the darling," Maura muttered.

It was true. Philippa's hair was a darker honey, and her eyes the startling McCoy blue, but her proud carriage and classical features were her mother again.

And the Randolph ironic grin always lingered near Philippa's lips.

The teapot on the wood stove in the kitchen sang. Maura shuffled out in her slippers to pour a cup. She wondered if Philippa would be lying awake, but decided she would be sound asleep by this time. Since Maura had cared for her as a baby, Philippa had been one of the best sleepers the Irishwoman had ever known.

"By my faith, that small one sleeps like an angel, or the Blessed Mother herself," Maura remembered telling her sister-in-law Kitty once. "Miss Celeste is saying that's a McCoy habit, but Philippa's mother was like that, rest her soul."

Maura shuffled back to her fireside to sip her tea.

Philippa raised and pounded her pillow. From the striking clock in the upstairs hallway, she knew it was an hour before that she'd gone to bed, anxious for a full night's sleep. She'd need it tomorrow. Maura had brought her hot milk. Philippa had had a warm bath. She'd donned a fresh nightgown.

Celeste had promised she wouldn't be disturbed on the morning of her wedding. "Shy as you sometimes are," Aunt Celeste had said, "Boston's most important wedding this season will be quite an ordeal, and we can't have you swooning halfway to the altar, now, can we?"

"Aunt Cel! *Swoon?* You've been reading too many trashy novels. My two long legs have never failed me yet, and you know it. Swoon!"

Celeste laughed. "It used to be fashionable."

"This is 1858."

Philippa caught her hands behind her neck, and frowned up into the darkness. Philip was enjoying his bachelor party tonight. Philippa sighed. Why did men think they had to get drunk with their men friends the night before they were married? Last week Bernice Foote's husband had been almost too hung over to get to the altar of the North Church.

Philippa wondered if Philip Morley would ever learn how little drink it took to make him tipsy and silly. They'd been engaged only a month, but she knew very well. Mrs. Morley did, too.

"My dear girl, when you and my son are married," the woman had confided the day before yesterday, "you will have to speak to him about spirits. The poor boy takes after his Uncle Frank, I'm afraid."

Boy? Philippa swore if she had a son, and he was in his middle thirties, she'd never refer to him as a boy!

Philippa's hand covered the soft rise of her womanhood through the silk of her nightgown. Aunt Cel had been frank when she explained a man's way with a woman, tacitly admitting that from girlfriends who had married, Philippa probably knew as much as she herself did.

Philippa didn't. She'd always shunned the subject of sex when it came up. "I've been a little prig!" she whispered to herself.

Tomorrow night . . .

Philippa examined her feelings and couldn't find fear among them. She'd be nervous tomorrow night, of course, and probably awkward, but Philip would understand.

Strange. There was no fear, true, but shouldn't she be curious? Shouldn't a little thrill of anticipation be warming her loins? Philippa felt neither.

"Now why is that?" she asked herself.

Truth is a strange thing, Philippa was to think afterward. It is always there, but sometimes we avoid it as long as possible.

It was as though a small door opened inside her head, and her childhood imp, Philippa II, was standing there with her tongue poked out.

"Where have you been?"

"Away, you ninny."

"Why away? I've needed you."

"You surely have!"

"What about Philip Morley?"

"He bores you stiff."

"He does not!"

"He does, too!"

Philippa jumped out of bed to stand, ramrod stiff and straight, in the warm darkness. A breeze from the window stirred her nightgown. More than two hundred people would come to the wedding, a hundred to the reception here at home. Two rooms downstairs were loaded with expensive wedding gifts.

Aunt Cel and Uncle Chris were proud of the match —in a quiet way, but, yes, proud. Could they ever understand?

I'm not marrying Philip Morley tomorrow!

"What are you going to do?" she asked herself.

She couldn't face Aunt Cel and Uncle Chris, or all those relatives and friends, not to mention Philip Morley, hung over from his bachelor party. Philip could be impossible when he wasn't going to get his way.

Philippa felt vibrant and alive, as if a trap had snapped closed just before she stepped into it.

I'll run away tonight!

"Maura has the second sight so far as Philippa is concerned," Celeste once told Christopher. "She always knows when the child is in trouble. Remember when Maura came back early from her honeymoon because Philippa was sick in bed for the first time in her life? It took both of us to nurse her through."

Maura couldn't sleep. She lay in bed, staring at the fire shadows flickering on the ceiling of her small room. She remembered how elated and excited she'd been the night before she married O'Grady, God rest him.

Cry about the O'Grady another time.

Philippa was in trouble.

Maura slipped into the robe Philippa had made with her own hands for her last birthday, and such a robe it was! The child would never be a seamstress. She and Kitty had giggled as they straightened the seams.

"The thought is what you count, Maura," Kitty said. "That one sewing is like a blooded mare put to pulling a plow."

Maura went through the night-quiet house, and upstairs to Philippa's room.

"What is it now, child?" she asked, when Philippa, fully dressed, opened the door at Maura's first light tap. "And just where do you think you'd be going at this time of the night?"

"I'm running away, Maura." Philippa was breathless, and her eyes danced with excitement. "I can't marry tomorrow, I can't face Aunt Cel or Uncle Chris and all those stuffy people. There's nothing else I can do."

"Is it you're afraid to perform your wifely duty, darling?" Maura hugged Philippa. "If that's it, we can talk tonight."

"That isn't it, Maura."

"What, then?"

"I don't love Philip as I should. All my friends are married, or marrying, so I guess I thought I should when Philip came along, and it was flattering to be his fiancé, but marry?" Color flamed in Philippa's cheeks. "I cannot!"

"You could stay and tell the man that."

"Yes, I could," Philippa admitted, "but you can imagine the scene. You know how much I hate scenes."

"As a toddler you certainly didn't," Maura said dryly. "I can remember once . . ."

"Maura, don't scold me!"

"Where will you go? Have you thought of that yet, darling?"

Like a good general, Philippa had plotted her line of retreat: New York, Washington, and from there a Baltimore & Ohio train to Harper's Ferry.

Last summer Belle Boyd's parents had rented Philippa's house, given Celeste by Philippa's mother, and deeded to Philippa last year so she would have an independent income.

"I'll go to Winchester, Maura. Belle has asked me to come visit, as I did last summer."

Lieutenant Jamie McCoy was stationed near Harper's Ferry with a marine detachment.

"I'll see my father again," Philippa said.

Maura gathered her robe and studied the girl. "I should be telling your parents . . . your aunt and uncle," Maura corrected herself.

"Please don't, Maura."

If Philippa was that determined, Maura decided, there was nothing to do but help her run away. She'd never cared too much for Philip. How she'd explain herself to Celeste and Christopher, Maura didn't know. Likely they'd fire her, and she'd have to sponge on Kitty O'Grady until she found another situation, but it couldn't be helped.

Cannons & Roses

Maura sighed. "Let me get on my clothes and we'll see to your packing."

Philippa kissed her. "I love you, Maura."

If you startle her, she'll scream and give away the game, Christopher thought.

He shrank into the shadows, shoulders against the wall, and as Maura passed, his arm snaked out, hand covering her mouth.

"It's all right," he whispered in her ear. "We need to talk."

Maura's eyes told him she understood. Releasing Maura, Christopher whispered, "Not here. Downstairs. I'll follow you."

Maura nodded.

"Mr. Randolph, you gave me a start!" Maura accused when they were in her room. "Holy Saints! My old heart is still jumping like a wounded fish."

Christopher grinned. "I'm sorry. Can I fetch brandy?"

"A drop or two wouldn't hurt."

"It never does."

Christopher brought back two glasses.

"How much did you hear with your eavesdropping, Mr. Randolph?" Maura asked. "We'd forgotten how lightly you sleep ashore."

"I overheard just about everything," Christopher said.

"You'll be stopping her I suppose?"

"No." Christopher grinned. "Surprised?"

He looks like a boy about to get into some mischief, Maura thought. "And why wouldn't you be, with the wedding all planned?"

"Philippa can get married anytime in the next ten

years, Maura. But only once can she run away, and between us, don't you think she can do better than Philip?"

"He's good Boston family."

"Yes."

"He's wealthy enough."

"Right."

"He's a good Christian man."

"Whatever that is," Christopher said.

Maura's eyes twinkled. "Philippa can do better."

Christopher laughed, then said, "Here's what I want you to do. Get her packed." He pressed a packet of money into Maura's hand. "I'll have the carriage ready, but tell her you ordered it."

Maura had counted the money. "Mr. Randolph, do you and Mrs. Randolph always sleep with a thousand dollars?"

Christopher chuckled. "Tips for the caterer's help tomorrow, Maura, and a going-away present for the bride and bridegroom. Tell her it's from you, out of your savings, will you?"

"What will you be telling Mrs. Randolph?"

Christopher scowled. "I wish to hell that I knew."

"You did *what?*" Celeste scrambled out of their bed. "You mean she's *gone?*"

Christopher sat on the edge of the bed, hands clasped between his knees. He wouldn't look at Celeste. "I helped her run away," he said meekly.

Celeste stared. "She's to be married today!"

Christopher looked up. "Now she can't be, can she? What are you going to tell Philip, not to mention his mother?"

"What am *I* going to tell him? You've got to be out of your mind!" Celeste stripped off her nightgown

Cannons & Roses

and threw it at him. "It's *my* turn to run away, but without your help, dear husband!" She began throwing on her clothes. "Of all the things you've ever done to me, Christopher . . ." Celeste paused to duck into her dress. Her head emerged from the dress, and she stared at her husband. "Did you put her up to this?"

Christopher raised his right hand. "I swear I didn't, and hope to die if I lie. I overheard her talking with Maura when I got up. Philippa's mind was made up, and you know how that is. Was I supposed to play the wicked uncle? Somehow I don't fit the part where our niece is concerned."

Celeste sank into a chair, eyes still on Christopher. "We've always spoiled her."

"Look, Celeste. Confess it. Aren't you just a little relieved we won't have Morley as a son-in-law? He'll go far in politics, I admit that, but even when he was at Harvard, he was called 'Mealy.' He still talks out of both sides of his mouth, as far as I'm concerned."

"Did you ever tell Philippa you don't like him?"

"What would have been the use while she thought she loved him?"

"You know, Christopher, for a man, you sometimes show good sense," Celeste said. She glanced at the porcelain clock ticking on her dresser. "Eight-thirty. Where do you suppose Philippa is now?"

"She caught the early train to New York, so she's nearly there by now, I'd guess. She'll be in Washington tonight, unless she takes a day to see the sights. Maura says she wired Bliss and Richard in Washington from the station, so they'll expect her, and see she gets on the B. & O. for Harper's Ferry. Jamie will probably meet her there."

"Bliss," Celeste mused. "In her last letter, she all but came out and said she sleeps with President Buchanan. Old Buck, she calls him. My sister, the *femme fatale*. Do you suppose she sleeps with our First Lady, too?"

"Am I supposed to answer that question?"

"No, don't you dare try." Celeste laughed. "What do we do about all the people coming to the wedding that isn't going to happen?"

"We could marry again."

"Not necessary," Celeste said. "I think I'll start by making an early call on Philip's mother."

"I'll get the word to Mealy," Christopher promised.

Celeste stood up, and turned her back. "Button me?"

Christopher slipped his hands inside her dress to cover Celeste's breasts while he nibbled at the nape of her neck. "Still love me?"

"I must. I put up with your morning lechery. But for now, just button me, will you? We are going to have a difficult day."

"Excuses!" Christopher sighed.

It had been another sleepless night for Old John Brown. The faces of the boys and young men he and his sons had called from their homes after Jim Lane's abortive raid on Lawrence, and siege of the fortified hotel there, had again haunted his sleep. He'd killed before the Osawatomie Massacre, but with a rifle or pistol.

In a sharklike blood frenzy, he and his boys had cut down each victim with those surplus navy sabers, leaving a trail of blood along Osawatomie Creek. The youngest boy had been just twelve. Visiting the proslavery family from the East, as it turned out.

An eye for an eye, a tooth for a tooth. Didn't the Old Testament say that? How was he to know the first reports about Lawrence were wrong, and that

Lane's Missouri border ruffians hadn't killed anybody?

That night had been a mistake, but he'd paid God for it, hadn't he? John Brown, Jr., was insane now.

John stared at the full moon overhead. When he and his chosen few, as he liked to think of his sons and the few free Negroes from Canada who'd rallied to his banner, had taken the Harper's Ferry arsenal, and distributed weapons to every male slave in Virginia, the holocaust would begin.

He'd be remembered in history as the man who finally conquered slavery in America, and the Secret Six who were now so niggardly with their money since he'd been driven from Kansas, would shower him with rewards.

Blood was on the harvest moon—the sign from God for which he'd waited. They'd strike the day after tomorrow.

2

Senator Richard Carroll and Bliss rented a suite at the Hotel Willard on a year-round basis, because an ailing Alicia Carroll at The Columns was being cared for by the servants, under the direction of Alicia's widowed sister, and Bliss couldn't stand association with the sick or senile.

"It just does something to me, Richard, that I can't help," she told her husband. "Sickness is morbid. Old age is worse."

After Mary Kay's suicide, Bliss couldn't stand Great Oaks, either, so Jeanette and DeWitt had moved back there, and DeWitt superevised both plantation acreages. At Jamie's suggestion, they'd fired Robert McAlpin out of hand, and permitted him to purchase Buck, as well as his quadroon mistress. With another elderly slave, purchased by McAlpin when an estate was liquidated in Memphis, the man had bought the Little Eva plantation on the Red River below Shreveport.

Part of his plantation was bottom land that Delray Bone had cleared.

DeWitt brought an enlightened policy regarding slaves on Great Oaks and The Columns when he returned to supervise the two plantations.

"The abolitionists are like irresponsible people who yell 'Fire!' in a crowd," DeWitt explained to Jeanette. "At the same time, we slave owners are like the Australian ostrich who buries his head in the sand."

Every slave in each work force was encouraged to earn money to buy his freedom; the more talented rented out in Natchez to carpenters, bricklayers, and hotels. Those without skills were given additional plots of land to grow vegetables for sale and some livestock. The industrious could be relieved of some plantation duties if they were anxious to harvest or work their garden plots.

Instead of white overseers, DeWitt trained the more intelligent male field hands to become drivers, but without the whip or the right to punish. DeWitt reserved discipline to himself, knowing that blacks were usually too hard on each other for the most minor infractions.

"Cruelty is born into Africans, I guess," DeWitt theorized to Jeanette.

Pregnant women beyond three months weren't permitted in the fields. Slave marriages were encouraged with a bolt of calico for every bride, a new pipe and pound of tobacco for each groom, and a feast for all hands on the first Sunday following the marriage, the ceremony provided by DeWitt himself.

This liberality was shocking enough to neighboring plantation owners, but DeWitt, following Senator Jefferson Davis's example, set up a *school* for his slaves! This, of course, was completely illegal—the Black

Cannons & Roses

Codes insisted it was a crime to teach any slave to read and write—but DeWitt stood his ground, pointing to Davis as an example.

Production increased nearly a hundredfold, and The Columns and Great Oaks became two of the most profitable plantations in the south.

The share Richard and Bliss got from these increased profits permitted them to live in Washington the year around, and entertain lavishly. Richard was becoming a minor power in the hard-core southern cabal of senators who spoke openly of secession if the North didn't leave slavery alone.

South Carolina's fire-breathers claimed Senator Carroll as one of their own. Geography was all that separated the promising young Louisiana senator from their vested interests and rebellious attitude.

At Great Oaks on leave, Lieutenant Jamie McCoy once confided to DeWitt Scott, "That silver-tongued rabble rouser, so help me, is going to bring the wrath of God down on our southern heads. He's as enlightened as those damned Yankee abolitionists yelling 'Freedom Now!' and to hell with the consequences. There's going to be war, Scott, if southern states stop quarreling among themselves long enough to make a united front, and try to secede."

"That bad?" DeWitt said. "I've been south too long now to remember what it's like up there, if I ever really knew."

In answer to Philippa's wire, Senator Richard Carroll was on the station platform to greet Philippa when her train from New York and Philadelphia pulled in an hour late. He had no trouble recognizing the tall, blond young woman who was chatting so easily with the rotund train conductor.

"My dear young lady, how extremely well you look after such a tiring journey," Richard greeted Philippa. Development of a pompous attitude toward all young women had grown with his carefully trimmed Van Dyke beard. "Is that one bag all your luggage? My wife can't travel up to Philadelphia without at least two trunks."

"It's everything, Uncle Richard," Bliss brushed his bearded cheek with her lips, and decided the sensation would be the same kissing corn silk. "How's Aunt Bliss these days? She hasn't written in ages."

"Busy with her social functions and charities," Richard said. "A senator's wife has myriad responsibilities, you know. Bliss is one of our most popular southern hostesses. She's been invited to the White House twice now."

"That's wonderful." Remembering overheard conversation between Aunt Cel and Uncle Chris, Philippa wondered if a lady served the president in bed by engraved invitation only. "When do I see her?"

"Probably late this afternoon," Richard said. "This is her day to visit hospitals for the indigent here in Washington, a pet charity of Bliss and Mrs. Jefferson Davis. There's a small reception arranged for you tonight in our hotel suite. How long will you be with us?"

"Just until tomorrow. I'm going on down to Harper's Ferry and the Shenandoah Valley for a long visit with my friend, Belle Boyd, and to see my father. It's sort of a sudden thing," Philippa confessed.

Richard raised his eyebrows. "Trouble at home in Boston?"

"No. Well, to be honest, yes, but not the family kind, Aunt Cel and I yelling, Uncle Chris putting his foot down, that sort of thing." Philippa hesitated, then said, "Oh, I might as well tell you now. I was supposed to be married the day before yesterday, but I found I couldn't stand the man, and since I'm a coward at heart, I simply ran away."

Richard's pompous mask slipped. "What a bratty thing to do to some poor guy," he said, "but, do you know? That's always funny to another man, unless it's happening to him."

"Is that really true?" Philippa asked.

"True."

"You men must be almost as mean to each other as us women."

Philippa felt she should have been flattered. The lion captured for her reception by an enterprising Bliss was aging General Winfield Scott, and the eagle-eyed old man had kissed her hand, then flattered her half to death with a twinkle in his eyes, before finding a corner couch where he could doze through the rest of the evening.

Across the room, General Scott's young aide, sunburned brick-red, wearing dark brown sideburns, but no beard or moustache, stood guard over the old man, staring down anyone so impolite as to notice when that elderly gentleman snored. It had been a cat-and-mouse game all evening, between Philippa and the aide, each trying sneak glances at the other while trying not to be caught.

What was his name? Philippa's feet hurt too much, and her back ached too badly, for her to remember. Damn that Boston shoe clerk! She should have known he wasn't impressed by the narrowness of her feet, that he didn't have these slippers in a larger size.

And tonight would be the first day of her time of the month! It never failed.

Cannons & Roses

Was it Brown or Smith? It was some name as common as that, Philippa was sure. General Scott had introduced them, and his false teeth fitted badly.

Bliss was flirting with some Frenchman, or was he Spanish? Philippa had forgotten. The people were beginning to thin out now, and she was glad of that. Philippa wondered how What's-his-name woke up the good general when it was time for him to go home to a hot toddy and bed.

She looked away quickly. He was staring at her again. Philippa hoped he liked her profile. General Scott had mumbled something about his being just back from fighting Indians. Philippa decided that was why he was so sunburned. His hair was black enough for him to be an Indian himself.

Richard had disappeared long ago.

What *is* his name?

So *that's* how he does it! The aide had just cleared his throat loudly. General Scott straightened, as wide awake as he'd been sound asleep a moment ago, and got to his feet stiffly.

"So it's taps for me, Captain Jones?" General Scott chuckled. "Lead the old warhorse back to his stable and Mrs. Scott."

"Yes, sir."

Keefer Jones! What a strange first name. Philippa couldn't remember hearing it before.

Keefer had forgotten his cap. It was on a table near the chair where General Scott had dozed. He hadn't so much as glanced in her direction before he left.

Philippa was let down until Captain Jones suddenly returned, tucked his cap under his arm, and crossed the room to her.

"Will you be in Washington long?" he asked.

"No. I leave in the morning."

Cannons & Roses

"Oh. That's a damned nuisance, isn't it?" He was irritated, as if such an abrupt departure was entirely her fault, and disappointed, too. "Good evening, Miss Randolph."

"Good evening, Captain Jones."

He turned abruptly and left the room.

Bliss had joined her niece. "What a dull young man," she remarked. "I wonder General Scott puts up with someone so ungracious."

"I think he's been fighting Indians," Philippa said.

"That accounts for it," Bliss said. "He probably has a squaw or two, and Indian brats out in the territories, but butter wouldn't melt in his mouth back here. Men are all the same." Bliss covered a yawn. "Did you have a good time?"

"Lovely."

"Richard will be glad to hear it. He said I shouldn't claim the reception was just for you, that we should tell you this was our monthly soirée." Jeanette smiled sweetly. "Whom did you leave in the lurch at the altar, dear? Anyone Richard or I know?"

"A Philip Morley."

Jeanette frowned. "Not the Massachusetts congressman? The very rich one?"

"That's Philip."

"How could Celeste ever let you do that?" Bliss asked, and she was shocked. "Nearly every debutante in Washington has her cap set for him! How could you be so foolish?"

Philippa sighed. "I suppose I'm talented in the foolish direction, Aunt Bliss."

"You can say you had amnesia."

"I don't think so," Philippa said in a tired voice. "Good night, Aunt Bliss."

She was glad her B. & O. train left early the next morning.

John Brown had chosen the detachment that would capture Louis Washington and his slaves, and bring them to the arsenal. "Make very sure you bring the dress sword presented to George Washington by Frederick the Great," he instructed Judah.

"Yes, Papa."

The old man scowled fiercely. "Harm no women this time."

"No, papa." Judah shifted uncomfortably. Why did the old man always make him feel like a sniffling kid? He was a thirty-two-year-old man, with a wife, such as she was, and six bawling kids, with the seventh on the way.

That dead Missouri woman knew how much of a man he was!

John stared around the circle of twenty-seven loyal followers, all but his six sons volunteers from the free Negro colonies in Canada he'd helped found.

They would set out in the early hours to light a torch that would send the south up in flames!

God had allotted His only begotten Son twelve followers, and one a traitor. Hugh Forbes was Brown's Judas Iscariot. Bitter because of a few dollars, he'd carried news of the plot to Steward and another northern senator, but the Secert Six New England abolitionist financiers and philanthropists had remained loyal and forthcoming with money. George Stearns, Franklin Sanborn, Thomas Higginson, Theodore Parker, Samuel Howe, and Gerrit Smith—all good and gentle men—would be proud of him.

God had stopped their ears to the perfidy of Hugh Forbes.

Brown's followers were gathered around a bonfire in the barnyard of the barren farm he had rented seven months ago. *Like Mount Vernon,* the old man thought, *these buildings will someday be an American shrine.*

Blood would begin flowing tomorrow: first a trickle, finally a flood that would wash the southern states clean of the Sin of Slavery. But tonight the seat of his projected empire, high in the mountains, was empty of human life. Deer grazed in moon-dappled high meadows, trout flounced in crystal streams, and all was quiet as nature awaited his God-ordained arrival, a new Moses permitted to enter the Promised Land.

Brown had lived and suffered for this moment of triumph.

Raising his fists, Old John Brown bellowed, "Let us all pray!"

A Maryland farmer was passing the farm in his buggy, half-asleep until Brown's deep voice shattered the moonlit quiet.

"Goddamn old humbug!" he muttered. "Praying again at the top of his leather lungs. There ought to be a law about crazy neighbors."

Judah Brown felt a shiver of excitement. The old man had made them pray like this before they hacked those people to death along Osawatomie Creek. If he got the chance tomorrow . . .

Jamie McCoy was up early, shaved and dressed, with his dress sword laid out. The wedding wouldn't be until noon, but as best man for his aide, Sergeant Robertson, Jamie didn't want anything to hold up the wedding. The youngster was nervous enough about marrying Old Jack's daughter as it was.

He wondered if Thomas J. Jackson, U.S.A., Ret., and military tactics instructor at V.M.I., would be

Cannons & Roses

sucking a lemon while he waited to give the bride away at that church in Lexington.

Jamie stared out the window of his small Martinsburg house. It was going to be a good day. Robertson had sweated rain. That was the trouble with sergeants —they worried too much.

Jamie grinned, but there was a core of sadness in him today. His marriage to Philippa had taken place on such a day as this, bright with hope and promising happiness.

He thought of their daughter for the first time in weeks.

After receiving the invitation to her wedding, and sending his regrets because he was waiting orders to take his Marine detachment to sea soon, Jamie had blanked Philippa out of his mind. She was too much like her mother.

There was the sound of galloping in the street. The rider pulled his horse to a skidding stop in front of the gate and dismounted.

"No one rides like that," Jamie muttered, "but Lieutenant J. E. B. Stuart."

The jaunty feather waving from the crown of the man's slouch hat proved it was Jeb Stuart.

What the hell does he want at this hour?

Jamie was downstairs and opened the front door just before Jeb's gloved fist struck it. "Hey, what goes on, Jeb? You're early for the wedding."

"Compliments of Colonel Robert Lee, sir." Stuart stiffened. "He wants you to join him in Harper's Ferry with a dozen of your best men."

Jamie returned Stuart's salute. "My compliments to Colonel Lee. I'll comply immediately." Jamie relaxed. "Now tell me what's up, Jeb. My sergeant is getting married at noon, and I'm best man."

Jeb Stuart's handsome boyish face lit up with excitement. "A party has seized the arsenal and has hostages, as we get the report. The Northern Virginia Militia is being called up, but you know militia. Bobby thinks we regulars will have to restore order." Stuart grinned. "Damned if this doesn't remind me of Kansas all over again. What do you suppose ever happened to Old John Brown?"

"Probably choked sucking an egg," Jamie said.

3

Philippa was supposed to change trains at Harper's Ferry, leaving the main B. & O. line that would wind through Cumberland Gap, and into Ohio, for a spur line that went down to Winchester where the Boyds were expecting her. Anxious to get out of Washington, before Aunt Bliss was too much on her nerves, Philippa had Richard put her on the earliest Monday morning train. She was dozing when brakes squealed, and the four-car train ground to a halt.

The hardware drummer in the next seat, a Mr. Squires, jolted awake when Philippa did. It was a gray dawn outside.

"Why are we stopping, Mr. Squires?" Philippa asked.

With his shirt sleeve, he rubbed condensed moisture from the window, to peer out. "We ain't in the station. We're across the bridge but out in the yards. I'll go see, little lady."

Philippa rose to let him get out of his window seat,

and watched his broad, suspendered back go down the aisle. He spoke a few soothing words to the worn-out woman with three young children and a nursing baby in her arms.

"Careful train crews on this line, ma'am," he said, chucking the sleepy baby under the chin. "They ain't like some."

The train jerked once, twice, then sat still on the tracks again. Philippa shifted to the window seat. When she peered out, she saw the engineer, the fireman, and the conductor, ahead by the baggage car, arguing with a tall, bearded man sitting a horse. In a ragged group behind him were other figures on horseback, some white, some black.

There was a flat bang, no louder than a handclap, and smoke curled into the air from a rifle. The bearded man on horseback wheeled his horse, shouted an angry command. The train crew stood like frozen dolls. With a handwave, the bearded old man waved the train on, and he dashed off into the morning darkness following his ill-assorted riders. All were armed with carbines and cutlasses, Philippa noticed.

The train backed, came to a clanking halt, waited, and when a switch was thrown up ahead, jerked forward, gathering speed.

Mr. Squires was back. His pudgy face was the color of freshly risen bread dough, and he sank into the aisle seat, gasping for breath.

"What in the world happened up there, Mr. Squires?" Philippa asked. "Who were those men? Train robbers?"

Mr. Squires mopped his forehead with a crumpled handkerchief.

"No, little lady. They thought this might be a troop train from Washington. A *troop train!*" His laugh was harsh and mirthless. "Poor nigger baggage handler poked his woolly head out of the baggage car, and a nervous trigger finger blew it half off! The old man apologized. *Apologized!*"

Mr. Squires slumped in his seat, closed his eyes, and blew out a sighing breath. "My wife, Ellie, wants me to quit the road and work for her father. My samples are in that baggage car. They could have blown *my* head off!" He turned his face toward Philippa. "Until I smell gunpowder, I'm a brave man, little lady. Her father really ain't a bad old cuss."

Because she was traveling in strange territory, Philippa assumed unexplainable delays, and even the offhand killing of baggage handlers, weren't cause for too much passenger alarm. She'd heard wild tales of the opening West. What had happened was an adventure she could share with Belle. She got off the train at the Harper's Ferry station to change for Winchester, hoping she'd have time for breakfast at the small hotel across from the station.

Men and women, carrying lunch pails, and chatting back and forth, were strolling past the station to their work in the arsenal and rifle works farther out on the narrow tongue of land where two rivers joined. Sheer mountains rose on either side of the sleepy town, blue with morning mist.

Her train wouldn't leave for two hours yet.

Philippa ordered eggs, sausage, toast, and coffee from a still-sleepy waitress. "Have you a newspaper?" she asked the girl.

"Two days old." The girl yawned. "Excuse me. The Richmond paper."

"Oh? May I borrow it?"

"You surely may. From the north, ain't you?"

Philippa nodded. "Boston."

Cannons & Roses

The waitress leaned her elbows on the counter. "I reckon you've read that awful book, *Uncle Tom's Cabin?*" she whispered. The waitress looked around the almost-empty restaurant, to make sure she wouldn't be overheard. "Is it as racy as they say?"

Philippa had browsed through a copy Uncle Chris brought home and had laid it aside as dull. Aunt Cel had laughed her way through the book.

Philippa knew it was about slavery, of course, so she misinterpreted "racy." "There's a lot about the relationship between Negroes and white people in it, I guess, but I haven't read it word for word."

"Oh, we all know that," the waitress said in an impatient voice. "They put you in jail for just having a copy down here, though. What I mean . . ." The girl's voice sank. "Is it *sexy?*"

Philippa's delighted peal of laughter echoed in the hotel restaurant. "I'm truly sorry!" she said. She wiped her eyes with a napkin. "No, as much as I read, it isn't," she told the girl. "Preachy, yes, but sexy? No."

The waitress made a disappointed face. "Oh, well, I won't mind waiting then," she said. "Five others are ahead of me to read the only copy in Harper's Ferry."

A tall young man who was faintly familiar to Philippa burst into the restaurant, stopped to look around, then approached the counter.

Philippa's waitress took his order before turning hers over to the cook.

Philippa remembered! He was the man who'd shot the baggage handler! She stared at his hawklike face, fascinated and repelled. He had a lantern jaw, needed a shave, and his face was pitted. But he wasn't armed now.

Why hadn't he been arrested?

Cannons & Roses

She decided there had to be a good reason. Maybe he was a secret operative, and the baggage handler was a murderous villain, wanted dead or alive. That had to be it, Philippa decided.

The waitress brought her breakfast. The girl was filled with barely suppressed excitement. "That man wants twenty-three roast beef sandwiches to go, and ten ham! Can you imagine? I asked him if he was feeding an army, and he said yes. The cook is out of her mind!"

Philippa didn't report the railroad-yard incident. She exchanged glances with the man. *He'll see I'm not a blabbermouth,* Philippa thought.

Judah Brown gave her a frosty smile. Philippa smiled back.

Wouldn't I like to be ripping the clothes off that young bitch, he was thinking. *I'd show her how much of a man I am!*

But Judah knew it could never be. Memory of the old man's beating out there in Kansas was still too fresh in his mind.

Afterward, sobbing and sick, he'd had to flog Old John with a harness strap, until blood trickled down his hairy back and flanks. That was nearly worse than the beating he'd been given.

Flogging your own father, and him seeming to enjoy it as he sang hymns!

It was after she'd had breakfast and read the *Richmond Advocate* that Philippa crossed the wide main street of Harper's Ferry, to sit in the railroad's waiting room and wait for the Winchester train.

Only then, when workers, still carrying their lunch pails, straggled from the arsenal and rifle works, to

Cannons & Roses

gather in puzzled clumps out in the street between the station and hotel, did Philippa realize something was wrong.

She didn't want to leave her valise, which was on the bench beside her.

A portly man wearing an unbuttoned floral-pattern vest hurried across the street from the hotel, pausing to talk and listen to each little group of workers. He kept shaking his head in disbelief.

In the station, he nodded a curt good-morning to Philippa, then crossed to the telegrapher's desk, and shook the thin young man with the green eyeshade out of his morning's catnap.

"Matt, they'll call me a fool and a humbug. Every other railroad president in the U. S. of A. will make me a laughingstock." He hit his forehead with the palm of his hand. "Why did I have to stop over here last night on my way to Washington?"

Matt had jumped to attention. "The bridges, sir. You was to inspect them today, sir."

The man stared at Matt, shook his head in disbelief. "At ease," he said, regaining his sense of humor. "Sorry I spouted off. Start to jiggle that key, and this is what you tell 'em in Washington. War Department, attention of General Winfield Scott. Urgent. Got that?"

"Yes, sir."

"Why ain't you scribbling it down?"

Matt tapped his forehead with a forefinger. "It's in here, you know."

The president of the B. & O. sighed. "I forgot. You're our mental wizard. Well . . ."

Matt waited, and so did Philippa, on the edge of the bench now, remembering with an effort not to start chewing her fingernails.

"Beg leave to report an insurrection here in Har-

Cannons & Roses

per's Ferry," he began dictating, then paused. "Oh, well, in for a dime, in for a dollar." The man sighed. "Rebels have seized the arsenal and rifle works, stop, holding hostages, stop, send help."

Without a change of expression, Matt sat down, tapped out the Washington signal, got a response, began sending the message.

Philippa rose when the man started to leave, buttoning his vest. "Sir?"

"Yes, miss?"

"What *is* going on?"

"I wish to Billy-Hell I knew! The mayor here sent for troops an hour or two ago, after our train was stopped and a baggage handler killed. The conductor and engineer reported to him, not me, you understand. They didn't know I was in town. They said some old man was going to seize the arsenal and rifle works, and, by God, I guess he did!"

"Is this serious?" Philippa asked, incredulous.

"I sure hope it is now! Bobby Lee is on his way, and he's bringing some of McCoy's marines, but the local militia don't think whatever crazy man is up at the arsenal and rifle works remembered to bring the rest of his army, whoever they might be. Have you ever seen militia in action, miss?"

"No, sir."

"If your train don't leave before *they* unlimber their squirrel guns, find cover! Good morning."

She watched him retreat to the hotel.

Matt spoke up from behind his telegrapher's key. "Mr. Otis Gardner forgot to tell you our local militia is mainly drunks. It's them we're going to need Fed troops to keep in line."

"Thank you," Philippa said. "I was getting confused."

"Last Fourth of July all of us civilians had to take cover," Matt said, grinning. "They run out of blank ammunition, but not whisky."

The army had furnished mounts for Jamie, his replacement, Israel Green, and ten marine privates, and they'd fallen in behind Colonel Robert E. Lee's 122nd First Virginia Cavalry, U.S.A. Green and Jamie were competent riders, but the ten marines Jamie had selected weren't horsemen.

They had volunteered from Rhode Island, Boston, and Connecticut, and were seafaring men. Lee's twenty laughing troopers shouted back encouragement as the column loped along the road between Front Royal and Harper's Ferry.

"Don't steer with the ears, Gyrene."

"That ain't no rudder, it's a tail."

"Three points starboard, sailor. That's a mare in yonder pasture."

Jamie's marines were giving as good as they got.

"Where's them foxhounds, southern boy?"

"Does your poor old daddy know you stole his horse?"

"Them fellows ain't wearing their iron pants this morning—ass armor so they don't get wounded when they gallop off—so I guess there won't be any trouble two marines can't handle."

Turner Ashby, slouched in his saddle, half-asleep as he rode, had his horse gaited beside Traveler. With half an ear, he listened to the back-and-forth behind him, amused.

At the dance last night, Belle Boyd had let him kiss her. Tonight he would see her again and meet her Boston friend.

"You'll just love Philippa Randolph," Belle had said.

"If she's the Queen of Sheba, or Cleopatra, maybe," Turner remembered saying. (That damned sneaky peach brandy!) "But you will still be my only true love, my lady, and I want your glove."

It was tucked inside his blouse.

"Hey, Turner."

Jeb Stuart had awakened.

Ashby's was a lazy, sleepy grin. "What is it, lackey?"

"Reckon we'll see action today?"

"No. False alarm. The damn Yankees ain't coming to get us yet."

Jamie kicked his horse and rode up beside Colonel Lee. "Sir, thank you for calling us out."

My great God! Jamie was thinking. *I'd give an arm and a leg to look that distinguished on a horse!*

He knew, dismounted, Robert E. Lee stood a mere six feet because of his short legs. But on a horse he was ten feet tall!

Lee smiled that always-gentle smile. "I thank you for coming along on this wild-goose chase. With luck, we'll get you back in time for the wedding."

"Thank you, sir."

Jamie dropped back to ride beside his men.

Harper's Ferry was in sight. It looked peacefully asleep in the October sun.

Louis Washington was confused. He'd lived for years, afraid of a slave rebellion, sleeping in a locked house from which even house servants were banished at nightfall. He'd slept with a shotgun under the bed since the Nat Turner affair in northern Virginia.

He'd had to present Frederick the Great's jewel-studded gift to his famous great-uncle, as if he sur-

Cannons & Roses

rendered a kingdom, but now sat opposite the seedy old man with the tangled beard, and they were both munching ham sandwiches.

God knows what was happening to his twelve slaves and his wife! But Louis somehow sensed there wasn't real danger to anyone's person. Yet why had they been brought here to the Harper's Ferry arsenal?

This was like a bad dream!

During the last half hour there had been desultory gunfire outside, and some return fire from this man's Negro and white followers. Louis had never seen an odder group than his captors.

Louis finished his sandwich (it wasn't sugar-cured ham) and cleared his throat. "Sir, you must have had a plan of some merit, bringing my wife and me, as well as our slave property here," he ventured in a mild voice. "The sword is an heirloom, but if that's all you want, you're welcome to it if you'll conduct us back to my plantation."

Brown had strapped on the sword. A strange light seemed to hover around the man's bearded face with those piercing eyes.

"Listen!" Brown said, cocking his head.

There was another sputter of gunfire.

"I'd say we're being attacked," Louis told Brown.

Brown roused. "Can't you hear slaves throwing off their yokes all over the south? It's the Day of Jubilee. Tomorrow we'll rest beside clear streams in the Promised Land, high up in the mountains where the southern sinners can never find us. Blood! It cleanses. Jehovah is a jealous God! He'll never forsake His chosen black people." Brown paused. "Are you still hungry?"

Louis Washington wiped his lips with a handkerchief. "I am not," he said, "but thank you for the asking."

Cannons & Roses

As if he were some sort of a magician, Old John Brown produced a hen's egg from the depths of his ragged clothing, nipped off the narrow end of the shell, and sucked at the contents.

Louis Washington vomited the sandwich he'd just swallowed.

I never could stomach ham that hasn't been sugar-cured, he thought, and wondered if he, his wife, and their faithful slaves would escape this madman alive.

4

*T*his strange morning, when Otis Gardner mentioned McCoy's marines, it didn't immediately register with Philippa that he was talking about her father's command, because Celeste and Christopher had raised her a Randolph. She was anxious to get down to Winchester as quickly as possible, and away from whatever was developing here. But before the Winchester local was called, the realization struck home.

The father she hadn't seen for a year was coming to Harper's Ferry!

Philippa crossed the street back to Harper's Ferry Commercial Hotel and rented a room. In doing so, she learned that Colonel Lee would set up his field headquarters here.

Before she left the station, Philippa had tried to telegraph Belle Boyd that her arrival in Winchester would be delayed.

"Them lines as well as all the others is cut now,"

the telegrapher informed her. "We're in a state of siege."

He offered his opinion that the North had declared war on the South, and that an invasion force was coming from Washington.

The desk clerk at the hotel had another opinion. "It's another Nat Turner slave revolt," he confided to Philippa. "They have a circle of fire around Harper's Ferry, and any troops coming to rescue us will have to fight their way in."

Philippa retired to her room, and took a long soaking bath before changing into her best dress. Revolution or war, she wanted to look her best. When Jamie finally arrived, he'd explain everything. Until then, she reserved judgment on the situation.

"Something must be wrong with me," she told herself. "This town's in a panic, troops are coming, those sniper rifles are popping out there, and I'm only mildly excited, anxious to see Daddy."

She found her Bible and sat down beside the window to read. Glass shattered and a wild shot thudded into the wall of the room behind her. She closed her Bible, gingerly brushed the glass shards from her skirt, and moved the chair over beside the bed.

She opened her Bible again.

And ye shall compass the city, all ye men of war, and go round about the city once. Thus shalt thou do six days.

And seven priests shall bear before the ark seven trumpets of rams' horns . . .

This morning, Philippa decided, Harper's Ferry must be Jericho.

Colonel Lee ordered the local militia to withdraw from positions they'd set up to pepper the armory and arsenal with rifle fire. Brown had seized a number of workers when they arrived for work, and no one knew how many hostages he was holding. As Colonel Lee sized up the situation, Brown was in an untenable position. Hostages were his only trump card.

North Virginia militia had begun to straggle into Harper's Ferry. Their fire-breathing commander wanted to storm Brown's position.

Colonel Lee commended him on his aggressive attitude (which wasn't shared by many of his men), but pointed out that a number of hostages would be killed.

"Our mission here as I see it, sir," Colonel Lee said, "is to get those people safely released, and to do so we must let whoever conceived this adventure realize how hopeless his situation is."

If there should come a time when a frontal attack was necessary, Colonel Lee assured the man, the North Virginia militia could have the honor of leading the sortie, if they so desired.

They were billeted in the town hall, with the local militia, and the ladies of Harper's Ferry brought sandwiches, cakes, pies, coffee, and lemonade. Colonel Lee had ordered all sale of liquor stopped, and there had been grumbling, but as the day progressed, a picnic atmosphere took over.

And nine months after the siege at Harper's Ferry, a surprising number of babies came into the world after hasty marriages.

Philippa met her father in the hotel lobby. The stunned expression on his face amused her. "Aren't you glad to see me?" she asked.

Jamie shook his head as if to clear it. "Well, sure I am, you know that, but it's been since last summer, and you're not the world's greatest letter writer, you know."

Philippa regarded Jamie's dress uniform and the ornamental sword. "Do you always come to war dressed like this?" she teased. "You're beautiful."

"One of my men was to be married."

Second Lieutenant Israel Green came up and nodded to Philippa. "Men accounted for, sir."

"Good," Jamie said. "I want you to meet my daughter. Philippa, Israel Green. He's under orders to assume my command at Front Royal. I'm bound for sea duty."

Jamie took off his sword and handed it to young Green. "I feel silly wearing the damned thing. Take care of it for me."

It was after midnight when Colonel Lee sent Jeb Stuart to the armory to bargain with Brown. He and Jamie had determined that a small, disciplined force should back Stuart's play, but stay out of sight.

The local and North Virginia militia had waived the honor of furnishing this storming force. Their commander had decided this was a federal affair.

After a brief discussion, Colonel Lee and Jamie decided the marines were a logical choice to do the job at hand.

The plan was simple. If Jeb Stuart discovered that the men inside were adamant, he'd step back, and the marines would burst through the partially opened door.

They knew Brown was in the rifle works now. Only there was fresh well water available. He'd moved his hostages into an adjoining room. Intelligence about what was going on had been ridiculously simple to obtain.

Sometime during the day, three of the Canadian Negroes from Chatham heard the word "treason." They hadn't bargained for that! You got hanged for treason. So they walked down the road and into Harper's Ferry. Colonel Lee had them served a meal in his personal quarters.

Israel Green's heart was set on leading the assault, if there was to be one. Jamie gave his permission, because younger than most of the men he would command, and Jewish, Israel needed to have their confidence before Jamie relinquished the command to him.

After a few minutes of talking with someone inside, through a crack in the door, Jeb Stuart came back to where Jamie stood.

"Would you believe it's Old John Brown inside there?" Stuart was thunderstruck. "I knew that crazy fool in Kansas!"

"So did I," Jamie admitted. "What the hell does he want here?"

"Not much. Safe conduct for his men and himself up into the mountains, rations for the journey, and permission for Louis Washington, his wife, and their slaves to be taken with him."

"That's Old Man Brown in there all right! What did you tell him?"

Stuart grinned. "I'm consulting with my superior officer."

Israel Green had been listening.

"This is it, Israel," Jamie said, matter-of-fact. "Let Jeb have another palaver. When he takes out his handkerchief to wipe his face, go in. Brown's the one with a full ebard. Use cutlasses. We don't want any hostages shot."

"Yes, sir!" The light of battle danced in Israel's brown eyes.

Cannons & Roses
* * *

In the short, bitter struggle inside the rifle works, four of Brown's followers died, and Brown himself should have been killed. He wasn't only because Green led the assault with Jamie's dress sword, instead of a navy-issue cutlass. Parrying a thrust from George Washington's gift, Israel slashed Old Brown's shoulder and laid open his ribs, but when Green thrust for the heart, Brown's breastbone snapped off the slender, blunt blade.

Brown left the armory on a litter.

"You damn-fool shavetail!" Jamie scolded Second Lieutenant Green. "I'm taking a new dress sword out of your pay."

"I'm sorry, sir, but I forgot." Green was shamefaced. "I hope you won't let the incident appear on my record."

"The only damned thing that's going to appear on your record, Israel, is a commendation for leading your men into there, with the loss of only a single man." Jamie sighed. "Do you want that dress sword as a souvenir?"

Israel grinned. "As a reminder, sir."

"You've got it. I'll send you a bill for my new one." Jamie thought a moment, then said, "This whole affair is ridiculous. A tempest in a teapot, a lot of sound and fury, signifying nothing."

"That's Shakespeare, sir," Green complimented.

"That so?" Jamie cocked a sarcastic eyebrow. "And I thought it was Thoreau, or maybe Ralph Waldo Emerson."

Israel Green flushed. "Sir?"

"Yes, lieutenant?"

"I always manage to say the right thing at the wrong

time, or the wrong thing at the right time. Do you ever have that trouble, sir?"

Jamie scratched his head, perplexed. "It hasn't been called to my attention yet, Israel, but I reckon I probably do. The bar's open. I'm buying the first drink."

Green flushed. "Sorry, sir, but I don't drink."

Jamie grinned. "You sure do have that knack, don't you?"

"I guess I have," Green admitted. "Sir?"

"What is it?"

"We've just put down the first armed rebellion in the United States since Shay's Rebellion and the Whisky War in Pennsylvania. I don't think Harper's Ferry is unimportant. I do think something evil has started here."

Jamie was thoughtful. "You have a good mind, Green," he said. "I won't argue the point. I'm only sorry you didn't kill Brown. Not that I'm bloodthirsty, but that sanctimonious old bastard is probably grooming himself right now in the role of a martyr. I knew him in Kansas, and so did Jeb Stuart. He's a horse-thief and a murderer, but abolitionist money floated this scheme, unless I miss my guess. There's going to be hell to pay!"

"Yes, sir. Sir? I think I'll let you buy me that drink."

"Come along," Jamie said. "Time's wasting."

Jamie escorted Philippa down to Winchester on the next day's train. He was moody and introspective most of the way.

Philippa reveled in the changing fall colors of the Shenandoah Valley, and was wise enough not to try to break through the wall of silence with which Jamie had surrounded himself.

Cannons & Roses

Over the years, Philippa had been with him for a few short periods. She couldn't find it within herself to resent the fact that he'd rejected her as a baby and child, but it hurt. With Jamie she always felt the interloper, never knowing what look or gesture would put that distant look in his eyes. She wanted to talk with him about it, but knew she never could.

Jamie finally broke the long silence that had been punctuated only by the clicking car wheels.

"What are you doing down here?" he asked.

"Do you want to hear my long story?"

"Well, if it isn't too long," he said. "We're just about to Winchester."

"A man wanted to marry me, and I thought I wanted to marry him, but on the eve of our wedding I changed my mind and left everyone in the lurch. End of story. The short version, anyway. Daddy, I just couldn't go through with it."

"What about Celeste and Christopher?"

"Maura O'Grady didn't want to tell me, but I wormed it out of her. Uncle Chris gave me a thousand dollars. I imagine Aunt Cel hasn't disowned me. Sooner or later, she and Uncle Chris always see things from the same angle."

"You just picked up and left?"

Philippa nodded. "Practically in the middle of the night."

Jamie shook his head. "You ought to be spanked. That's a hell of a trick to play on any man."

"I know."

"How long do you intend to stay in Winchester?"

"I'll be with the Boyds at first. I've already graduated from a female seminary, but there's a Washington College for Women in Lexington, isn't there?

Daddy, I can't go back to Boston just yet. After what I did, I don't know if I ever dare."

"Your mother was a Virginian." It was the first time Philippa had heard Jamie mention her mother, and she was touched. "If I weren't up for sea duty, we could have a long visit, but I'm off to Newport News the day after tomorrow. But the Boyds think as much of you as they do of Belle. I'll come back here on leave."

"You really want me to stay?" Philippa asked.

"I want you out of the north," Jamie told her. "With this man Lincoln running for president, and I guess there's no way to stop him, something very ugly is shaping up. You've just seen the curtain rise in Harper's Ferry. Old John Brown is a crazy man, but watch your northern benighted abolitionists make him a hero. I don't want you up there, Philippa. I want you down here where I can keep an eye on your future."

"You know something, Daddy?"

Jamie studied her face. "Yes, you're a very beautiful young woman, and I pity the poor devil you left at the altar."

"There, damn it!" Philippa fished in her reticule for a handkerchief. "You've made me cry."

Jamie slipped an arm around Philippa's shoulders to hug her. "Stop it, you little minx." His voice was husky. "McCoys don't cry, and neither do the Randolphs, so blow your nose and settle down. We'll be in Winchester in ten minutes."

Belle Boyd was anxious. When Philippa didn't come in on the train yesterday, she'd been worried and had tried to wire Harper's Ferry, only to learn the wires

Cannons & Roses

were cut. At the day wore on, rumors about the uprising there trickled down to Winchester. Belle was furious that her Boston friend should receive such a welcome to the south.

Maybe Philippa would turn back.

Belle and Philippa were the same height, and Belle's spun gold hair complemented Philippa's dark honey. Each moved with a prowling grace, and they selected dresses to wear when they would appear together, that would nearly match, but not quite.

Today Belle wore a spray of small red roses at her throat. Together, Belle might wear a spray of yellow roses to Philippa's pink or red, the next time red to Philippa's white.

Philippa had her mother's dashing style on a horse. When the mood was on her, Belle rode like a Comanche.

Last summer they'd discovered they were distantly related—second or third cousins, they never could figure out exactly which.

Each girl was a beauty in her own right, but together Belle and Philippa were overwhelming. They were nicknamed the Rose Princesses.

Most important, their personalities were complementary. Belle was happy-go-lucky, Philippa thoughtful and introspective. But just beneath each girl's surface lurked a gamin streak that scotched affectations and conceit.

"Damn those Yankee abolitionists!" Belle irritably slapped a boot with her riding crop. "Maybe Philippa knows now why we've got to get away from the northern states, or forget the southern way of life."

Belle had a strong feeling that time was running out, that there would be no more shameful compromises

Cannons & Roses

with a people who might elect an ugly ape like Lincoln to sit in the White House and plot the destruction of the south.

Turner Ashby had put it neatly the other night: "Time's coming soon when we're going to ride over to Washington and teach these Yankees some manners. South Carolina is right. Virginia should lead secession, but if she won't, we'll play second fiddle awhile."

5

Belle was a graduate of Mount Washington Female College in Baltimore, and had made her debut in Washington society, but at heart she loved the Shenandoah Valley, particularly the small town of Martinsburg. It was only a few days after Philippa's arrival that Ben Boyd announced that their new Martinsburg home was finally finished. Belle persuaded her mother and father that she should stay on in Winchester with Philippa and one servant, an elderly Negro woman called Beulah Land.

Turner Ashby and Jeb Stuart teamed up to escort the girls to dances and other social functions, and the handsome couples were the talk of the valley.

In Stuart, Philippa discovered the southern gentleman cavalier, as if he'd just stepped out of the pages of a Walter Scott novel. There was always a subtle glint of mischief in his eyes, but there was a frank regard for womanhood there, too, which sometimes reminded Philippa of knightly gallantry she'd read about.

The staid and sometimes stuffy boys in Boston she'd known suffered in comparison with Jeb Stuart, but Philippa was careful not to fall in love.

"Yes, Jeb is charming enough," she confided to Belle, "and exciting, too, but he always seems to be looking over my shoulder for something or someone else. Do you notice that about Turner Ashby?"

"If I did, I'd slap him silly," Belle said.

Philippa laughed. "I bet you would, too."

Belle grinned. "Turner knows it."

"He and Jeb make quite a pair."

"I'd say that," Belle agreed. "I don't know two other men who could wear a feather with those slouch cavalry hats, and not get to be tagged as . . . well, odd. You know what I mean."

"No, I don't," Philippa confessed.

"Well, sometimes men love each other," Belle said in a candid voice. "Like one of them was a wife," she explained.

Philippa's eyes widened. "I never heard anything so ridiculous! Do you know what you're talking about, Belle?"

Belle nodded. "Turner explained it to me, and did you know that men blush, too?" Her laugh was guilty. "I pretended to be *so* dumb. One of his officers and a young private had to resign because they were having an affair. The man killed himself, and Turner had to lie to his family."

During the months they lived together in Winchester, Belle and Philippa became the toast of the valley. Both had always gotten on well with their peers, but neither girl had ever established a warm, mutual friend-

446

ship. The slight difference in their ages—Belle was three years older than Philippa—didn't make any difference.

Philippa had watched her Uncle Chris become increasingly disillusioned with the abolitionist as well as the antislavery cause.

"These do-good rascals are as extreme as the people they slander," she'd heard him tell Celeste more than once.

Garrison, Harriet Beecher Stowe, and her preacher brother, particularly disgusted him. He'd stopped backing abolitionist causes.

The Shenandoah had been cleared of Indians and settled by Virginia pioneers unable to compete as independent farmers with the gang-labor plantations of northern Virginia. Prosperous, small farms checkerboarded the floor of the valley.

Prosperous families like the Boyds owned one or two slaves, but these usually considered themselves family members. Beulah Land was typical.

She cooked for Belle and Philippa, unless her rheumatism was bad, and then they cared for her. She scolded when she wasn't petting the girls. Beulah Land was a stricter chaperone than Belle's mother would have been.

"That Ashby man, he got an eye on you, Miss Belle," she'd say, "but you just mind your manners. Don't go give him no cause to think you ain't a lady. You been brung up strict, you stay strict, hear?"

Or Beulah Land would tell Philippa, "Since your ma ain't here, you goin' to listen to this old nigger, Miss Philippa." Beulah Land could never get it through her head that Celeste was Philippa's aunt. "You goin' to stay as strict as Miss Belle, hear?"

John Brown's raid at Harper's Ferry had shocked

Philippa more than she wanted to admit. She'd seen the dead carried from the rifle works.

Philippa had seen Brown with his blood-stained bandages and that crazy look in his eyes. More than once she woke up hearing the snap of the rifle that killed the Negro baggage handler, and seeing the puff of smoke from its barrel.

Before Harper's Ferry, if anyone had called for her opinion, Philippa would have said the southern states were too touchy, and just imagined they were being persecuted. It was what she'd learned in school, and to a certain extent from Uncle Chris.

After Harper's Ferry, Philippa's opinion turned around. That rabid abolitionist talk was being put into practice. And the idolization of John Brown all through the northern states disgusted her. It was frightening, too.

Flushed into the open by a congressional investigation, the Secret Six reacted variously. Gerrit Smith fled to Canada. All of the others claimed they didn't know Brown would strike directly at the government and squirmed off the treason hook. All of them still felt they'd contributed to a righteous cause.

Philippa drew the logical conclusion. Anything that would injure the southern states was laudable. John Brown had been just a bit too zealous and had used bad judgment.

What had seemed like a threatening but distant cloud on the southern horizon when she was in Boston, here in Winchester became a towering storm about to break.

Philippa was quickly infected with Belle's flaming southern patriotism. This soon became evident in letters to Celeste and Christopher, as well as the few she wrote her father.

Cannons & Roses

It was Jamie who replied: *As a military man, when and if the break comes, I face a hard decision as do most of my friends. You don't have to make that decision, Philippa. Sister Celeste and Christopher are right: you should go back to Boston.*

"What are you going to do?" Belle asked when she'd read the letter.

"Stay here," Philippa said. "This is my house. I've made more friends here in a few months than I ever had in Boston. This isn't only a house now, it's becoming my home."

"Good for you!" Belle grinned. "Together we stand. You've joined the southern race."

Captain Keefer Jones was twenty-five, the only son living of Minerva and Maxwell Jones of St. Louis. A lie about his age got him into the army when he was only sixteen, and thus escaped the family enterprise, a leather-goods manufacturing business. Keefer had always been a solitary boy, more interested in birds and animals than people, a fact that worried his parents. When they learned he'd enlisted in the cavalry, they decided not to stop him.

"Keefer needs to associate with men," Maxwell Jones said. "The army will be good for him."

His mother wasn't so sure, but she didn't try to interfere.

Private Jones first came to the attention of his commanding general, Philip Sheridan, when he was on a patrol.

"Sir, that's no owl that hooted out there," he said to his sergeant. The troopers were setting up camp in a ravine after a hard day's ride. "It's a Kiowa."

"Son, this here's Arapahoe territory," Sergeant Baird said indulgently.

Cannons & Roses

"I smell Kiowa war paint," Keefer said.

Sergeant Baird was an old-timer on the plains, too experienced to ignore even a green trooper's hunch, so he deployed his men just before the Kiowa war party swooped into the ravine.

Keefer slipped away from the main body as soon as it was evident that the Kiowas were overmatched.

Keefer chose a concealed flanking position, cocked his Spencer carbine, and waited for their headlong retreat from the ravine. When the Kiowa whirled their horses, Keefer picked off three of them before they could get away and tore a brave who tried to ride him down off his pony. After a desperate fight, he killed the Indian with his own tomahawk.

"Sir, get that young 'un out of my troop," Sergeant Baird told General Sheridan. "He's making my veterans look like greenhorns. Don't you think Old Ben Thompson could use him?"

Mountain Man Thompson was Sheridan's head scout. A bearded giant with one ear (the other was bitten off in a fight), Thompson was rated the best scout—if the most cantankerous—west of the Mississippi. He took a liking to the youngster. Until he was twenty-two, Keefer scouted for Sheridan.

For months at a time, he and Thompson roamed the prairies together, scouting hostile tribes. Keefer learned all the tricks. From just a whiff of faint woodsmoke, he could determine the direction and approximate distance of a fire. He learned to forecast weather by animal actions and to sort out the individual members of war parties by their moccasin prints.

Thompson taught Keefer the fine art of stealing ponies from the tribes, and how to survive in dry country for days without water by chewing cactus and other desert plants. Once he and Thompson had to kill one of their mounts and drink the scummy green water from its belly, an Apache trick.

"Better for your guts than skull-bust whisky," the older man assured him. "There's nourishment in this stuff."

When General Scott queried Sheridan about an aide experienced in scouting he could trust with an important mission, Keefer received orders to report to the U. S. Army's commanding general in Washington. Sheridan didn't tell Keefer the reason for the transfer.

Scott appointed Keefer his personal aide so he could study the trooper. Did he drink too much? Did he have too many friends? Was he inclined to talk too much? What was his way with women?

John Brown was finally hanged, and flags flew at half-mast in every northern state. There were prayers for his immortal soul from nearly every pulpit. Mass meetings were held to mourn Brown and his followers. Men and women wore mourning bands.

The southern states stopped quarreling about secession. Adding insult to injury, that crude country ape desecrating the White House talked about sending supplies and more men (it was said) to Fort Sumter. General P. T. G. Beauregard in Charleston brought up more cannon for his ring of fire around Sumter.

Colonel Robert E. Lee prayed, but no longer for peace. Should he resign his commission and offer his services to President Jefferson Davis, or keep the oath he swore when he graduated from West Point? It was a soul-rending decision for Lee.

Old Jack prayed, too. He chewed his lemon and asked for humility, and that he would never have to fight a battle on Sunday.

General Winfield Scott called Keefer Jones in for

a solitary midnight conference in the deserted War Department building.

"The Shenandoah Valley is a loaded pistol pointed at our heads, Major Jones." Scott was alert and at his didactic best. "The Army of the Potomac is being formed, as you know, and its purpose is the invasion of Northern Virginia when hostilities break out."

Scott limped to a map of eastern United States on the wall of his office."

"A moment, sir," Keefer said. "You've forgotten my rank."

"Not likely," Scott grumbled. "The ink of my signature on your promotion voucher is scarcely dry. Now, let's get to the business at hand." He touched the Shenandoah Valley. "See here? A determined southern force coming up this plain between the Alleghenies and the Blue Ridge mountains can cut the B. & O. railroad, cross the Potomac, strike east at Baltimore, severing the railroad there, then capture this city. You know how uncertain we are of Maryland."

Keefer studied the map. He remembered Philippa Randolph had been on her way to Winchester. With a start he realized she must have arrived in Harper's Ferry when John Brown's raid was in progress. No women were reported killed, so that was some relief.

"Are you with me, Major Jones?" Scott asked.

"Oh, yes, sir."

"You are a scout. Penetrating Indian territory is a different problem than the one I propose, but your guile and cunning should be as effective ferreting out the secret war plans of our southern brothers. The Valley Army of the Cenfederate States, their strengths, weaknesses, tactics, commanders, morale, and battle plans, if possible, will be your responsibility."

"I'm to become a spy, in other words, General Scott."

"I prefer the word 'scout.' "

"Am I to decide how I'm to establish myself in the valley, and gain the confidences I'll need?"

"You're to do just that, and review your plans with me within the next forty-eight hours. You are dismissed, major."

Cavalry needed saddles and other leather goods. Keefer started with that premise in his small Willard Hotel room. His father's company did a brisk business in saddles and bridles.

So far as Keefer knew, Jones Leather Manufacturing Company had no representatives east of Ohio. Why not set up, say, in Winchester, as a factory representative selling saddles?

Cavalry in the Shenandoah would be the right arm of the Valley Army. It was cavalry terrain.

He'd grow a beard to look older than his years while he waited for sample saddles from his father's factory. Western Missouri would probably go for the south, one way or another, but there was, Keefer knew, much proslavery and prosecession feeling in and around St. Louis.

General Fremont, California's hero, would be in charge of that army department. Regular army men despised Fremont and his overly ambitious wife. Only the public considered him a knight in shining armor. Shipping saddles from Union-held St. Louis to the Confederacy should be no problem. Fremont's procession of vultures were probably already headed there.

Cannons & Roses

It would be just a matter of who to bribe, and how much to pay.

So far so good.

But why choose Winchester, with Philippa Randolph, who might recognize him, there? She was a Boston Randolph. If she remained south, Philippa's sympathy would be for the Union, despite her relationship to Senator Carroll.

Keefer decided she might be able to help him in his clandestine mission. In any event, he hoped to see her again. Hoped? The word wasn't strong enough. Somehow, some way, somewhere Keefer Jones was *determined* to see Philippa again.

Along the way, Keefer had had his fair share of girls and women. But across that hotel room, at the reception, something had happened that deeply disturbed him. Keefer didn't know whether his previous attitude toward women was typically male, if it was simply normal that he wanted a shapely one as a stallion wants a mare in heat, or a bull wants to cover a cow.

Bad simile, he decided, because from any woman, be she Indian squaw, saloon girl, or a willing local girl wherever he'd been stationed, Keefer wanted—and got —more than that. Friendship, too? It was partly that.

"You make me feel as if I could matter," that woman in New Mexico territory had told him. "It ain't just bluff?"

Keefer had assured her it wasn't. "We're two human beings doing something we both enjoy, I hope," Keefer told that one. "So you do matter to me right now, and very much."

"Keef, you spoil them dames, treating the whores as if they was ladies," a bunkmate had once accused. "Bet you get your money's worth, though."

Cannons & Roses

Philippa. She was virgin, and probably very shy with men. Keefer knew that from across the room. But she aroused a different lust within him, and this is what disturbed him. He wanted *all* that this one had to give with her slender body, but also everything she could share with him from her mind and memory.

Keefer decided this was what the poets meant when they used the word "love."

Keefer hoped for Philippa's sake, as well as his own, that she'd packed up and returned to Boston. Love was an emotion he couldn't afford now, or into the near future.

Then why am I praying, he wondered, *that Philippa Randolph is still in Winchester?*

6

Johnston had routed the Army of the Potomac at the first Battle of Manassas (the Federals called it Bull Run) when reinforcements arrived posthaste from the Shenandoah in time to rout McDowell's exhausted troops. P. T. G. Beauregard, conquerer of Fort Sumter, and the darling of Charleston, whose troops had borne the first shock of the Union offensive, claimed credit for the victory. So did Johnston.

Pretty socialite Rose Greenhow kept her counsel, but knew exactly who made that Confederate victory possible. Forty-eight hours in advance, she'd furnished Beauregard the complete Union battle plan, accurate to the last detail.

The young officers who'd drawn the maps and written the orders were honored guests at Widow Greenhow's Sunday-evening salons, always asked to stay over for quiet chats when the rest of the guests had gone. In Wild Rose they had discovered someone who would listen for hours to all the details of their grueling, thankless work.

Rose's narrow-fronted brick house on Sixteenth, only a few blocks from the White House, was more than just a leak in Union security, it was a flood gate. Even Allan Pinkerton didn't suspect how many top officials, even cabinet members, confided in Wild Rose.

Rose and Mrs. Katherine Brady, foremost madam in Richmond, and once Philippa Randolph's confidant, were close friends.

That first Battle of Manassas convinced southern civilians it was as they'd suspected, the Federals didn't have a stomach for war, and it would all be over within a month. The Confederate War Department wasn't so sure. Neither was Jefferson Davis.

Rose Greenhow reported that General Banks would soon invade the Shenandoah to prevent another Confederate flank attack when the Army of the Potomac, under new leadership, would strike for Richmond.

General McClellan was the new leader. To one of her coded messages, transmitted by couriers, she added that the handsome little general, darling of the discouraged Federals along the Potomac, who promised to lead them to Richmond, couldn't stand the sight of blood. It amused them in Richmond as it had amused Rose.

General Thomas J. (Stonewall) Jackson, now in charge of the Valley Army, which included Turner Ashby's 4,000 cavalry, Jamie McCoy second in command, didn't laugh or even chuckle when he read Rose's coded postscript.

Rose had given him the measure of McClellan.

He was Stonewall Jackson since Manassas, and his brigade was the Stonewall Brigade. The harried and

Cannons & Roses

vexed southern general who's said, sarcastically, "While we charge, damn it, there stands Jackson like a stone wall," had nicknamed the wiry little man.

"McClellan," Jackson confided to Turner Ashby, "is a spit-and-polish general, but he don't know war is killing the other fellow—not trying to step around him so nobody gets hurt."

Rose Greenhow wrote Kate Brady a note on her lavender-scented stationery.

Dear Kate, she wrote. *Suggest you select a house in Winchester for your nieces, so those lusty Federals have someone to whom they can confide. Is Vivienne still with you? The tales she tells of her abused octoroon slave childhood will draw much sympathy and, of course, interesting information.*

The note was signed, *Love, Wild Rose.*

Kate Brady left her Richmond house in charge of her protégée, Emilia Williams, a willowy blonde from the north with the face of an angel.

She took Vivienne with her to find a suitable location in Winchester for the entertainment of Banks's officers when they arrived.

By pure chance, she selected Philippa Randolph's house as the one she had to have.

Vivienne Robidaux had never been a slave. The handsome young woman with ebony hair that reached the backs of her dimpled knees was the offspring of a handsome New Orleans quadroon woman and her Spanish protector, Juan Esteban Filhiol. She'd been educated in Spain.

There she'd fallen in love with a cave gypsy near Madrid, borne him a child, learned their dances, and

Cannons & Roses

returned to New Orleans. Kate Brady had met her there.

Vivienne returned to Richmond with Kate and became a feature attraction in her establishment, dancing, singing in a high, clear voice, and entertaining gentlemen who could afford the best.

Vivienne managed to look virginally innocent when clothed, but with banked sensual fires, and could be exquisitely wanton. She'd been a favorite companion of Philippa's mother.

Philippa's house wasn't large. It was built of red brick and sat back from the side street, screened by a weeping willow. A white picket fence surrounded it, and the mullioned windows had been imported from England by her mother's father. The sharply slanted slate roof made it resemble a cozy English cottage, brought to Virginia from a yew-shaded lane in Cornwall.

Kate and Vivienne were passing in an open carriage when Vivienne said, "There it is, Kate. Please stop, driver."

"Yas'm." The driver pulled up his horse. "Dat place belong Miss Philippa Randolph, that northern lady so popular with quality folks here. She don't go home when de war come because her's got our southern blood in her pretty veins."

"Wait," Kate instructed the driver.

Beulah Land met them at the door.

"Miss Philippa, she out in the back garden with the roses," Beulah announced, when she'd answered Kate's knock. "Who are you ladies?"

"Friends of her mother," Kate said. "Don't bother to announce us. We'll join her in the garden."

These two ain't quality ladies, Beulah Land thought.

Trash? No. Too well dressed, too soft-spoken.

Younger one, she ain't all white.

Beulah Land squinted at the carriage driver on the box for some hint. Staring at an imaginary spot above Kate's and Vivienne's heads, he rolled his eyes.

So *that's* who they are!

"Miss Philippa, she tan me, you walk all that way," Beulah Land said. "She ailing, it time for her morning tea. I tell her you here."

Vivienne started to speak, but Kate touched her lips with a gloved finger. "Please announce us," she said. "It's such a lovely morning. We'll wait here on the stoop."

"Uppity nigger!" Vivienne said when Beulah Land disappeared into the house, locking the door behind her.

Kate laughed.

"Miss Philippa, two women come, say they friends of your mother," Beulah Land told her mistress in the rose garden.

"Oh, good. Where did you leave them?"

"On the stoop, and I lock the door."

"I take it you don't approve of our company?" Philippa said. "Show them into the parlor and make tea. Hurry."

Philippa put her roses in vases, and brushed her hair before going to receive her company. Her mother had confided to Aunt Cel about her friendship with Kate Brady. From Beulah Land's reaction to her visitors, Philippa had guessed who they were.

"Mrs. Brady?" she said from the parlor doorway.

Kate looked up, surprised. The resemblance stunned her for a moment. Vivienne was speechless, too.

"Sometimes it unsettles me that I seem to look so

much like my mother," Philippa said. "I never knew her, you know. She died when I was born. Is your tea all right? Beulah Land makes it a bit strong."

"Just right," Kate said.

Vivienne nodded.

Philippa seated herself and poured her own cup of tea. "Why are you here in the valley just now?" Philippa asked. "We understand the Federals will come to Winchester soon. Some folks are packing to leave."

Kate Brady decided to be as frank with the daughter as she would have been with the mother, and said to Vivienne, "Wouldn't you like to see the back garden?"

"I certainly would."

As soon as Vivienne was gone, Kate moved her chair closer to Philippa's. "My dear, I take it that your sympathy is with the south in this war."

"Yes. I was at Harper's Ferry, you know, and my father resigned his commission to ride with Turner Ashby. I'm here in Winchester to stay, Mrs. Brady, and do everything I can to see that the south wins freedom from the north."

"I'll be just as honest with you," Kate said. "I need to rent this house." She told Philippa why, but without mention of Rose Greenhow. "Of course, we can't put you out on the street," Kate finished. "What can we manage in that regard?"

"I could stay with my friend, Belle Boyd, in Martinsburg," Philippa said, "but I'd rather stay right here. Maybe there's something I can do to help The Cause."

"Maybe there is," Kate agreed.

Philippa blushed. "Mrs. Brady, I haven't had any experience with men, so I don't see . . ."

Kate laughed, but not unkindly. "You'll get none in any establishment of mine," she said. "Not the sort you have in mind. I'm not a procuress, Philippa, so you can rest easy."

"I didn't think you were, if you were my mother's friend. Do you know Belle Boyd?"

"No. I don't have that pleasure."

"She and I are planning to help the Confederacy when the Yankees come. She knows this whole part of the valley, and we ride together so I can learn the terrain."

"I believe we're all going to keep busy," Kate said.

As an apprentice, before he joined the army, Keefer Jones had learned saddlery. He came to Winchester with a neat, pointed beard, wearing clear-glass octagonal spectacles, and clothes a size too large. A lift in his left boot gave him a slight limp. Twice he'd spoken to Philippa on the street, lifting his hat, and there hadn't been a flicker of recognition.

Keefer felt like a voyeur, being so near Philippa, and remaining unrecognized.

He'd rented a small empty store on the main street, but near her cottage, and slept in the bare room above it. Selling saddles, he discovered when he arrived in Winchester, was too ambitious a project for a spy. Repairing saddles, and occasionally building one to order, filled a real need for Turner Ashby's troopers and kept him in close touch with the rank and file as well as the officers.

"Gideon" was his password through the Federal lines on the banks of the Potomac. He made occasional trips in a creaky secondhand wagon over into Maryland to obtain leather and findings for his saddle work. These were also an opportunity to mail carefully coded messages to Winfield Scott.

Keefer traveled once to Richmond. At the War Department, he boldly approached a Major Ainsworth, and offered his services as a spy. "Joshua" was his password through Confederate lines.

Keefer furnished Scott exact figures on the number of soldiers in the valley, their commanding officers, their equipment, their morale. After each trip up into Maryland, Major Ainsworth was forwarded the same information from Winchester, but carefully distorted by Winfield Scott to give Richmond a false picture.

Keefer knew to the day and hour when Banks would invade the valley to protect the expedition that McClellan was finally mounting to capture the Confederate capital, and win the war. What he couldn't find out were Old Jack's plans in that contingency.

Keefer couldn't find out because even Stonewall's staff didn't know. It was gossip in the Valley Army that at the proper time and place, Old Jack would consult God before he moved.

Keefer learned the ragtag Valley Army had two opinions of Jackson. Half considered him insane, the other half inspired. When his troops marched, he marched, too, or rode a mule, wearing a mended Federal uniform left over from his army days.

He was totally unself-conscious in the presence of his troops. Sometimes he had a word with them, other times he ignored them.

Jackson issued orders deploring swearing. He despatched directives about how and when to wash their feet. They were advised to spend the sabbath in prayer. But their main grudge against Jackson was his marching orders.

Thirty miles was an average day's march, regardless of sweltering heat, or pouring rain.

Exhausted soldiers would sleep while they marched, or crawl into a ditch to doze off. The Valley Army, with

Cannons & Roses

its trail of stragglers, was Jackson's despair. They'd volunteered to fight Yankees—not to march—and discipline was a problem. Only a few wore any kind of uniform. Weapons were everything from standard-issue single-shot rifles, to blunderbusses, and even a few antique fowling pieces.

Close-order drill was a joke.

Officers were elected by the men and voted back into the ranks if they took their duties too seriously. The arrival of Richard Taylor's Louisiana Tigers added a new element to the army with which Jackson had to cope.

Taylor, the son of Zachary Taylor, raised his regiment in New Orleans, drafting jailbirds, drifters, and criminals who'd decided some distance from the Crescent City police might be a good idea. A fastidious man himself, General Richard Taylor managed to gain the full confidence of his men, and had whipped them into shape. In their colorful Zouave uniforms, on marches they dared other units to keep up with them.

This was good. But the Tigers believed in living off the country through which they happened to be passing. Unless Taylor was present, they raided orchards and fields, stole chickens and pigs, until Shenandoah residents feared them more than they did the Yankees.

As far as the Tigers were concerned, the Shenandoah was foreign territory. Valley girls and women were fair game.

Yet the arrival of the Tigers put a punch into Jackson's Valley Army that hadn't been there before. Rawboned farm boys tried to imitate the swagger of the older men from New Orleans, and to outswear them— an impossibility.

Jackson wagged his head more than once over the Tigers, and probably wondered why they'd been brought

Cannons & Roses

to the Shenandoah to plague him, but in the back of his mind he must have realized the time would come soon when he'd need every man of them.

The one time Keefer and Winfield Scott met in Hagerstown, Thomas J. Jackson was the main topic of their discussion of Confederate strengths and weaknesses.

"Is the man competent?" Scott asked.

"I really can't say for sure," Keefer replied. "Nobody really knows him, and that includes his staff. I get all sorts of impressions. A Turner Ashby leads his cavalry, and I made a special saddle for Turner just last month. Turner and I did some drinking together. He writes Jackson off as some sort of religious crank."

"Have you met the man?"

"Not yet, and it's not likely that I will. He's a loner. Even his own staff doesn't seem to know him well." Keefer thought about Jackson for a moment, then said, "The man is either a military genius, or an idiot in the wrong place at the right time."

Scott left Hagerstown convinced that generals Banks and Buell would have no trouble handling Jackson and his ragtag army if McClellan could finally be persuaded to move on Richmond with the Army of the Potomac.

Banks and Buell, he decided, would be able to sweep into the Shenandoah, occupy Winchester and Martinsburg, as well as Front Royal, then reinforce McClellan in his thrust toward Richmond.

The threat to Baltimore and Washington that Lincoln feared so much would be scotched. If Jackson was fool enough to be lured into battle, so much the better. He'd be outnumbered two-to-one, by a much better equipped army, especially in artillary.

Back in Winchester, Keefer Jones was having serious

second thoughts about what he'd told General Scott about Jackson. Without being able to put his finger on the reason, Keefer thought he may have badly underrated Jackson. But there was nothing he could do about it now.

General Jackson had fresh orders from Robert E. Lee in Richmond. At all costs, his Valley Army must occupy Banks and Buell to prevent them from releasing part of their forces to reinforce the Army of the Potomac.

For the moment, Old Jack laid aside his Bible to concentrate on the *Maxims of Napoleon*. One thing immediately impressed him. To harass the divided forces of Banks and Buell—and they would be divided, he knew—accurate and timely information as to the exact location of each command would have to be available, and, if possible, their intentions.

Ashby had mentioned someone named Belle Boyd, and her friend, who promised to supply such information. Jackson wasn't much impressed—war was man's business—but any scraps of information would help.

7

*F*ormer governor of Massachusetts, and before that Speaker of the House of Representatives, stodgy little Nathaniel P. Banks, with the drooping walrus moustache that hid his mouth, was one of Abraham Lincoln's political generals. He cut a ridiculous figure in uniform, and was nicknamed "Codfish" by the Federals in his command. But a staff of competent young officers staffed Banks's army of occupation.

Jamie McCoy and Turner Ashby were the last Confederates to leave Winchester. The pair sat their horses near the town's southern limits while the Federal cavalry rode in from the north.

"Here come the blue-bellies," Turner said.

Both men were in a reckless mood. For the past three days, they'd been screening Jackson's strategic retreat down the valley, ahead of the blue tide.

Turner was astride the black stallion only he could ride. Jamie sat his husky piebald mare whose explosive bursts of speed had saved his neck more than once in the past three days of brushes with Federal cavalry.

Only a few minutes before, he'd said good-bye to Philippa at the Randolph cottage.

"If they fight as well as they march, we're in trouble," Jamie said.

Turner snorted. "They proved at Manassas they can run even better than they march."

Belle, Philippa, Kate, and Vivienne were on the cottage porch, only partially screened by the willow. Belle was in her riding costume, ready to ride backroads and lanes to Martinsburg after spending the night with Philippa.

"Damn them!" she'd mutter as each blue-clad company swung by. "Damn them, damn them, damn them!"

Kate was regal in her best Cantonese silk dress. Vivienne had dressed for the occasion in a revealing red dress. Chin resting on a hand, elbows on the porch railing, the warm valley between her barely concealed breasts rippled at each passing column. As if there'd been a shouted "Eyes left!" command, heads swiveled, and dusty Federal faces grinned.

Vivienne stared thoughtfully off into space.

Only a few minutes before, Jamie had brushed a hasty kiss on Philippa's cheek. "We'll be back," he'd assured her. "Stay out of trouble, will you?"

Philippa had promised she would.

Now she watched Turner Ashby and her father, wondering what sort of game they were playing with the advancing Federals.

Across the street, slouched against the trunk of an elm tree, Keefer Jones watched Philippa. She wore a prim gray dress with a high neck for this occasion, and lacked only a Quaker bonnet, but Keefer found her much more exciting than he did Vivienne.

She has to be mine!

It was a litany with Keefer now. By this time he knew she was as much a rebel as Belle Boyd, and he damned the war.

Keefer wasn't too preoccupied to notice four troopers from a company of cavalry turn their horses into a side street at a whispered command.

It was a clever and lethal move, Keefer realized. They would circle through back streets and come around, flanking Ashby and McCoy. Only a few minutes before, Keefer had watched Jamie kiss Philippa good-bye.

Keefer's decision was instinctive. Philippa loved her father and Keefer loved Philippa. He couldn't see her father trapped and killed. He took a few quick steps toward the foolhardy Confederates, then swore and broke into a run.

Ashby swung his carbine to his shoulder and kept Keefer in his sights. Jamie touched his arm. "Watch it," he said. "That's Jones." With a grin, Jamie waved a gauntleted hand. "You'd better find a tree and get behind it, Jones," he called.

Keefer skidded to a stop. "Behind you!" he yelled back.

It was just enough warning. Both Jamie and Ashby whirled their horses as the four Federal troopers spurred their horses out of a side street, and charged at a gallop, carbines blazing. Their quick movement spoiled the Federals' aim.

Turner snatched his carbine from the saddle boot and shot from the hip. He had the satisfaction of seeing one Federal rider knocked backward over the rump of his horse.

Cannons & Roses

Jamie's carbine jammed. Clubbing it, he knocked the first Federal to reach him to the ground, then hooked an arm around the second man's neck, dragging him out of the saddle.

At point-blank range, Ashby had killed the second Federal charging him. Pulling his stallion back on its haunches, he took careful aim and shot the Federal Jamie had unhorsed with his clubbed carbine. The bullet shattered the man's face.

They kicked their horses into a run.

Jamie kept a stranglehold on the Federal he'd snatched from the saddle. The Valley Army had taken its first prisoner.

Keefer was sick to his stomach, and retching. Three men dead, one Federal captured, and it was his fault.

The leading file of marching troops were unlimbering their rifles, firing wildly after the disappearing Confederates. For the first time in this war, Keefer heard the whistle of bullets. He hit the ground and tried to embrace it.

Just my luck, he thought, *to get killed here by my own side!*

"Cease fire!" It was the high, clear voice of a young officer. "Can't you see they're out of range?"

It was one of the cadets who'd enlisted.

"Thank God for West Point!" Keefer breathed. Then he got to his feet, dusted himself off.

Had anyone seen him warn McCoy and Ashby?

Philippa had seen it all. Hand covering her mouth, she stared at the dead blue lumps in the dusty street, and their milling horses. She'd seen and faintly heard Keefer's warning. Now she watched him trying to calm the horses and keep them from trampling the dead men.

Cannons & Roses

Belle had seen, too. "Isn't that the fellow who makes saddles?" she asked.

"Yes, it is," Philippa answered. "I think he just saved my father's life."

They were calling up a wagon to remove the bodies so the triumphant march through Winchester could continue.

A short, portly man, flanked by a young officer, opened the gate in the picket fence, and came up the gravel walk to the porch. The sad, drooping moustache made Philippa want to giggle.

Sweeping off his cap, he nodded quickly to Belle, then Philippa, finally Vivienne, and his eyes lingered for a moment on her cleavage before he addressed Kate.

"General Nathaniel P. Banks of Massachusetts, at your service, madam." Philippa hadn't heard that nasal Yankee twang for a while, and she winced. "I'm requisitioning your house for Union headquarters. You and your . . . daughters, madam? . . . will vacate the premises immediately."

"This is Philippa Randolph's house, sir." Kate nodded toward Philippa. "You may know her people in Boston."

Banks flushed. "Randolph?" He squinted at Philippa. "You wouldn't be Christopher Randolph's niece?"

"I am," Philippa said coldly.

"Well, I'll be damned!" He gently punched the palm of his left hand once, twice, three times. "My compliments, Miss Randolph, and you are now under the protection of your country's flag. Your uncle is a good friend and staunch political supporter of mine. May we have the honor of using your house for my headquarters here in Winchester? You and your friends will not be bothered, I assure you."

Philippa and Kate exchanged glances. Kate nodded.

Cannons & Roses

Philippa turned back to Banks. "You will be welcome in my home," she said, and dazzled him with a smile. "Any friend of Uncle Chris is a friend of mine."

Belle fluttered her eyelashes. "Sir, I need a pass to return to my home in Martinsburg. I was here visiting when your troops entered Winchester."

Banks turned to his aide. "Captain Yates, make out a pass for me to sign. It will always be my policy," he told Belle, Kate, and Philippa, "to treat you ladies of the Confederacy with every courtesy. As you've seen, I've brought a well-disciplined army to the Shenandoah, to protect your fair sex from the ravages of war." Banks clapped his cap on his head, stood to attention, saluted. "Good afternoon, ladies."

Vivienne finally stirred. "General?"

"Yes?"

Vivienne lifted her breasts, to settle them in her bodice, and Banks's eyes bulged.

"You wouldn't know, sir," Vivienne said, in a lazy drawl, "but here in the south, evening begins after our noonday meal. Good evening to you, sir."

The three other women forgave Banks his ignorance with indulgent smiles.

The man flushed beet-red. *These damned southern women!* "Yates," he snapped, "see to our accommodations here."

"Yes, sir." Yates handed Banks a scribbled pass to sign.

Banks dashed off his signature and handed it to Belle. "Good evening!" he snapped, and turned on his heel.

The women watched him mount the horse another aide held at the gate. Another company was passing, bayonets sparkling in the afternoon sun. The horse danced and Banks nearly lost his seat.

Captain Roderick Yates was a Harvard graduate, where he'd been reading law until Fort Sumter—a ruddy-cheeked Vermont boy of eighteen. He stopped suppressing his grin when Banks had ridden off.

"My compliments, ladies," Yates said.

"For what?" Belle asked, all innocence.

"The good general rode away from here a little angry," Yates said, then was serious. "Miss Randolph, the general and I will quarter here. Have you room enough?"

"We have," Phillipa told him.

"The rest of his staff will be down the Valley Pike, at the local hotel. Will your woman of color serve our meals? We'll provide our own rations, of course."

"She will," Philippa promised, "and Beulah Land is a better than adequate cook."

Later Beulah Land complained to Philippa. "I'm a Boyd nigger," she said, "and Master Ben, he don't hold with these damn Yankees that come down here, disturbing our peace. Why do I have to cook for them?"

"Beulah Land, listen carefully," Philippa told her. "Our soldiers need to know what these Federals plan to do. Vivienne, Kate, and I want them to think we're friends."

Comprehension dawned. Beulah Land snickered. "You going to spy on them!"

"Shush." Philippa touched a finger to her lips.

Before she left for Martinsburg, Belle Boyd showed Philippa The Closet. Philippa's spacious bedroom was on the second floor, at the front of the cottage. Beneath it was the parlor.

When Ben Boyd had the old-fashioned ceiling gas fixture removed, to light the parlor with more modern wall sconces, they'd loosened a board in the closet to Philippa's room.

The gas-pipe hole in the parlor ceiling hadn't been filled.

"What you do," Belle explained, "is lie flat on your stomach and put your eye—or your ear—to the hole. You can see everyone in the parlor—and hear every word spoken." She laughed. "I found out what a spoiled brat my parents thought I was. I used to plague them by reciting supposed dreams about things they'd never told us children. But I was smart enough to quit that before they caught on. To this day they think I used to have second sight."

"Now all I have to do," Philippa said, "is get them to use the parlor for strategy conferences."

"That's right," Belle said. "Then, some way, you'll have to get what you know to General Jackson."

Philippa had a gentle mare lent her by the Boyds. For some reason Philippa could never divine, she was named Nectar.

"Nectar and I will find him," Philippa promised.

It would be called the Battle of Kernstown. General Banks would claim the credit, but tough Major General Shields baited the trap for the Valley Army.

At nightfall the pursuit of Jackson's forces ground to a halt at Kernstown, two miles south of Winchester on the Valley Pike.

At Strasbourg, further south on the Valley Pike, Jackson rested his main force while Ashby scouted the Federal left, Jamie McCoy the Federal right west of Kernstown. Turner Ashby was no longer the Virginia cavalier. Leading a patrol into Maryland from Harper's Ferry, Turner's younger brother had been surrounded

Cannons & Roses

by Federal cavalry, and, hopelessly outnumbered, tried to surrender. The Federals chopped the boy down and stabbed him to death.

Turner was now a cold-blooded killer. He led his men, their horses on the run, through the Federal encampment just after dusk, cutting down anyone in his path, then looped back to Jackson and reported that ground east of Kernstown was being held by a token force. He had taken no prisoners to question.

Jamie McCoy brushed with Federal pickets, but didn't drive them in. In the confusion and darkness, his troopers captured two young pickets. The scared boys were eager to tell their captors everything they knew.

"It looks as if Banks is recalling most of his forces, sir," he reported to Jackson. "They must be moving to reinforce McClellan."

Jackson squinted across the map-strewn table in his tent at Jamie. "McCoy, probe that right flank at dawn," he ordered.

"Yes, sir."

"Prisoners lie," he reminded Jamie. "The only intelligence I want is what you see with your own eyes. Remember that."

"Yes, sir, I will," Jamie said.

Jamie rode his men around the Federal right the next morning, estimated their strength at less than 500 men, with no artillery, and reported back to Jackson. It was Sunday morning.

Ashby engaged the left flanking force in a brief firefight that morning, while Confederate troopers sneaked north to check the road that led across the Blue Ridge mountains into northern Virginia. It was crowded with traffic, moving east.

It began to look as if Jamie's first report was correct, but Jackson still wasn't satisfied that Winchester was his for the retaking. But his orders were to hold as many Federals in the Shenandoah as possible.

Not wishing to break the sabbath, he planned to attack Monday morning.

The closet floor was hard and Philippa was tired. In the parlor below, Captain Yates and the man they called Shields pored over maps, while Banks sat in the rocking chair smoking a cigar, sipping wine, and rustling a newspaper, eyeglasses on the end of his nose.

It was late Sunday morning. A messenger galloped up to the house and dismounted. With his spurs jangling, he strode into the parlor and saluted Shields. "Message, sir."

At Shields's crowing laugh, Banks laid aside his newspaper. "What is it?" he asked.

"The old fox evidently believes our geese are flying east, leaving the nest unguarded," Shields told his superior officer. "He's coming up the pike to make sure. Our cavalry scouts report he's only a mile from Kernstown."

Banks beamed, and lit a fresh cigar. "Good."

"The column we started east is doubling back right now," Captain Yates reported. "Reinforcements for our left flank have split off. We'll have the right flank beefed up by late afternoon. Artillery is wheeling in place."

Philippa was suddenly wide awake. Now everything she'd heard that had made no sense added up. They were setting a trap for the Valley Army!

She eased the board back into place and crawled out of the closet. Vivienne was stretched full-length on the bed. "What's happening?" she asked in a sleep-husky voice. "My turn to watch and listen?"

"No." Officers were already riding up and dismounting, clanking into the cottage and crowding the parlor. "They've set a trap for General Jackson. I have to warn him."

Vivienne raised on an elbow. "How will you manage that?" she asked. "The Federals are spread out between us and Jackson's forces."

"I have to try," Philippa said.

8

*A*shby was assigned the task of brushing aside the Federal left flank and hitting the eastward bound column he'd sighted that morning. He immediately ran into trouble. The weak force he'd skirted past had been heavily reinforced and now had artillery backing. They were spaced out over a two-mile front.

When Ashby tried to break through with a pell-mell, hell-for-leather charge, rifle fire and canister tore great bloody holes in his ranks, and his troopers fell back and took shelter.

Jackson had dispatched Jamie with a small force to turn the Federal right flank. Scouting ahead, Jamie discovered infantry moving up and artillery already in place. He sheltered his troopers in the woods, and rode back to Jackson, who was with the middle force, coming up the Valley Pike.

Taylor's Louisiana Tigers were being held in reserve that Sunday afternoon.

Cannons & Roses

"Sir, we're in trouble," Jamie reported. "I need reinforcements if we're to take any ground."

The sound of cannon and rifle fire rolled over them from the east, and Jackson guessed that situation without a report from Ashby.

"You'll have them, sir," he told Jamie.

"God almighty!" Private Eakins, newly arrived from the Army of Northern Virginia remarked to his new friend, Buddy Atkins of Tennessee. "I thought you said Old Jack respected the Sabbath."

"Don't believe anything I say," Buddy replied. "He's marched me so far in this damned valley, my brains are in my feet."

"Mine, too," Eakins said. "Know what they tell me?"

"Yup. Run, run, run."

Eakins nodded and pointed south. "That way."

"Don't tempt me!" Buddy told him.

Philippa had slipped from the house to saddle her horse. Vivienne joined her to help pull up the girth. The ground floor of the cottage was jammed with officers now.

"Are you going to ride in that dress?" Vivienne asked.

"Have to," Philippa panted.

"Which direction are you riding, Miss Randolph?"

Philippa and Vivienne whirled around, to find Keefer Jones slouched in the stable doorway, one shoulder against the door jamb, arms crossed on his chest. He was clean-shaven, without his glasses, and in a new uniform. Philippa recognized General Winfield Scott's aide—not the seedy older man who'd warned her father and Ashby.

"I ask," Keefer said, "because there's a bit of a battle shaping up out there. That isn't thunder you hear, it's

Federal artillery, and what sounds like firecrackers going off are rifles."

Philippa mounted and reined her horse around. "Get out of my way."

Keefer grinned. "Please?"

Philippa kicked her horse. Keefer had to jump back, or be ridden down.

She was on the Valley Pike, cantering south, skirts hiked up around her thighs, shoes kicked off, hair streaming, when Keefer rode up beside her.

Pickets blocked the road ahead—they'd reached the outskirts of Winchester.

"Halt!"

Philippa reined in when the soldiers raised their rifles.

"I'm escorting her through, fellows," Keefer said. "My responsibility."

"Yes, sir."

Their horses paced each other in an easy canter. "Where are we going?" Keefer asked.

Philippa was trying to cover her bare thighs, but without much luck. "Why don't you leave me alone?"

A side road ahead wound through the hills, avoiding Kernstown, and then rejoined the Valley Pike. Philippa intended to take it.

All the cannonading and rifle fire was east, to their left. The side road was now jammed with troops moving west.

Philippa reined in, and so did Keefer.

They were half a mile north of Kernstown.

"Listen. You're Captain Jones?" Philippa said.

"Major Keefer Jones now, and at your service, Miss Randolph."

She touched the back of his hand that rested on the saddle pommel.

"Major, my father has been wounded, and he may

be dying." Philippa tried to sound convincing. "I must reach him! He's with General Jackson," she explained. "Can you help me?"

Keefer grinned. "You really don't recognize me, do you?"

"Why, yes, we met in Washington."

"Your father isn't with Jackson, he rides with Turner Ashby, and they both damned near got their heads blown off the other day. A fool Yankee warned them in the nick, and got three Federals killed, one captured. That's pretty heavy on my conscience."

Philippa gaped, and a hand jumped to her throat. "You're a spy! I know you now."

Keefer grinned. "What are you, so cozy in Banks's headquarters?"

"I could kill you!"

Keefer unsnapped his holster and handed over the heavy Colt with its long blue barrel. "Help yourself."

Philippa shunned the revolver. She tried to smooth her skirt down. "Will you arrest me?"

There was a sound like tearing cloth, then a concussion that shook the ground. When the shell exploded only a few yards away from the pair, Philippa's horse reared. She snapped back, over the rump, and hit the ground with her shoulders and the back of her head.

She'd been stunned.

Keefer grabbed for the reins of her horse, but missed. The mare raced back up the road toward Winchester. Out of the saddle, he cradled Philippa. "You all right?"

She stared up at him, moved her head to clear it, then said, "I think so."

Jackson knew he'd sprung a Federal trap, but instead of ordering a withdrawal, he decided to batter and bloody his opponent, bearing in mind he was supposed to tie down as many troops as he could.

Before galloping off with Jamie, he sent for the Louisiana Tigers to come up for an assault on the Federal right. The feint at the Federal center in Kernstown was stalled.

There was a chance of turning that right Federal flank, driving them back to the Valley Pike. Jackson was going to take that chance.

Jackson would have sworn at Ashby, had he been a swearing man, for leaving him in the dark about what went on over at the Federal left. But he trusted Turner Ashby not to break and run.

It was the middle of Sunday afternoon.

Ashby's men were dismounted and fighting for their lives as wave after wave of Federals tried to sweep them away. Casualties were mounting with each new Federal assault. Ashby himself was wounded in the arm. His troopers were running out of ammunition. But damned if he was going to retreat!

The gentle slope ahead of their position was littered with dead and screaming wounded. Federal cavalry was gingerly circling their right flank. Ashby took a company back to where they'd tethered their horses in a gully.

"Mount up."

A headlong charge of screaming Confederates scattered twice their number, and the threat to Ashby's flank was gone. But that charge cost thirty-one men. Ashby took the survivors back to the main battle.

Darting out from behind their rail fence barricade, troopers were stealing rifles and ammunition from the Federal dead and wounded.

Cannons & Roses

Ashby ordered the horses brought up. He told his few remaining officers, "They'll run over us if they come up that slope one more time, so we'll charge down it and pray to God they'll think reinforcements have arrived."

Horses were jumped over the barricade, and with sabers drawn, the Confederates deployed as they charged. The high-pitched rebel yell shattered Federal nerves. Shaken by the afternoon's fighting, the Federals broke and ran.

Ashby halted pursuit, wheeled his command, and raced off to find Jackson.

The Federals rallied. They slogged up the slope again, only to find Confederate dead and wounded huddled behind the rail fence.

It was late Sunday afternoon.

Federal artillery was up on the right flank, plastering Jamie's men, when he and Jackson arrived. The Federals had the high ground. The Louisiana Tigers had come up.

The high ground was a steep ridge crowned by a stone fence. Federal cannon were behind the wall, and it was lined with infantry.

"We must have that ridge, sir," Jackson told Richard Taylor. "Without it, we can't pull back."

The Confederates were sheltering in a wooded area, but their only retreat was across open fields, with their right flank exposed to withering enemy fire.

Taylor deployed his battle-hungry men. Their Zouave uniforms were dusty and threadbare, but they were still the most military unit in the Valley Army, and proud of it. They finally were going to get a chance to fight, instead of standing around in reserve.

Cannons & Roses

At a close shell-burst, a few Tigers broke ranks to find cover.

"Goddamn it!" Taylor exploded. "Do that again, and I'll keep you standing here until sundown!"

Jackson touched his shoulder. "You're a very wicked man to take the Lord's name in vain on His sabbath."

Taylor stared at Jackson a moment, then said, "You'd better pray for my immortal soul."

"I will, sir," Jackson answered. "I will. Now give me that ridge."

Taylor moved his men out.

They went in perfect formation, closing holes ripped in their ranks by canister, and the spaces left by men dropped when they came within rifle range. they walked at first, then trotted toward the enemy, finally raced up the last steep slope, exploded across the stone wall, bayonets twinkling in the late-afternoon sun, sabers flashing as Tigers ripped in among the cannoneers. The hand-to-hand melee rolled down the opposite slope of the hill, to the banks of a creek, before buglers sounded recall.

The Pelican State flag was planted on the ridge. With the Federals routed, Tigers immediately began to rifle the pockets of the dead. But they stood to attention and tried to look innocent when Richard Taylor caught them at it.

The Battle of Kernstown was over by late Sunday evening, except for pockets where Confederates had been cut off, and had decided against being captured. In a ditch, with their horses dead, Philippa and Keefer were in the middle of such a pocket.

Captain Bill Grace had the honor of leading the feint toward the Federal center. Carried away, Bill took his company through Kernstown like a hot knife through butter, then discovered that the Federals had closed ranks behind him and his fifty men, with reinforcements coming down the Valley Pike from Winchester.

Herman Ulbrecht built his farmhouse back in 1760 from fieldstone, and designed it as a fortress against Indian attacks. Bill Grace and his men holed up in the house and outbuildings, within easy rifle range of the Valley Pike. Their sniper fire had deprived Kernstown of reinforcements they didn't really need all day.

Philippa and Keefer had ridden by a stalled column of Federals, sprawled along both sides of the road, half a mile short of where they'd gone to ground. It wouldn't have meant anything to Philippa why these men were there, not moving toward the sound of guns. It should have registered with Keefer, but he was too intent on Philippa.

So they'd ridden into a lull, and the shower of shells that killed Keefer's horse, and spooked Philippa's mare, were an example of expert Federal marksmanship at this point in the war. The Ulbrecht house was only a quarter of a mile away, on the brow of a hill, surrounded by an apple orchard.

When the shelling finally stopped, a company of Federals behind them opened up on the stone farmhouse. Incoming fire was returned. The air sang above the ditch in which they'd taken cover as if it were full of lead hornets.

It was a deep enough ditch so they could sit up, and Keefer's arm was around Philippa, her head was on his shoulder, their feet were propped up on the opposite bank, and Philippa had stopped worrying about her muddy, torn dress.

Keefer had shrugged out of his jacket and folded it for a cushion, so he was bare to the waist.

Cannons & Roses

The sun was down and they slapped at mosquitoes. Keefer needed a shave. Philippa's face was daubed with dry mud. They'd exhausted all the polite conversational ploys an hour ago. Keefer knew all about Aunt Celeste, and Uncle Christopher. He'd heard about her school friends. He knew why she'd adopted The Cause. Philippa had admitted that there was a lot she had to learn about being an effective spy.

Philippa knew General Winfield Scott used snuff. She'd learned how to tell a Kiowa from a Sioux by their smell. Keefer had explained how to steal ponies from Indians. (Before trying, you had to go without a bath for three days, then smoke yourself in the campfire. The proper war paint helped.) She knew his mother did the best needlepoint in all St. Louis.

Desultory sniper fire droned over their heads. Federals with itchy trigger fingers were all around them in the darkness.

Keefer chuckled.

Philippa looked up. "What's funny?"

"Codfish Banks," he said. "I was just thinking how much I'd hate to be trapped in this ditch with him tonight. I was reporting to be on his staff this afternoon. I wonder if he ever missed me."

"I have to go to the bathroom," Philippa said.

"Serious?" Keefer asked.

"Not too, but urgent," she told him.

Keefer pointed up the ditch. "You go that way, and keep your pretty head down. I'll go south a few paces."

"All right."

"Philippa?"

"Yes?"

"I'm in love with you."

"You've picked a fine time to tell me that!" she

said. She patted his cheek. "Don't be long. I'm scared."

"Know something?" Keefer said. "I am, too."

"You all right now?" Keefer pressed the length of Philippa's body against his and found her mouth with his lips.

Her hands pressed the back of his head.

A ragged Federal volley sizzled the air above their heads, like bacon frying. But the war had moved away into another dimension, and a remote one.

Keefer's hands moved all over Philippa's firm body, under her clothes, and she moaned but didn't resist. She arched up her hips when he worked to get her skirt up.

"Let me," she whispered, when his clumsy fingers tugged at the waistband of her underwear.

Deaf and blind with a stronger lust than he'd ever felt before, Keefer couldn't help himself. The first thrust was hard, drawing a squeal of pain. But she didn't push him away. Philippa locked her heels in the small of his back. With a strength he'd never suspected, she drew herself to him, and what they did together lasted a century.

When it was over, and they finally lay back, Keefer saw starpoints in her eyes. The expression on her face stung his eyelids with tears.

"I'm sorry," he panted.

She didn't answer. He watched her catch her breath, and brushed her lips, then her forehead with quick, light kisses.

"I said I'm sorry," Keefer repeated.

Philippa's eyes focused. "Sorry?" She didn't understand the word. "You've got tears in your eyes, but am I not the one who's supposed to cry? It's like that in books."

Cannons & Roses

Keefer smoothed hair away from Philippa's forehead, and kissed her there. "I wasn't gentle," he said. "I always swore I would be with the woman I love."

"This wasn't the time or place for gentle," Philippa told Keefer.

A bullet shredded the air just above their heads, followed a second later by the report of the rifle from which it had been fired.

"If we get out of this ditch alive," Philippa said, "I'll always remember that sound." She laughed. "It isn't the sort of music I imagined for my wedding night."

9

*H*alf of Bill Grace's men were wounded. Four were dying. Three were dead. The Egan family who now owned the farm had fled into Kernstown when the fighting began, and the kitchen was well-provisioned, but the last of that food was gone now. Snipers had them cut off from the well.

"They'll come howling down on us, Bill, soon as the sun comes up," one of his men told Grace. "What you reckon we ought to do?"

Bill Grace was wishing someone else had been given command. "I don't rightly know, and that's a fact," he said. "I been praying, but it don't seem to help."

It was just beginning to get light outside. The last hour had been ominously still. Bill wandered through the house, checking his men posted at the windows. All of them were running out of ammunition. Back at his command post, in the kitchen, he perched on a stool, head in his hands.

* * *

"Our best chance is the farmhouse," Keefer told Philippa. She huddled in his jacket, but still shivered in the early morning coolness. "The Federals have the place ringed, and we'll be shot down if we try to break out."

"Can't we stay here until it's finished?" Philippa asked.

Keefer was staring up at the Blue Ridge mountains, silhouetted by the coming dawn. "Fog," he breathed. "It's rolling down in clouds. If we try to make the house," he thought out loud, "we'll be out of one trap, and into another. If the morning fog is thick enough, they could miss us when they move in."

"So we stay?" Philippa asked.

Keefer slipped an arm around her shoulders. "We stay."

"I have an idea," she said. Philippa was wriggling out of her torn white petticoat. "Find me a stick."

"What are you going to do?"

"Surrender." Philippa's laugh was half-hysterical. "That's what we women do in a situation like this. Instead of getting ourselves killed, we surrender. A stick, Keefer."

Keefer thought about it. What Philippa said made some sense. A woman's petticoat, waving in the morning breeze, would tempt any encroaching Federals to investigate first, and shoot afterwards if it was necessary. He crawled up the ditch, looking for a stick.

Bill Grace had made up his mind. The wounded were as comfortable as he could make them. He'd gathered his remaining men, both able-bodied and walking wounded, in the farmhouse kitchen.

Cannons & Roses

"I figure it this way, boys," he said. "We got fog coming down. Maybe somebody's prayers got answered, I don't know. I'm going to try to get through before the fog lifts. Any want to come with me?"

A few tired, hungry, and thirsty men raised their hands.

"All right," Bill said. "The rest of you get up some kind of white flag when it comes dawn."

Four men filed out of the stone house after Bill and began working their way toward the Valley Pike through the apple trees.

Federal troops, in groups of three, were working their way up toward the house through the orchard, to be in position for a quick rush at dawn.

In the thick fog, Bill and his men passed two of these groups. Both trios challenged.

"Shut up, you damned fools," Bill replied to the first challenge. "Captain's orders."

It worked, so he answered the second challenge the same way. They finally reached the Valley Pike.

The fog, stirred by a breeze, was beginning to thin.

"Well, I'll be damned!" Bill had spotted Philippa's petticoat, waving in the morning breeze. "Look there, fellows."

A minute later, Philippa and Keefer found themselves staring into the muzzles of Confederate rifles, and Bill had found a way to get his four men and himself back behind Confederate lines.

"What you do, blue-belly, is take this here rifle, which ain't loaded," he told Keefer, "and march us five right through Kernstown. We're your prisoners, see? Only we ain't."

"Why would I do a thing like that?" Keefer asked, and thought he knew.

"Because I'll have my horse pistol against the spine of your lady friend," Bill told him, with a wolf's grin that showed tobacco-stained teeth, "and if you ain't convincing, it goes off."

"I'll be convincing," Keefer said. "You hurt the lady, though, and I break your damned neck."

"She won't get hurt if you do just as I say," Bill promised. "You got my word."

Kernstown was jammed with wounded men from Sunday's battle. They lay on litters, up and down the main street, waiting for hospital wagons to come down from Winchester. The farmhouse siege had stopped all traffic up and down the Valley Pike. In the general confusion, Bill Grace's ruse worked, and the Valley Army had another legend.

Clear of the Federal lines, Keefer became a prisoner, and so did Philippa.

Keefer and Philippa were locked into adjoining cells in the Strasbourg jail, and she'd sent for Jamie. When he finally came, shoulders slumped from weariness, eyes bloodshot, Philippa was never so glad to see anyone before.

"Daddy, get us out of here!" she pleaded. "I can't stand this filthy place."

"How in hell did you get in here?" he asked. "I thought you were safe in Winchester."

"I had some information for General Jackson, and tried to get through the Federal lines," Philippa said. "Keefer was helping me, I think. Anyway, we got trapped in a ditch . . ." She stopped. "Can you get us out of here?" she asked.

"Don't I know you, major?" Jamie asked Keefer.

"He saved your life the other day—yours and Turner Ashby's," Philippa volunteered.

Cannons & Roses

Jamie snapped his fingers. "Sure!" Then he scowled. "But you weren't in uniform."

"No, sir, I wasn't," Keefer admitted. "It's a rather long story."

"What are you to my daughter?" Jamie asked.

"A friend," Keefer said.

"I love him," Philippa declared.

Jamie raised his eyes. "I'll be damned!" he told no one in particular.

Banks was claiming a major victory, but in the same telegram to Winfield Scott, he asked to be reinforced. With replacements for his extensive casualty list, and another regiment, he promised to crush Jackson's Valley Army. He'd need more artillery, too.

There was no chance to reinforce McClellan now. Now Phil McClellan had another alibi for not moving faster toward Richmond.

"Nat Banks and this Stonewall Jackson remind me of a neighbor back in Illinois who fought a wildcat with his bare hands," Lincoln drawled when he heard the news from Scott. "Fellow was chawed and gnawed by the cat something fierce, and like to have died, but he claimed he'd won the fight because the cat run off."

"Jones is a very mysterious fellow," Jackson told Jamie and tapped a telegram from Richmond that was on his desk. "They tell me he's been spying for us, but we find him in a Federal uniform, and people who knew him in Winchester say he had a saddle shop there. Most of his business was with my men, and he made frequent trips through the lines over into Maryland."

"Has he been questioned?" Jamie asked.

Jackson stroked his beard. "Not yet."

Cannons & Roses

"My daughter says that she loves him."

Jackson fumbled through the pockets of his rumpled blue uniform until he found a fresh lemon.

"Excellent for your digestion, sir," Jackson told Jamie, holding the lemon up for his inspection. "What is your opinion?"

Jamie was confused. "About lemons for my digestion?"

"No. Is it a girlish fancy, or does your daughter love this man?"

"My God, I don't know," Jamie said.

"Thou shalt not take His name in vain," Jackson lectured.

Jamie flushed. "Sorry, sir."

"I hear he saved you and Ashby during our retreat from Winchester."

"Yes, sir, that's true."

"You must not be so foolhardy again, McCoy. I need you and Ashby." Jackson unbuttoned the collar of his uniform. "We'll release your daughter from jail. You have her parole."

"Thank you, sir, but what about Jones?" Jamie asked.

Jackson shook his head. "A mysterious fellow. Information just received from another charming young lady says he's wanted for desertion from General Banks's staff."

"That should be in his favor," Jamie said.

"Do you think so?" Jackson's eyes showed contempt. "You may have heard. I had one of our men shot last week for just such a crime, and that poor fellow went home to his wife and four children. Discipline, sir. It's the backbone of any army."

Jamie waited. Never before had he found Jackson in such a talkative mood. "My men feel we were badly whipped the other day. I am well satisfied with the outcome of the battle, although we didn't retake Winchester. Here in the valley we're saving Richmond. I want you and Ashby to tell your men that. They have no reason to be ashamed."

"Yes, sir."

"Question Jones," Jackson said. "Report back to me."

Jamie closed the door of the jailer's cramped, stark office. Philippa was in the care of the woman owning the Strasbourg boardinghouse he and Turner Ashby frequented for meals and civilian conversation when they were in town. Mrs. Taliaferro had been told to furnish whatever clothes his daughter needed. Jamie sat across the small, scarred table from Keefer and stared at the man his daughter professed to love.

Jamie intended to dislike this man. "Let's find out just who the hell you are and what sort of game you're playing," he said bluntly. "I want to know, particularly, what your relationship with my daughter is. Are you hiding behind her skirts?"

Jamie couldn't help admiring the way Keefer's steady eyes met his stare.

Keefer cleared his throat. "What Philippa means to me isn't your business."

"Damn it, man!" Jamie smacked the table with his hand. "She's the only daughter I have."

"So she tells me."

"Why did you pull that stunt in Winchester? You got three Federals killed, and one captured. Whose side are you on anyway?"

"Right now I just don't know," Keefer said. "My own side, and Philippa's, I guess. I'm already sick of this God-damned war! Fighting hostile Indians is one thing. Trying to kill men like yourself is something else. I've forgotten why it's necessary. Do you remember?"

Jamie wanted to say yes, but found he couldn't, so, elbows on the table, he masked his eyes with his hands, and wondered if he'd ever feel rested and fresh again.

Hate of Keefer Jones for being young and in love was sour in Jamie's throat. Philippa's mother's presence in this grubby little room was almost tangible. She'd crept very close to him in the past few days, and now he knew why.

"Are you all right, sir?" Keefer asked.

Jamie dropped his hands. "No."

"Can I do something?"

"Yes."

Keefer didn't ask what he could do. "You really want to know if I love Philippa. I do, and with all my heart. I play no games so far as she's concerned. Do you know the West?"

Jamie nodded. "Texas and Kansas."

"You know how the wind blows, then, and what it smells like in the morning, how the stars burn down at night, and what it's like to see forever, and wonder about God, and why He made so much distance for us. Sometimes I think I know why, and other times I'm not sure. Maybe Philippa can tell me. I want to find out if she can. God! I don't give a damn about anything else!"

The two men sat across the table from each other for what seemed like a long time, each lost in his own thoughts.

Keefer broke the silence. "I want her to have our children. I want her to be beside me during the night, so I can touch her and know I'll never be alone again. There's so much to tell her!" Keefer took a deep breath.

"And here I sit, making a God-damned lovesick fool out of myself."

"Where can you take her?" Jamie asked.

"West," Keefer said. "Away from here."

Jamie looked over his shoulder, half-expecting his Philippa would be standing behind him. She wasn't, yet he knew she was still in the room.

And he suddenly realized it was nearly time for him to join her, wherever she might be. He could tell her why he wasn't there when the baby was born, and while she died.

She would understand.

It was going to be all right.

"Sir?" Keefer said.

"I'm going to let you walk out of here," Jamie said. "On my own authority." He told Keefer where to find Philippa in Strasbourg. "Take her and get the hell west any way you can. Do you need money?"

"No."

Jamie rose, and extended his hand. "Good-bye."

Keefer took the offered hand. "I hope you won't be in trouble," he said.

Jamie shrugged. "Jackson will probably have me shot, but it doesn't matter."

Jamie McCoy didn't know how near the truth he'd come. When Jamie reported he'd released Keefer Jones, Thomas J. Jackson went into one of his rare cold rages, his usually gentle face turning hard as stone and gray as granite.

"Have this man confined to quarters," he said to his chief aide, Sandie Pendelton. "You, sir, are stripped of all rank," he told to Jamie. "You'll face a court martial immediately."

Cannons & Roses

Jackson then vented pent-up fury on Turner Ashby. "Draw up orders relieving Ashby of his command," he instructed Pendelton, while Jamie stared in amazement. "Grounds, insubordination, failure to report, unable to maintain proper discipline."

"But, sir," the good-natured Pendelton protested. "Without McCoy or Ashby, and after the battle, there isn't a general officer to take over the Valley cavalry."

"Assign them to Ewell and Richard Taylor. Split the division, sir."

Sandie saluted, exchanged startled glances with Jamie, and left Jackson's tent to carry out the orders he'd just been given.

"What goes on in there?" another aide, waiting outside Jackson's tent, asked Pendelton.

"Old Jack's having a crazy spell," he answered.

The repercussions were immediate. Ewell wrote Richmond and resigned his commission rather than take half of Ashby's command. Richard Taylor tried to reason with his commander and very nearly got himself on the court-martial list.

More than half the Valley cavalry went absent without leave, and when challenged for a pass, touched their carbines and said that their weapons were all the permission they needed.

The Valley Army's morale hit an all-time low, and they ceased being an effective force. All of this happened within a week.

Robert E. Lee returned Ashby's resignation. He quietly back-filed Jackson's orders to court-martial Jamie. In their place, he issued orders, countersigned by Jefferson Davis, transferring Jamie to Jeb Stuart's cavalry with the Army of Northern Virginia. He explained to Jackson, in a polite personal letter, that when

Cannons & Roses

the Army of Northern Virginia was his command, which it would be soon, he wanted Jamie McCoy.

Officers of his temper and caliber, sir, Lee wrote Jackson, *we must forgive much these days.*

In a few months, Jamie and Jeb Stuart would both die in a minor skirmish at Yellow Tavern. Within the year, Turner Ashby would be dead, shot through the heart, and Jackson himself would die at Sharpsburg, shot out of his saddle by one of his own men in the morning fog and confusion.

Without apology, or explanation, Jackson canceled his rash orders, treated Ashby with the same courtesy he'd always shown officers he outranked, and wrote a short letter to Lee commending Jamie and suggesting a promotion was due.

Sandie Pendelton wrote his wife: *Praises be! Old Jack is over this latest crazy spell. But it will be just our luck that some fool will call him "Stonewall" to his face.*

10

*P*hilippa didn't like the withdrawn woman who was Keefer's mother, and she was afraid of his father. Their modest home, with its dark draperies, and polished antique furniture, reminded her of a museum, lacking only *Do Not Touch* signs.

She would rather have been married in a tomb!

Philippa and Keefer had finally reached St. Louis after a wearisome and nerve-wracking trip on the sorry railroads of the south. It had taken them a long three weeks. In that time, Keefer hadn't touched Philippa. She felt as if she'd suddenly become a vestal virgin.

Because Keefer was listed as a Federal deserter, it would have to be a very quiet wedding.

Tomorrow they'd be married by a Reverend Spooner, a dour man Philippa had yet to see smile. Only Keefer's parents would be in attendance. Tonight she was alone in the guest room with its craggy, dark-wood furniture and hard bed. Her wedding gown was Keefer's mother's, altered to more or less fit, and Philippa hated it. The smell of mothballs was all-pervasive.

She laid on the bed, face down, and bit her fist, fighting tears and feeling more desolate than she ever had before in her life.

"I'm making a mistake!" she whispered. "Keefer doesn't love me, and I don't love him—not now, not ever."

She wanted Celeste and Christopher to come and get her.

"Damn!" She beat the pillow with her fists, and let the tears come.

It was getting dark, and the small room with too-large furniture was filled with shadows.

Someone touched her shoulder. Philippa caught a sob in her throat and looked around to find Keefer's mother towering over the bed in the gloom.

"Finish your crying, child," the woman said.

Philippa sat up. "I've finished." She tried to clear her tear-dimmed eyes with the back of her hand. "What do you want?"

"Just to be alone with you a few minutes. We'll never have this chance again. I want to know you, Philippa, because I want to love you. Do you find this strange?"

Her voice was different, and her face somehow softer, and more vulnerable, Philippa realized when Keefer's mother lit the lamp, and adjusted the wick. This done, she sat beside Philippa again, this time with a protective arm around the girl's shoulders.

"You must love Keefer deeply to give up everything you've always had for him, Philippa. He's told us nothing about you. As you've found, we're not a demonstrative family. So you can tell me whatever you wish."

"There's really not much to tell." Philippa had cleared the tears from her voice. "My mother died when I was born."

Deep into the night, Philippa told Keefer's mother about herself, her childhood and growing years, the man she'd run away from, about Jeanette and DeWitt, and Great Oaks.

Philippa laughed about herself in ways she never had before. She told her something of their night in the muddy ditch, under fire, but not all—yet Philippa knew the older woman guessed what she hadn't said, and searched for censure in those calm eyes, to find understanding.

Keefer's mother asked no questions and made no comments.

"So I guess that's just about everything about me," Philippa finally said. "Please don't think I'm going to talk your son to death. I can't remember when I've used so many words to say so little. I'm just not a very interesting person."

"I find you to the contrary," the older woman said. "In case you've wondered, my husband and I are grateful you're taking Keefer away from this terrible war. We're not very patriotic, I guess."

"I have wondered," Philippa admitted. "Not about your patriotism," she added hastily.

"You'll make Keefer the fine wife he needs," the woman said. "Now you must be very tired. Let me tuck you in."

Impulsively, Philippa kissed her. "I love you," she said.

"Child! Don't make me cry," Keefer's mother scolded.

* * *

Cannons & Roses

Reverend Spooner finally managed a smile when he finished reading the marriage rites and told Keefer he could kiss his bride. From the moment Philippa had seen the nervous strain in Keefer's face, before the ceremony, and noticed the way his hands trembled when he checked his vest pocket to make sure he still had her plain gold wedding band, all remaining doubts about her love for him melted.

In their place came serenity, and a quiet but warm flow of love that suffused her whole being. Philippa was radiant. The glow in her face, and love for Keefer in her eyes, dissolved his father's last secret doubts about Philippa.

It was after the ceremony that he told them of his wedding present. "I've reserved a room or two for you at the Missouri Hotel," Mr. Jones told them. "Mother and I find this house comfortable enough, but it somehow doesn't serve young love."

His "room or two" turned out to be the bridal suite in the fashionable hotel, secluded on the top floor, with a view of the Mississippi. Keefer could buy nothing. A selection of the finest champagnes, wine, brandy and whisky were already in the bridal suite.

They would stay three days before starting up the Missouri River for Independence, their jumping-off place into the West. The hotel's chef consulted with Philippa about their meals.

"Your husband, he has been in the army, yes?" the French chef asked.

"At one time," Philippa said cautiously.

"From here you go to the West, yes?"

"Yes," Philippa said.

"Then I suggest, while we are honored by your presence, a properly prepared buffalo steak for at least one meal."

"That sounds all right."

"This unfortunate war has stopped our supply of fat oysters from Louisiana," the chef apologized. He sighed. "Such a waste, this war to free slaves. Instead of oysters, may I serve you, baked in wine, the excellent whitefish from Lake Michigan, brought down the river packed in ice? I make an excellent sauce to go with this dish."

"I think Keefer likes fish. Coming from Boston, I do, too. We'll have the whitefish, monsieur."

The chef beamed. "A supper of quail prepared in white wine, another of grouse, and the wild turkey—have you ever tasted him?"

"No, I haven't," Philippa said.

The chef kissed his bunched fingers. "A wild rice dressing, madame. And so-tender small new potatoes, prepared in cream sauce."

They would be served pheasant under glass, squab, dove, a *bouillabaisse*.

Finally the chef said, "Madame is so obviously used to servants—does she know how to cook?"

"I haven't had much practice," Philippa confessed.

"Fortunate!" the chef beamed. "Will you do me the honor to visit my kitchen, my empire, my domain? Since you have not much experience, I can teach you the small things about preparation of food that make so much difference. The American women!" He made a clucking noise. "Boil, boil, boil! Fry the steak. Ugh. No finesse. You, madame, I see as a woman with the good taste. Part of you is French, no?"

"My grandmother comes from Santo Domingo. But how could you know?"

"Ah!" The chef grinned and winked. "It would be obvious only to a Frenchman."

Philippa promised to visit his kitchen.

Cannons & Roses

"That man flattered me right out of my good sense," she confessed to Keefer that night. "When he gets the bill for our meals, your father is liable to faint."

"Don't worry about my father," Keefer said. "Food is fine, but I'm hungry for something else."

They'd had their wedding night, and it had been a tender time, Keefer always considerate, and, to Philippa's amazement, shy. It was as if he were apologizing for their first fierce interlude. He'd left Philippa only partially satisfied, and more than a little puzzled.

Here she was, willing and eager to explore every dimension of sexuality, both her own and Keefer's, and her husband treated her like a fragile toy.

"Let me guess," Philippa flirted.

Keefer slapped his hands together, then stabbed a forefinger at Philippa. "You have it."

"Have I?" Philippa pretended surprise.

"You've guessed what I'm hungry for," Keefer said. "I can see it in your eyes. They get a smoky color."

"How can you tell in the dark?" Philippa asked.

Keefer gently touched the tip of each breast, through the fabric of her dress, then slid his hands down to clutch her slender waist and draw her to him. His kiss didn't beg, it demanded.

"Kissing is fine," Keefer said, when they paused to catch their breaths, "but aren't you a bit uncomfortable in all those clothes?"

"Well, now that you mention it," Philippa said, and turned for him to unbutton her dress.

Keefer carried her to the bed before he undressed. Unlike the night before, he didn't turn down the gas fixtures. His desire for her was fierce. Philippa met each new demand on her sexuality, then matched it with one of her own.

She found she'd been barely initiated in the arts of

sexual pleasure! But she was a most willing neophyte.

Her abandon was a pleasant shock to Keefer.

It was a night with only snatches of sleep, locked together. In another day they would be on the river, heading out into an uncertain and probably dangerous future. But tonight they were safe, unafraid, and alone.

They made the most of it.

"We haven't talked about exactly where we're going from Independence," Philippa said when they were finally satiated. "Of course I haven't asked. For some strange reason, I trust you, although why I should I really don't know. Any man who would seduce a poor, frightened girl in a muddy ditch . . . well!"

"I had some cooperation, you know," Keefer said.

"Fie! I was bewildered. And helpless."

"Sure." Keefer grinned and stroked her hair. "Have you heard of San Francisco?"

"Gold!" Philippa exclaimed. "We're going to dig for gold!" She clapped her hands. "I've always wanted to be rich."

Keefer raised himself on an elbow to look down in her face. "Don't be greedy. I'm a pretty good saddle and harness maker, and I have to make us a living, remember? I also have a dream. I want to be a rancher, and own land farther than I can see. I want more horses than I can ever ride, and more cattle than we can eat in a lifetime, and that includes the sons and daughters we're going to have. I hear they keep so busy trying to strike it rich out there, no one has time to make what they need."

"You're going to open another saddlery?"

"Right. On our way to San Francisco, we'll see the land we want. When this Civil War is over, there's going to be a western rush. The Indians will be swept away. They haven't got a chance! I've seen the beginning." Keefer's eyes were alight. "When that rush comes, from the North, if they lose, from the South, if the Federals win, we'll be there, on our land. If we have to fight to hold it, we will. We're going to start a dynasty, Philippa!"

"Do you know something?" she asked.

"What?"

Philippa cupped his cheek with her hand. "A kiss and I'll tell you."

"Glad to oblige."

It was a long and tender kiss.

"I truly believe everything you've just said," she told Keefer. "Together there just isn't anything we can't do. You'd better believe that, husband!"

"Can you shoot?" he asked.

"Not yet. But I'm going to take cooking lessons tomorrow."

"Today," Keefer said.

Philippa groaned. "Where did last night go?"

"*You're* asking?"

"Oh, yes, I remember now. You were hungry."

"You'll have to learn to use a rifle," Keefer told her. "There are quite a few Indians between Independence and San Francisco."

"You'll teach me to shoot."

Keefer paused, then asked, "Aren't you afraid?"

"Not really, not yet. Oh, I suppose I will be sometimes. But you'll be there."

"I will be," Keefer promised.

It was late in the season, and most of the wagon trains had left Independence, Missouri, so they'd reach the Sierra passes before winter locked them out of the land beyond.

Cannons & Roses

The bustling prairie town didn't seem to know a war was raging back east.

Their trip up the Missouri, on a shallowdraft steamboat, had been wearing on Philippa and Keefer, without much of the privacy they wanted, but fortunately it was uneventful.

Philippa wore buckskins now and had cropped her hair short. From the deck of the boat, she'd become proficient, even by Keefer's standards with a Sharps and the new repeating Winchester carbine.

She'd sunburned on the slow upriver trip, and then tanned. Twice hostile Kiowas had fired on their boat. Indians fascinated Philippa. At the landings, she'd seen their squaws and phlegmatic babies, their tepees and the travois—two poles used to transport game and household goods instead of a wheeled wagon.

Philippa had smelled them, too—a combination of wood smoke, sweat, and a musky odor she didn't find unpleasant.

Latecomers to Independence were camped around the town, disappointed that most of the trains had already left, optimistic that they could somehow be on their way before too long.

Keefer bought four horses and two mules. Within a few days, he'd outfitted Philippa and himself for the long journey ahead. Out here, she'd discovered, Keefer was a different man. There was a new quickness in his step. He spoke with more quiet authority. For the first time, Philippa was seeing a man who not only knew exactly what he wanted, but also knew how to get it.

So she wasn't surprised when he ducked into their tent and said they'd leave tomorrow with a train of six wagons, and that he would be wagonmaster.

"I've picked carefully," he said. "No babies or small

Cannons & Roses

children. Families, though. I learned something out here when I was scouting and fighting Indians."

"What was that?" Philippa asked.

"In a fuss, pick a family man to side with you if you want to survive."

"That makes sense," she said. "Can their women shoot?"

Keefer grinned. "Those who can't will show up tomorrow for their first lesson from my wife."

"Well, thanks!" Philippa said. "You might have asked me."

But she was flattered.

Ten days later, the Keefer Jones party left Independence for the long trek west. Philippa rode beside her husband, at the head of the train, leading her spare horse, and one of the pack mules carrying their outfit.

Every woman in the party could handle a rifle, and most of the girls. They all envied Philippa her freedom from skirts and petticoats, as well as her strapping young husband who carried their lives in his hands. Eastern notions of what was fit and proper for a girl or woman had been left in Independence.

It was two weeks after their departure from Independence that they met War Eagle and his party of war-painted Sioux braves one late afternoon.

Warning his people to keep their weapons loaded and cocked, Keefer rode out to parley. War Eagle wanted whisky. As politely as he could, in sign language, Keefer told him there wasn't any. (Keefer had personally searched each wagon on the eve of departure to make sure that only medicinal liquor was aboard.)

Ammunition? Some. Keefer shared what he could. War Eagle claimed they were out after buffalo to feed their hungry wives and children.

Cannons & Roses

War Eagle's party rode off over the western horizon. Keefer circled the wagons and camped on the spot.

"They'll hit us at dawn," Keefer told Philippa. "Now watch me break every military rule they teach at West Point. Never divide your force, for instance. That's useless when you fight Sioux—or the Kiowa, for that matter."

During the night, Keefer set the men and boys digging a full circle of rifle pits around the circled wagons. In the tall grass, they were indistinguishable from the flat prairie. An hour before dawn, he posted two men in each pit.

Each was armed with the repeating Winchester that Keefer had insisted they buy in Independence and learn to use.

The attack came exactly at sunrise. War Eagle's party raced their ponies toward the circled wagons, screaming the Sioux war cry.

Philippa commanded the women, girls, and boys. Keefer was a third party in one of the rifle pits. Philippa's people held their fire until the warriors were in the circle, then let her command open a withering fire.

That was Keefer's cue, and he fired three quick shots in the air. His orders were followed, and only the men in pits behind the Sioux opened up. Philippa's volley had stalled the attack, and six ponies were riderless. Fire from Keefer's men routed it. When survivors kicked their ponies in a rush around the circled wagons, to escape the bullets from behind them, they'd fled headlong into intense fire from the opposite half of the rifle-pit circle.

Thirty-seven Sioux had attacked. Thirty-one riderless ponies scampered away from the ambush. War

BIG IN SIZE, BIG IN STORY, FROM DELL—

Nothing Could Stop *The Polreath Women* in their drive for the ULTIMATE REWARD

ELIZABETH, the matriarch—her love for Lord John Polreath is surpassed by only one other passion...

PATIENCE, the scapegrace—she becomes the toast and the scandal of New York and London, and despair of her family, until one fateful night...

HOPE, the rebel—bearing her dead step-brother's child, she alone can save the Polreath heritage.

Set in England and America in the turbulent nineteenth century, embracing the Civil war, the rise of a great shipping empire and the emergence of women as a force in the world, here is a saga novel in the grand tradition of R.F. Delderfield's GOD IS AN ENGLISHMAN.

Cannons & Roses

Eagle and five braves dropped their weapons to surrender. All were wounded.

"I didn't know Indians gave up," Philippa said. "Books I've read . . ."

Keefer grinned and wiped a powder smudge off her nose. "Don't believe everything you read."

Her eyes widened. "I didn't really think of it until now," she said, "but I could have been *killed!*"

Keefer laughed and kissed her. "Mrs. Jones, you'll do."